BY C. W. GORTNER

The Romanov Empress

The Romanov Empress

A NOVEL OF TSARINA
MARIA FEODOROVNA

C. W. Gortner

BALLANTINE BOOKS / NEW YORK

Published in the United States by Ballantine Books, an imprint of Random House,
a division of Penguin Random House LLC, New York.

BALLANTINE and the HOUSE colophon are registered trademarks
of Penguin Random House LLC.

LIBRARY OF CONGRESS CATALOGING-IN-PUBLICATION DATA
Names: Gortner, C. W., author.
Title: The Romanov empress: a novel of Tsarina Maria Feodorovna / C. W. Gortner.
Description: New York: Ballantine Books, 2018.
Identifiers: LCCN 2018006314 | ISBN 9780425286166 (hardback) |
ISBN 9780425286173 (ebook)
Subjects: LCSH: Maria Feodorovna, Empress, consort of Alexander III, Emperor of Russia,
1847–1928—Fiction. | Romanov, House of—Fiction. | Russia—History—Alexander III,
1881–1894—Fiction. | Russia—History—Revolution, 1905–1907—Fiction. | Empresses—
Russia—Fiction. | Russia—kings and rulers—Fiction. | BISAC: FICTION / Historical. |
FICTION / Biographical. | FICTION / Literary. | GSAFD: Biographical fiction. |
Historical fiction.
Classification: LCC PS3607.O78 R66 2018 | DDC 813/.6—dc23
LC record available at https://lccn.loc.gov/2018006314

Printed in the United States of America on acid-free paper

randomhousebooks.com

2 4 6 8 9 7 5 3 1

First Edition

Map and Family Trees by C. W. Gortner

Book design by Victoria Wong

For my mother,
who introduced me to the splendors
of the Romanovs

Fame and misfortune live in the same courtyard.

—*Russian proverb*

The Royal Family of Denmark

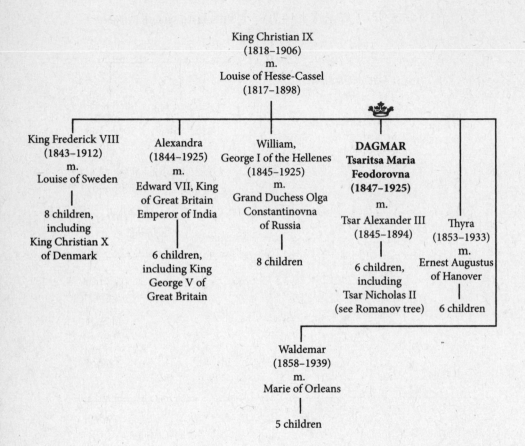

King Christian IX
(1818–1906)
m.
Louise of Hesse-Cassel
(1817–1898)

King Frederick VIII
(1843–1912)
m.
Louise of Sweden

8 children,
including
King Christian X
of Denmark

Alexandra
(1844–1925)
m.
Edward VII, King
of Great Britain
Emperor of India

6 children,
including King
George V of
Great Britain

William,
George I of the Hellenes
(1845–1925)
m.
Grand Duchess Olga
Constantinovna
of Russia

8 children

**DAGMAR
Tsaritsa Maria
Feodorovna
(1847–1925)**
m.
Tsar Alexander III
(1845–1894)

6 children,
including
Tsar Nicholas II
(see Romanov tree)

Thyra
(1853–1933)
m.
Ernest Augustus
of Hanover

6 children

Waldemar
(1858–1939)
m.
Marie of Orleans

5 children

The Imperial Romanovs of Russia

TSAR ALEXANDER II
(1818–1881)
m.
1) MARIA OF HESSE AND BY RHINE, Tsaritsa Maria Alexandrovna
(1824–1880)

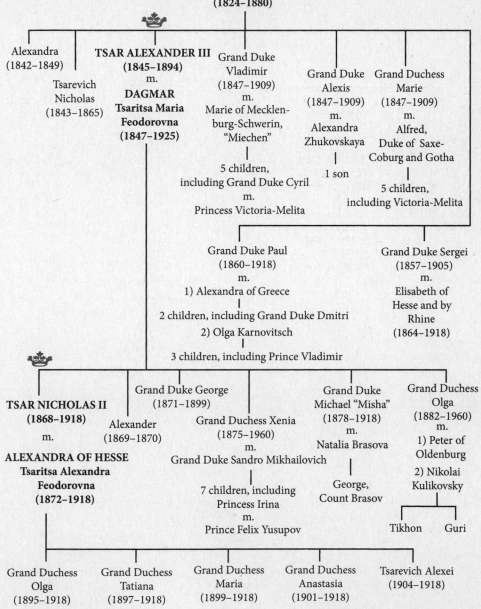

Alexandra
(1842–1849)

Tsarevich
Nicholas
(1843–1865)

TSAR ALEXANDER III
(1845–1894)
m.
DAGMAR
Tsaritsa Maria
Feodorovna
(1847–1925)

Grand Duke
Vladimir
(1847–1909)
m.
Marie of Mecklen-
burg-Schwerin,
"Miechen"

5 children,
including Grand Duke Cyril
m.
Princess Victoria-Melita

Grand Duke
Alexis
(1847–1909)
m.
Alexandra
Zhukovskaya

1 son

Grand Duchess
Marie
(1847–1909)
m.
Alfred,
Duke of Saxe-
Coburg and Gotha

5 children,
including Victoria-Melita

Grand Duke Paul
(1860–1918)
m.
1) Alexandra of Greece

2 children, including Grand Duke Dmitri

2) Olga Karnovitsch

3 children, including Prince Vladimir

Grand Duke Sergei
(1857–1905)
m.
Elisabeth of
Hesse and by
Rhine
(1864–1918)

TSAR NICHOLAS II
(1868–1918)
m.
ALEXANDRA OF HESSE
Tsaritsa Alexandra
Feodorovna
(1872–1918)

Grand Duke George
(1871–1899)

Alexander
(1869–1870)

Grand Duchess Xenia
(1875–1960)
m.
Grand Duke Sandro Mikhailovich

7 children, including
Princess Irina
m.
Prince Felix Yusupov

Grand Duke
Michael "Misha"
(1878–1918)
m.
Natalia Brasova

George,
Count Brasov

Grand Duchess
Olga
(1882–1960)
m.
1) Peter of
Oldenburg
2) Nikolai
Kulikovsky

Tikhon   Guri

Grand Duchess
Olga
(1895–1918)

Grand Duchess
Tatiana
(1897–1918)

Grand Duchess
Maria
(1899–1918)

Grand Duchess
Anastasia
(1901–1918)

Tsarevich Alexei
(1904–1918)

NORWEGIAN
SEA

ARCTIC

NORWAY

SWEDEN

BARENTS
SEA

KARA
SEA

COPENHAGEN

BALTIC
SEA

FINLAND

SIBERIA

POLAND

ST.
PETERSBURG

MOGILEV

TSARSKOE
SELO

URAL MOUNTAINS

IMPERIAL
RUSSIA

KIEV

MOSCOW

UKRAINE

KAZAN

PERM

CRIMEA

YEKATERINBURG

YALTA

TOBOLSK

BLACK
SEA

GREATER CAUCASUS

ABBAS-
TOUMAN

TURKEY

CASPIAN
SEA

KAZAKHSTAN

IRAN

0   250   500   750 km
0   250   500   750 mi

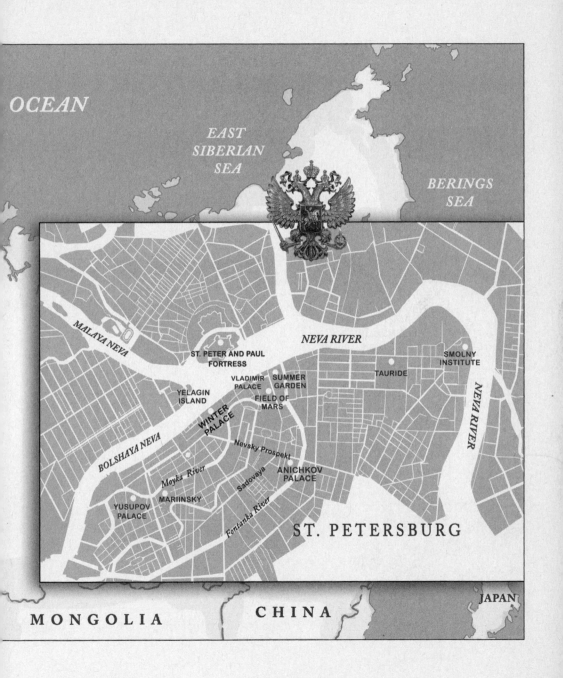

PART I

1862–1866

The Yellow Palace

She comes! The Maid of Denmark . . .
To be our Queen of Love.

—MARTIN TUPPER

CHAPTER ONE

"We should dress alike," I said on that afternoon when life changed forever. I didn't yet understand how profound the change would be, but I could feel it as I sat riffling through the heap of boxes sent by Copenhagen's and London's finest emporiums, packed with satin-bowed shoes and beribboned hats, silk undergarments, dresses, corsets, shawls, leather gloves, and cloaks made of fine cashmere or Scottish wool.

"Alike?" Standing on a footstool as Mama and her maid flapped about her, lifting items to her face and slim figure to determine which best suited her, my sister Alix regarded me in bemusement. "As if we were twins?"

"Yes." I tilted up two of the boxes beside me on the settee. "Look. You have an extra pair of everything now. We could dress alike and see if your fiancé can tell us apart."

Alix's thin brows knit together. Her little frown pleased me; it showed my sister was not as immune to the absurdity of the situation as she might feign. Before she could reply, however, our mother issued her tart reprimand, with that faint irritation she employed whenever I did or said something inappropriate, which, for her, was becoming all too frequent.

"Minnie. That is enough. Dress like twins, how absurd." Mama clucked her tongue. "As if His Royal Highness the Prince of Wales were blind. Why, you and Alix are nothing alike."

"Are you certain?" Though I meant to sound nonchalant, I heard the challenge in my tone. "We might not be alike, but he's only met her once. He might not even recognize her when he sees her again."

Mama went still, a ruffled petticoat in her hands. Looking at that creamy white silk, I had to swallow a surge of anger. Times past, we could never have afforded such a petticoat or indeed any of these other fancy things littering the room. We made our own clothes, and mended them, too. We'd been happy in our little yellow palace in Copenhagen, relishing summer outings to swim in the sea, our gymnastics competitions, and musical evenings after frugal meals, where we'd served ourselves at the table. Luxuries had never mattered, not when we had one another. Our family was our greatest gift. Yet here we were, smothered in visible proof of our impending dissolution.

How could so much have changed in so little time?

"Of course His Highness will love her," said Mama. "It's his duty as her husband, as it is hers as his wife. Whatever has come over you, to be so contrary on the very day of Alix's fitting for her trousseau? Can't you see she's nervous enough as it is?"

My sister watched me from the mirror. If she was nervous, she did not show it. She looked tired and pale, the shadows under her cool-gray eyes betraying her fatigue, but she was composed—so much, in fact, that her steady gaze unnerved me. Despite her unflinching stance, she must realize I spoke the truth. It was impossible to predict if her marriage would bring her happiness or heartache. But she'd never admit it aloud, not before our mother, who'd labored so long for this elevation in our fortune, the latest in a sweeping tide of change that had left me feeling stranded, struggling to stay afloat.

"I was only saying . . ." My voice trailed off as Mama gave me a glare.

"We know what you were saying, Minnie. And I tell you, it is enough."

Exasperated, I crunched the tissue in the hat box beside me. "Perhaps I should go out for a walk," I muttered. "Seeing as I'm not needed here."

"If you cannot make yourself useful, yes, you should." Mama turned back to my sister. "Fresh air will no doubt improve your mood and take that unpleasant sting out of your tail. I'll not have you distracting your sister with nonsense when we've so much to do."

Fresh air and a minimum of nonsense were Mama's solution to

everything. She was nothing if not sensible, no matter that in the last year we'd experienced enough upheaval to turn any other sensible woman's head. But Louise of Hesse-Cassel never indulged such weakness. She'd first showed this obdurate trust in her own judgment by defying her family to marry my father, her second cousin, Christian of Glücksburg, an impoverished princeling of no particular account, with whom she'd settled into a penurious but pleasant existence, raising us with a sensible disregard for pretension. She might now be poised to become Queen of Denmark, with Papa's surprising inheritance of our childless king's throne, while preparing to send her eldest daughter off to marry Great Britain's heir, yet she approached these monumental tasks as she might the daily cleaning of the parlor. And that sting in my tail, as she called it, confounded her, for it was something no child of hers should display, especially in light of our newly exalted circumstances.

Tugging at my voluminous skirts, I marched to the door, pausing there. I hoped my sister would call me back. I wanted Alix to say something, to show she still needed me. But when she remained silent and I glanced defiantly over my shoulder, I found her smothered in the silk petticoat, Mama ordering the maid to fasten her stays, as if Alix were a doll.

Or a lamb for the sacrifice.

To me, my sister's upcoming marriage was much the same.

WE WERE NOT born to grandeur. Mama had often reminded us of this in our childhood, so we wouldn't expect more than we had. Those born into riches are not so fortunate, she would say as she sat with Alix and me, instructing us in our embellishment of homemade bonnets or darning of underclothes. Those who begin their lives with everything cannot appreciate the rewards of aspiration. Wise advice, for no one had reaped more reward in aspiration than Mama, but scarce comfort to me now as I traversed the Bernstorff Palace, passing statuary and mirror-paneled walls without a glance, my heels echoing on the parquet floors and my wide-hooped skirt soughing in my wake.

We'd moved to the palace a month ago, once it was determined that Papa would become Denmark's new crown prince. Nestled on spacious grounds outside Copenhagen, the palace was suitably elegant, much larger than our yellow home within the city. The beautiful gardens were one of the few changes I'd welcomed, with their magnificent lime trees and walking paths. My younger brother, Valdemar, and little sister, Thyra, loved it here, let loose to dirty their feet and scramble under the hedgerows. But I was nearly fifteen now, too old for childish games, though as I escaped into the garden I wished I were not. I longed to be a child again, free to run and hide.

Raising a hand to my brow, I realized I'd forgotten to fetch a parasol or hat. I risked getting too much color. Imagining my mother's reaction to this, I strode forth, thinking I should also undo the scratchy net confining my thick curls at my nape and incite a scandal. Only there was no one here to be scandalized. The gardens stretched before me in verdant emptiness, until I neared the Swedish-style villa that served as a teahouse and saw a familiar figure in a dark suit pacing outside it, cigar smoke drifting in a cloud about him.

Papa.

Grasping up fistfuls of my skirts and not caring that my ankles showed, I raced across the lawn to him. He turned, startled, smoke curling from his mouth under his impressive new mustachios. He had grown them to appear more distinguished. I found them funny, for his wispy brown hair was thin on top, a sparse fleece offsetting that thicket on his face. And future king or not, he still had to smoke outside, because Mama deplored the smell and had begged him to cease indulging "that disgusting vice."

"Finished so soon?" A smile lightened his careworn face. It hurt me to see that he too had begun to change. Ever since it was decided he would succeed our ailing king, Papa had shed his lighthearted air, as if the burden of the crown already weighed upon him.

"Not for hours, I should think." I wrinkled my nose at the pungent odor of tobacco enveloping him. "They still have mounds of things to sort through. There mustn't be a single dress left in all of Copenhagen. Mama said I was being contrary, so I left."

"I see." A smile creased the corners of his mild light-brown eyes. "And were you being contrary, my Dagmar?"

It was his chosen name for me, one of the several with which I'd been christened, and my favorite, for everyone in the family but him called me Minnie. Dagmar was a unique name that set me apart, once belonging to a legendary queen consort of our country.

I shrugged. "I don't see why there must be such a fuss."

He laughed. "Your sister is about to wed Queen Victoria's son and heir. One day, God willing, she'll be queen consort of Great Britain. Most consider it a grand fuss, indeed."

"Perhaps for Mama and Queen Victoria. As for Alix, how grand it is remains to be seen." As I saw his expression dim, I added, "I'm only worried for her, Papa. Alix has been acting so strange. She just seems to accept all of it without question."

He exhaled, leaned down to stamp out his cigar on the path, and then tucked the butt into his jacket pocket. "She doesn't need to question. It's a very prestigious match, which your mother encouraged and Queen Victoria approved. Alix knows she must fulfill her duty."

His statement took me aback. I believed I knew Alix better than anyone, yet I hadn't paused to think that, indeed, my sister had always shown an exemplary sense of duty.

She was almost three years older, and we had grown up together, sharing a bedroom and our lessons. Our eldest brother, Frederick, was sent abroad to study, and our second brother, Willie, was enrolled in the Danish Military Academy, while our youngest sister, Thyra, and our third brother, Valdemar, were still children. Alix and I had therefore cleaved to each other in a home always lacking for funds and dominated by our mother, who, when our family reunited for the holidays, lavished her attention on our brothers.

I'd always resented how much due she gave Freddie and Willie, even if Alix told me it was natural, as a mother always valued her sons more. I didn't see why, seeing as we, the daughters, helped manage the household while the sons were away. Yet unlike me—I hated the endless chores—my sister never protested. At night, we whispered together over our work-chafed hands, our narrow beds pushed side by side. We promised each other that one day we'd buy a house of our own by the Sound, with floors we'd never scrub. We'd own a hundred dogs and paint the hours away, for we were both skilled with watercolors. All that changed once she'd accepted Prince Albert Edward's proposal. She became someone else, no longer my devoted sister; suddenly she was Mama's favorite, inundated with etiquette practice, dance lessons, or dress fittings, preparing for a new life in another country, in which I'd play no part.

"I barely see her anymore," I said, avoiding my father's eyes. "Mama always has important letters Alix must write, people they must visit, or something she must try on. I feel as though she's left us already."

"Have you told her as much?" he asked gently. "Perhaps this contrariness of yours has made her think you're angry with her."

Again I paused. Was I angry? I supposed I must be. I certainly did not like how willingly she'd acquiesced to this marriage and forsaken our confidences.

"Do I seem angry to you?" I said.

"Always." He pinched my cheek. "You're our rebellious one."

"Rebellious!" I exclaimed. "Just because I don't want everything to change? Our life has been turned upside down, Papa. I never expected any of this."

He sighed. "I see how trying it is for you. I am sorry for it. But marriage is an essential passage in life, Dagmar. We must leave those we love behind to start a family of our own." He paused. "You're almost fifteen. Have you never considered it?"

"Of course I have," I replied, though I hadn't. Marriage might be inevitable, but until now it had also been easily ignored. "But how can Alix marry someone she barely knows? Bertie of Wales saw a photograph of her and asked for a meeting; it was only at Easter that they were introduced, remember, when we all went to Rumpenheim together. The tsarina was there with her eldest son; I thought Alix liked the tsarevich. Nixa certainly seemed to like her, while she and Bertie barely said three words to each other. Yet now she loves him enough to marry him?" When my father didn't answer, I pressed on. "You must have loved Mama when you married her."

"I did." His face softened. "Your mother was so vibrant and determined. I fell in love with her at once. She wasn't unlike you in her youth. She knew exactly what she wanted."

I refused to be placated. At this particular moment, I wasn't pleased to be compared with my mother, who had connived to upend our existence.

"But before I met your mother, I tried to woo Victoria," Papa added, with a grin.

I was astounded. "You did?"

"Not only me. Dozens of princes tried. She was the most eligible bride in Europe. And I was rather bold, despite my lack of means. I wrote her letters and offered to visit, hoping I might win her hand. Alas, she disdained me, and several others, to marry Albert of Saxe-Coburg and Gotha instead."

"Who died," I groused. "Leaving her a widow to meddle in our affairs."

"Now, now. You mustn't blame the queen. It is true the tsar's son expressed interest in your sister, but Alix didn't want to live in Russia, where she doesn't speak the language."

"They speak French at the Russian court. See? Alix doesn't know anything! She hates rain, too, and I hear it rains all the time in England. Whatever will she do when she cannot step outside without getting wet?"

"We'll have to make sure she brings plenty of umbrellas." Papa gave me another smile. "I know this isn't easy for you, but casting doubts now will not reassure her."

I winced. Being too engrossed in my own feelings, I hadn't given Alix's feelings any thought. I moved closer to my father, seeking comfort as he slipped his arm about my waist and kissed my brow. "Again without a hat," he said. "Your mother will be furious."

"Add it to her list of grievances," I replied, and his laughter rumbled in his chest as he guided me along the path, his arm about me, enclosing me in a sense of safety that made me realize I feared losing him, too. I knew our king was ill and that hasty preparations to confirm Papa as crown prince were under way. What would our life be like, with him on the throne and Mama as queen, with hordes of retainers and officials surrounding us day and night?

I shivered at the thought. He tightened his hold on me. "What else troubles you?"

I felt foolish. Any other girl would welcome this rise in her station, the chance to call herself a princess and be the senior daughter, now that her sister was leaving. "Must we move to the Amalienborg Palace after we return from Alix's wedding?" I asked.

"I'm afraid so. King Frederick has granted me the immense honor of becoming his heir, but it was no simple task. It took months for everyone to reach agreement. His Majesty now insists we must live according to our rank." He looked down at me, for I was short in stature, like my mother, while Alix was tall and willowy, like him. "Our yellow house isn't suitable for a future king and his family. We'll keep this palace for the summer and then you'll have your own suite in the Amalienborg. Won't that be nice? Apartments of your own, to do with as you like, after sharing a bedroom all these years?"

"With Thyra there?" I referred to my nine-year-old sister, who followed me around in adoration whenever she wasn't romping with our little brother. "She'll move in with me the moment she can. I don't mind," I said. "I wouldn't know what to do with an entire suite."

"More unwelcome change, eh? We'll have to muddle through it as best we can."

I nodded glumly as he released me, searching his jacket. He was about to extract his cigar butt when he suddenly peered toward the palace. Following his gaze, I saw my mother waving at us from an upstairs window.

"It seems they finished sooner than we thought," said Papa. "Well. Let's go behold your sister's trousseau. Do be kind to her. Remember what I said; Alix isn't like you. She doesn't express herself easily, so find a time to speak with her alone. She needs your support more than ever. I don't want you at odds when we depart for England."

"Yes, Papa," I said.

But I wasn't sure I wanted to hear what my sister might say. What if I discovered she wouldn't miss me as much as I wanted her to?

CHAPTER TWO

Supper was held in the chandeliered hall. We now had liveried footmen with white-gloved hands to serve our soup, baked salmon,
succulent greens, fresh-baked pies, and decanters of claret wine—a feast
that could have fed our entire family for a week. I observed Mama instructing the servants with perfect poise from her chair, as if she'd been
ordering legions about her entire life. My younger siblings, Valdemar
and Thyra, scrubbed clean of their garden frolic and perched on gilded
chairs at the huge linen-draped table, were uncharacteristically subdued,
as if bewildered by the array of silver forks, spoons, and knives beside
their plates.

"The small fork is for the salad," I whispered to Thyra, nudging the
utensil. "The larger one for the meat and fish. You move from the outside in. See?"

My sister nodded, a bow twined in her dark-gold curls. Like me,
Thyra had large, expressive brown eyes and a snub nose; she took after
our father, while little Valdemar was fair, with the gray-blue eyes and
pale complexion of our mother and Alix.

As we ate, Mother spoke in a low voice to Papa, no doubt about the
trousseau and arrangements for the trip to England. I could barely hear
her, though in the past at our yellow palace we'd engaged in rambunctious discussions over meals. It was yet another sign that our life was no
longer the same, and when four-year-old Valdemar suddenly declared,
"I want to go to England!" he plunged us into silence.

I clutched my napkin to my mouth to suppress a giggle.

"Children are not invited to weddings," chided Mama. "You will stay here with Thyra and your governess until—"

"No." Valdemar thumped his fist on the table. "I want to go!"

Mama glanced at Papa, who, like me, appeared as if he might burst out laughing. "Christian, my dear, please inform our son that such outbursts are not to be tolerated."

Papa composed himself. "Valdemar," he said, trying to sound stern, "listen to your mother."

My brother's expression crunched up. Alix patted his hand, murmuring. Valdemar looked at her, uncertain, before he echoed, "A new train?"

Alix nodded. "I promise. I hear they make lovely toy trains in England."

I had to stop myself from retorting that they made lovely ones in Denmark, too. We had a train set left by my other brothers, which had worked wonderfully until Valdemar stomped on it one day in a tantrum. Then, to my astonishment, Alix turned to our parents. "I don't see why he shouldn't come with us. It is my wedding, after all. I'd like for our entire family to be there."

Who knew? I hadn't heard her state an opinion this entire time. I sat more upright in my chair as Mama battled her own uncomfortable surprise.

"But we've so much to attend to. Queen Victoria's family will all be there, as well as other important guests. I cannot possibly look after the children."

"Minnie can look after them." Alix shifted her gaze to me.

I found myself assenting. "Yes. Of course I can."

"Good. Then it's settled," said Papa in audible relief, which earned him a tight-lipped look from Mama.

Valdemar might have let out a triumphant whoop had Mama not given him a warning look. He busied himself with his plate, making a mess of the baked fish until Alix took up his fork to assist him; as she did, she gave me a quick, grateful smile. It melted away my hesitation. If she wanted all of us to be there, she must harbor doubts. I resolved to find time to speak with her.

After supper, Valdemar and Thyra were sent protesting upstairs to bed, while we gathered in the drawing room. Papa served himself a cognac and Mama took up her embroidery. As she threaded her needle, she said, "Minnie, play something for us." We had a large piano in the palace, not like the decrepit pianoforte in our yellow house, but as I sat on the stool and began to play, my fingers seemed to be all thumbs. I kept making mistakes, attuned to Alix where she sat by the window, looking out as twilight enveloped the grounds.

"Minnie, is that Handel you're mutilating?" said Mama testily. My hands paused.

Alix turned to the room with a sigh. "It's been a long day. I think I'll retire."

"At this hour?" Mama said. "Why, it's not even dark yet."

But Alix drifted over to her and Papa to kiss their cheeks. As she moved to the drawing room doors, I bolted to my feet. "I'll go with you," I announced, and before Mama could call me back, I followed Alix into the corridor.

She didn't seem to notice me trailing behind her until I touched her sleeve. She started, coming to a halt. In her wary look, I saw she knew what I was about to say.

"Are you too tired to talk with me?" I said.

She smiled. "I was wondering when you might ask."

"You might have asked instead," I said, and then I bit my lip, not wanting to start out on a sour note. "I suppose you've been too busy."

"Entirely. I had no idea planning a wedding required so much effort. If I have to see one more dress or hat . . ." She met my eyes. "Shall we go upstairs to my room?"

"No," I said impulsively. She had her own bedroom now; I didn't want to behold the piles of new things to be packed for England. "Let's talk in the gallery."

The gallery was an airy black-and-white-tiled passage that ran the length of the garden side of the palace. We found it submerged in gloom, the plants like feathered beasts in their porcelain jardinière, crouched over the white wicker furniture I detested because bits of the framing always snagged my dress and—

Alix broke into my hesitation. "You can sit down. If you pull a thread, you can have it fixed. No more sewing by candlelight; we now have others to do our mending."

I plopped onto the nearest chair in defiance. I couldn't tell if she was mocking me. "I suppose you enjoy having servants."

"Why shouldn't I?" She perched opposite me. "It's refreshing not to suffer broken fingernails and needle-pricked thumbs." She met my stare. "Don't you?"

I shrugged. "Servants talk. They have eyes and ears. I'd rather my every minute not become the subject of backstairs gossip."

She looked down, fiddling with the lace trim on her cuff. "You sound angry, Minnie."

"Do I?" I bristled at her echoing of what Papa had said. "Perhaps I have good reason."

She lifted her gaze. In the shadows of the gallery, her eyes seemed immense in her drawn face. "What reason?"

I wanted to remonstrate that I was angry because she was marrying someone for whom she couldn't possibly hold any affection, because I knew it was Mama's fault, that she'd forced Alix to do her duty. Not knowing where to begin, I heard myself say, "Why did you say yes?"

She went quiet, not looking away but with that distance once again surfacing in her gaze. It emboldened me to add, "You cannot possibly care for him. You hardly know him."

Her tone was measured. "Do you think I'd have agreed to marry him if I thought he were unsuitable? No," she said. "I do not know him yet, nor do I know if he will make me happy. But he requested my hand and will make me Princess of Wales. I considered it very carefully before I gave my consent."

"Your consent? Or Mama's consent? Alix, I always thought . . ."

"What?" she said. "What did you always think?"

I grappled with my words, taken aback by her gravity. "I . . . I don't know. I just thought we'd both marry when we fell in love, like Papa and Mama did."

She smiled. It rent me, that subtle creasing of her mouth—so stoic and resigned, like when she faced one of our mounds of endless darning. "Minnie, we're not children anymore, eager for Herr Grimm to tell us bedtime stories. Papa will be king. We must marry where we can do our country honor. Denmark might not be a powerful nation but we still have enemies, Prussia foremost among them. That devil Bismarck wasn't pleased that Papa was chosen to succeed to the throne over his preferred candidate. The time is past for fairy tales."

"Fairy tales?" My voice lifted. I stopped, took a calming breath. My dutiful sister, who'd never paid attention to the world outside, was suddenly talking like a diplomat. "This isn't about fairy tales. The tsarevich—don't you think marrying him will do us honor? The Russian empire is more powerful, I daresay, than the British. And Nixa loves you."

"Loves me?" Mirth colored her voice. "Nixa Romanov does not love me."

"No? Well, he gave a very good impression of it. I saw how he looked at you at Rumpenheim, where you met stodgy Bertie of Wales. Nixa barely spoke to anyone but you the entire time. Papa told me he would have asked for your hand, but you said you couldn't live in Russia because you don't speak the language. Alix, they speak French at the Romanov court. Your French is much better than your English."

"I only said that to spare Nixa embarrassment. He was only going to propose to me because his father ordered it. Tsar Alexander doesn't want his son to take a Prussian bride."

"You're not Prussian."

"No. But Nixa didn't want me." She regarded me with unsettling candor. "Can it be that you truly have no idea?"

Suddenly I found myself short of air; I almost flinched when her hand touched mine.

"You were the one he couldn't stop looking at when we were at Rumpenheim," she went on. "He was enraptured. The entire time he spoke to me, all he did was ask about you. He wanted to pay suit for your hand, only Papa wouldn't hear of it. The tsar had sent his son to woo me. I simply saved everyone the trouble by making it clear I wasn't interested."

I stared at her, speechless for one of the few times in my life.

She patted my hand. "Oh, Minnie. Are you so blind? Everyone noticed it. Even stodgy Bertie, as you call him, remarked that Nixa was behaving like a lovestruck swain."

My memory plunged back to our time in Rumpenheim. I recalled bracing morning horseback rides, idle lunches under pavilions on the castle lawn, dancing and games of whist in the evenings. Yet much as I tried, I couldn't summon a solid recollection of the Russian heir; he was vague, a nondescript figure in polished boots. I had known his mother, the tsarina, for years. She'd been born a princess of Hesse-Darmstadt, from the ruling branch of my mother's family, but I'd always found

Empress Maria Alexandrovna rather forbidding, with her patrician mien and sad yet sharp eyes that seemed to pass unspoken judgment on our threadbare ways as she sat enveloped in sables we could never afford. She and Mama exchanged regular letters, however, and the empress made a point of summoning us whenever she came through Germany or Denmark on her way to her annual vacations in Nice. Thus, we had met her eldest son, Nicholas, or Nixa, as he was known, on those occasions when he accompanied her. He was just another boy to me: polite and privileged, not given to familiarity. In fact, I couldn't remember him paying me any mind. And during our time in Rumpenheim, I'd been so focused on his interest in Alix, I'd apparently neglected to actually *look* at him. I didn't like that I'd failed to notice what my sister now claimed everyone else had.

"Don't be absurd," I said. "He wouldn't ever want me if he could have you."

Alix withdrew her hand. "This isn't a competition. He fell in love with you. He only left Rumpenheim without proposing because Papa wouldn't have him turn your head unless the tsar first sanctioned the match. Nixa Romanov will never be my husband. However," she said, as if stating an irrefutable fact, "he might be yours."

I was so unsettled, I didn't know what to say.

"You should consider it," Alix said. "Nixa seemed determined and assured Papa the tsarina will support the match, as will Mama. And perhaps Tsar Alexander will approve, seeing as you're not a Prussian princess, either."

"I'm not a princess at all! Papa hasn't even been crowned yet."

"We're already princesses in the eyes of the world." Something in her tone sent a shiver through me. "You must grow up now, Minnie. See the world as it is, not as you'd like it to be. As the daughters of the King of Denmark, we will be sought after as royal brides."

"Not you," I reminded her. "You belong to Bertie of Wales now."

"I do." She came to her feet in a rustle of gray silk. "My future is decided. Yours, on the other hand, is not. You must choose wisely. Listen to your heart, but also use your head. Love may conquer all in sonnets, but love isn't necessarily what will keep us safe."

I gazed up at her, rooted to my seat. Of everything she might have said, this was the last thing I'd expected to hear. "Safe?" I breathed. "You chose Bertie for . . . safety?"

"Among other things. Even if Nixa had proposed to me, I still would have said no. I really don't want to live in Russia. I'm not like you; it's not my nature to be adventurous." She paused. "Are you still angry with me?"

"I was never angry," I whispered.

She smiled again, only this time her smile was imbued with forbearance. "Oh, you were. Quite angry, I think. You mustn't be. We are still sisters. I'll always love you best."

I wanted to embrace her. I half-rose, tears stinging my eyes, overwhelmed by what she'd told me, by my own ignorance of the intrigues that sought to ensnare us like some invisible machine, grinding efficiently in secret, to wreak havoc on our lives.

Before I could touch her, Alix stepped back. "Not now." Her voice caught in her throat. "We'll have plenty of time to say goodbye. Just not yet."

She walked from the gallery. As she disappeared into the palace, climbing the staircase to her room, I did not let myself surrender to the chill inside me.

I was losing my sister to safety. In the immensity of this knowledge, I didn't spare another thought to the revelation that the Romanov heir might seek to marry me.

CHAPTER THREE

We returned to Copenhagen and our yellow palace, to its sagging chaises draped in shawls to hide the horsehair stuffing sprouting from the sides, to the musty rooms with their framed watercolors painted by us, and to the faded drapery, which we'd washed countless times and repaired ourselves.

As glad as I was to be home, nostalgia permeated me as the days sped past. This palace where we'd roamed as children had begun to fade like a ghost, receding into its own tired walls as the future seeped ever more into our present.

Mama and Alix were inseparable, closeted together for hours, overseeing details of her trousseau or visiting aristocratic matrons who'd suddenly discovered our existence and clamored to host a luncheon for the future Princess of Wales. Papa was often gone, as well, attending the court at the ailing king's behest, leaving me with the children to idle away my time, as the daily chores that once occupied my time were now undertaken by our new servants.

Reading aloud from our battered fairy-tale books or playing games with my little brother and sister kept me from outright melancholia. Yet I still worried over how they'd fare, so young still and about to be catapulted into public notice as members of a royal family. I wanted to shield them, even if there was nothing I could do; I could scarcely shield myself. At night, I lay awake, concocting fanciful means of escape. We'd board a ship in disguise and sail to the colonies (which colonies, I did not know), where we'd become ordinary people (doing what, I had no idea). Or Papa would realize he didn't want to rule and would reject the crown, returning us to life as we knew it, because Queen Victoria would hardly want Alix to marry her son then, and—

I might have laughed at my own delusions had I not known what lay ahead. And as winter descended upon Denmark, the impending March of 1863 and Alix's departure inched ever closer, whispering its inevitability with the flurries of wind and snow.

Then, all of a sudden, our reprieve was over. Before I could collect my thoughts, the house erupted in a pandemonium—trunks packed and transported to the ship, Mama marching around barking orders at the harried maids as they flung sheets over our furnishings, turning our palace into a shroud. It was truly a ghost now.

"Are you scared?" I whispered to Alix on the night before we left, after I'd lain in wait for hours until Mama departed her room, so she and I could share some time alone.

She shook her head. "Why should I be?"

But she was afraid. I could see it, in her pinched lips and the way she held up her chin as we boarded our train to Brussels, from where we took Queen Victoria's royal yacht, dispatched especially for us. Our fellow Danes crowded the dock to bid her farewell, waving and shouting her name. I had to bite down on my laughter. No one had ever called out our names before; it seemed ridiculous.

My amusement turned to awe upon our arrival in England.

Here, Alix was greeted with panoply. Though the early-March rain fell upon us like cold blades, making us shiver in our new apparel—which had come at considerable expense, as Mama didn't cease to remind us—thousands of Queen Victoria's subjects mobbed the route into London, cheering Alix in her covered carriage. She rode with Mama and Bertie, who'd welcomed us with a sardonic smile on his mustachioed lips and, I detected, a distinct trace of feminine perfume on his frock coat. Riding with Papa in the carriage behind my sister, I tore my gaze from the cheering British, all of whom seemed immune to the icy downpours, and looked at my father.

He mouthed, "Umbrellas," forcing me to once again stifle my laughter.

Umbrellas, indeed. Alix would need dozens of them.

We boarded a train from Paddington Station. It was past nightfall by the time we reached Windsor Castle. After another carriage ride to the castle, delayed due to more throngs of well-wishers trying to catch a glimpse of their new princess, my feet were freezing and my hands were icicled in my new calfskin gloves, though I barely noticed the discomfort as we staggered from our carriages into the castle.

Instead, I felt anxiety at meeting the queen. Victoria was famous throughout the world. She'd ascended to the throne in her eighteenth year, and under her rule the British had embarked on a relentless expansion of her domains, claiming distant India and bringing luster to her crown. Yet her devoted marriage to Prince Albert, with whom she'd had nine children, had been shattered by his untimely death, plunging her entire empire into mourning. As isolated as we'd been, even I had heard of her soul-rending grief, my mother remarking that had it been up to the queen, she'd have been entombed with him. I imagined her as an ancient goddess—stern, unforgiving, draped in black—and my first sight of her only confirmed it.

She stood in the entrance hall encircled by her attendants, a collection of wide belled skirts and frilly caps. She stood out not because she wore black—they were all dressed in varying shades of her somber hue—but because her quiet command immediately drew the eye. She wasn't tall; in fact, she was much shorter than I expected, but no one could mistake her for anyone but who she was. Victoria Regina stood as if the world moved around her, not as though she moved within the world.

Drawing up the veil shielding her features—evidently, she'd still not abandoned her grief—she blinked at us through her watery eyes before she said peevishly, "Wherever have you been?"

Silence fell. I wondered where she thought we had been, until her son Bertie stepped forth to say, "The people."

With a terse nod, as if this were sufficient explanation, the queen directed her gaze to Alix. Before my sister could drop into an overdue curtsy, Victoria enveloped her in an embrace. "At last, you are here," she said, as if she'd done nothing but pine for Alix's arrival.

We all did our obeisance. As the queen clutched my sister, I had to look away to avoid the sight of those plump black-sheathed arms wrapped about Alix like raven wings.

Victoria held on to Alix for so long, I feared she might smother her. When she drew back, tears glistened in the queen's eyes as she rebuked,

"You are very late. Dinner will be served within the hour. I suggest you go up to your rooms to change. I cannot join you; this waiting has exhausted me. I will see you tomorrow."

And with that, the queen turned and walked away, her collection of funereal attendants at her heels, along with a herd of surprisingly docile spaniels.

Alix glanced over her shoulder at me. She did not look scared. She looked resigned.

THE ENSUING WEEK was filled with activities leading up to the wedding. I couldn't get near Alix in public, while hundreds surrounded us, with the queen herself the focal point around whom everyone must shift. Yet I watched Alix and Victoria develop an unmistakable affinity. The queen wasn't given to displays of affection, but over dinner or tea or one of her interminable walks in the enclosed gardens, with those spaniels who were never far from her side, she would set her fingers on Alix's arm just so—a maternal, possessive gesture that indicated as far as she was concerned, like everything else she put her name to, my sister now belonged to Britain.

Which didn't ease my indignation one bit.

Papa was virtually ignored, treated as a negligible guest, although he was the father of the bride, our king's heir, and Duke of Schleswig, Holstein, and Lauenburg—in title, if not practice. I wondered if his prior futile courtship of Victoria was something the queen did not care to recall. She only deigned to speak with him when protocol required, and since she established protocol, they spoke infrequently. Mama was too preoccupied to take umbrage, fussing over Alix whenever she had the chance and chasing after Thyra and Valdemar, both of whom slipped my haphazard charge over them to race through the castle, playing hide-and-seek with the children of Victoria's daughter, Vicky, Crown Princess of Prussia, startling the servants and jangling the disembodied suits of armor in their niches.

One clear day (or as clear as it could be in England), we went out riding. Papa was an expert horseman from his time in the Danish Horse Guard, a position he'd held in order to support us with its meager salary before he became the king's heir. He'd insisted we all learn to ride as children; Alix was fond of horses but preferred placid mares, while I had no such fears. To me, nothing equaled the thrill of being on horseback, the power and speed of it. It was the closest I could ever get to flying, and I took to the excursion with vigor, joining the gentlemen and ladies for a jaunt outside the castle on the royal stable's numerous mounts. I was proud to see Papa acquit himself, gaining even Victoria's begrudging praise as he demonstrated his skill at the reins for her in the courtyard.

I had to devise a makeshift riding outfit, however. No one had given any thought to whether I might be expected to show my skill on horseback, and as I had no suitable cap, I simply coiled my hair into a net and braved the queen's astonished look.

Victoria did not ride, retreating to her study, but her younger son, eighteen-year-old Alfred, did. He'd been lurking in the background, a pouty-lipped youth with his mother's tepid blue eyes and a permanent scowl. He seemed put out by everything except food and drink, both of which he consumed prodigiously. Conniving to ride alongside me, he bumped his leg against mine and caused my horse to pull at the bit.

"Enjoying the party?" He leered. Not sure which party he referred to, I smiled and spurred ahead to join Alix and Bertie. Despite my initial misgivings, I'd taken a liking to my future brother-in-law. Well traveled and cosmopolitan, Bertie had shown an affability toward Alix that reassured me that if he wasn't any more in love with her than she with him, he was at least resolved to cultivate their mutual respect.

We returned to the castle in considerably better spirits from being outdoors. As I made my way to my room to change for tea—a solemn ritual in which Victoria demanded we all preside—one of her ubiquitous funereal attendants intercepted me.

"Her Majesty wishes to see you."

A private audience was highly unusual, but there was also no question of pleading for a moment to tidy up. When the queen summoned, one must oblige. Brushing a hand over my rumpled skirts and wincing at the smell of horse on my fingers, I followed the lady through Windsor's tapestry-hung corridors to a wainscoted study. After knocking on the door, she left me stranded on the threshold.

"You may enter," the queen called out.

I stepped into a frigid room where I could see my own breath.

Though there was a fireplace, it was scoured clean. The room was over-stuffed, like most of the castle, where bric-a-brac accumulated without discernible purpose, priceless medieval objects perched beside tables spilling over with silver-framed daguerreotypes or porcelain figurines, the walls cluttered with smoky paintings, and corners heaped with marble busts or books.

She sat at her escritoire, before a stack of paper, her pen in hand. I'd heard that she was a dedicated correspondent, spending hours each day penning missives to relatives and dictates to governors in far-flung places of her empire. She didn't look up when I entered, leaving me with my gloves and discarded hairnet crushed in my hands before she said, "I'm told you have an excellent command of the saddle."

"Thank you, Your Majesty." Should I curtsy at the compliment? My legs were sore from riding. If I did curtsy, how low must I descend before I could painfully rise again?

Her pen scratched on the paper. "Do you often ride like that?"

"Yes, Majesty. In Denmark, I try to ride as much as I can—"

"No." She glanced up with a piercing look. "Like *that*."

At first I had no idea what she meant. Then, as she lowered her eyes, I understood.

"I had no cap, Majesty." I resisted the urge to pat down my disheveled curls.

"So it appears." She went on writing. Then she sanded her letter and said, "You might have asked for one. I'm quite sure we could have provided a cap, Dagmar."

"Minnie," I said, and as I heard myself correcting her, I thought I must be mad. "Only my father calls me Dagmar."

"Does he?" Her expression was inscrutable. "Is he very fond of you?"

What type of question was this? *Fond* of me?

"He's my father, Majesty. He loves his family. And we love him."

Something forlorn seeped across her face. I wanted to bite off my tongue. A husband, who was a loving father to his children—she had lost hers.

"That is as it should be." She came to her feet, moving to a set of upholstered chairs before the unlit hearth. "Come. Sit with me. I wish for us to talk further."

I sat beside her. The chair felt enormous, swallowing me whole, the cushion icy. How could she sit at that desk all day, in a room that could have stored slabs of meat?

"Alfred tells me you ride like an Englishwoman," she said.

I smiled, assuming it was another compliment. The English must do everything better than anyone else, according to her.

"And he says you're enjoying your time here," she went on. "Are you?"

Did she doubt her son's word or was she testing my appreciation of her hospitality? Considering how she'd disregarded my father, suspicion flared in me. I restrained it, saying only, "It's a beautiful country, Majesty, but it does rain quite a lot."

"Rain is healthy. For the body and for the field."

"Yes, that is true." How tiresome. Had she called me for a private audience to discuss my lack of a suitable hat and the insufferable weather? At this rate, I'd never make it to my room in time to wash, change, and be back in her cavernous hall for the obligatory tea.

Without warning, she said, "Alfred is quite taken with you. I'm certain you haven't noticed. But you should know that not long ago I considered you as a bride for him."

She had? It came almost as much of a surprise as Alfred being taken with me, for I hadn't noticed; even if I had, I couldn't admit it. To her, a proper lady must never notice a gentleman's interest. But as I recalled Alfred's leering remark, I nearly rolled my eyes. If that was how her son expressed interest, he had something to learn. Still, the revelation, which she'd calculated to spring on me in private, took me aback. Was conquering my sister as she had India not enough? Did she think Danish princesses came in pairs, like shoes or gloves?

"I wish to hear what you think," she said, with faint reproof. "I fear it wouldn't be a suitable match now, but your response will dictate whether I choose to speak with your father. It is important to me— *vital*—that no one marry against their wishes."

I doubted my wishes had any bearing on it. Danish princesses might come in pairs, but she had plenty of other brides to choose for her son. Swallowing against a throat gone dry from the cold, I replied, "I do not know His Highness at all, Your Majesty."

"That could be remedied. You can stay with us for a time after the wedding, as our guest. Your sister would be delighted. I've placed Sandringham and Marlborough House at Bertie's disposal, so there'll be plenty of room. Naturally, I'll furnish all your expenses."

"My expenses? We're not so impoverished, Majesty. My father will soon be King of Denmark."

My indignation burst out before I could detain it. In the leaden silence that ensued, I saw her nearly invisible fair eyebrows lift a fraction.

"You have spirit," she said. "I was once a spirited girl. Too spirited, some might say."

Again, darkness veiled her gaze, sinking into her eyes, drawing down the corners of her mouth. The death of her beloved Albert haunted her.

"Majesty, I'm honored by your consideration, but with my sister living so far from our country, I'd not wish to visit another such loss upon my parents."

"Yet every girl must marry." She regarded me with an impassive expression, as if nothing, not even outright refusal, could affect her demeanor. When I did not reply, she said, "Yes. Entirely too much spirit, I'm afraid. And the will to match it. Well, then. We shan't speak of this again. You must run along now, lest you be late for tea."

I dipped a curtsy and went to the door. She did not move from her chair, staring into that empty hearth, but as I made to leave, I heard her say, "I pity the man who does marry you, Dagmar of Denmark. You'll not be easily tamed."

It sounded like an indictment. And it pleased me.

I SNEAKED INTO Alix's room after another staid dinner, over which, like her teas, Victoria held absolute charge—a solemn affair punctuated by dishes drenched in brown sauces and innocuous conversation over the tinkle of crystal glasses and silver forks.

My sister now sat in her robe on the bed, with her hair unbound, gazing in bemusement at the elaborate wedding dress set on a dresser dummy in the corner—a confection of white Honiton lace and silver tissue, garlanded with silk orange blossoms. Beside her was an open coffer filled with ropes of pearls, a diamond tiara, and other jewels, all of which she was expected to wear for the ceremony, as ordained by the queen.

"Look at this." She held up a gem-studded pendant. "Do you recognize it?"

I peered at it. "Is that the Holy Cross of Dagmar?" I asked incredulously.

"A copy," replied Alix. "But identical in every detail to the original. King Frederick sent it to me as a present. He wanted to attend the wedding, but Her Majesty thought not."

Of course Victoria thought not. Our childless king and his current mistress, a common woman without a drop of royal blood, were naturally not welcome. The replica of the thirteenth-century jewel revered in Denmark was beautiful, however. Extraordinary, in fact, and more valuable than anything either of us had ever owned. My sister was about to dwell in the heart of luxury, even if she risked a lifelong chill, as Victoria seemed unwilling to recognize that fireplaces were meant to be used, flinging open windows wherever she happened to be, to let in all that healthy British air.

"She's rather an ogress, isn't she?" I fingered the delicate lace trim on her wedding gown, which felt like shredded meringue. "She has everyone in terror of her. Did you see her at dinner tonight?" I lowered my voice to imitate Victoria's querulous tone: "*Alfred. Enough wine. We have other guests who wish to partake. Vicky, please keep that boy's elbows off the table. Bertie, must you talk of India? We are eating. I do not wish to hear about elephant tusks.* She certainly knows how to keep her brood in place."

Alix frowned. "She's their mother. It is what a mother must do."

She sounded irritated. Thinking she was upset that I'd not kept closer watch over our younger siblings as promised—especially after one of their romps in the drawing room, when they'd stepped on Victoria's favorite spaniel and made it yelp—I said, "You'll not miss Mama. The queen sounds just like her, though Mama is prettier."

"You mustn't say such things," said Alix, but a smile crept over her mouth. "She summoned you today to a private audience. It's unheard of; everyone was talking about it. Alfred went to Bertie later. He seemed upset."

"How could you tell? He always seems upset. It must be his digestion. He eats too much."

Alix chuckled, to my relief. "Entirely. He'll grow obese before he's thirty. Did the queen ask you about him?"

"As a matter of fact, she did." I gave her a pointed look. "She told me Alfred was taken with me and she'd considered me as a bride for him but didn't believe it would be a suitable match." I paused. "Did you tell her about Nixa?"

"About his interest in you? No. She only knows that I refused him. She said it was very sensible of me. She thinks Russia is a barbaric land, too harsh on foreign brides."

"She must mean Danish ones. The Romanovs have wed plenty of German brides in the past, and none died of their barbarism that I'm aware of."

"Perhaps she's worried for you," said Alix.

"Why should she be? Whom I marry is none of her concern. And if Alfred is so interested, he should have said so—to me. Not have his mother do it for him."

"I doubt she expected him to show any interest." Alix paused. "If you'd said yes, you could have stayed here with me."

I was surprised. "Is that what you want? Are you having second thoughts now that you're here?" I almost added that after meeting Victoria, I'd certainly have second thoughts.

"I am not. But remember what I told you: Listen to your heart—"

"And use my head. I haven't forgotten."

We gazed at each other, the short distance between us suddenly seeming too wide, almost unsurpassable. "I don't know what I'm going to do without you," I finally said, lowering my eyes. "It's never going to be the same again, is it?"

"No." She came to me, clasping my hands. "But *we* will always be the same. Minnie, promise me that we'll never change. We'll always be loving sisters, no matter what."

"Stop it. You'll make me cry before the wedding."

"Promise." She pressed my hands tighter. "I must hear you say it."

"Yes." A lump filled my throat as I whispered, "I promise. Sisters forever."

"No matter what." She bent her head to kiss my fingertips. Then she reached up and set her palm against my cheek. "You are so strong. Stronger than you know. You refused Queen Victoria today. What other princess would dare do that?"

I refrained from saying that she certainly had not done so. What was the use?

Alix came to her feet. "And you mustn't worry about me. I know I will be happy here. Bertie is so kind. We have our entire life ahead of us."

It was as much reassurance as I could expect. At this time, what else could she do?

"That must be a relief to everyone concerned," I said, as she returned to the coffer and shut its lid. "Imagine the uproar if you decided to cancel the wedding."

Alix went still. Then she started to laugh, and I had to laugh, too.

CHAPTER FOUR

The wedding wasn't grand, but it was crowded, held in St. George's Chapel at Windsor, which could accommodate nine hundred in the pews.

I was proud to see that my sister, in her wedding gown and pearl-and-diamond parure, a gift from Bertie, outshone even the queen's daughters. Alix had never looked more beautiful, an opalescent vision beside her florid husband, who looked quite pleased with himself.

They would honeymoon at some manor called Osborne, where the queen had honeymooned with her late Albert. After the wedding reception and breakfast in the Waterloo Gallery, Victoria disappeared as soon as Alix went upstairs to change. I waited anxiously for my sister, knowing she'd soon depart by train. When she reappeared, she had everyone, including me, gazing in awe at her, in her white velvet and ermine wrap.

"Regal" was the only way to describe her. "Hurriedly" was the only way she could say goodbye. They were running late, as everything tended to do at weddings. Before I could say a word to her, her kiss grazed my cheek and she and Bertie were racing out of the castle with their respective households for the carriages to the station. Behind them went the nine hundred guests.

We departed the next day, without seeing the queen again. I hoped I'd never see her again. While I was glad to leave, I worried for Alix, who now must endure married life under a tyrannical mother-in-law.

UPON OUR RETURN to Copenhagen in mid-March 1863, more un-expected change fell upon us.

Following the overthrow of their Bavarian-born king, Otto, in late fall of 1862, the Greeks had rejected Otto's brother as his successor. A list of candidates for a new monarch, including Victoria's son Alfred, was drawn up; to everyone's surprise, my seventeen-year-old brother, Willie, who'd seemed destined for a career in the Royal Navy, was elected by the Greek National Assembly on March 30. He took the title of George I of the Hellenes, and after his ceremonial enthronement in Copenhagen, he departed for Greece in October, marking another elevation for our family. I felt badly for him. Kingship aside, he'd been obliged to do his duty as Alix had, accepting a crown he hadn't asked for that took him far from us. It only strengthened my resolve to stay put.

No sooner had Willie left than Papa was summoned to our moribund king's bedside. Frederick's notoriously extravagant life had finally caught up with him. He succumbed in November, just as he'd lived—noisily, and without remorse.

My father became King Christian IX.

We moved into the Amalienborg Palace—a ramshackle edifice in dire need of renovation, which Mama proceeded to undertake with her habitual industriousness and economy. I was now officially Princess Dagmar of Denmark. When I declared I found the title ridiculous, Mama reproved, "Much as you might dislike it, a princess is what you are."

"Well, I don't feel like one," I said, which made her purse her mouth.

Papa provided me with my promised suite of rooms; as predicted, Thyra clamored to share it with me and I agreed. I couldn't bear that echoing expanse without Alix at my side to make it feel like home.

Conflict plagued Papa soon after. Prussia and Austria contested Denmark's titular possession of the duchies of Schleswig, Holstein, and Lauenburg on the base of Jutland Peninsula between the North Sea and the Baltic Sea. Otto von Bismarck, Prussia's minister president under King Wilhelm, declared war on us and seized the duchies, claiming we held them illegally. Despite his futile attempts at mediation to regain the duchies, Papa was excoriated by our newspapers for our loss, rousing my hatred of the Germans.

This weakening of our standing also exerted immediate impact upon me.

Mama summoned me to her new study, which was heaped with fabric samples and architectural plans for the palace renovation.

"I've received a letter from His Imperial Majesty Tsar Alexander II. He approves his son's suit. He proposes to send Tsarevich Nixa forthwith. Isn't it wonderful?" she said, waving the letter at me. "He'll come here to propose in person. That's not usually done," she went on, as I stood there, silent. "It's a great honor. Prospective brides are always invited to the Romanov court to be assessed, but His Highness will come instead to—"

"Assessed?" I interrupted. "How so?"

"To determine their suitability. Minnie, are you not elated? It is a great honor," she repeated.

"So you keep saying. But if the prospective bride is deemed unsuitable, what then?"

Her foot tapped under her hem—an impatient tempo on the warped wood floor (she'd had the old rugs removed), which I was unable to see yet couldn't ignore. "You're not being called upon to be assessed. Nixa has seen you already. You are deemed suitable. He thinks so, and now so does his father, the tsar."

I set the letter aside. "Isn't this rather sudden? After Prussia has humiliated us and stolen our duchies, I should think I'd be deemed most unsuitable indeed."

I saw her near-imperceptible recoil. As I glanced at the disorder on her desk, evidence of her plotting, I wondered how many letters had gone between her and the tsarina—two queens organizing the future of their progeny, regardless of political calamity, like countless queens before them.

"Your father's situation has nothing to do with this," she replied at length. "A princess must still marry, regardless of who stole what from whom."

"I see," I replied, for she'd never admit otherwise. "Yet Nixa barely knows me. Apparently that also poses no impediment."

"There are none. What impediment could there possibly be?"

"Me." I met her aghast stare. "I am the impediment. Or shall I have no say in whom I take as a husband, as Alix had no say in hers?"

Mama's face closed like a trap. "She had her say. Plenty of say, I can assure you."

"Then will you allow me the same?"

For a moment I thought she might start berating me for my ingratitude, poking a hole in her carefully laid plans. Instead, she said tightly, "Naturally. Your father and I would never force you."

I nodded. I meant to take her at her word. More important, I knew Papa would take her at her word. If I did not find the tsarevich agreeable, there would be no wedding.

⁓

HE ARRIVED IN early summer, as Denmark burst with wildflowers and melted snow gushed in the rivers. We'd moved to Fredensborg Palace outside Copenhagen, by Lake Esrum, as Mama deemed the orangery and baroque gardens the ideal setting for our encounter.

I didn't know what to expect. As I had told Alix, they spoke French at the Romanov court; it was sophisticated, renowned for its grandeur—more Western than Eastern, despite its Oriental roots. But for me, Russia had now adopted that barbaric menace Victoria had accorded it. I imagined endless winters under snow-filled midnight skies, with fur-swathed heathens downing vodka and smashing the cutlery. Anything that added to my determination to find the tsarevich unworthy became grist for my imagination, until my fear assumed such epic proportions even I had to admit not all of it could possibly be true.

Still, I clung to my resolve. Alix had been wrong. I wasn't adventurous. I had no desire to abandon my country, my family, or my faith—as a Lutheran, I'd be expected to convert to Russia's Orthodox Church—for a land steeped in myth and frozen tundra.

I supposed he'd arrive with Cossacks flanking him; instead, my first look at him—my first *real* look—occurred as he walked alone across the gardens toward where I sat under an oak tree, a book in my lap.

My eyes at half-mast as I succumbed to drowsiness, I suddenly heard his footsteps approach. I jolted upright, my book slipping from me. At first, I thought the male figure walking toward me was my father, who, since the loss of his duchies, was given to perambulations in the afternoons to rest his mind. Mama hadn't been specific about when the tsarevich might arrive, and I'd anticipated some sort of production to herald it.

Yet here he was—the Russian heir, standing paces away, his head tilted quizzically as I scrambled for my upended book, at first not thinking anything, then, as awareness went through me, leaving the book where it lay to lift my face to him.

He was handsome. I couldn't deny it. The Romanovs were a handsome family. But he wasn't large; he looked too slim in his fitted jacket and gray striped trousers, his crisp white shirt open at the neck, without a cravat—an informality that struck me moments before he leaned down to retrieve my book. As his gray-blue eyes met mine, he said softly, "I regret to disturb Your Highness. Please, accept my apologies."

His thick hair was dark, with coppery highlights in its depths. His features were angular, and he had a slight quirk to his mouth when he spoke, a subtle imperfection that gave him an elfish air. Despite everything, I found myself intrigued. He was behaving as if he had no right to be here and must explain his intrusion.

Listen to your heart.

Hearing Alix in my head, I ventured a smile as he turned my book over, smoothing its crumbled pages. "*Enoch Arden* by Lord Tennyson. In English." He handed it back to me. "Do you enjoy reading poetry in foreign languages, Princess Dagmar?"

I still hadn't grown used to my title, although the way he spoke it in his Russian accent (he'd learned some Danish, which impressed me) wasn't unpleasant.

"My sister Alix sent it to me," I said. "She says everyone in London is reading it. Enoch is lost at sea and finds upon his return that his wife, who thought him dead, has married his childhood friend. Enoch never tells her who he is, as he loves her too much to spoil her happiness. He dies of a broken heart. It's sad. I'm not sure I like sad poems."

"Neither am I, though in Russia, sad poetry is a national pastime." As he smiled, I realized that he'd not introduced himself, as though we were friends who'd happened upon each other, which again proved disconcerting.

None of it fit into my idea of how our encounter would be.

"You look surprised," he said, as I came to my feet. He was tall but not too tall. I found I could look him in the eye without craning my head too much.

"I am." I saw no reason to lie. "I hadn't thought to see you today."

"But you knew I was due?" He seemed worried that I hadn't, so I made myself nod and then, with his gaze still fixed on me, I said, "You've found me idling away my time. My mother will not approve. She had hoped our meeting would be more dignified."

"Then we shall not tell her." He was looking so intently at me that I wondered if I had a grass stain on my face. "You are not as I thought."

"Oh?" Had he decided this wasn't a proposal he cared to make, now that he'd seen me in person again? It must be one thing to admire a girl from afar as she ran about unawares, as I had at Rumpenheim, quite another to come face-to-face with her and decide whether to marry her. Without realizing what I was doing, I raised a hand to my hair, finding to my chagrin that the frayed ribbon tying it back had nearly slipped off. Suddenly I wanted to be that girl he'd first seen and been enraptured by, as Alix had claimed, and I cursed inwardly at my disregard for the seriousness of the occasion. I should have prepared, as Mama had chided countless times, greeted him as befitted my station in life. He'd think me slovenly, in my worn day dress with my hair unbound, reading poetry in midafternoon under a tree, without a hat or—

"Yes," he said. "You are different. More . . . vibrant."

Incredulous laughter escaped me. "That isn't what Mama would say."

"Then she does not see you as I do." Before I could react to his remark, which I wasn't sure he intended as flattery, he said, "I've come a long way in hope of this moment. I planned it all in my head and yet . . ." He smiled once more. He had small white teeth, but the top one was crooked, overlapping its neighbor—another perfect imperfection.

"You are disappointed," I said.

"Oh, no." He moved so quickly to me, I thought he might take my hand. He didn't, his fingers flexing at his side as if he struggled to curb the impulse. "Not in the least. Are you?"

It was the moment I had dreaded. Now would be the time to send him on his way. I sensed he wouldn't express offense. He was too well

trained to cause me any discomfort. He'd simply retire, as he had all of
Europe to choose from.

Instead, I heard myself say, "No. Not disappointed."

His smile widened, brightening his face. He was rather pale; he did
not seem to be someone who spent much time outdoors.

"Shall we walk?" I asked, and as I winced at my forwardness, for the
gentleman should always lead, he stepped closer, so close this time that
his slim fingers brushed mine.

"I would like nothing better," he said.

⁓

HE STAYED WITH us for a month. We went riding in the morning—
despite his delicate appearance, he was an avid horseman—and boating
on the lake. We took walks in the garden without a chaperone (proof
that everyone knew he was a serious suitor) and he spoke to me of Russia, as if he somehow intuited that I harbored unspoken trepidation.

I found myself fascinated by his descriptions of the Romanov empire, of steppes inhabited by Mongol tribes, and of the rugged mountains of the Caucasus, populated by rebel Circassians whom the tsar
had vowed to tame or annihilate. He had me basking in the balm of the
Crimea on the Black Sea and running wild like a lynx in the wilderness
of Siberia. He danced me through the ethereal beauty of St. Petersburg,
under the shimmering pale sky—those white nights I knew about, as
we had them in summer in Denmark, but which he turned into such a
magical occurrence, he made me long to see them in Russia. He spoke
of his father's historic emancipation of the serfs, which freed the peasantry from centuries of servitude to landowners and made Tsar Alexander II beloved in his realm.

"In Russia, we have many princesses and princes," he said, "but
within our royal family, we are known as grand dukes and grand duchesses."

"Like in Prussia," I said. "How curious. Do you have many of
them?"

He chuckled. "According to my father, too many. He wants to curtail our autocratic privilege, but his brothers—my uncles, the grand
dukes—will have none of it. They don't want anything to change, al-

though," he said, taking my hand, as he was now apt to do during our conversations, "it must. My father says if we are to survive, we have to leave the past behind. A Romanov's duty is to serve Russia first, before himself."

I admired his love for his country; it was something we shared, as I loved mine. He asked me many questions about Denmark and I eagerly obliged, but as I heard myself extolling our small nation's accomplishments, and silently comparing them to the might of Russia, I began to realize we didn't have much else in common. Besides being heir to the most powerful empire in the world, Nixa was very well traveled, having been throughout Europe and all the way to Asia, and very erudite, as only an imperial prince could be. I felt keenly my own lack of learning and experience, my reading of insipid poetry, my silly watercolor painting, and my covert cartwheels on the lawn when Mama wasn't looking. The differences between us stretched as wide as the Gulf of Finland, and while he didn't seem to mind, surely his mother the tsarina would.

And indeed, as I soon discovered, if Nixa had disconcerted me, his mother would even more so.

That remote empress who'd spoken only a few innocuous words to me was altogether changed. She arrived on her way to Nice for her annual respite; when I greeted her in the drawing room under Mama's watch, she embraced me with delight, kissing both my cheeks in the French style and holding me at arm's length, looking me over with her keen yet melancholic gaze. "How lovely you are, Minnie dear. Such a tiny waist and those big black eyes—why, you're enchanting."

I was? I couldn't help but glance at Mama, who sat suffused with pride. I recalled that Nixa had first been ordered by his father to woo Alix. Had the tsarina also deemed my sister "enchanting"? Was this her polite way of easing any awkwardness? Born a princess herself, Maria Alexandrovna—her imperial name, as adopting a Russian name upon conversion to Orthodoxy was required of a foreign bride—had presided over her husband's court for many years. She couldn't be oblivious to the delicacy of our situation.

"Has she ever sat for a daguerreotype?" she said, turning to Mama.

Mama gave a forlorn sigh. "Not in several years." She didn't add that photography was novel and expensive; we'd never had enough money to hire an official photographer, if we could have even found one in Denmark.

"Then we must remedy that," said the tsarina. "I must have a portrait of her to show Alexander. I'll send for someone in France. There have been remarkable improvements. Sitting now for a daguerreotype isn't nearly as arduous as it used to be. Would you like that, my dear?" she asked, returning her smile to me.

I nodded. She had me sit beside her, engaging me in small conversation that expertly avoided any pitfalls. I left feeling as puzzled as when I'd arrived. It was nice to be admired, but once again, nagging doubt overcame me, causing me to withdraw from Nixa, not overtly but in a subtle manner he eventually noticed.

He hadn't yet proposed. I appreciated his tact, not blurting it out until he'd earned my affection, until one night after supper, as everyone retired to the drawing room, he tugged at my sleeve and drew me into one of the screened alcoves in the corridor.

Before I could ask him what the matter was, he said, "Do you not love me?"

"Love you?" I regarded him in astonishment. "We've only just met."

He lowered his eyes. "But I thought . . ."

"Nixa." Though I'd been mindful to never touch him first, I did so now, lightly setting my fingers on his sleeve. Feeling him tremble, I left my hand there. "What did you think?"

"I thought that you . . ." He appeared to have trouble finding the words. Then he squared his shoulders. "I thought you might wish to be my wife one day."

I considered him in silence before I said, "I believe I might. One day."

"Then you would say yes if I . . ." He looked so eager now, yet also so braced for rejection, I wanted to laugh. But laughter wouldn't be appropriate. He'd gone visibly taut, his entire person strung like a wire, until I said, "If you ask properly, I think I would."

He clumsily embraced me, careful not to press his lean figure too close to mine. I heard him whisper in my ear, "I'm afraid to ask."

"Yet you must." I drew back. "A girl must always be asked."

"Will you marry me?" he breathed, and I feared he might actually drop to one knee.

"Yes," I said.

For I wanted to—which was the most unexpected thing of all.

⟶⟜

OUR ENGAGEMENT WAS greeted with joy by my parents and the tsarina; by the time Nixa left with his mother to continue to France, the news had winged its way to England, where Alix, who had delivered her first child in January, a son, was so elated that she insisted on coming to visit us once she persuaded Victoria. Though her delivery was already six months past, the queen apparently worried over the health of everyone in her family, mandating that as a new mother, Alix must undertake as little travel as possible.

"Alix says Bertie wants them to attend my wedding," I read aloud from her letter.

Papa smiled. "That would indeed be noteworthy. No member of the British royal family has set foot in Russia in many years; Victoria and Alexander are not on the best of terms. Just think, your marriage could be cause for a détente between the two empires."

"Never mind that." Mama snatched my sister's letter from me. "Politics are of no account here. Two young people have fallen in love and are blessed to have found each other. If Their Highnesses of Wales wish to celebrate the blessing in person, so be it."

Papa winked at me. I saw that while he was happy for me, it also saddened him to know I'd leave his side for a foreign land. I vowed to spend extra time with him, though his duties as king were such that it was a challenge to see him at all.

As for Mama's refusal to exalt political benefits to the match, it didn't matter. Nixa had chosen me, for me. I'd not made it a simple task, but in the end he won my heart—not because he was the tsarevich but because of who he was inside. I fell in love with Nixa Romanov himself, with his gentle spirit and noble soul.

That love buoyed me as months separated us, our distance bridged by the exchange of frequent letters. The photographer from Paris arrived and I sat for my portrait. I did not view the finished product until weeks later when a framed copy arrived, the original having been sent to the tsarina. I was dismayed by my image, dressed in a high-necked white gown and my hair in contrived ringlets, my enormous eyes over-powering my monochrome face. Mama declared it a perfect likeness. She hired her own photographer for our court and dispatched our por-traits by special courier to St. Petersburg in profusion.

In return, Nixa sent his portrait and those of his relations, so I could put faces to the names of my future Romanov family. One portrait, in particular, of the tsar and tsarina surrounded by their six sons, who ranged in age from Nixa's twenty-one to Grand Duke Paul's four, along with their surviving daughter, eleven-year-old Grand Duchess Marie, caused me to laugh and point at a hulking figure who seemed to stand apart from them, though he was in fact beside Nixa himself.

"Look! He must be a Cossack."

Mama remonstrated, "Honestly, Minnie. That's not a Cossack. He's Grand Duke Alexander, Nixa's brother. In the family, they call him Sasha. He's only seventeen months younger than Nixa. He and Nixa are very close."

"Are they?" I peered at that stolid figure, who towered over the oth-ers. "Nixa barely mentioned him to me. And he doesn't look like any of them."

Nixa also sent a box of books for me to read, including Russian fairy tales of witches, dancing bears, and immortal sorcerers; poetry by the celebrated Pushkin, which I didn't find sad at all; and novels by the lit-erary idol Tolstoy, as well as a Russian primer so I could become ac-quainted with the language. He wrote that the Russian embassy in Copenhagen would provide an Orthodox priest to instruct me in my new faith, as my conversion to Orthodox Christianity was a require-ment and not anything I could protest. As Mama assured me, "In Rus-sia, they still revere our Savior."

Late at night, I sometimes woke from a restless sleep. As I listened to my little sister, Thyra, breathing beside me, I tried to conjure Nixa in my mind and see him in his milieu, in that great Winter Palace where generations of his ancestors had lived, with its fabled Malachite Room. I tried to envision the first pristine snows, the joyous sleigh rides as the people took to the frozen outdoors, and to hear the crack of ice as it overpowered the Neva, turning its shallows so solid that one could strap on skates and glide across it.

I couldn't maintain these illusionary images for long. They appeared and vanished like smoke, leaving me disorientated, with an uneasiness that began to gnaw at me.

"Nerves," Mama said when I confided in her. "A new bride's nerves are an instrument of torture if she lets them get out of hand. You mustn't dwell on what you do not know. Think only of how much he loves you and let the future take care of itself."

She behaved accordingly, occupying me with plans for my trousseau, which included evening gowns by the renowned couturier Charles Frederick Worth, whose sumptuous creations were the height of fashion. I did not ask how we could afford such extravagance, as his atelier was in Paris, but in this matter Mama was immovable. I must travel to my nuptials dressed in the latest styles, so no one could say Denmark was behind the times.

Monsieur Worth sent dresses on cunning miniature dolls, including the corsets—elegant mannequins that Thyra squealed over and Mama forbade her to touch. After making our selections, Mama told me we'd travel to Paris to have the gowns fitted in person. I grew excited at the thought of arriving in Russia, dressed like one of those idealized dolls.

We had just purchased our passage to Paris when my entire world fell apart.

CHAPTER FIVE

Mama entered my room with the telegram. Having returned to Copenhagen, I was packing, or trying to pack, clothes strewn all over the bed as I debated what to take. We would travel to Nice after our sojourn in Paris; the tsarina was already there, having left St. Petersburg earlier than usual due to an unspecified ailment. Mama had told me that Maria Alexandrovna suffered from weak lungs and required regular proximity to the sea. She had various seaside palaces in Russia, but apparently she required proximity to a sea beyond her husband's domain. Nixa had joined her there so we could spend time together before my trip to Russia; when I noticed the paper in Mama's hand, I didn't think anything of it.

"Did Her Imperial Majesty send word again?" I asked, holding up my battered straw hat. "Do you think this will do for our time at the villa? I know it's early spring, so it won't be too hot, but I don't want to get any spots. Or would a parasol be better?"

Mama said, "Minnie." The quiet in her voice, under which lurked a slight quaver, immobilized me where I stood. The hat crunched in my hands, its straw gone brittle.

She didn't move from the threshold—not because she didn't want to, but because she apparently couldn't. Her hand came up against the doorframe as though she might fall.

"Nixa," she said, and the hat dropped from my fingers. "He's had an accident."

I didn't say a word. I looked at her stricken expression, at that slip of paper in her hand, and the room capsized around me.

"He was thrown from his horse," Mama said, still in that awful hushed voice. "He developed pain in his back. He couldn't walk. Then fever set in. Her Imperial Majesty summoned a specialist from Vienna. Minnie, he has spinal meningitis."

She might have cited any disease; it made no difference. As her words plunged through me, consumed by the pounding tempo of my heart in my ears, I reached out for something, anything, to hold on to.

Mama rushed to me, catching me about my waist and lowering me onto the bed, where I sat limp, voiceless, staring into nothing.

"He has asked to see you," she said. "Oh, my child, we must make haste. He has already received the Last Rites. The tsarina begs us to come at once."

⌒

I HAD NEVER been to France, and I didn't see anything when I finally went. We traveled by train for four days, through odious Germany. The tsarina sent tickets for the best class; from Dijon, her own imperial train conveyed us to Nice, with the French emperor Napoleon III ordering all other trains canceled to abet our passage. In an upholstered walnut-paneled compartment as luxurious as a palace, equipped with uniformed servants, I sat by the window and watched the French countryside slide past without marking a single sight, as if I were rushing through an interminable tunnel.

Mama spoke little. No words could ease my agony. I'd fallen in love and pledged to marry; now my fiancé was being taken from me. Even if she had tried to console me, I wouldn't have listened. I nursed the fissure in my heart and prayed over and over, in tandem with the clattering wheels on the rails: Let it not be true. Let him recover. Give me a miracle to heal him. Do not let him die.

I believed if Nixa died, I would die, too. Like Victoria with Albert, I would want to join him in his tomb, for I couldn't envision my life now without him.

I believed this with every fiber in my being.

I was still so very young.

⌒

THE TSARINA WAITED at the entrance to her splendid Villa Bermont, nestled among orange groves and fragrant acacia, overlooking the Mediterranean—a vista that assaulted me with its cruelty, that such a beautiful place could be the scene of such devastation.

In her bruised eyes and grateful embrace of my mother, I saw we were not too late. I also knew, without anyone saying it, that God would not answer my prayers.

"He asked to see you as soon as you arrived," the empress told me.

"I must change first," I heard myself whisper. I sounded so remote, not myself at all.

"Nonsense." Mama prodded me toward the tsarina, who brought me through the airy villa, which smelled of the sea, to his room.

"He's not in pain," she whispered when I paused at the doorway. "He's been given laudanum. Go to him, my dear. He has waited longer than—" Her voice fractured.

Longer than he should have. Longer than God had intended for him to wait.

I moved to his bed. His eyes were shut, his skin so pale he almost blended with the sheets, his skull incised under his skin, as if what had claimed him was determined to devour him to his bones. I choked back tears. I mustn't cry before him. He mustn't see me disconsolate; he must take strength from my presence, know that I—

"Minnie."

His voice reached me across the distant murmur of the sea outside, the room's windows left ajar to admit the air. Though he couldn't see the water, he could hear it.

I sat on the stool by his side, taking his hand. His skin was cold, shocking me. And in his red-rimmed gaze as he raised his eyes, I saw fear. He might not suffer visible pain, because of the drug, but he felt a deeper pain, inside.

Nixa knew he was doomed.

His parched lips opened. "No," I said, retrieving a glass of water from the bedside table. "Don't speak. I am here. I will not leave you."

His hand clutched at mine. He avoided the glass I tried to set at his lips. "Listen," he rasped. He had no strength, but his fingers dug into my palm. I leaned closer to him, smelling his fetid breath, his unwashed body soaked in perspiration. "You must listen to me. I must tell you . . . I . . . I failed you. I spoiled your happiness. Like Enoch."

"No. You haven't. Never."

"Yes." His hand was crawling to my wrist, gripping me. "I—I am lost to you. We cannot marry. I promised you . . ."

Without knowing why, as if something inside me sensed an unseen presence, the pad of a footstep nearby, I turned my head to the door. No one was there.

I returned my gaze to Nixa.

"Sasha," he said. "Promise you will marry him instead. He's my brother. He—he will love you as much as I do. More so, because of me."

I might have pulled away in disbelief, but his fingers were wrapped about my wrist like icy vines, and his face—dear God, his face. He was *beseeching* me.

"Promise me, Minnie."

I couldn't utter the words he needed to hear. I wanted to, for his sake, but I felt as though I was tumbling off an endless cliff toward the sea and I would never reach the water; I would forever flail and twirl in the empty air until I disintegrated.

He went limp. His fingers unraveled from my wrist, and he lay so still, I thought he must be dead. But I saw his chest moving almost imperceptibly and I did not move from the stool, watching him as he drifted away, like Enoch on his boat.

MAMA STEERED ME to rooms prepared for us, while the tsarina resumed her watch over Nixa. A servant brought a meal to our room, which I couldn't look at, much less taste, and as I undressed for bed, Mama asked, "Did he say anything to you about Sasha?"

I met her sorrowful eyes, wondering how she knew. "Why would he?"

She regarded me strangely. "He said nothing?"

"No. *Why* do you ask?"

She must have heard the hysteria seeping into my voice, for she took a wary glance at our closed door, just as I had in Nixa's bedroom, before she said, "Because Sasha is here. He came as soon as he heard of Nixa's illness."

"He's here?" I recalled that eerie sense of being watched as I sat with

Nixa, the sound of a footstep outside the door. Revulsion curdled in me. "Why hasn't he presented himself?"

"The tsarina thought it best to give you time with Nixa first. You'll meet him later. Tomorrow, perhaps," she added, stumbling over her own words as she realized that what she was trying not to say was I would meet him at the death vigil, if Nixa survived the night.

I turned to my bed, wanting to escape, to forget everything.

"Shall I wake you if . . . ?" I heard Mama whisper.

"Yes," I said.

The door clicked shut as she left me alone.

I did not sleep. I invoked oblivion, but I felt that unseen presence as if it stood at the foot of my bed—the stranger whom my fiancé had begged me to marry in his stead.

WE GATHERED AT Nixa's bedside early in the morning. April sunshine gilded the sea, but the windows were shut now, the room suffocated by the smell of musk mixed with champagne, a concoction the Viennese specialist employed to rouse Nixa from his stupor.

Two Orthodox priests—bizarre to me in their black cassocks adorned with golden-brocade *epitrachelion* stoles and their flat-rimmed *kamilavka* caps—stood by the bed, one of them chanting. A chased-gold censer swung in the other priest's hand, its myrrh-scented fumes adding to the smothering atmosphere. When Mama and I entered the room, I had to avert my gaze from the priests' somber bearded faces as Nixa agonized toward his final hour.

Then I caught sight of him: Grand Duke Sasha, motionless beside his mother.

The tsarina sat crumpled on the stool, still in the same dark dress she'd been wearing when we arrived, indicating she'd spent the entire night here. She did not look up as Mama and I stepped past the weeping ladies-in-waiting and other guests—all Russian aristocrats, I assumed, vacationing in Nice, who must have known the imperial family intimately to be present. It seemed disrespectful, a travesty. This was not a performance. It was the tragic end of a young life.

Clenching my fists, I assumed my post by the tsarina. When she felt me near, she reached for my hand. I did not uncoil my fist, so she clung to it.

I glanced at her second son. Had I not known he was Nixa's brother,

I would never have believed they were related. Unlike Nixa, Sasha's solid build gave him the appearance of ungainliness, and he was so tall, he slouched. His head pressed forward from his thickset neck; under his already receding hairline, his blue-gray eyes were narrow, his mouth small and grim, offset by an incongruously wispy mustache. To me, he possessed none of Nixa's refinement.

He didn't return my glance. But when Nixa sensed me there, he shifted his glazed eyes to me and he whispered, "Isn't she charming?"

If he was asking Sasha, his brother did not answer. The priest continued to chant, and my tears blurred everything. At the final moment, I tore myself away from the tsarina to kneel by the bed. "Don't leave me," I said, my voice breaking.

He sighed. His last breath.

The tsarina let out a small cry. I half-turned on my knees, her despair sundering the hush. A trim, tall man with a balding pate, graying mustachios, and thick sideburns stepped forth to comfort her. Sasha stepped aside. I went still. That tall older man . . . he seemed so familiar to me. And when he murmured, "Maria, my *solnyshko*," recognition gripped me.

Tsar Alexander. He was also here.

My fiancé lay dead, yet I searched frantically, furiously, for my mother. I found her behind the tsarina, among the women holding handkerchiefs to their faces. She averted her eyes. I knew then that these strangers around me, whom I'd thought vacationing aristocrats, were the imperial family itself.

I couldn't bear it, the humiliation of being left unaware, when they knew, every one, what I had just lost. As I staggered to my feet, my skirts tangled about my ankles, and someone gave a stifled gasp, perhaps fearing I'd pitch backward onto the corpse. Sasha lunged forth. With a firm hand, he caught me by my shoulder, compelling me to stay upright.

I looked into his cast-iron eyes. Before I could utter my gratitude, he hissed under his breath, so that only I could hear: "I *promised* him. Remember that."

He released me and moved away, into chilling silence.

My mother guided me from the room, away from the loving future I had thought would be mine.

. . .

THERE WAS NO further mention of Nixa's last request. I did not admit what he'd asked of me, hiding it within me during the torchlit procession to the Orthodox church. After the mass, the coffin was taken by Russian warship to the funeral obsequies in St. Petersburg.

Their Imperial Majesties came to say goodbye before I departed with Mama, who insisted we must travel to Rumpenheim so I could grieve and rest. Handing me the Orthodox Bible that had belonged to Nixa, the tsarina held me close. "He will always be with us, my child," she whispered. "In us now resides his memory. As long as we remember him, he will live forever, in heaven and in our hearts."

I curtsied before the ashen tsar, who kissed my cheek. In a quavering voice that betrayed his deep inner grief, he said, "You are always welcome in our family. We grieve for your loss, too." He tried to smile at me, but his blue-gray eyes, Nixa's eyes, were dark with sorrow. I could see that the unexpected death of his eldest son and heir had devastated him, much as it had me.

He stepped aside, his shoulders stooped, as his third son, Grand Duke Vladimir, embraced me with a warmth that nearly made me weep. Vladimir possessed some of Nixa's allure, only his was more masculine, his robust build contrasting with his mother's sensitive brown eyes. I felt his sincere affection, though we'd never met before, when he said, "You must come to St. Petersburg soon," and I saw the tsarina flinch.

Sasha didn't make an appearance. As the tsarina accompanied us to the train, she told us that the new tsarevich was inconsolable, so overwhelmed that he refused to speak to anyone. He had already departed Nice to accompany his brother's coffin to Russia.

On our way to Denmark, my mother plied me with cakes and tea I refused to touch, murmuring endearments meant to provide solace, reminders that Nixa and I had loved each other so much and I'd given him such solace in the end. I let it all wash over me like the whisper of those waves outside Nixa's window, which I knew I would never forget.

I promised him. Remember that.

It haunted me. For though I'd failed to make the same promise, I felt bound by it.

CHAPTER SIX

At Rumpenheim, I fell ill with a recurrent fever that proved mysterious to our physicians but not to Mama. She understood that grief was overtaking me like a dark shade, and she refused to let it triumph. She roused me to walks in the gardens, which made me cry because the trees reminded me of the oak where he'd first come upon me. She forced me to ride, but that also made me cry, because I remembered that being thrown from a horse had precipitated his death. She sat me beside her for hours in the parlor, doing needlework that was soon wet with tears. She unpacked the dresses that arrived from Paris, paid for and finished without me, but I'd lost so much weight, none of them fit; and the sight of those sublime gowns in pale-pink satin, white and cream silk, intended to enhance my luster in Russia, made me cry all the more.

Finally she set aside her attempts at distraction. "He is gone," she said abruptly one morning. "Nothing you do can change it."

I stared at her. "Don't you think I know that?"

"Then, why? Must you die, as well? Is that the reason for this intolerable malaise, this refusal to do anything, even eat, pecking at your food like a bird? I will not have it. You loved a man and you lost him, as many women do. Your death will do nothing but bring further grief. Do you intend to have us put you in your grave?"

"*What* would you have me do?" I cried, though I'd never raised my voice to her before.

"I would have you live. Mourn him, but live. Nixa wouldn't want to see you like this. He wanted only for you to be happy."

"He told me he spoiled my happiness! He—he said he had failed me." I buried my face in my hands.

She moved to me, setting her hand on my shoulder. "He wasn't to blame. You are not to blame. It was God's will. The sooner you accept it, the easier it will be. Please try. For me. For your papa. For your brothers and sisters. We're all so terribly worried for you."

My sister . . .

I lifted my face to my mother. "Alix. I want to see her."

"Then you shall. I'll write to her this instant."

"No. Not in England." The mere thought of facing Victoria, who'd expressed pity for the man who married me, made me quail. "She must come here."

"Yes," said Mama. "She will."

⁓

ALIX ARRIVED, ACCOMPANIED by her husband, Bertie, and their son, Albert Victor, as well as their new baby boy, George. My sister informed us that given the circumstances, she had insisted on making the trip despite Victoria's objections, and her loving presence at my side helped to ease my sorrow. Bertie had gained so much weight, he looked portly to me, with his ruddy face and mustachios, his tight frock coat straining at his stomach. But he was solicitous, offering me his condolences, and clearly a proud father, inadvertently causing me to smile when, as he held up his little George, the babe passed gas. Horrified, Mama declared, "Whatever are you feeding that poor child?" Bertie replied calmly, "Mother's milk. It seems the boy has inherited my Hanover intestines."

Alix had also put on flesh, but on her, it added to her beauty. She seemed content in her marriage. She took me under her charge, stating we mustn't talk of anything serious; this was our reunion, and we must make the best of it. What the best entailed were plenty of meals to fatten me up, games of cards, poetry readings, and playing the piano together. There were also trips to our various palaces to watch Mama fuss over the dirt on the windows, with me laughing out loud for the first time since Nixa's death when Alix stomped her foot to prohibit Mama from attacking the grime herself, reminding her that she was a queen and had servants to do it.

Alix healed me. Her presence did what nothing else could. "Even in the midst of a cataclysm, life goes on," she said, as we sat embroidering a bassinet cloth for her baby. "You are still so young, with so much to look forward to, once you move past this time of pain."

"Such as what?" I asked. "I am—what do the French call it? *Une demoiselle à marier.*"

"You are that. *Une princesse* to marry, in truth. Have you thought of it since . . . ?"

We did not speak his name; it was tacit between us, but in that moment, lulled by our needles and thread, by George gurgling at her side, I suddenly wanted to unburden myself of my secret and be cured of its wound, so I could feel whole again.

I told her about Nixa's exhortation and what Sasha had said to me.

My sister's eyes widened. "You did not promise in return?"

I lowered my gaze. "I should have. I regret it now. He left this world without it."

"You mustn't. He was dying. He did not know what he asked."

"No," I said quietly. "He knew. Sasha took his words to heart; he made certain to let me know. Nixa must have truly wanted it."

"And you?" Her eyes were fixed on me. "Is it what you want?"

"I don't know. I cannot know, I suppose, unless I . . ."

"Unless you marry him," said Alix. "But then, if you discover it's not what you want, what remedy can there be? A divorce or a separation would be unthinkable."

I tried to summon a smile. "Yes, a scandal would not do. Mama would never allow it."

"Then we must make inquiries. You must know for certain what Sasha intends. There has been no correspondence? No formal request or . . ." Her voice drifted off as I shook my head. "Of course not," she said. "Or if there was, Mama has kept it from you. She won't say anything until she thinks you are ready to hear it. Are you?"

I went quiet. "I honestly cannot say," I said at length. "I suppose if he does intend it, I should be prepared. Nixa—" My voice caught. I swallowed, forcing myself to continue, to utter his name aloud. "Nixa surprised me. I do not wish to be surprised again."

She smiled sadly. "I understand."

THERE HAD BEEN letters, Mama confessed. Many letters, in fact, between her and the tsarina during the official year of mourning; even the tsar had expressed his approval. As for Sasha, he hadn't volunteered any opinion in public, but Mama hastened to clarify that the rumor he'd forsaken a mistress was unfounded. As soon as my mother spoke, I saw that she wished she hadn't. I frowned. Clearly, the rumor had some truth to it; regardless of whether Sasha had given up his mistress to prove his constancy, it seemed to me evidence enough that he was only committed to the marriage out of obligation, but Alix saw it differently. To her, it was clear that he had decided to dedicate himself entirely to me.

"All young men have dalliances," she told me. "And many never give them up. If he has, it's an excellent sign of his character. Minnie, he's waiting for you. Now, you must decide."

She refrained from repeating her counsel to listen to my heart but to also use my head, yet it was implicit. I now had a second chance to marry the tsarevich and live in Russia as his wife, the tsarevna. Such an opportunity wouldn't come again. Still, I hesitated, riven by doubt, until Alix left for England and I had endless hours to ruminate, sleepless nights to play that deathbed scene over and over in my mind.

Mama once again took the matter in hand. "He's prepared to come here for a visit and state his proposal in person. I needn't remind you of how unusual that is."

I was preparing for bed, brushing out my hair in the mirror, having dismissed my chambermaid, Sophie, as I never seemed to have much for her to do. Regarding my mother's reflection in the glass, I asked, "How long have you known?"

"I did not—" She checked herself. "I will not lie to you. When we went to Nice, the tsarina told me. Nixa had made his wishes known to her and Sasha. I did not think it right to inform you at the time. You were in no position to consider it."

Just as I'd suspected. I set down my hairbrush. "He's a brute. He hissed at me like a serpent, with his brother not yet cold on that bed." When she frowned, I went on, "What do you think I should do?" I wanted to avoid her questions, which would invariably lead to the revelation that Nixa had asked the same of me and I'd denied him my answer.

"How can I advise you? You've suffered so deeply. . . ." She let out a sigh. "He is not Nixa. But he isn't unkind. He may be brutish, as you say, at least in his outward appearance, but it's hardly his fault. As the second son, Sasha was raised to serve in the Imperial Guard. No one ever thought he'd find himself in this position."

"Just as no one thought I would find myself in mine," I said.

"Indeed. Yet you could do so much for each other. Love isn't everything in a marriage, providing there's mutual trust and respect. And love can grow in time between those who are committed to nurture it. The tsarina assures me that Sasha is committed."

"Is forsaking a mistress sufficient proof of his commitment?" I asked tersely, before I could curb myself.

Mama gave me a pensive look. "Minnie, I understand your reluctance. I realize Nixa's death has been very hard on you, and you were never one to accept change easily. But you must still marry and bear children, have a home of your own."

"Is that enough?" I quailed at her stoic tone but strengthened my voice anyway. "A home and children of my own, with the hope that one day there might be love? I am still a princess of Denmark, as you've reminded me many times. Surely, marrying a Romanov isn't my only opportunity to be a wife and mother."

Mama sighed. "You are still too young to understand the realities of this life. Though you did not marry Nixa, to many you are now a widow. And there is only one tsarevich."

As I recoiled at this harsh reminder that I was somehow compromised by the death of the man I had loved, she went on, "Marriage to Sasha can change everything for you. He can accord you a station in life that will make you one of the most important women in the world. If love comes in time, it's a blessing, but the marriage itself is still a great honor," she said, making me wince, for these were the very words she'd used to coerce me to Nixa. "He'll be tsar one day, God willing, and God grant his father many more years to reign. As his tsarevna, and later as his tsarina, think of everything you can achieve. You could help Denmark immeasurably. Even from behind the throne, a woman can rule."

"Rule?" I finally turned my gaze directly to her face. "I don't want to rule."

"You will, regardless." Again, the candor in her voice unsettled me. "It is what royal wives must do. Do you think your father would be the king he is without me? I am the whip that prods him. I am his ears and eyes, his conscience and counsel; without us, most men would stay little boys. Our family has become who we are because of me, because I never ceased to aspire for more than what we had."

Suddenly I understood. "Willie. Did you . . . ?"

"I did. I gained your brother the crown of the Hellenes by promoting his candidacy to Victoria. She's one of our few who can wield her power in the open, but she's still a woman. And a mother. She knew the Greeks were considering Alfred for their next king, and she was loath to surrender him. She readily agreed to my suggestion to offer up the Ionian Islands, a prized British protectorate, to sway the votes in Willie's favor. This is the influence you can possess: to affect nations and benefit your bloodline—but only if you choose wisely."

She didn't await my reply. She left me at my dressing table, astonished and appalled. Yet also admiring. For the first time in my life, I no longer saw her as my demanding mother. I saw her as a woman who'd forged a place for us out of nothing.

Though I couldn't let myself admit it, she had made my decision for me. I would marry Sasha and assume my destiny, as Nixa had wanted for me.

Even if I was not in love.

⁓

OFFICIAL CONFIRMATION ARRIVED, bearing the Romanov double-headed eagle seal in gold wax. Per the custom, I must wed in November, the traditional month for a tsarevich's union. Mama marshaled her resources, confining me to hours of daily study with my Russian tutor and the Orthodox priest sent to instruct me in my new faith. Then Alix wrote that she was again with child, her third, and the queen had put her foot down, forbidding her from travel, so she couldn't attend my wedding in Russia.

Mama sniffed. "Victoria is not pleased by your betrothal, seeing as you turned down her Alfred."

I made no comment. Though I was unhappy that my sister must suffer for it, I rather enjoyed that I'd rattled Victoria again.

Long before I was ready to say goodbye, my departure was upon me. I traveled with three ladies-in-waiting, as well as my maid, Sophie, and a black spaniel named Beauty—a gift from Papa. "To have something alive from Denmark with you," he said, which brought me to tears as I embraced him before boarding our newly refurbished royal vessel, the *Slesvig*. My brother, Crown Prince Frederick, would escort me to Russia as our representative, but Mama and Papa had demurred; they couldn't afford the expense. The prohibitive cost of my trousseau and dowry had depleted our treasury.

Now I embraced her. After so much gone between us, in that moment neither of us could speak. Mama drew back, whispering, "Remember who you are." Then she relinquished me to Freddie, who took me on board.

In the harbor, two Russian warships loomed like steel leviathans, my official escort into the tsar's domains. Gun salutes fired from the ships, and the band on my vessel struck up our patriotic anthem:

In Denmark I was born, 'tis there my home is,
From there my roots, and there my world extend.
You Danish tongue, as soft as a mother's voice is,
With you my heartbeats oh so sweetly blend . . .
'Tis you I love, Denmark, my native land!

I sang along, Freddie and my ladies beside me on the deck, Beauty cradled in my arms. Leaving my homeland tore at my heart.

But my homeland, I knew, would never leave me.

PART II

1866–1881

White Nights

Это очень высокий к Богу
Это очень высокий до царя

It is very high up to God.
It is very far to the tsar.

—Russian proverb

CHAPTER SEVEN

My favorite story in the books Nixa had sent me was a fable that claimed Russia glowed with the red-gold hue of the firebird because an evil sorcerer, beset with envy by the weaving talents of a peasant girl, cursed the girl. Transforming her into a firebird, he tried to steal her away. But the firebird died as he bore her aloft, her feathers drifting from the sky to scatter across the land, where the fertile soil drank them up and reflected their color in the leaves of Russia's trees, wildflowers, and the traditional garb of the *moujik,* the peasants.

And firebird red, I would find, *was* the hue of Russia—that deep scarlet of blood, of health and prosperity and good fortune. It suffused every home, marketplace stall, and cathedral, where revered icons were illuminated by red-glass lamps on filigree chains. Red was also the color of houses, troikas, carriages, and sleighs. Red in the tracery of beloved apples on doors, on gables, eaves, and walls; delicate red stitched in kerchiefs and *sarafan* sleeves; bold scarlet on the wood utensils finished in shiny lacquer; and elegant blood-red piping on the uniforms of the Cossacks marching in procession to celebrate my arrival.

Red wasn't the only color of my new land. My arrival in St. Petersburg preceded the first snows, and in the crystalline sharpness of the air, this astonishing city dubbed the Venice of the North glowed with a myriad of pearlescent hues—turquoise, pear green, ivory white, ethereal blue, and pale pink—on the onion-shaped cathedral domes, palace façades, and whimsical shop signs, with bridges over the swath of the Neva River and numerous canals connecting the islands to the mainland. I had never seen anything like it. Straining my eyes toward the city from the deck of my ship, I was overcome by awe. Nixa had described it to me, but to see it thus, in person, made me feel as if I'd come upon a strange and wondrous place, a vision of paradise.

I was not allowed to disembark. Instead, the tsar and tsarina, along with my betrothed, Sasha, and his brothers, Grand Dukes Vladimir, Alexis, Sergei, and young Paul, as well as his sister, precocious Grand Duchess Marie, came on board my ship to welcome Freddie and me. To my astonishment, the tsar himself presented me with a common pewter platter of bread and salt—Russia's traditional welcome—even as immense fireworks exploded over the harbor, turning the night sky into a glittering fiery firmament.

The following day, escorted by Hussars on horseback, my brother and I were taken through the city in open carriages, the populace cheering and falling to their knees when the tsar passed, as if he were a god. Their cries of "God save the tsar!" roared over us; to me, it was evidence of the deep love that Russians bore for their rulers. Yet the tsarina turned to me in our carriage and said, "For the people, your arrival is a good omen. You've come to us in the month of the Feast of the Cross, when St. Andrew's cross fell from the sky."

I smiled warily. It sounded like superstition to me, and I'd been raised a Lutheran, a faith that didn't traffic in idolatry. Yet I wanted to see more, to explore this magnificent city. To my disappointment, we returned to the harbor directly after our procession, boarding the luxurious imperial yacht *Alexandria,* which had anchored overnight by my ship.

Sailing the gulf of the Baltic Sea bordering the city, we were brought to the tsar's summer estate of Peterhof, an imposing collection of palaces built on a high bluff by the shoreline. I couldn't fathom the size of it, with its immense stately formal gardens and variety of cascading fountains. While the main palace itself was in fact not that large—only thirty rooms—to me it was as if all of Denmark might fit into its frescoed dining hall.

Departing Peterhof, we went farther inland by private train to the sumptuous ice-blue and gold Catherine Palace in the village of Tsarskoe Selo, another extravagant imperial summer retreat, enclosed by gardens of placid beauty. Here, we tarried for six days. By now I was exhausted, in desperate need of respite, my mind a whirl of impressions and tangled emotions. I felt dwarfed by the grandeur of my surroundings, by the realization that I'd come to a land whose wealth far surpassed anything I had known, but I was even more disquieted by my impression that as delighted as the tsar and tsarina were at my arrival, Sasha was not.

He had barely said a word to me. His voluble brother Vladimir made up for his taciturnity, taking me on a dizzying tour of the Catherine Palace and adjacent Alexander Palace, comprised of vast marble staterooms, painted chambers, and salons. Vladimir took pride in showing me the ostentatious suite of formal rooms known as the Golden Enfilade, including a breathtaking ballroom dripping in gold baroque tracery and crystal chandeliers.

In the Amber Room, I paused in amazement. Faced entirely with sculpted amber panels backed with mirrors and gold leaf, the chamber emanated a preternatural saffron glow. As I struggled to imagine the years of cost and craftsmanship required to construct such a marvel, tentatively touching a translucent panel surmounted by a stucco angel bathed in gold, Vladimir said, "This room was a gift to Peter the Great from the Prussian king Frederick William I. It was originally made for the Berlin City Palace, but Peter so admired it, the king offered it as part of their alliance. Peter's daughter Empress Elizabeth had it installed here. It's been expanded over the years. There are now over six tonnes of amber in this room."

"But doesn't amber chip easily?" I said. "How did the artisans create this?"

"Heated carefully in an oil bath, amber becomes flexible," said Vladimir. "Pieces of it can be joined by coating the surfaces with linseed oil, heating them, and then pressing them together while hot." He laughed. "We Romanovs spare no expense. If you think this is impressive, just wait until you see our Winter Palace in St. Petersburg."

I whispered, "This must be what Versailles looks like." It was the only palace I knew of to compare; I'd heard plenty of stories about the French Sun King's legendary abode.

Trailing behind us, his boots striking echoes upon the inlaid marquetry floor, Sasha muttered, "See this?" and when I turned to him, surprised, he lifted his fist. "In here," he said, "in this simple Russian hand, I could bend all of Versailles like a horseshoe."

"Oh?" I was so pleased to hear him speak, it hardly mattered what he said. "Now that, I'd like to see."

Vladimir laughed. "Do not tempt him. He'll do it."

That very night during the state dinner, Sasha took up a silver table platter before the court, and with an unblinking stare at me, he twisted it like putty in his fingers. Tossing the crumpled platter aside, he declared, "Thus has Russia nothing to envy of any land."

"He wants to impress you," said Vladimir, when he escorted me onto the dance floor. "He fears you'll find him a poor substitute for Nixa."

I made no response, though I found it disconcerting that Sasha believed displaying his muscle in public would incite my affection. Resisting a pang of overwhelming homesickness as I thought about wedding a man capable of such an act, I gave myself over to the exhilaration of the dance. Here, I could excel. I'd practiced so much, I was scarcely out of breath after two quadrilles and my favorite, the sprightly Polish mazurka.

"You'll win Russian hearts everywhere by dancing like this," Vladimir breathed, perspiration beading his flushed face. "To know how to dance in Russia is a feat one should never underestimate. It would appear Denmark has nothing to envy, either."

I found myself thinking it was a shame he wasn't my bridegroom, for Sasha sat out all the dances, beating his palms on his thighs and stomping his feet to the music but making no effort to accompany me.

The next day, we returned by private train to St. Petersburg.

In open landaus, we rode down the wide Nevsky Prospekt thoroughfare to the Winter Palace. Crowds again crammed the route— cheering, doffing their caps as they caught sight of us. At my side, Sasha sat quiet, looking trimmer in his blue Imperial Guard's uniform, his wispy mustache detracting from his stony jaw, his slightly protuberant blue-gray eyes reserved, as though the panoply around us was a tedium he must endure.

As our carriages swept through the Narva Gate, which commemorated Russia's victory over Napoleon, and into the vast Palace Square, dominated at its center by the red granite Alexander I obelisk, my breath caught in my throat.

Directly before me reared the Winter Palace.

Girding the river embankment, the palace stretched as far as my eyes could see—a colossus of vibrant vermilion, punctuated by white and gold-crowned pilasters. As the sun gathered strength, it blazed upon the palace, turning the enormous white-framed oblong windows into reflective pools. I shielded my eyes, gazing up at the roofline bristling with bronze statues. It should have seemed overwrought, a baroque monstrosity; yet it was somehow almost airy, like something out of a fairy tale.

"Over a thousand rooms," Sasha said.

I started, turning to him. "How does anyone ever find anyone else?"

"They manage. We'll not live here. After we wed, we'll reside in the Anichkov Palace. It is nearby but not too near. I prefer to keep my distance from the court."

My smile felt tepid on my lips. Did he mean to reassure me?

To the blare of heralds trumpeting on gold bugles, we entered the palace. Inside, it was even more daunting: endless alabaster halls lined in mirrors, galleries populated by thickets of lapis lazuli, onyx, and malachite pillars, and tiered staircases made of slippery whipped-cream marble that were difficult to climb in my heavy wool skirts.

Sophie hastened behind me, with Beauty tugging at her leash. Suddenly, at the top of a stairway, the group divided. The men turned one way while the women, headed by the tsarina, whisked me into the labyrinthine west wing, into a suite of apartments of red brocade, with upholstered chairs and settees, gilded bureaus and tables, and a canopied bed large enough to sleep ten. I could only stare at it, recalling how in winter, Alix and I had doubled up at night on one of our rickety cots, stuffing wool in the window crevices to stanch the drafts.

The tsarina remained with me while her ladies vanished into an antechamber. I stood limp, perspiration sliding under my ankle-length coat. Somehow, my belongings were here, stacked in a corner. That pathetic collection of trunks resembled a bedraggled anthill compared to the excess I'd just seen. It made me feel like a supplicant; without warning, I had to bite back a mortifying onslaught of tears.

Beauty barked, her moist dark eyes fixed on me, her tongue lolling out.

"She's thirsty," I said to Sophie, who appeared as bewildered as I was. "She hasn't had anything to drink in hours."

"Eau pour le chien," ordered the empress. One of the women in the antechamber entered moments later with a basin, which she set before my spaniel. My dog lapped it up, dripping water onto the lush red carpet.

"You too must be thirsty and tired," said the tsarina. Her acknowledgment of my discomfort, uttered in a soft voice, brought the tears brimming to my eyes. Blinking through a watery haze, I whispered, "I . . . I don't know what to do, Majesty."

"Oh, no." She came to me. "No 'Majesty' here. Just Maria." She took me in her arms, pressing her cool hand at my nape. As I set my head against her bony shoulder, I felt the absence of my own mother so much that a stifled sob escaped me.

Removing a handkerchief from her skirt pocket, she dabbed my cheeks. "There, now. If you like, we'll visit him tomorrow. We will go together to pay our respects."

She had misinterpreted my sorrow. She thought I wept for Nixa, when to my shame I'd scarcely thought of him, missing my home more than I'd imagined possible.

I nodded. "Yes. I would like to . . . see him."

"He's across the river in the fortress, in the Cathedral of Saints Peter and Paul." Her hand slipped from my neck to clutch mine, her fingers icy now, as if the mention of his grave had leached all the warmth from her body. Although her voice trembled, I detected a hint of steel within it. "You'll adjust in time. It's never easy at first, coming to this land, but we adjust, my child. We must. Do not let yourself be overwhelmed. You are a Romanov now. You must accept your role and embrace it. There is no other way to survive."

She released me. "I'll see that you're properly attended. You've much to prepare for in the coming days: your conversion to our faith, your trousseau, and the marriage itself." She drew away with a wan smile. "I know you'll surprise us all."

As the tsarina moved into the antechamber, Sophie hurried to assist me. My fingers were numb inside my gloves as I tried to unbutton my coat, though the room—indeed, the entire palace—was stifling, heated by an immense tiled *pechka* in the corner: the ingenious Russian stove, mounted on clawed feet and blasting warmth like a demonic kiln. I felt as if I'd suffocate if I didn't divest myself immediately of extra layers.

A trim youthful woman with auburn hair and an arresting, if not beautiful, face entered the room. She curtsied. "I am Alexandra Apraxine, Princess Obolensky. My husband the prince is head steward of His Imperial Highness's household. I will serve as your chief lady-in-waiting." She smiled. "If it pleases Your Highness, you may call me Tania in private."

I sighed in relief at her unexpected informality. "And you must call me Minnie."

"Minnie," she said carefully, as the name was unfamiliar to her. Then she helped Sophie relieve me of my coat, hat, gloves, and muff and proceeded to unpack my luggage as I sat upon one of the uncomfortable red brocade chairs and watched her lips purse when she smoothed out my wrinkled linens.

"I'm afraid my lace isn't as fine as what you must have here," I ventured. In fact, I almost said, nothing I'd brought—save for my Parisian gowns, packed in their satin-lined boxes—must be as fine as anything they had here.

"No matter," said Tania. "His Imperial Majesty has seen to it already. It is customary for the tsar to provide a trousseau for his daughter-in-law. It only awaits your inspection."

"Today?" I couldn't bear to face more evidence of my family's penury.

"Tomorrow afternoon, after your visit to the Peter and Paul Fortress with Her Majesty," she said. She instructed Sophie on the proper storing of my things, though at this point I thought they might as well throw away everything except my Worth dresses.

Tugging Beauty onto my lap, I buried my face in her fur. She smelled of the cold outside and the linseed oil permeating the palace woodwork. I tried in vain to find the scent of home upon her, to capture it in my memory, overcome by fear that I'd forget too soon.

But while she was something alive of Denmark, she now smelled only of Russia.

CHAPTER EIGHT

It was a simple tomb before the lavish iconostasis—a white marble sarcophagus, fenced by grillwork, with his name and dates etched on a plaque on the railing, the sarcophagus itself adorned with the curious triple-barred Orthodox cross in gold.

Grand Duchess Marie had insisted on coming with us, chattering without cease about everything that came into her mind during our ride across the bridge over the Neva to Zayachy Island, where the cathedral spire, topped by an angel, towered over the rest of the city. But the moment we entered the incense-drenched church, where tapers flickered and icons gazed from under the lime-green vaulted ceiling frescoed with depictions of a long-fingered Christ, Marie went quiet, holding on to her mother's hand.

We knelt before the tomb. There were no pews or cushions for our knees—Orthodox services were held to a standing congregation—and in our dark cloaks and dresses, we passed unperceived among elderly women in shawls, lighting tapers and praying nearby.

I had brought a wreath of roses from the palace, which had a seemingly constant supply, arranged in vases on tables and marble tureens in the halls. Placing them by the tomb, I whispered my Orthodox prayer for him, carefully memorized.

I heard the tsarina weep.

Later, as we returned to the palace, the river choppy now, a winter chill in the air, Grand Duchess Marie asked, "Did you love my brother Nixa very much?"

"Yes." I smiled to conceal the sorrow her question roused in me. "I did not know him for long, but he was very kind to me. We . . . we were going to be married."

"But now you'll marry Sasha instead." She frowned. "Do you love him, too?"

Lost in contemplation as she gazed out to the river, the empress appeared oblivious. Still, I cast a quick look at her, taken aback by her daughter's perceptiveness.

"I will," I finally said. "It is my duty as his wife."

Marie considered this. "Well, if you love my brothers, then we must be sisters."

I leaned to her and kissed her cheek. "Then we are," I said softly.

MY TROUSSEAU, LIKE everything else, was staggering in its abundance. It filled an entire hall, set out on linen-covered tables and watched over by the turbaned Turks who guarded the tsar—sables, ermines, and lynx cloaks; coats, mantles, jackets, and dressing gowns; boots made of embroidered leather and gloves lined with fur; colorful shawls, delicate silk stockings, and exquisite silk undergarments; and piles of the ubiquitous lace handkerchief, essential for a Russian bride. Their fine quality confirmed that they indeed surpassed anything I had, even if I doubted I could bring myself to blow my nose with them.

"Must I inspect *all* of it?" I asked Tania in dismay. The tsarina had retired to her apartments, her persistent cough causing me to fear she'd caught a fever from the upset of visiting Nixa's tomb. Marie accompanied me, however, flitting among the tables, fingering articles as if they were toys, and making silly expressions at the stone-faced guards.

"Not all," said Tania. "Or indeed any of it, if Your Highness approves."

"I . . . I approve," I said haltingly, but I spent several hours examining the trousseau anyway, enthralled by its largesse and aware I owed all of it to my father-in-law, the tsar.

THE NEXT WEEKS were regimented by scheduled activities from the moment I woke to the hour when I was permitted to collapse into bed, my head reeling.

My conversion to Orthodoxy consisted of a somber two-hour ritual that obliged me to abjure and curse my Lutheran faith, spitting three times as I choked on the incense wafting from the swinging censers suspended from chains around me. Because I had to submit, I reasoned that having faith in God was more important than how one went about it. Adopting my new Russian name of Maria Feodorovna—the patronymic meaning "Gift of God" and common to most foreign-born brides—I was anointed and led to kiss the icons before my first Orthodox communion.

At the gala held in my honor that evening, I was announced for the first time by royal decree as Her Imperial Highness Grand Duchess Maria Feodorovna. I was dressed in a shoulder-baring blue gown with a white satin sash and a star-sapphire brooch, and I wore the traditional Russian headdress, the crescent-shaped *kokoshnik,* glittering with diamonds and pearls. By the time the dancing began, I felt my attire weighing on me like lead. I danced in it nevertheless and took pride in it.

But the ritual for my wedding ceremony I found completely incomprehensible, overseen by the haughty master of court ceremonies, who took my lack of knowledge as a personal insult. Tania was at my side every minute, advising me, translating into French when the master lapsed into ill-tempered German. I'd never bothered to learn German as well as I should have, considering almost everyone at the Romanov court spoke it, in addition to French. Russian, in fact, was the one language I rarely heard. It simply wasn't spoken at court, Tania told me, making me wonder why they'd eschew their native tongue.

Yet I knew from my laborious history reading that Peter the Great sought to bring Russia closer to Europe, and his successors had upheld his tradition. The Romanov line was not even fully Russian anymore; Catherine the Great had been born in Prussia, wedding into the Romanov family before she staged a coup to claim the throne. In its manners and way of life, the imperial court functioned like every other in Europe, only in Russia, its magnificence was overlaid by ancestral Slavic customs I was expected to learn in all their intricacy. And as I struggled to master them, I wished I had someone in whom to confide. Though my brother was still here, he was occupied by his own obligations as the crown prince representing our nation, often absent on visits around the city with Vladimir and the tsar's officials. And I barely saw Sasha, save for the state dinners and receptions. He did indeed stake his distance, which only roused more anxiety in me. I'd never felt more ill equipped or alone. After the banquets and galas, in the privacy of my bedchamber I succumbed to despair. How was I going to survive? How could I bring Denmark honor by being a wife to a man I scarcely knew, who would one day, may it be many years hence, become tsar himself?

On the morning of November 9, which dawned with the first fall of snow, I was finally herded into the Malachite Drawing Room for the ordeal.

Robing me in my bridal attire took three excruciating hours. While the hairdresser licensed especially for the occasion plied my dark locks into the side curls once favored by Catherine the Great, I watched in the full-length mirror—which had belonged to Peter the Great's niece and was the sole mirror a Romanov bride could use—as Dagmar of Denmark was submerged in folds of Russian silver tissue and the ermine-trimmed crimson mantle. Catherine the Great's diadem was perched on my head, with its centerpiece pink diamond, and sur-mounted by the diamond arches of the bride's crown and silvery veil. Jeweled bracelets and ropes of pearls encircled my wrists and throat.

The effect was captivating but so heavy that it proved a test of my stamina as the tsar and my brother escorted me on the processional walk to the royal chapel. Under my grandeur, I was soaked in perspira-tion, so nervous that I swayed, feeling momentarily faint as I mounted the red-draped dais beside Sasha in his blue-and-silver regimental uni-form.

Without a shift in his countenance, he reached out a steadying hand. I went still, as if paralyzed, remembering how he'd steadied me after Nixa's death.

I promised him. Remember that.

The metropolitan recited the service while we circled the altar three times. I wondered what Sasha felt, compelled to marry me because of a promise made to his dying brother. As I snuck glances at his stolid pro-file, I asked myself if he would care for me at all or come to loathe me because I'd spoiled his life, made him assume his duty not only as the tsarevich but also as my husband, responsible for begetting heirs on me, for my comfort and welfare—a woman who had loved his late brother, whom he himself did not love?

I was still thinking of this when the ceremony ended. The prayer for the imperial family was recited, my name included. The tsar and tsarina stepped forth to kiss our cheeks. The tsarina whispered to me, "Remember, you are now one of us."

Outside, the salute of one hundred guns rattled the palace casements, informing the people that they had a new tsarevna. We were taken through the enfilade of corridors past bowing courtiers to a balcony bunted in red velvet, overlooking the square. As we emerged into the icy air, snow drifting about us, the people assembled below—an anonymous mass, thousands for as far as my dazed eyes could see—lifted a resounding cheer. At first I couldn't discern what they chanted, until in a sudden rush I understood the Russian words:

"God save our tsarevna!"

In that instant, as I beheld the people of my newly adopted country, crying out my newly bestowed title, a rush of heat surged in me, erasing the chill of the air. It was inexplicable, unexpected, but I truly realized then that in marrying the heir to Russia, I'd done more than bind myself to a stranger. I had bound myself to a dynasty and an empire, to centuries of women before me who'd done their duty for their country. I was no longer the impoverished daughter of a once-negligible family, a princess of no power. I was indeed a Romanov now, with all the challenges, privileges, and obligations my rank entailed.

"Show Mother Russia that you love her, too," Sasha said to me. He took my hand, raising our arms together as the people's cries reached us in rapturous acclaim.

"God save Your Imperial Highnesses!"

No longer Dagmar of Denmark. I was Her Imperial Highness Maria Feodorovna now.

I WAS PERMITTED to discard my mantle for the reception. Freed of its burden, I looked forward to the gala, attended by the entire imperial family and hundreds of the aristocracy, all of whom had secured coveted invitations to sit at the dining tables in the chandeliered Nicholas Hall, with its Corinthian columns and immense windows. By custom, we did not dine with the guests; we ate apart in a separate hall, then the tsar went to mingle with his guests, who were forbidden to rise in his presence—an informality I found unusual, given how everything else was governed by strict protocol.

The presentations were interminable. The tsarina had provided Tania with the guest list, and Tania had prepped me on the proper pronunciation of names, corresponding titles, and tidbits of personal information, such as an eldest son's rank in the Preobrazhensky regiment or a daughter's recent marriage. I thought this surfeit of knowledge would fly right out of my head, yet I found myself recalling everything as each nobleman and his wife came before me. And by their delight at my inquiries, I saw I made a favorable impression.

"A very good start," whispered Tania before I followed the tsar out to our dining chamber. "They'll not forget how gracious you were. Word will travel; nothing moves faster in society than gossip. When the Season begins, everyone will be desperate to invite you. This is how Your Highness will conquer society: name by name, and salon by salon."

It sounded tiresome, but, then, I'd been on my feet for over twelve hours and was famished. Even Sasha, who'd stood stiff beside me during the presentations, gave me a cursory look as I dug into the first course of roast venison in plum sauce. "Not a dainty appetite, I see."

"Should it be?" I paused, my fork halfway to my mouth.

"Perhaps in Versailles," he retorted. "Not here."

With our appetites sated, we went into an adjacent hall for the dancing, which Sasha and I opened with a mazurka. It wasn't an easy dance. He stepped on my toes and seemed put out by all the attention. As soon as it ended, he pulled me aside. But then Vladimir bowed before me, red-cheeked from the wine, and Sasha glowered as I took my turn with his brother, whose gracefulness cut a swath through the dancing couples. It went on until well after midnight, leaving me invigorated. Dancing always had a salubrious effect on me; with my vitality restored, I now faced the next ordeal—my wedding night.

By tradition, a Romanov groom and bride spent their first night away from court, at the tsar's private dacha. I had hoped this custom might be discarded, given the cold and snow, but it was not. Accompanied by our new household, Sasha and I were bundled into a coach drawn by eight fleet horses and driven at breakneck speed out of the city into the countryside. The Russian night poured like ink upon the world; as we neared the torchlit estate, I heard a wolf howling somewhere in that vast snowbound wilderness.

The traditional offering of rye bread and salt welcomed us. Tania brought me to private apartments, where I was divested of my gown and dressed in one of the embroidered night-robes from my new trousseau. Then I was taken into the garlanded nuptial chamber, with its bed on a silver dais. After kissing the blessed icon held to my lips, I was slipped between the sheets, damp from a sprinkle of holy water, and left alone.

I heard my heart in my ears as I waited. And waited. Pulling up the luscious bearskin coverlet, I sank into it, almost drifting to sleep before the door opened. The room was dark, but whoever accompanied him bore a candle, so that he loomed, enormous, on the threshold. He had to dip his head as he entered to avoid hitting it on the lintel.

"Well?" Sasha planted himself before me, his hands on his hips.

I was so astonished that words failed me. He wore a turban, like one of the Turkish guards, replete with a peacock plume. On his large frame hung a metallic dressing gown that resembled armor. I lifted myself upright in bed as he stepped forward with a chime. His feet were shod in Oriental slippers, with tiny bells on their curled tips.

I tried to stop myself. I felt it roil up inside me, an uncontrollable release of fatigue, disbelief, and mirth, but before I could curb it, my laughter erupted, and once I started I couldn't stop. Tears leapt to my eyes, cresting over my cheeks as he stood, stunned, his face turning white, then molten, his eyes narrowing to slits.

"It is the custom for the tsarevich's wedding night," he growled. "Would you make a fool of me?"

As the memory of his hands twisting that silver platter passed before my eyes, I sobered at once. "Never a fool," I said. "But you must admit, it is . . . unexpected."

"I'm a buffoon." He shot a furious glance at the door, which his unseen attendant had closed after he entered, leaving the candle on a side table. "That mincing master of ceremonies will regret it. I told him I don't care if it's the custom, I'll not be made—"

"Forget the custom." I eased over in the bed. "Come here, Sasha."

I'd not spoken his name aloud with any intimacy until this moment, and I gauged its impact, the way he lowered his eyes, his hands bunching fistfuls of his ludicrous ensemble.

I was as unprepared as he was for this moment. All the rituals upholstering our marriage outside these walls would avail us nothing now. Here, we were husband and wife, expected to do what married people did. I wasn't entirely ignorant of the requirements, but he held the advantage. If the rumor was true, he'd had a mistress. I was untouched.

"Not if you laugh," he said. "If you laugh, I will . . ." His voice drifted into awkward silence, as if he wasn't sure what he could do without forsaking his dignity. I liked it. I liked that even if he could be uncouth, he was not without his sensitivity.

"I won't laugh," I promised, and like a man readying to plunge into cold water, he gripped the dressing gown and heaved it over his head, knocking off the turban in the process and depositing both items with a noisy clatter onto the floor. It must have been heavy; underneath, his linen nightshirt was wet, yet when he clambered into the bed, I smelled no odor on him, not a hint of sweat. He smelled clean, like soap.

He had bathed before coming to me.

We lay side by side, without moving, before I heard him say, "I know you do not yet care for me, but if we can only . . ."

"Yes?" I turned to him. The candle was guttering, tossing little light. In the encroaching darkness, his profile seemed etched. I could have traced it with my fingers.

"If we can only try," he said. "I want us to be happy, Maria."

"Minnie," I replied. "Everyone calls me Minnie."

He went silent. Then he said, "I prefer Manja. Here, we use it for Maria, but it also can mean rebellious. . . . You remind me of it."

I had to smile. "My father also called me rebellious. Manja it is. And, Sasha," I added, "I also want us to be happy."

What else could I say? We were married. Nixa was gone. I did not want the shadow of my love for him lingering between us. I had made my choice. This was the man to whom I'd pledged myself, for better or worse, in sickness and in health, to love and to cherish. He needed me as much as I needed him; he was as bound to our vows as I was.

He reached across the space between us to tentatively touch my breast. I closed my eyes. He caressed me, edging closer, such a large man, reduced to uncertain tenderness, hovering in hesitation before he pressed his lips to mine. Our first true kiss. It did not stir any passion in me, but I didn't find it unpleasant. His breath was clean, like his person.

I felt his arousal against my thigh. He murmured, "You're so small. Like a child. I . . . I don't want to hurt you."

"You won't." I reached down my hand. "Only, be gentle . . ."

He was gentle. And I did not dislike what we did.

To my surprise, I did not dislike it at all.

CHAPTER NINE

Winter was magnificent, providing one didn't stay outside too long. I had experienced harsh winters in Denmark, but the Russian winter was a different beast. Not that most Russians seemed troubled by the bone-piercing cold or months of snow, the glacial winds shrieking across the Neva, freezing the river and canals. Russians delighted in building ice hills and flying down these on toboggans, like pagans. No one, however, liked to walk much. Colorful sleighs and hired *drozhki*—a kind of open carriage—or the distinctive troika, drawn by three horses and designed to race across drifts, abounded, driven by bearded coachmen in fleece-lined caftans. Yet the streets remained busy as ever, people going about their business while fire cans warmed each corner. And in every well-to-do home, built with impermeable walls, burned the remarkable Russian stove, condensation beading the double-paned windows behind stout shutters and thick drapes.

The city burst into frenetic life as the Season took hold. Events started toward midnight, lasting well into dawn. Galas, operas, balls, plays, and symphonies were held in blazing halls, theaters, and palaces, with fortunes spent on fuel for the stoves, beeswax candles, and gas for the chandeliers. Lavish boards were heaped with delicacies brought up from storehouses, where a wealth of meat and fish had been kept frozen on ice blocks from the prior winter. Only in Russia had I ever heard of food being frozen, and I was astounded by the abundance: succulent salted sturgeon and trout, partridge, grouse, venison, ham, and sausage, as well as grains, dried fruits, and nuts, accompanied by tender asparagus and vegetables nursed in indoor greenhouses. Hospitality was a

Russian virtue, and winter was the time to eat, drink, and celebrate. Winter was for rejoicing, and Russians loved joy.

Sasha and I took up residence in our Anichkov Palace at the intersection of Nevsky Prospekt and the Fontanka Canal—a commodious house that included, to my delight, an enclosed garden and a large pond. From my new palace, I took to my troika to visit the aristocracy. As Tania predicted, everyone was eager to receive me, invitations arriving daily at my door. Sasha grumbled that "were it up to those empty-headed fools," I wouldn't set foot at home until the Neva thawed, but I felt obliged as the new tsarevna to let myself be entertained, while Tania emphasized the importance of instilling goodwill, particularly with the tsar's three brothers, his two sisters, and their respective families.

I reveled in the attention. The conversation, held in French, was never tedious, everyone enthralled by the latest opera, play, or novel. The food was delicious, and the music, by Rimsky-Korsakov, Mussorgsky, and Borodin, sublime. I wore beautiful new gowns, ordered by the dozen from Paris and St. Petersburg fashion houses. With my curled hair adorned with feathers, bejeweled combs, or pearls, jewelry sparking against my skin, I danced the nights away without a care, for there was nothing improper in it. Unlike some ladies, I invariably returned home. Sasha might grumble, but he didn't impede me. One of us had to attend society and, as he said, "Better you, my Manja." He too had his entertainments, places he went with his brother Vladimir and their fellow officers. I refrained from asking what these pursuits entailed. Prince Obolensky, Tania's husband, kept watch over him, and like me, Sasha always came home, albeit bleary-eyed from vodka.

Protocol, however, obliged him to accompany me to the state galas at the Winter Palace, where thousands flocked, the Nicholas Hall searing with heat and adorned with parterres of roses and allées of laurels. Sasha detested it. Frowning, tugging at his uniform, he always drank too much. Once drunk, he lost his timidity and would play the tuba with the orchestra; he had a fine ear for music and played quite well, when sober. More often than not, he ended up in an inexplicable fury, compelling me to whisk him back home to tuck him into bed before I returned to the palace to finish out the night.

I had everything I could have dreamed of—wealth, position, the entire city at my feet. For my first Epiphany, the traditional time for gifts, I held my first ball at my palace, overseeing the preparations for weeks in advance and marshaling my slovenly maids. Dirt and disorder, I found, were the norm in Russian households. The linen closets alone presented a mess of disorganization, the maids baffled when I joined them to sort and discard the worn or moth-eaten to replace it with the crisp and new. Ladies of quality, let alone a tsarevna, apparently didn't occupy themselves with the management of their homes, but my childhood of chores under my mother came to the fore.

"These floors must be scrubbed," I told my staff. "And the rooms dusted thoroughly every day. You wash yourselves, yes?" I added, as they stood with their mouths agape. "Well. A house must also be maintained. It is where we live."

In contrast, bodily cleanliness was a Russian obsession, with public steam baths available throughout the city for men and women. My private bathing room was fully equipped, and Sasha bathed every two days, even in the dead of winter. I was therefore confounded that such a fastidious people could allow inches of cinder dust from the stoves and hearths to accumulate unnoticed on every surface. I developed a ruthless reputation for impromptu inspections and sniffing of the linens, but in time my staff learned that if they wanted to remain in my employ, they must do as I instructed. Those who persevered reaped the reward, for my annual income as tsarevna was substantial, apportioned by the tsar himself, and I believed in paying my servants well.

In winter the days were short, with long nights, but homes and churches remained aglow with candles and song. By January, the dim daylight expanded, reluctantly at first, for the ceremonial Blessing of the Waters, when we joined the tsar on the Feast of the Epiphany in procession to the river, where a hole dug into the ice revealed the Neva's murky depths. After the metropolitan dipped his staff in to bless it, a goblet of this briny water was given to the tsar to sip, and the people rushed to fill up their buckets, for the blessed water was deemed miraculous. By April, the icebound Neva cracked, and cannons were fired from the fortress to herald the advent of spring.

In this perfect world, all I lacked was a child. But Sasha and I enjoyed regular intimacy, and I was confident I would soon bear fruit.

I was nineteen years old and the tsarevna.

How could anything I desired be denied?

CHAPTER TEN

"Are you walking with us today?" thirteen-year-old Marie asked. I found the grand duchess in the antechamber of the tsar's study, her big blue eyes shining with anticipation. Her father's daily strolls along the promenade of the Quai de la Cour alongside the Winter Palace were a time-honored spring routine. After reviewing his state affairs, Alexander would take walks outside, dispensing with ceremony to greet his subjects. He believed Russia's Little Father, as the tsars were dubbed, must never seclude himself, and his request that I join him today was an honor.

"I am." I smiled at Marie in her white frock and beribboned sun hat, her chestnut-colored hair plaited. "How pretty you look." I didn't see her as often as I would have liked. Her youth precluded attendance at the winter galas, as it did the presence of her even-younger brothers, Grand Dukes Sergei and Paul, both of whom, like her, studied under tutors, only the boys did so in preparation to enter the regiments. So I was pleased to find Marie here, perched on the ottoman with the tsar's red Irish setter, Milord, petting his ears and sticking her tongue out at the turbaned attendants protecting the study entrance.

She heaved a dramatic sigh. "Finally. Winter is *so* boring."

I sat beside her. "You'll not be a child forever. Once you are a woman, winter won't seem that way."

Her young face made the perfect moue of distaste. "Mama is still in Nice. She hates winter, too."

"Yes. The cold is very hard on her," I said. Marie was still too young to realize that her mother's health had grown increasingly frail or that the tsarina's frequent retreats to the Crimea or Nice, ostensibly to seek a warmer clime, were, I suspected, as much motivated by her cough as the need to escape the social demands of St. Petersburg. "But now that it's spring, she'll be back soon. And this summer, we'll go to Peterhof and Tsarskoe Selo. Won't that be lovely? All those wonderful gardens to run around in."

I wanted Marie to have gardens, to play and laugh, to enjoy her final years of childhood. I realized now that I'd been fortunate growing up as I had, without strict etiquette. For while Marie was lively, given to racing about the palace, sliding down the marble banisters, and joining the liveried servants taxed with polishing the floors by skating along them in padded slippers, life as a grand duchess wasn't easy for a child, especially one whose mother was absent for long periods of time and whose father oversaw an empire.

"I suppose," she said, with that mercurial indifference children had. She leaned closer to me. "If the Nihilists don't force us to flee to the fortress of Gatchina instead."

I regarded her, taken aback. "Whatever makes you say that?"

"Papa was just yelling about it to one of his ministers. They don't want him to take his walks outside anymore. The Nihilists have threatened him again."

A chill went through me. To hear such news from her was bad enough, but I'd had no idea that this nebulous group of anarchic discontents, who'd adopted the epithet of "Nihilists" to promulgate their gospel of social revolt, had threatened the tsar. I'd heard talk of them in the salons, of course. But nearly everyone dismissed them as rabble-rousers and libertarians with too much time on their hands, taking up the banner for the downtrodden and the serfs, left by the emancipation without land, obliged to pay taxes and immigrating in growing numbers to the cities in search of employment.

"You mustn't let such things worry you," I said. "It's not—"

My words were cut short by the tsar's emergence from his study. Spare and tall, my father-in-law wore his old frock coat, his cravat and hat, a walking stick in his gloved hand. He beamed at Marie, who rushed to hug him, and then at me. "Always so prompt, my dear," he said through his bushy mustachios. "You should have had them inform me you were here."

"Them?" I glanced at the attendants, who remained impervious as pillars.

He chuckled, taking me by the arm. As Marie and Milord trotted beside us, we traversed the palace, his personal guard accompanying us to the side entrance but no farther, at his command. He didn't move in his usual direction toward the promenade along the Neva, however, turning us instead toward Sadovaya Street. In his ordinary clothing, with his plain black fedora on his head, he went unnoticed, pedestrians passing by without a glance. Past the Mikhailovsky Castle, used for military training, the Summer Garden came into view—an oasis of greenery on its island between the Fontanka and Swan canals.

"The gardens today?" I asked.

Alexander gave a grim nod. "If we can evade those imbeciles following me." He did not elaborate on which imbeciles; as I cast a nervous glance over my shoulder, he tightened his hold on me. "Come. We can enjoy privacy here. I'll not be deprived of it."

Marie skipped ahead with Milord. "Not too far," Alexander called out, as we walked under the elm trees, past fountains of colored marble. "I've been advised the embankment is no longer safe," he said to me. "It appears nowhere outside the palace is safe anymore, if my ministers are to be believed. Such hens they are, always fussing over me."

"Marie overheard the fuss," I said, flipping open my parasol to shield my complexion.

"Did she?" He patted my arm. "She's not a child anymore. Living as we do doesn't allow it. She hears too much. The servants talk. Everyone talks. As I said, such an ungodly fuss. You'd think that a Nihilist assassin awaited me on every corner."

"So, it's true?" I came to a halt. "Have they actually threatened Your Majesty's person?"

"Do you doubt it? My dear, Russia is not what it seems."

I met his gaze. "I don't understand. *Who* are these Nihilists to threaten their tsar?"

He looked pained, glancing to where Marie chastised Milord, who'd elected to urinate in the middle of the path. "Their name says it all: The

Latin *nihil* means 'nothing.' They reject authority, proposing anarchy as a means for change. They despise our monarchy, our aristocracy, and our Church. Like the mobs during the French Revolution, they would tear asunder everything we stand for."

I felt as if a shadow fell over us, though the sky above was clear of clouds, that immense crystalline spring sky of Russia. "That's absurd. You freed the peasants and abolished serfdom. You are the Tsar Liberator. Your people adore you."

He sighed. "My people are not Nihilists. They merely want to go about their lives with a minimum of hardship. These rebels are discontents. Intellectuals, mostly, who've adopted the fervor of revolutionaries. They're not always aligned in their views, from what I'm told, but they believe I freed the serfs to provide slave labor for our new factories. We do whatever we can to suppress them, but they sow terror in the hope that I'll either grant reforms or abdicate. Preferably abdicate. They have no use for a tsar."

"It cannot be allowed. It's treason!" I exclaimed, and Marie glanced over at us.

Alexander waved her on ahead. "Much as I lament to say it," he said, "treason it might be, but not everything they promulgate is baseless. The serfs are indeed suffering. I released them from centuries of servitude, but releasing them from the bonds of tradition isn't so simple. I failed to see what the result might be. Without landowners to answer to, they've been cast adrift, exploited when they come here to seek work, as many are illiterate. Had I known as much, I may not have been so determined to change their way of life. Few can welcome change if they reap no benefit in it."

I couldn't imagine what he described. Recalling the people on their knees in the snow as he'd passed in his carriage, I had to wonder at my naïveté. Had I failed to mark the darkness festering under my gilded new life? And then, as I realized we were here, alone in the garden, I said in alarm, "Surely if they're a danger to you, we shouldn't—"

"No, no." He shook his head. "I won't cower in that pile of stone, nor have guards dogging my every step. When our fate comes, we cannot escape it." He steered me down the path, toward Peter the Great's little Summer Palace, perched beside an artificial lake at the far end of the garden. "You mustn't worry about such things," he went on, echoing my own words to Marie. "The Nihilists are a nuisance, but they've not killed me yet."

"God forbid." I might have crossed myself had I not been holding the parasol with one hand while my other hand was resting upon his arm.

"Indeed, but they don't believe in God." He let out a curt laugh. Then he went quiet, his stick tapping on the path before he said, "I wish to talk to you about Sasha. Are you happy with him? Please don't say what you think I should hear. I get enough of that already at court. Tell me the truth. Is he a loyal husband to you?"

Though he didn't say the actual words, I understood. "Yes. He has his habits, but not that." I searched my father-in-law's face. "Why?"

"No reason. Only that he protested rather vehemently at first when told he must give her up before marrying you." He clicked his tongue against his teeth, making a remonstrating sound. "Marie! Let Milord do his business wherever he likes." As he watched his contrite daughter proceed to the lake bordering the Summer Palace, I grappled with sudden disquiet. Sasha had indeed forsaken a mistress; the tsar had confirmed it. And the knowledge squeezed my heart. I'd seen no evidence of any indiscretion. He went gallivanting with Vladimir at night, but surely it could not mean . . .

"Minnie?" Alexander's voice brought my gaze back to him. "If you tell me that a mistress is no longer a concern, I'm very pleased. Sasha kept his word."

Uncertainly, I said, "We still don't know each other well, Majesty, but Sasha . . . he has been kind to me."

"Kind. Hardly what I'd call a healthy endorsement from a newlywed wife, though I suppose kindness in a marriage is underrated. Do you love him?" Alexander said abruptly.

"I . . ." My voice faded. I did not want to lie, as he had requested honesty. "I will learn to love him. In these matters, love requires time."

"It does. For some." His face underwent a subtle change, a sadness that softened him, so that he appeared both younger and much older. "I once loved my wife very much."

The melancholic admission disturbed me. He spoke as though he did not love her anymore, but how could that be? They'd been married over twenty years, had eight children together, suffering the loss of a daughter early in their marriage and then Nixa's death. I would have thought such trials could only bring them closer. But then I recalled the tsarina's absences, her apparent need to escape. Did she also seek to escape her husband?

He paused, chuckling as Marie ran up to him to take from his coat pocket a bundled handkerchief, which she ran back with to the lake, scattering breadcrumbs. Huddled in the middle of the water to avoid the stalking hound, the ducks ignored her.

"She'll never lure them with Milord there," Alexander said. "But she'd stay all day with those crumbs if we let her. She's stubborn. Like Sasha. Did you know his brothers call him the Bullock?"

"Bullock?" The nickname was so apt, I had to smile. "It fits him. He does have a bull's temper. And its obstinacy."

"You know him better than you think. When he was a boy, his tutors despaired. They assured me he had no mind for learning. They recommended I entrust him to the regiments and let the military discipline him. Who would have thought he'd become my heir instead?"

He sighed, watching Marie stomp her foot at the ducks' refusal to cooperate. "Now he must learn. Sasha is not prepared to assume my throne, should these dire warnings of my demise come to pass sooner than expected. I cannot leave this empire to a man who doesn't know how to rule. Our modern age shows no mercy to crowned fools." He returned his gaze to me. "Will you help him?"

"Me?" I said in surprise. "Majesty, I'm not very well educated myself."

"But you read. You like books. And you win people's hearts. Don't deny it. I've already heard plenty from my brothers' wives, who speak only about how fashionable and clever you are. The grand duchesses do not flatter any woman lest she overshadows their own considerable accomplishments. You could provide him with a tutor, see that he does more than follow Vladimir's lead. Young men can be so impetuous, and Vladimir doesn't set much of an example. Wine, ballerinas, racehorses: What Vladimir alone spends will bankrupt me. Sasha needs guidance. He is not Nixa."

"No," I said quietly. "He is not."

"You could find someone he trusts. He had plenty of tutors at court, so perhaps one of them would be appropriate. He must be led to it without suspecting, like a—"

"A bull to the pen," I said, with a reassuring smile to ease the bite in my words. "I suppose it would do him no harm to read more than the newspaper."

"And teach him some moderation," added the tsar. "Sasha drinks too much, and he mustn't endanger his health. Unlike Vladimir, who can indulge himself to his heart's content, Sasha will inherit the throne, and his son after him." He paused. "I hope to hear of that blessed event soon, my dear. A tsarevich needs a son. More than one, if you can manage it."

"We are trying," I said awkwardly.

"And we must leave the rest, as we say, to God's will." He looked past me, his eyes narrowing. "Ah. I see they've finally found us."

Turning about, I saw two men in plainclothes dart behind the willows. I let out a gasp. Alexander said, "Gendarmes sent by the palace. My ministers will not be dissuaded, but I have other plans and must elude them. Would you mind if I left you and Marie in their care? They'll have a carriage nearby, no doubt, to see you to the palace."

Before I could reply, he pulled down his hat and strode away, past the Summer Palace into an elm-shaded avenue that led to the other exit. Within minutes, he had vanished. The two gendarmes emerged from their hiding place, obviously uncertain as to what to do now, with me standing there and Marie looking after her father, abandoned by the dog, which had bounded after the tsar.

"He has Milord to protect him," I told her, ruffling her hair as she turned her frown to me. Her hat hung on its ribbons down her back; her frown deepened when the gendarmes escorted us back to the front gates, where a covered carriage indeed waited. As we settled into it, Marie glared out the window. When I reached over to tug down the blind and give us privacy, she snapped, "It's no use now. The Nihilists won't hurt us. It's Papa they want, and he went to see that woman."

I stared at her. After the unexpected revelations of today, I wasn't sure I wanted to hear more. "You're mistaken, my child. Your father merely wants to walk on his own. Being the emperor is a very difficult charge and—"

"What do you know?" she interrupted, reminding me in that instant of Sasha. "He visits her all the time when Mama is away. He even took me once to see her."

"Her?" I felt a drop in the pit of my stomach.

"Yes. His mistress." Marie turned away to stare out the window as the coachman cracked his whip and the horses pulled the carriage into the road.

From my window, I saw the two gendarmes racing back into the garden, but I knew they wouldn't locate the tsar. Alexander was gone by now, on his way to a rendezvous with a secret of his own—one I'd never suspected he harbored.

I WANTED TO ask Sasha if he knew. I assumed he must, if his sister did. But I wondered if he might not, as he was rarely attuned to gossip. Before I could decide what to do, my husband distracted me: As soon as I entered the dining room, he handed me a letter that had arrived from my mother. I read it quickly.

"My brother Willie is coming to visit us. With Bertie and my sister Alix!"

I was so excited that my discomfort over the tsar's secret faded, for I missed Alix so and I'd been worried about her. Freddie had returned to Denmark after my marriage, but our family exchanged regular correspondence, thus I'd learned that Alix had given birth to a daughter, Princess Louise. Shortly after the birth, my sister contracted rheumatic fever. Concerned over her health, I was immensely relieved to now hear she was well enough to travel.

Sasha made a skeptical sound. "There must be more to it."

"Mama says Willie must take a wife." I folded up the letter. "His Greek advisers insist on an Orthodox bride, as he hasn't converted and they must be reassured he intends to raise his heirs in the Orthodox faith. Mama has asked Alix and me to help in the search. We must inform the palace at once. There are important arrangements to be made."

"If Queen Victoria has granted her approval to let her heir and his wife set foot here, you can trust that the palace is already informed," said Sasha.

He returned to his newspaper and poached egg. He'd risen late, having gone out last night. As I recalled how he'd staggered in at four in the morning, so drunk he could barely stand, suspicion flared in me. But then I remembered how he'd nuzzled my throat, slurring, "Minnie, my Manja," and had tried to yank me into bed, to which I put a halt, advising him to sober up in his own quarters and we'd see each other in the morning. Only we hadn't, because his father had called for me and I left before Sasha woke, as the tsar was an inveterate early riser—

Recalling what I'd learned today, I was reassured. Sasha had given up one mistress and was far too clumsy to hide another. If the tsar had not succeeded in doing so, how could my husband?

"Well," I said, "if Willie seeks a bride, we must oblige. A wife will do him wonders."

"Not to mention wonders for Denmark and Russia. As for Willie or Greece, or indeed Great Britain, it remains to be seen."

"Oh?" I eyed him until he lowered his newspaper. He had a bit of egg yolk caught in his mustache. "Do you not think a wife can improve matters, husband?"

"Not me. I do not doubt it at all," he said. "Come here, my Manja. On my lap." He parted his broad thighs under his robe, which hung open, barely fastened around his thick waist, revealing his manhood rising inside his drawers.

I laughed. "None of that. Finish your breakfast, then go upstairs to bathe and dress. My family is coming. We've much to do. We can attend to our needs later. But not," I added, again remembering my talk with his father, "before we find a suitable tutor."

"Tutor?" He regarded me as if I'd told him to run naked down the Nevsky Prospekt.

"Yes. For both of us. We must educate ourselves properly. I want to learn more about—about everything. And you need to read something other than that newspaper or the menu of whatever tavern you happen to frequent with Vladimir. You will draw up a list of names, so we can interview prospective candidates."

He glowered. "I don't know any prospective candidates."

"You must. Did you not have tutors at the palace?" I said, and then I cursed my ineptness, for according to the tsar, his tutors had despaired over him.

To my relief, he muttered, "There was only one I liked. I don't think he liked me."

"He will like you now. Write to him. Say we wish to see him. At once."

⁓

HIS NAME WAS Pobendonostev—thin to the point of emaciation, with a gimlet stare behind his wire-rimmed pince-nez, and a spine so straight I couldn't imagine him ever bending at all. After much prodding from me, Sasha had begrudgingly informed me that Pobendonostev was a lawyer and former divinity student, appointed by the tsar to educate his sons, and the tutor Sasha had admired and sought to please. I now noticed the man sniffing as he entered our drawing room. Fresh flowers were arranged in vases, and I'd filled the corners with potted ferns in Chinese urns; he regarded all of it as though nature was something with which he had no traffic and didn't care to revise his opinion.

"My boy," he said, and I was astonished to see Sasha almost cower in his seat. "I must admit, this comes as a surprise." He turned his arid smile to me. "Your Highness."

I poured him a cup of tea, which wasn't something I did for anyone these days except my husband. "We wish for a man of learning and standing to assist us with a curriculum of study, Monsieur. I understand you are highly qualified, having taught the tsar's own sons."

"I still instruct Grand Dukes Paul and Sergei. It is my greatest honor," he said, sipping his tea. The brew was Russian, served from my samovar after steeping to its requisite tarry flavor. His lack of expression indicated it met his exacting standards. "Alas, I fear I did not succeed with Sasha. Did I, my boy?" He glanced at my husband. "Despite all my attempts, our tsarevich went out into this world with the shabbiest of intellectual outfits."

Though not taken by his supercilious tone, the metaphor impressed me. "We've both had shabby outfits, I'm afraid," I said.

Sasha grunted. "I can read and write. That should be enough—"

I preempted him with a touch of my hand on his thigh.

Pobendonostev sat quiet, as if debating my offer. I wasn't deceived. To help prepare Sasha for his future was too enticing. As he claimed he had failed once, his pride would not permit a refusal.

"History, to start, I should think," he said at length. And then, with startling passion, he declared, "Outside our cities, Russia is a wasteland, where ignorance and superstition abound." He paused for dramatic emphasis. "The peasantry is easily misled. They must always obey the tsar, because the tsar is appointed by God to rule over them."

I smiled, though his words made me shudder, reminding me of the Nihilist threat Alexander had described. Still, I saw Sasha nod reluctantly in approval. Pobendonostev's reverence for the autocracy was something my husband shared.

"History it is," I said. "If you'll provide me with a list of books, I'll see to it."

"Books, yes." He finished his tea, standing with an eagerness that belied his rigidity. "I'll provide you with the list within the week, Your Highness. I am honored by Your Highness's request. I believe this will be a very satisfactory arrangement."

As soon as he left, Sasha exploded. "He thinks I'm a fool! *Your* request, he said, as if I wasn't even in the room. He always disdained me. He was the one who advised my father that I was fit only for the regiments. Satisfactory for him, perhaps, but *not* for me."

"Sasha." I sighed. "You told me you respected him. He has exemplary credentials."

"I did respect him. I wanted so much to earn his praise that my brothers mocked me. 'Look at the Bullock,' they said, 'waiting for Pobendonostev to yoke him.' I tried to prove them wrong, but he told Papa I would never learn—" He turned from me, actually trembling with the recollection of his childhood denigration.

I stepped to him. "Sasha, you're not that boy anymore. You're the tsarevich now. You need only apply yourself. You'll soon see how well you can do. And I will study with you; we will learn together as husband and wife. We must be prepared for when the time comes."

He shook away my comforting hand, my tender words. Shooting one of his ferocious glares at me, he spat, "You should get back to changing the bedsheets for your sister's visit," and he stormed out, slamming the drawing room doors so hard that the watercolor landscapes I'd brought from Denmark tilted on the wall.

I sighed. He'd stay angry for a while, but he knew I was right. He must learn to rule. His future, *our* future, depended on it.

Not that being right would make my task any easier.

CHAPTER ELEVEN

Willie, Bertie, and Alix arrived in late May 1867, in the midst of the shimmering white nights, when the sun did not fully set and St. Petersburg radiated translucence. After rounds of galas, we traveled to Peterhof, where Alix and I could finally find time to gossip together.

"Didn't you worry Bertie would become embroiled in a scandal?" I asked, as we sat on the seaside palace terrace, enjoying the salt-tinged breeze from the nearby Baltic. To everyone's surprise, Sasha had taken an immediate liking to Bertie, escorting the Prince of Wales and my brother, along with ever-willing Vladimir, about the city. Their vodka-fueled escapades in the notorious Novaya Derevnya—the island quarter on the Neva where mandolins, gypsies, and drink circulated in profusion—had splashed headlines across international newspapers.

Alix shrugged, as if unperturbed. "More so than he has in London? I think it improbable."

"Did he dance like a Hussar on tavern tables in London or wear a fur hat and eat piroshkies from vendor stalls?" I said archly. "I hardly think Victoria will approve."

"No, she will not." She didn't meet my gaze. "But I prefer it to his other antics."

Taken aback, I wanted to press her for details, but I saw her gaze follow her husband, who walked in the garden with Willie, Sasha lumbering beside them. My own husband had caused me some fear of scandal himself, with his resolve to regale Bertie with proper Russian hospitality.

"Why do you ask?" Alix turned to me. "Do you worry over Sasha?"

Now I was the one to look away. "He's the tsarevich. Everything we do is reported. The journalists and society are ruthless here."

"Journalists and society are ruthless everywhere. And you needn't worry on his account. His heart is entirely yours. I've never seen a man more in love with his wife."

I paused. "You truly think so?"

She smiled. "Oh, Minnie. Still blind as ever. You should heed talk less and open your eyes more. He adores you. In fact," she said, lowering her voice, "I'm surprised you've not yet borne him a child. Is anything amiss, besides this preposterous suspicion of yours?"

"No," I said, more sharply than intended. "I haven't conceived, but we are trying."

"Well." She inclined to my ear and whispered, "As long as you're trying."

I drew back in mock outrage at her suggestive tone, and then we both broke into peals of laughter, causing the tsar and tsarina seated nearby to glance at us.

"Her Imperial Majesty has lost too much flesh since I saw her last," Alix said. "And that cough of hers . . . I hope it's not serious."

I refrained from glancing at the empress, who'd arrived back at court like a specter, requiring frequent attendance by her physicians. Lowering my voice, I said, "The doctors fear it might be consumption."

"Oh, no." Alix looked pained. "Poor woman. Such a dreadful illness. It goes on for years and is incurable. The tsar must be beside himself, after so many years of marriage."

Though I longed to confide what I'd discovered about Alexander, I held my tongue. I sensed something different in my sister, a reserve that did not affect us directly yet lingered, like a veil that mustn't be lifted. Her mention of Bertie's behavior in London made me question the tactfulness of sharing the tsar's indiscretion; I wasn't so blind as to ignore her intimation that Bertie may have also strayed from the marriage bed.

I elected to change the subject. "Now that we're here, let's consider a bride for Willie. He's not done anything thus far to find one on his own, with all that carousing in the city. What about the tsar's daughter? I know Marie is only thirteen and Willie is twenty-one. But they might be engaged under the condition that he wait until she reaches the proper age."

"She pays him no mind," said Alix. "Unless he's rowing her and Olga out in that boat on the lake. Poor Willie must have a terrible shoulder strain by now." She paused, eyeing me. "I believe he likes Olga better. How old is she?"

"Nearly sixteen." I returned her stare. "Do you really think . . . ?"

Alix laughed. "As I said, still blind as ever. Minnie, every time she's present, Willie can't take his eyes off her. And she's suitable enough. The daughter of the tsar's own brother, raised in the Orthodox faith."

"Yes, but . . ." I considered. "We'd have to ask her father, Grand Duke Constantine, and the tsar, of course. I'm not certain they'll approve."

"Maybe we should ask Willie first," said Alix.

I didn't believe Willie would be interested. Constantine's daughter Olga was very timid and not especially beautiful, though she had the lovely Romanov eyes. The eldest daughter in a rambunctious clan of six, she'd lived a sheltered existence, like all girls of her rank. To me, she seemed as immature as Marie. Yet when we approached Willie, he admitted he'd developed a fondness for Olga, and Grand Duke Constantine was so enthused, he waved aside any doubts. While somewhat discomfited by Willie's choice, Alexander expressed no objection if the girl agreed. As for Olga, when questioned by Alix and me, she blushed, murmuring she was honored, making me doubt she understood what marriage entailed. Willie was delighted, however, so Alix and I plunged into the wedding plans, producing a magnificent affair at the Winter Palace in October of that year. Willie took his new bride to meet our parents in Denmark on his way with her back to Greece.

After five months of being with my sister, I wept when Alix left. I clung to her at the dock as she murmured to me, "Love Sasha as much as you can, Minnie. He might not be as sophisticated as Nixa, but his heart is full of you. You cannot ask for more in this life."

I didn't know when I would see my sister again, but I took her advice to heart, setting aside my worries over Sasha's fidelity and dedicating myself to our instruction by Pobendonostev, social obligations, and my household.

By the time the snows had buried St. Petersburg and Christmas chants soared in the cathedrals, I discovered I was finally with child.

———⌒

I WOKE BEFORE dawn of an early-May morning—the sixth of that month—gasping in sudden pain. Reaching down between my legs, I felt drenching wetness there; breathless as another sharp pang overcame me, I frantically rang the little bell on my bedside table.

Tania and Sophie stumbled in, blinking, their night bonnets askew. They slept in the chamber next to mine; we'd come here to the Alexander Palace in mid-April to prepare for my delivery, a move I'd delayed as long as possible, loath to leave my Anichkov for the tedium of the isolated country estate. I kept protesting that I was pregnant, not an invalid. Only the tsarina's insistence that my child must be born in Tsarskoe Selo had persuaded me to take residence in this lavish suite facing the gardens, appointed for my confinement.

"Sasha," I gasped to Tania. "Fetch him. I . . . I think it's time."

Despite everyone's assurance that the way I carried my belly indicated my child would be a boy, I had told myself I didn't care. Son or daughter, I'd love it the same, but when Sasha came barreling into the room, where Sophie mopped my brow as I groaned in pain and the midwife prodded between my thighs, he went white and began shouting to no one in particular, "Alert the Winter Palace this instant! My wife is about to give birth to my son. Tell them to make haste."

Between crests of pain that sucked the very air from my lungs, I managed to say, "Haste? Why? I can give birth just as well without—"

"No." Sasha glared at Tania. "See that she's not left alone for a moment. My father and mother must be present to attend the birth."

As he stormed out in a fluster, bellowing orders again at the footmen in the corridor and thereby alerting the entire palace staff to my ordeal, I grimaced. "Must I delay until they arrive?"

Tania nodded. "It is the protocol, Your Highness."

Two hours later, the tsar and tsarina arrived to hold vigil in my room, alongside Sasha, to my embarrassment. By the tenth hour, just as I thought I'd gladly yank the child out myself, I felt its sudden release. The umbilical cord was severed. I heard a resounding slap on wet buttocks and a wail of protest. As I collapsed onto my sweat-sodden pillows in a fog of fatigue, I heard Sasha declare: "A son!"

The tsarina said mournfully, "Born on the feast day of St. Job. We must pray that God does not test him like poor Job in the forge of calamity to prove his faith."

I wanted to retort that surely God had tested his mother enough in labor, but I was too exhausted, and the empress was ill, her consumption now a confirmed secret among the family. I pitied her, knowing the deep anguish she still felt over Nixa.

"Let me see him," I whispered. Tania set the baby, cocooned in white cloth, on my chest. As his little fist clenched at my breast, a feeling unlike any I had known overwhelmed me.

My child. My son. He was here at last. He was mine.

"We shall name him Nicholas," Sasha said, "in honor of my grandfather." He paused, looking suddenly at me. He had turned away during most of my labor, prowling the room as I heaved and cried out but never really looking at me. Now he did. "Manja?"

I passed my weary gaze from him to Alexander, who stood with his arm around his wife. He smiled at me. "It's a fortuitous name for a tsar."

"Yes," I whispered. "Nicholas it is."

TO ME, HE was perfect, with Sasha's gray-blue eyes and silky tufts of my dark hair, which would lighten as he grew older, and a little body that smelled soft, like cream. I was dismayed when informed I must employ a wet nurse. I wanted to nurse him myself and crept to his bassinet whenever I could, dismissing the wet nurse to let him suckle at my aching nipple. I had plenty of milk; my pregnancy had been uneventful, despite all the precautions taken out of fear that I might suffer from milk fever or other ailments that killed new mothers. The tsarina's superstitious comment about his birth had also perturbed me; I did not share her pious mysticism, but I couldn't help believing that nursing my son gave us both a talismanic protection.

For the christening, I dressed Nicky—as we all called him—in a hand-embroidered cotton-and-lace gown I made for him, his bib stitched with his name and birth date. The tsar gave him the traditional Romanov gold cross and issued an effusive proclamation: a three-hundred-gun salute from the fortress and free champagne everywhere, from the great palaces to the aristocratic mansions and dockside taverns.

Sasha strutted about in pride. But in private, he said to me, "Isn't he rather small? My mother remarked he looks half the size Vladimir and I were at our births."

"Every babe is different. I am small. I'm also strong. Did I not carry him for nine months? He will grow into a Russian bear, like you."

Sasha gave uncertain assent. "Still, we mustn't coddle him too much. When I was a boy, we slept on cots, bathed in cold water, and had no luxuries to give us airs. My father, as you know, still has his apartments kept in the strictest order." His gaze roved about our drawing room, which was crowded with potted plants, Japanese lacquer screens, and knickknacks I'd bought on whim at the local bazaars, framed photographs on every table, the walls covered in paintings. I liked the clutter, especially in winter. It felt cozy to me, as a home should.

"He's a baby," I said. "He'll not be sleeping on a cot anytime soon."

Sasha chuckled. "My swan has become a lioness. Woe to anyone who interferes with her cub."

Truer words had rarely been spoken. I was determined to rear my son personally, following my own childhood example by not engaging menials to keep him out of my way. I even used my need to care for my child to postpone my studies with Pobendonostev, which in any event weren't serving me, as the tutor had dedicated all his efforts toward Sasha. Despite his grumbling, my husband had avidly taken to the instruction, so much so that he didn't even make a mention of my absence. With the extra time from not attending those grueling afternoon lessons, I caught up on my correspondence while Nicky napped. Letters between my mother and me became a weekly occurrence, with her imparting advice on weaning and nutrition and warning me against swaddling, for it stunted a babe's natural growth. I did everything she advised, battling the wet nurse. Being a mother was an all-consuming gift and chore I relished. I liked nothing better than to bundle up Nicky and take him in my carriage to show him off to his cooing great-aunts and -uncles or to promenade with him in his pram, the tsar at my side, on the Quai and in the Summer Garden, though I now insisted on a gendarme escort at all times.

I was so engrossed in caring for my boy, I didn't feel the need for any more children, though it was expected. And within weeks of my recovery from labor, Sasha was again visiting my bed.

The love that Alix advised me to nurture but I had not yet fully felt began to flourish in this time. Despite our differences over how Nicky should be reared, having a child brought us closer, and I found myself welcoming my husband's affections, his burly arms and tender touch. He was the only lover I'd known, but I couldn't imagine any other— attentive and sensitive, attuned to my pleasure more than his own. When he had me moaning aloud, he liked to whisper, "I'm told if a woman is pleased, she breeds sons," making me pull him deeper into me even as I replied, "What nonsense."

I soon became pregnant again. Almost a year to the date of Nicky's birth, I bore another son, this time named Alexander, after his grandfather the tsar. He was a beautiful babe, too, larger than Nicky, to Sasha's proud satisfaction.

"Now sisters," he said, cradling little Alexander in his arms. "Boys need sisters."

I rolled my eyes at him. "Not yet. Mothers need respite."

"Would you lock the door on your own husband, wife?" he growled.

"If necessary," I replied, but he knew I would not, and I smiled to see him kiss Alexander's plump cheeks and our newborn son's attempt to reach for his mustache.

"This one is strong," Sasha said. "A true Romanov. I'll teach him to shoot boar."

I reasoned it was natural for him to favor the more robust proof of his manhood, although it made no sense to me. Even if he was smaller, Nicky was healthy and well formed, too.

As our second son's first birthday approached in 1870, we were due to depart for Denmark to visit my parents. Sasha had expressed keen interest in seeing my country, and I was eager to show it to him. Then little Alexander developed a high fever; in a panic, Sasha sent word to the palace. When the imperial physician dispatched by the tsar emerged from the nursery to say sadly, "I fear it is meningitis, Your Highness," I gave such a piercing cry that Sasha recoiled helplessly.

"He's only eleven months old! He hasn't fallen from any horse." In my disbelief at hearing the same illness that killed Nixa, I barely heeded the physician's grave explanation that the disease did not require an injury. Ripping myself away, I bolted into the nursery, refusing to allow anyone near him.

I sat by his crib and dried his puckered brow over and over of that horrible sweat as he writhed and lamented before lapsing into silence. Seeing Nixa again in that villa, his wasted face and imploring eyes, my entire world shattered.

Everything inside me, everything around me, went black.

I did not know he was gone until Sasha entered and I felt his hand, trembling, on my shoulder. "Manja, my love. Come now." His voice caught. "Nicky . . . he needs you."

My son had been sequestered in the Tauride Palace with his nurse-maid, out of fear of infection. Lifting my eyes to Sasha, I whispered, "Don't let them take him away."

Sasha hoisted me up from my stool by the crib and led me to the door; when I started to turn around, he tightened his hold on me. "Do not look back."

Bereft, I could not attend his funeral. Sasha saw him entombed in the St. Peter and Paul Cathedral, and from her retreat in the Crimea, where she was fighting her own deadly battle, the tsarina sent me a heartrending letter of condolence, reminding me that God sometimes takes from us what we most love.

Crumbling the letter in my fist, with a wail I flung it aside. That evening, Sasha came home to find me on the floor. Tania and Sophie said they'd tried to rouse me as he roared at them to get out. They had tried. But in that dreadful moment, envisioning my perfect babe lying cold and still under a white sarcophagus, all I wanted was to die myself.

"Manja." Sasha dropped beside me to gather me in his arms. "You mustn't do this to yourself. God must love us very much to have called our little one to His side."

"God took him from me, just as Nixa was taken," I wept. "God does not love me."

He cupped my face in his palms. "You must never utter such a blasphemy again. God indeed must love you above others, to ask of you such sacrifice." As I flinched at his quiet chastisement, he said, "I also grieve for our little boy, but you—you are my life. Without you, this world means nothing to me."

Sudden tears swam in his eyes; I'd never seen him cry before. He lowered his gaze, whispering, "I know I'll never be Nixa for you," and I recognized then what I hadn't yet admitted. In some unbidden moment I failed to mark, I had fallen in love with him—with his stolid presence and awkward vulnerability, with his persistent devotion to me, although he had no need, for, like his brothers, he could have had plenty of other women. Yet in all this time, even if he'd no doubt heard that Sasha the Bullock was fortunate to have wed his dead brother's fiancée, not once had he wavered. Not once had he reproached me for the secret flame of Nixa's loss in my heart, which our son's death had laid bare.

He had given me his heart instead. His great bull's heart, with all its insecurities.

"Sasha," I said.

His expression faltered, as if he braced for a thrust. "It doesn't matter if you never love me as I love you. Nicky and I . . . we both need you so."

"I do." My voice caught. "I do love you, my husband."

He slowly let out his breath, as if he had carried a knot inside him, and drew me to his chest. "We will have more children," he said. "I promise you. Many more. We shall fill this house to the rafters with their laughter, so one day you can remember our lost boy without so much sadness."

His tender avowal fractured me, so that I found myself saying, "Take me home."

He murmured, "We are home, my love. Russia is our home."

"I want Denmark. I want my country. My parents."

He tightened his arms about me. "Then we shall. We will go as soon as it can be arranged. I'll ask leave from my father."

It was then, in that moment, as we held on to each other like survivors of a cataclysm, that I gave myself entirely to him. In the next few weeks, as we prepared to travel, I forced myself for his sake and for our Nicky, who was confused, sensing my grief, too young to understand the loss he must have felt at seeing the nursery emptied of his dead brother's crib.

I had to be strong for both of them. For just as I was to them, they were my life.

CHAPTER TWELVE

My mother and father welcomed us with joy. Assuming charge of me as they always had, Mama commandeered plenty of meals and fresh air to fortify my body and spirit.

"Why, you are skin and bones!" she exclaimed. "We can't have you wasting away. You've a son and husband to look after."

My sixteen-year-old sister, Thyra, wasn't there. She'd fallen in love with a Danish army officer—an unfortunate choice, as he was in no position to wed a princess. Mama had to intervene to break up the affair, sending disconsolate Thyra to Athens to spend time with Willie and his wife and hopefully mend her broken heart.

But Alix arrived with Bertie and their young children, my sister having given birth to her second daughter, Victoria, the same year as I had Nicky, followed the year after by her third daughter, Maud. She was pregnant yet again, she sighed, but it was still early enough that she'd defied the queen's usual mandate against travel. As we walked through the gardens at Fredensborg, my son tottered after Alix's George, who was three years older and quite the tyrant, ordering Nicky and his own older brother, Albert, about with a peremptory tone.

"My George thinks he must assert himself," said Alix. "The second son is always the most demanding, because he knows he's not first—" She cut herself short, taking my arm. "Forgive me. I didn't think. Having a child every year has made me an addle-brain."

"Don't apologize." I blinked back sudden tears. "Your children are so beautiful. You and Bertie must love them so much, and look—" I said, to dispel the shadow that fell over her eyes. "Sasha is besotted. What a great Russian fool he is."

My husband was on his hands and knees on the lawn, clad in his rumpled linen jacket and baggy *moujik* trousers—as soon as we were away from court, he refused to wear anything else but that old jacket, worn pants, and scuffed boots—as the children squealed, clambering onto his broad back, assisted by Bertie, who guffawed as Sasha crawled to and fro, shaking his head and mock-biting at the children's legs.

"He loves children. He's like a big child himself." She turned to me. "Have you given any thought to when you might try again . . . ?"

I swallowed against a knot in my throat. "Yes. Soon. We both want more children."

Her smile deepened. "Children are our consolation. Until they grow up and leave us, we must get out of bed every day for them, no matter what."

I sensed distance between her and Bertie—nothing I could elucidate, but present nevertheless. One evening, Alix retired early; the men emptied the cognac and smoked too many cigars, finally staggering drunk up to their rooms. Left alone with Mama in the drawing room, I ventured, "Does Alix seem unhappy to you?"

My mother was darning socks. She still mended her and Papa's clothes, which had so dismayed me that I insisted on giving them funds to replenish their meager livings. Without looking up from her needle, she replied, "You must never ask her."

"Why? Did she say something to you?" I wasn't sure I wanted to know. I had come to love Bertie, not only because of his fondness for Sasha but because he was everything I might have wished for in a brother-in-law—affable and never rude, a champion against Prussia in England. France and Prussia were on the verge of war, and Bertie's outspoken speeches about the need to curtail German aggression hadn't pleased Victoria in the slightest.

Mama gave a troubled sigh. "Nothing directly. But enough to know she must look the other way. Bertie is a good husband, but like every man, he has his weakness."

"You mean mistresses," I said flatly, bringing her gaze up to mine.

"As I said, you must never ask. It would serve no purpose other than to humiliate her. He loves her, regardless. More so, I think, than he even knows."

I returned to my reading, but the words blurred before my eyes and I excused myself, going upstairs to the children's room. The boys shared a bed, tumbled together like puppies. Alix's girls were next door to her, with their nanny, so she could hear them if they cried in the night. After I smoothed Nicky's hair and disentangled George's possessive arm thrown over him, I padded down the corridor to Sasha's room. We did not share the same rooms, even in Russia. He kept his own apartments, which were austere, while I had mine, which were not. He came to my bed whenever we sought intimacy, but we'd agreed to an amicable balance by maintaining separate beds.

Now I could hear him snoring from behind the door. I went in anyway, undressing to my shift. Sliding into the bed, hot as a kiln from his body, I curled beside him. He grumbled, moving closer to me. His manhood poked the small of my back. Hiking my shift, I eased him into me.

"I want a child, Sasha," I whispered as he bucked into me. "I want another son."

⁓

As the last of the autumn leaves drifted across the *prospekts,* I knew. I found myself beset by malaise, a retching in the morning that sent Tania into a fluster. I didn't say anything to Sasha until late November, when our personal physician examined me and confirmed it. Despite our joy, and perhaps because of the loss of our second son, Sasha became impossible, wanting me to seclude myself and abstain from any strenuous activities.

"With the Season upon us?" I said. "Your mother has gone to the Crimea. Who will open the gala at the Winter Palace? Your father needs me, the tsarevna, at his side. And there I will be."

Irate but unable to detain me, short of bolting the doors, he squeezed into his blue-and-silver uniform and elk-skin breeches and trudged with me to court, where, in the flush of my new condition, I contrived to dance, flirt, and converse. Sasha glowered, steadfast at my side; even Vladimir remarked he'd never seen my husband quite so resolute.

"Have you given him cause to doubt you?" he teased as we danced across the Nicholas Hall under the cut-crystal chandeliers.

"Never," I said. "And isn't it high time that you, brother-in-law, ceased cavorting about and found yourself a proper arrangement?"

"What? Are two ballerinas from the Mariinsky not proper enough?"

"Honestly." I rapped my fan on his shoulder. "Your father complained to me only last week that your gambling debts are outrageous, and if you don't marry and start behaving as a grand duke should, he'll cut you off. Whatever will you do with your ballerinas then?"

Vladimir threw back his leonine head and guffawed. But his mirth soon faded. "I must get myself a wife," he admitted. "Papa has made it a nonnegotiable condition of my continued solvency. So I'll go abroad on a grand tour—it's what we grand dukes do—and see if I can find one. Wish me luck, Minnie. Such a pity you're already taken." He winked at me, the rogue. "I'd have married you without a second thought."

"You're incorrigible. I wish only luck for the lady. She will need it."

As he bowed and I left him to rejoin Sasha, who waited for me with a scowl, Vladimir called out, "Lucky lady or not, I'll not give up my ballerinas."

Of that, I had no doubt.

⁓

WHILE CHUNKS OF melting ice flowed from the Neva to the sea and the Summer Garden burst with May bloom, I took to my bed, again in Tsarskoe Selo. After only a few hours, I delivered my third son, christened George. Sasha paraded with him yowling in his arms. He was robust, a proper Romanov baby, and his arrival helped ease my lingering sorrow over the death of our little Alexander; we now had two surviving sons.

Nicky, however, remained small, to Sasha's discontent, and cleaved to me rather than to his father. Though our firstborn was still very young, Sasha grew too strict with him. I came upon them one morning, after Sophie alerted me, to find poor Nicky standing naked in the tub, shivering, as Sasha doused him with a pitcher of cold water.

"Are you mad?" I shoved my husband aside to envelop my trembling son in a towel. "He's four years old. What in God's name were you thinking?"

"To make him strong." Sasha jutted out his lower lip, as he always did when confronted with a problem, be it soggy cabbage at the table or a demanding lesson from Pobendonostev. "He must learn that life is not soft cushions and Mama's loving arms."

"You're a brute. You could have given him pneumonia. If I ever catch you doing this to him again, *you* will learn just how cruel Mama's loving arms can be."

He went out, slamming the bathroom door. Nicky whispered, "Papa hates me."

"No. No, my sweet boy. Papa doesn't hate you. He's just—he's . . ."

"A brute?" Nicky said, and I laughed, coddling him. "Yes," I said. "A big *moujik* brute. Shall we send him out to thresh wheat?"

My son tilted his head, as if he thought it a good idea. From then on, I made certain that Sasha did not bully him.

"Do you want him to grow up to fear you?" I asked Sasha, who scowled.

"Better that he fear me than grow up to be like Sergei," he retorted.

I paused. His younger brother, Grand Duke Sergei, was fifteen, a year from his majority of age, and exemplary, fluent in several languages, including Italian, as he'd insisted on reading Dante in the original. He also had musical talent, playing the flute in the Winter Palace orchestra. Tall and thin as a stork, Sergei was strikingly handsome, with the incised cheekbones of a Renaissance prince and hazel-green eyes that, like a cat's, tended toward amber in the right light.

"And what is so wrong with Sergei? He's studious, accomplished, and—"

"You don't hear what I do." Sasha heaved himself to his feet. "My brother Paul has told me . . . things. Things I will not repeat. But mark my words," he warned. "Nicholas will not be like Sergei. Not if I have any say in it."

There was no arguing with him when he was in a mood. Besides, whatever Paul had conveyed couldn't possibly be as terrible as he made it seem. The tsar's youngest sons, Paul and Sergei, were inseparable; they'd grown up together, traveling with their mother to the Crimea and Nice until she became too ill. In the palace, they shared lessons, trying to find their way in a world dominated by their older brothers, Sasha, Vladimir, and Alexis.

As for Nicky, I'd not let anyone instill fear in him. My firstborn was not like a Romanov. I already sensed it, and I did not think it a defect. Quite the contrary, in fact.

We had more than enough swaggering Romanovs already.

CHAPTER THIRTEEN

Vladimir returned from his tour of Europe, where he'd made an endless succession of casino owners, hoteliers, actresses, and their respective entourages exceedingly happy.

He came to see me at my Anichkov. Sasha was out, walking Beauty and his hunting terrier, Moska. As we drank tea, Vladimir exposed his new monogrammed emerald and onyx cuff links. I had to roll my eyes at his inability to restrain himself until he suddenly announced, "I found a wife."

"You did?" After the adventures he'd described, in addition to the tsar's fury when the bills from the Continent arrived, I thought finding a wife had been the last thing on his mind.

"Yes," said Vladimir. "She suits me. Apparently, I suit her more. She was already betrothed, but she broke off her engagement to marry me."

I suspected this enterprising lady had gleaned the advantages he presented. A profligate husband, with his imperial income and penchant for ballerinas and racehorses, was the sort some women preferred, as it left them with ample time to indulge their own interests.

"And who is this fortunate lady?" I asked.

He sucked at the inside of his teeth. "You'll not like it."

"Whyever not? I thought you might never marry at all, given your present course."

"She's German," he said, and before I could react, my hand freezing on the samovar, he went on quickly, "Duchess Marie of Mecklenburg-Schwerin, daughter of Grand Duke Frederick II. Her father has Slavic blood; his great-grandmother was a daughter of Tsar Paul I. But her family is also friendly with Chancellor Bismarck and the new kaiser."

I sat back, without pouring him more tea, regarding him in disapproving silence until he groused, "Everyone wanted me to get a wife. Must I be judged for her birth?"

"Not by me. I'm quite sure you know best." But my tone of voice indicated otherwise, and he reverted to a plaintive tone, which was entirely wasted on me.

"Minnie, there aren't many princesses willing to come here as you did and adopt our ways. I realize France's defeat by Germany must leave a bad taste in your mouth, but please don't begrudge me. I've heard enough about it from my father."

"The bad taste in my mouth is of no concern here," I said. "Is His Majesty opposed?"

"Not in theory. But in practice . . ." He fiddled with his cuff links. "She will not convert. She says she owes her highest obedience to God, and God wishes her to remain a Lutheran."

"How like a German, to have personal assurance of our Almighty's wishes."

"You'll be kind to her when she arrives?" he said. "You are the tsarevna. I'm depending on you."

"*If* she arrives. Conversion for a Romanov bride has never been an option."

"Oh, she'll arrive," he said. I couldn't tell if he was confident or perplexed. "Marie may think she knows what God wishes, but if He disagrees, she will ignore Him."

"She sounds enchanting," I said dryly. "I look forward to her arrival."

⁓

MARIE OF MECKLENBURG-SCHWERIN refused to convert, but such was the pressure brought upon Alexander, who wanted Vladimir settled, and by the duchess's father, who had an intractable daughter on his hands, that eventually an agreement was reached. For the first time in one hundred fifty years, a Romanov grand duke would marry a woman who did not embrace the Orthodox faith.

Sasha was enraged. Like Bertie, he had absorbed my family's anti-Prussian sentiment, for I wasn't reluctant to express it, particularly after the catastrophic war that cost Napoleon III his empire and laid brutal siege to Paris, crushing my hope for a Prussian defeat that might restore our lost Danish duchies. Now Sasha vented his spleen on Vladimir, snubbing him at the Winter Palace and informing their father the marriage would be an "abomination," until I had to remind my husband that, sometimes, we must swallow what we cannot chew.

"Vladimir will be the one doing all the swallowing," he said. "That German cow will lead him by the nose and spend every last ruble he has."

"Perhaps, but she'll be Grand Duchess Vladimirovich, so we must accommodate."

Only she was not Grand Duchess Vladimirovich. She adopted the patronymic of Pavlovna, to exalt her Romanov descent, and arrived in 1874 to turn our lives upside down.

⁓

I DIDN'T WANT to like her.

Since the loss of our Danish duchies, hatred of Germany had taken root in my soul. Adding to my disgust with the marriage was the fact that the tsar presented his new daughter-in-law with a hundred-carat emerald once owned by Catherine the Great, in addition to the five-carat ruby from Vladimir, as well as a magnificent suite of emeralds that rivaled any I owned. Watching the statuesque Grand Duchess Pavlovna glide down the aisle of the Kazan Cathedral, adorned like an empress, I took savage glee that all the jewels in the Romanov vault could not detract from her square-jawed Germanic face, although I had to concede she had expressive brown eyes and an arresting presence, despite her overly plump figure.

And, like her or not, the tsar made it clear he expected me to befriend her—in fact, do more than befriend her. "She's headstrong," he said. "She wanted Vladimir and now she has him. What she'll do with him is beyond me, but I don't want her making a spectacle of herself. See to it that she understands what's expected of her. I detest vulgarity."

It was a telling remark on his new daughter-in-law, so once she and Vladimir returned from their monthlong honeymoon abroad, I took it upon myself to visit her at Vladimir's palace, which fronted the embankment near the Winter Palace in the most exclusive district of the city. I entered the foyer to the cacophony of workmen, high scaffolds mounted against the walls, and tarps covering the floors.

She swept down the main staircase, dressed in a bustled green silk gown, her curly auburn hair, lighter than my own and frizzier, barely contained by diamond-studded combs. After a perfumed embrace and tiny kisses on both my cheeks, she led me upstairs to her drawing room, where her Limoges tea service was set out and the thick, gilded double doors muffled some of the noise.

"Renovations," she informed me unnecessarily in her accented French. Like a German, she'd not bothered to refine her pronunciation; I would discover it only added to her charm. "This *schloss* desperately needs a feminine touch. New furnishings, new floors, new upholstery— all of it. Vladimir barely stayed here. As you can imagine, he left it in utter disarray."

"I see." I resolved to say as little as permissible. Let her talk and reveal herself. Seated on a baize settee opposite me, she waved her maid out as soon as the girl had served tea, then directed her full scrutiny on me. Her gaze was piercing, almost intrusive in its intensity.

"You must tell me everything. I do so want us to be friends."

"Everything would take a very long time," I replied. "Perhaps you can tell me how you find Russia. I remember when I first came here, everything seemed so strange."

"Did it?" She sipped her tea, then reached for a silver case inlaid with seed pearls. Snapping it open, she removed a thin black-papered cigarette and lit it with a match, blowing smoke through an affected pout of her lips. "I don't find Russia strange at all."

I stared at her.

"Oh, do you want one?" She extended the case. I did not smoke, but the way she proffered it felt like a challenge, so I took a cigarette, lighting it and immediately coughing when the acrid smoke hit my throat. My eyes watered; as I placed the cigarette in a crystal ashtray on the table between us, she reclined with hers between her fingers. "I do love a cigarette with tea. It's the style in Paris and Berlin. All the princesses smoke these days."

The mention of Berlin was deliberate. I made myself take up my cigarette and inhale. The attempt sent me into such a coughing fit that she half-rose, alarmed, until I managed to say, "It's stronger than I'm used to."

"It's Russian tobacco," she purred. "What were you smoking?" But then she smiled. "You didn't smoke before, but now you will. I admire a woman who doesn't let herself be bested."

"I had no idea it was a contest," I said, but despite my resolve to remain aloof, I began to rather like her. She wasn't what I'd expected. There was no Teutonic aggression here, only a firm sense of who she was. In a woman of only twenty, it was refreshing.

"It's always a contest between women who are wed to brothers," she said. "I hope we can move past the obvious and become friendly rivals instead."

"Rivals?"

"Why, yes. I intend to be a premier figure in society here." She leaned toward me. "You cannot imagine how very dull my existence was before I met Vladimir. He rescued me from a life of endless subservience and boredom."

The former I doubted. She did not strike me as a woman who could be subservient to anyone. "Vladimir is certainly a prize," I said, and she must have detected the irony in my voice, for she laughed—a startling guffaw that had nothing false about it.

"A prize, indeed. He's a reprobate. I know about it already, so you cannot shock me. The ballerinas, the horses, the gambling debts—he told me everything. I insisted on it. One must be very sure of the bank before one opens an account."

"He has led a colorful life. You'll have your work cut out for you, I'm afraid."

"No. *He* has his work cut out for him. I've been quite clear on my expectations. It's up to him to fulfill them. If he thinks I'll abide the debts, he's mistaken."

"And the ballerinas?"

She shrugged. "One cannot tame a beast, only train it to do one's bidding."

I chuckled. I couldn't resist. "Train Vladimir. You *are* fearless."

"What is there to fear?" She extinguished her cigarette in the ashtray, where mine smoldered in a column of ash. "He's my husband.

Providing he can obey a few simple rules, he's free to do as he pleases. If he cannot, I'll take a lover of my own. A wife can, you know."

As appalling as her words were, I wasn't appalled. She spoke with such forthrightness, as if stating the terms of a transaction. Yet I must have looked astonished, for she pointed at the case. "Have another. It takes time, but after a while, the smoke feels pleasant." And as I did, coughing just as much but determined to master the vice, she asked in a dulcet tone, "Have I shocked you?"

"Not in the least. Did you expect to?"

"I had hoped." She shrugged again. "That I have not bodes well for us, Minnie." Taking up the teapot, she refilled my cup. "You must call me Miechen."

SHE MEANT WHAT she said. That Season, the gates of her still-unfinished palace were thrown open to welcome the aristocracy. I realized at once that while I was the undisputed first lady at court by virtue of my status as tsarevna and the tsarina's now-chronic absence, in St. Petersburg at large, Miechen intended, as she'd warned, to establish her claim.

Ill-tempered because I'd forced him to join me tonight and don his gold-and-green Preobrazhensky uniform for the occasion, Sasha took one look around the newly restored foyer and grumbled, "Did she strip the Winter Palace of its gilding?"

"It is rather ostentatious," I agreed, for it was, her renovations consisting of multicolored marble and gold cherubs everywhere.

Sasha practically gnashed his teeth when Vladimir and Miechen came to greet us, passing his virulent gaze over her person as she gave him a careless smile. In contrast to my discreet white silk and diamond-and-pearl choker, she flaunted a dramatic carnelian silk gown in the most current fashion, her round white shoulders powdered and, most shockingly to Sasha, bare; her arms were sheathed in long satin gloves, with as much jewelry as she could ladle on, including that impressive suite of emeralds. The effect was indeed vulgar, as the tsar had feared, but she seemed utterly unconcerned with what my husband or anyone else thought, leaving Sasha to glower at his brother as she hooked her arm in mine and swept me into her crowded salon.

Throughout the evening, champagne, cognac, and wine flowed. Caviar, smoked salmon, and various imported pâtés circulated with abandon, borne on gold platters by servants liveried in distinctive mulberry with Miechen's grand ducal crest. Sasha made no effort to conceal his distaste, but Vladimir appeared content, resigned in a manner I'd not have thought possible, rotating around his wife like a star in her orbit and naturally, with his own erudition, enhancing the overall ambiance of sophistication.

"I cannot understand what he sees in her," said Sasha, hours later as we returned home. "She's a parvenu. Their palace is ghastly and that buffet dinner was a debauchery. She will bankrupt him before their first anniversary."

"He knew who he was marrying. She did not deceive him."

"She will yet," he retorted. "A woman like her always does."

Miechen roused both my admiration and my envy. She had dictated the foundation upon which her marriage would be built; she did not fret over dalliances yet somehow managed to rein Vladimir to her will. Moreover, she had a husband who complimented her, who loved society and to admire and be admired. My sudden resentment of Sasha's aversion to balls, his habit of ranging around at home in his tattered apparel, caused me to reprimand him. Once he caught me in a fit of pique after an argument, sneaking a cigarette in my parlor. I was so flustered when he came through the door that, as I spun around to face him, I thrust the cigarette behind my back.

"There's smoke coming up behind you," he said. "Be careful you don't catch fire."

I became a daily smoker. Miechen had been correct: I did grow accustomed to it, but I restricted my intake to four cigarettes a day, and never in public. I didn't want anyone but Sasha to know, although sometimes when I kissed my sons good night, Nicky wrinkled his nose. "Mama, you smell like a cigar."

Miechen's influence wormed its way into me like poison. I had the disturbing sensation she was gauging me, judging, when we invited her and Vladimir to our palace, as if she was deciding whether we had the right to be who we were. She never said anything denigrating, but I found myself purchasing new gowns by the dozens, discovering that designs by Worth's rival, the rising Parisian couturier, Félix, were not among any she owned, as she preferred to expend lavish sums solely on Maison Worth. She admired my décor, even asking where I'd bought my Japanese screens, as she needed something like them. But while mine graced my drawing room, in full view of everyone, hers were placed in her private dressing room as a backdrop to her bountiful silk-upholstered boudoir.

I couldn't decide if we were friendly rivals or friendly at all and I doubted she cared. That I did care was the most upsetting part, for I should not.

One day, I would be Empress of Russia. As well she knew.

CHAPTER FOURTEEN

As I rode through London with Alix at my side, Bertie and Sasha ahead of us in another open carriage, the English people applauded, and for once, not a drop of rain fell upon us. I had to smile to recall my first visit here.

I'd been only Dagmar of Denmark then, the younger sister of the new Princess of Wales, my suitability as a bride queried by Victoria for her son Alfred. Now I had returned as Her Imperial Highness Maria Feodorovna, paving the way for the unexpected betrothal of the tsar's daughter Marie to none other than Alfred himself, now titled Duke of Edinburgh. When Alix wrote to tell me that Alfred had been infatuated with Marie during a reunion of German relatives in Hesse-Darmstadt, my first thought was that he obviously couldn't control his carnal impulses. Had he not been taken by me during my own sister's nuptials? Nevertheless, after much negotiation, both Alexander and Victoria gave their consent, signaling an unusual conciliation. London newspapers speculated that the two empires had agreed to uncross their sabers over various domains in Asia. St. Petersburg newspapers promulgated a British plot to undermine Russia, as usual. To emphasize that the marriage was a love match, not political, Victoria agreed that Sasha and I should pay a visit.

"Let's wave to them," I now said to Alix, who raised an eyebrow but did as I suggested. The crowds, surprisingly voluble for the British, cried out our names.

I laughed, leaning back against the upholstered seat as we made our way toward Buckingham Palace. "What a lark." I motioned to our matching pin-striped gowns and jaunty bonnets trimmed with artificial cherries—it had been my idea that we dress alike to confuse everyone.

Alix gave a dry chuckle. "At last, you got your wish. But I'm quite sure the queen will know who you are when she sees you."

"I should hope she will," I replied, smiling.

Victoria, of course, wasn't present to welcome us, having retired to Windsor Castle to avoid the uproar of our visit. I determined to enjoy myself, regardless. At a ball held for us one evening, Alix and I again dressed alike, in identical blue satin and jewels, dancing with each other's husbands—both of whom had grown out their beards to abet our ploy—as the guests scrambled to perch on chairs, tables, and even the edges of potted plants to catch a glimpse of us.

From Windsor, Victoria dispatched a terse note that she was mortified at the news of our childish behavior.

We stayed in England for three weeks, touring the royal estates before spending a few obligatory days at Windsor with Her Majesty, who looked to me very aged and querulous, regarding me through her watery gaze as if she couldn't quite believe her eyes.

"She never thought you'd marry Sasha," Alix confided, as we huddled together in her bed like when we were girls in Denmark, for despite the summer balm, Windsor was still inhospitably dank. "She didn't want Affie to wed Marie, either, but Bertie told her the world is changing and we mustn't be at odds with Russia."

"I hope Alfred agrees," I said. "Did you see his face tonight when Sasha cornered him after dinner? I thought he'd start to cry as Sasha warned him to make sure he accorded Marie the respect she deserves."

Alix tugged the blankets up to our chins. "He needn't worry on her account; we shall see to Marie's every comfort."

Her remark left me troubled. On our return voyage to St. Petersburg, Sasha gave voice to what I couldn't elucidate. "It's a mistake. My sister has no idea of whom she marries. She just wants to be a bride, but what kind of life can she have on that dreary island, with a boor as a husband and miserable queen as her mother-in-law?"

"You certainly hunted and ate to your heart's content." I prodded his stomach. "You've gotten fat off the dreary island's game."

"I enjoyed Bertie, Alix, and the pheasants," he retorted. "Not the rest."

I found Marie in a fever of impatience, desperate to hear my counsel on the queen, England, and her future groom. I found myself repeating Alix's words to her. What could I do, with preparations for the wedding in the Winter Palace already under way?

"My sister Alix is so looking forward to your arrival," I assured her. "She will see to your every comfort."

Marie was so nervous, she was oblivious to the fact that I failed to mention she'd also have a husband to care for her. I wondered if Sasha was right about her motives.

Only weeks after her wedding and departure for England, Marie was writing to the tsar to complain. The queen had refused to let her light a fire in her rooms at Balmoral, and when Marie appeared at dinner wearing the diamond *tiara russe* given to her by her father as a nuptial gift, Victoria bristled, declaring it "too good" while pointedly looking over at her own daughters, none of whom, Marie wrote, "own anything so fine." She was homesick and miserable, and the tsar summoned me in despair.

"I shouldn't have allowed it," he said. "I was against it at first. But Marie implored me. She said she loved him."

"And you believed her? She's only twenty and has lived her entire life in this palace! What can she possibly know about love?"

He let out a wretched sigh. "I didn't wish to deny her. Remember, she's my only daughter, and I vowed I would never force her to marry someone she didn't love."

I told him I would write to ask my sister to assist Marie. I knew it would take time until, like all brides in a foreign land, Marie learned to compromise. But as I left Alexander in his study, I heard the tsarina's words in my mind.

It's never easy at first, coming to this land, but we adjust, my child. We must.

Unfortunately for Marie, I feared the adjustment might vanquish her Russian spirit.

⁓

DARK-EYED AND ELFIN, my daughter, Xenia, arrived in the spring of 1875. I refused to seclude myself in Tsarskoe Selo, insisting on giving birth in my bed in my own palace. As she was a daughter, there was less fanfare surrounding her birth.

Sasha, however, was greatly moved. He doted on Xenia, her arrival softening his authoritarian control over our sons. He bought her dolls, lace gowns, pretty caps, and even a miniature wood pony, which he plopped her upon, holding her upright and rocking her back and forth as she squealed. With two sons and now a daughter, our family life absorbed us so much that I scarcely paid heed to the anarchy just outside our gates . . .

Until a Nihilist assassin attempted to kill the tsar as he walked in the Summer Garden. The gendarmes, whom Alexander now couldn't evade, threw themselves upon the villain before he could fire his pistol, but the resulting panic ended Alexander's informal strolls. Sequestered in the Winter Palace, he was obliged to wear a bulletproof vest under his clothes whenever he rode out in his fortified carriage, because, as he sadly told me, "They would hunt me down like a wolf."

"He's done this to himself," Sasha declared. "My father has spoken of authorizing a constitution, allowing a Duma to restrict our autocracy. Pobendonostev says it would be the end of everything we stand for. Autocracy, orthodoxy, and nationality are the three pillars of Russia, where the tsar is ordained by God to rule, not to tear down God's rule."

I now bitterly regretted having endorsed our tutor, especially as I'd never resumed my lessons with him after Nicky's birth, so I'd been left somewhat unaware of the man's pernicious influence on my husband.

"If he says that, he's a fanatic. It doesn't conform to the world we live in now," I said, as he stared at me in amazement. "Sasha, your father once told me the serfs are suffering. For lack of land, they're forced to come here to work in factories, where they barely earn a living. Many are illiterate and are exploited because of it."

"It has always been that way in Russia. Would you question our divine right to rule this empire as we have for centuries?"

I realized I'd made a blunder but now felt the urgent need to pry open his constrained view, which could only create more dissension with the tsar. "Ruling as you have for centuries is the reason the Nihilists exist. Your father doesn't intend to uproot everything the dynasty stands for, but he recognizes there must be adjustments. Surely we cannot go on this way, waiting for the next villain to shoot at him."

Sasha glowered. "He may not intend it. But his talk of a constitution gives them plenty of incentive. What he fails to do, they'll do for him." He thrust a pamphlet at me. "See here."

I lowered my gaze to read the smeared ink on cheap paper:

People of Russia—victims of oppressors—go out with your pitchforks and return with them lit by the flames of the great houses, with the money that is your due in your pocket.

A bolt of fearful rage went through me. "Where did you get this?" I asked, even though I already knew. "Did Pobendonostev dare bring this filth into our house?"

"They're churning these out on illicit presses all over the city. He wanted to show me that the Nihilists urge our own people, your suffering serfs, to rise up against us."

I was horrified. I sympathized with the plight of the poor, even if I now recognized how little I truly knew. Dwelling in a world that rarely offered a glimpse of how the thousands around me lived, I'd assumed it was not my affair, that the tsar was the one to enact the law and see to his people's welfare. Now I faced the terrifying possibility that should the Nihilists succeed in their zeal, everything I knew and loved might be destroyed.

"They should be executed for it," said Sasha. "Hung in the palace square to show that we'll not abide sedition. Instead, my father, whom you defend, pardoned that cretin who tried to shoot him and let him loose to run back into the rat holes they gnaw in garrets all over this city. Next time, they'll not miss. Next time, they will kill him—"

"Sasha, hush," I said. Nicky had paused in his playing with his toy soldiers on the carpet by the hearth, looking up at us with a troubled frown.

"Let him learn now," Sasha said. "Let him understand that the tsar holds power solely by the grace of God and cannot place trust in his own people."

I longed to dismiss Pobendonostev, only Sasha wouldn't permit it. Instead, he gave the horrid man leave to invite into our very drawing room all sorts of people with notions I couldn't fathom—university professors and gaunt writers in threadbare coats, spouting ideals of freedom in direct conflict to Pobendonostev's ideals. I was repulsed after one of these writers, with wine on his breath, leered at me and said, "In this very palace, Madame, how many families do you think could live comfortably?"

"One," I retorted, irate, resisting the urge to say I was "Your Imperial Highness" to him. "Mine. Do you suppose we should rent out our rooms?"

"This is why you cannot understand what is right before you." The man turned with a deriding laugh to the others, all of whom regarded me as if I were an inept child. I saw Sasha's face darken in rage at the gross dishonor done to me. Then he glanced at Pobendonostev; the tutor's sardonic smile made Sasha hold his tongue. I understood perfectly then. Our tutor deliberately surrounded us with the very thing he detested, to prove that only chaos would result if we allowed radicals to have their way.

The very next day, desperate to escape the brooding atmosphere at home, I fled with my children to visit Miechen at her palace. Here, her legion of staff oversaw my sons and her own year-old son, Cyril, the boys running about in a toy-laden nursery the size of a small ballroom, replete with the ubiquitous gold tracery on the ceiling.

"That tutor will cast us into disfavor," I said, smoking one cigarette after another, my strict quota forgotten. "Alexander is furious. He berated Sasha for entertaining revolutionaries in our salon!"

"How unpleasant," said Miechen. "I regret to add to your distress, Minnie, but there has been talk in society, too."

"Talk?" My voice cracked in disbelief.

"Yes. Of how at the Anichkov, anyone may enter, even a Nihilist, providing they've read Dostoyevsky and disdain a cravat." She gave one of her self-deprecatory shrugs. "Not that I condone such talk, mind you, but I can't help overhear."

"That—that is outrageous," I whispered. In her eyes, I saw a flicker of malice, a satisfied gleam that she'd discovered a vulnerability in my otherwise ideal existence.

"It is," she said. "I certainly would never tolerate it. Nor would I risk incurring His Majesty's displeasure to indulge a man whom I hired and pay."

"He's a servant." I came to my feet. "Servants do not determine who enters my home."

She gave me a cold smile. "I sincerely hope not."

Ordering my maid to gather up my boys and Xenia in her bassinet, I returned in a whirlwind of indignation to my palace. The moment Sasha came home from his regimental duties, I confronted him in the foyer, before he'd unbuttoned his overcoat.

"Would you see us defamed and banned from court to satisfy Pobendonostev? You will cease these gatherings at once. Inform our tutor that he may continue his instruction of you in a limited capacity, but we will not see any of those miscreants in this house again."

His eyes narrowed. "Do I hear my wife dictating to me?"

"You do." I turned on my heel. "And unless you care to see your wife and children take residence elsewhere, you will abide by her dictates."

⁓

POBENDONOSTEV DIDN'T PROTEST. He'd accomplished his goal: to set Sasha on a path of inflexibility that put him in opposition to the tsar, whose emancipation of the serfs and resultant miseries had given rise to the Nihilists. I could barely remain polite to him, so infuriated that I couldn't just throw him out on his ear that I went to see Alexander myself, barging into his study unannounced.

"Minnie." He looked up from his desk, amid his papers with his pen in hand and old Milord snoozing at his feet. When he saw my expression, he said, "Do not say a word in Sasha's defense. He has gone beyond forgiveness. These gatherings in your salon and that fiend Pobendonostev, filling his ears with venom—how could you permit it? I'm very disappointed. Not even Miechen, for all her extravagance, has contrived to hurt me thus."

"I have no excuse," I said. "Only that you asked me to guide Sasha. Since Pobendonostev educated him in his childhood and has continued to instruct your sons Grand Duke Paul and—"

"Not anymore. That man is now forbidden to set foot in this palace. I should dispatch him to Siberia and see how he likes it, teaching convicts to disrespect their emperor."

I took a step toward him. "The gatherings are over; I've told Sasha that I will not allow them. What else I can do? With Her Majesty so rarely at court, perhaps she has additional duties I can assume. I wish to make amends."

"Can you?" Alexander set his pen down, passing an ink-stained hand over his weary face. He had aged. The toll of the Nihilist menace, his wife's illness, and, no doubt, the secret mistress were taking a toll on him. "My brother Nikolai has abandoned his wife to take up with a common woman. My other brother Constantine, whose own daughter wed your brother, is rumored to be an occultist, inviting prophets and *strannik* into his home, all of whom urge him to usurp my throne. My daughter, Marie, is desperately unhappy in England. And as if all that weren't enough, the Balkans are in an uproar and the Ottomans of Turkey have just declared war against us. How do you intend to amend any of it?"

"I don't know." I gazed at him helplessly. "Surely I can do something."

He considered me. "I've always been very fond of you. You're my favorite daughter-in-law because you never interfere in what doesn't concern you. I am sorry Sasha has taken this stance against me, for he misunderstands the gravity of our situation. I cannot allow our empire to career into revolt when there's a solution at hand—a constitution and Duma, approved by the people, to stem the criticism and save us all. I once told you I feared I made a mistake in liberating the serfs, but I've come to understand that my mistake was not liberating all of Russia. However, I'm heartened you do not share my son's disapproval of me."

He tried to smile, although it came out more like a grimace. "My wife is the president of the Red Cross; it's an honorary position, but with war breaking out we will require the Red Cross to assist us in our time of need. I'll authorize your assumption of her duties while she retains the title. But," he said, as I eagerly nodded, close to tears at his continued, if frayed, trust in me, "be forewarned that, like everything else, the organization is not as it should be. I've heard complaints of missing funds, poor management, and overall apathy. No official in my empire seems to think he need be honest if he can get away with it."

"I oversee my household. I can manage the Red Cross."

He sighed. "I wish it were the same thing."

CHAPTER FIFTEEN

"This is the ward for unwed mothers." The head matron of St. Petersburg's Red Cross paused with me on the threshold of a large, poorly lit raftered room, where row upon row of wasted women on iron cots emitted a din of wretched coughing. As I started to step inside, I smelled the stench even through my protective sanitary mask—a putrid miasma of unwashed flesh, open sores, pus, excrement, and antiseptic.

The head nurse held me back. "They have influenza and typhoid. It's not safe, Your Imperial Highness."

I peered into the room. The rows seemed endless. "So many?" I was deeply shaken. I had assumed the Red Cross duties for the sake of reconciliation with Alexander, but I also had hoped to prove my own charity toward the unfortunate. However, I'd not counted on this searing display of the plight of the poor, the likes of which I'd never imagined. In my tour of the hospital, I'd seen enough to make me want to weep. Not only was the need overwhelming, there seemed to be no way to relieve it. Confronted by such misery, I couldn't avoid understanding why the Nihilists would want us dead. While we dwelled in splendor, Russia suffered right under our unseeing eyes.

"These are not even a quarter of those in the city," said the matron. "We care only for the very sick. Most are prostitutes or factory workers. Their children, many soon to be orphaned, are in the lower ward and are twice as many. Your Highness, every hour of every day we must turn away many more in need of our care. We haven't sufficient beds or staff to accommodate all of them."

I thought I must go in, offer whatever solace I could, but the matron steered me back to the administration office, where I sat before her
desk in limp disbelief.

"As Your Highness has seen, we lack funds," she informed me,
standing over her stacks of papers. "We do not know where the monies
allocated to us by the imperial ministry end up, but they do not come
here. In our current state, we cannot pay our doctors. We're on the
verge of closing. It's a disgrace."

Looking at the mildew-stained walls, feeling the wind whistling
through the cracked window frames, I could see she wasn't exaggerat-
ing. The entire place was falling apart.

"I'll see the funds administered," I said. "I will speak to the finance
ministry at court myself and bring the monies here in person, if necessary."

She gave me a grateful nod, but I detected the skepticism in her
voice. "We are indeed blessed to have Your Highness's concern."

I was determined to prove they had more than my concern. It took
months of disentangling the bureaucratic knots that had resulted in
more than half of the Red Cross funds being redirected into unscrupulous pockets, but I pursued it relentlessly, summoning ministry officials
to demand an accounting. If anyone tried to evade me, I threatened to
inform the tsar. Word soon spread, until the mere mention of my in-
volvement sent malefactors scurrying for cover. I wasn't interested in
punishment—I didn't have the power to enforce it, though I wished I
did—devoting myself instead to reorganizing the Red Cross and seeing
it funded as it deserved, including donating substantial sums from my
own income. Eventually those who oversaw the funds understood that
if anything went awry, they'd answer for it—to me.

I hardly cared that my efforts elevated my profile, with newspaper
editorials penning praise for my interest in something other than fashion or galas and intimating other grand duchesses might do the same,
easing some of the backlash against our Romanov indifference. I went
to the hospital every day, enrolling in courses to become certified as a
nurse, and did rounds on the wards, ignoring Sasha's outrage that I
endangered my health. I marshaled my children to help prepare care
packages for the destitute who queued up for hours outside charity
centers, and I paid for major renovations to a new ward, founded in my

name. I wanted to establish educational centers, so that impoverished women would have options other than working as seamstresses, factory employees, or prostitutes, but my plans were suspended by the war with Turkey.

Under my administration, the Red Cross rose to the challenge, sending medical supplies, infirmary units, and other necessities to the front by train. Sasha was dispatched at the head of his regiment; he might end up in battle, which worried me greatly, but I didn't waver in my work. I'd finally found the means to be useful to my adopted country, to give back to Russia something of what she'd given to me.

Being a member of the imperial family came with obligation. I had discovered mine.

⁓

THE WAR EXACTED tremendous casualties. The tsar's own nephew was killed in battle, and Sasha was also involved in the fighting, causing me tremendous anxiety before I received word that he was unharmed. Every man in the imperial family sound enough to do his duty had been obliged to present himself for the cause; we were fortunate that more did not perish. By the end of 1877, the Turks had suffered unsustainable losses and our army had reached the Ottoman capital of Istanbul. Fearing Russia might bring about that ancient city's fall and thereby reap more conquest than was acceptable, the British sent a fleet of battleships to deter our navy from invading the capital. Under pressure to negotiate a settlement, the tsar agreed to terms in which the Turks renounced their hold on their provinces of Romania, Serbia, and Montenegro, with Bulgaria granted autonomy. As a result of Alexander's conciliation, Prussia wasted no time in occupying Bosnia and Herzegovina, and Great Britain seized the former Ottoman holding of Cyprus.

And whatever victory the tsar might have claimed was marred by a national corruption that helped abrogate his disagreements with Sasha. My husband was the sole commander in the field not accused of the wholesale embezzlement of funds that had resulted in army boots and coats arriving at the front made of threadbare fabric, of bread baked with sawdust, rotting meat, and bayonet blades so weak they broke apart, costing countless Russian soldiers their lives. Alexander charged

Sasha with a commission to investigate abuses of power; all high-ranking commanders, including the senior uncles and Vladimir, came under scrutiny. The voluminous report Sasha prepared made the very color drain from his father's face. The grand dukes and Vladimir were heavily fined, the newspapers printing the scandal on the front pages.

"They merely neglected their duties," Sasha said. "They all blame their subordinates, forgetting they put those subordinates in charge. Of course, while the cats looked the other way, the mice felt free to plunder at will." He snorted. "Now let's see how high Miechen holds her head this Season, once she discovers Vladimir's income has been reduced to a pittance and no one wants to be seen anywhere near their palace."

In the midst of all this upheaval, I found myself again with child. I despaired at the inconvenience, as due to my pregnancy and the unrest abroad, I couldn't attend my sister Thyra's unexpected wedding to Prince Ernst August, titular heir of the German duchy of Hanover. Prussia had recently annexed Hanover, so my sister had in fact wed a titled prince without a realm. I had to wonder at the haste of it and suspected our mother had arranged it to remove Thyra from any further unsuitable liaisons.

My third son, Michael, or Misha, as we called him, was born in December of 1878. Our child seeded in war would be our most gentle, as if his very nature resisted the violence preceding his birth. Nicky and George nicknamed Misha "Floppy" because, as he grew older, he had a habit of throwing himself onto the nearest chair as if the weight of his body were too heavy for his spirit. I loved him with all my heart, and Sasha, perhaps because Misha had been born after he himself had witnessed the horrors of war, favored him with a tenderness he'd thus far only shown toward Xenia.

With three growing boys and a daughter, I submitted to the inevitable and, at Alix's recommendation, hired an English nanny, Mrs. Franklin. I still personally attended to my children, however, insisting on suppers together and reviewing their educational progress. In time, Sasha would have his way and the boys would experience the hard cots, cold baths, and firm discipline that he believed necessary to fortify their character, but while they were young, there was always affection in our home, warmth and playtime, and plenty of love.

I never wanted any of my children to feel unloved.

⌒

PRIVATE SUNDAY LUNCHEONS with the tsar at my palace were my idea. As he and Sasha groped toward mutual accord, I thought they needed time together without ceremony, and Alexander fascinated my children, who greeted him formally as "Your Imperial Majesty Grandpère" and then clambered into his lap. Alexander patiently endured their chatter and was taken with soft-eyed Misha, who always sat close to him.

I knew Alexander was grieving. The tsarina had returned from Nice for the last time; installed in her apartments in the Winter Palace, she would only leave them again in her coffin.

I had gone with Sasha to visit his mother and been deeply affected; the tsarina had wasted to mere bones, gasping for air as she coughed up bloodied clots, but Sasha showed no sympathy for his father's suffering at the impending loss of his wife. If the subject was raised, my husband went silent and Alexander didn't reproach him, making me wonder if Sasha had at long last discovered the tsar's adultery.

If I had any doubt, Miechen made sure to dispel it. Although she'd endured a frightful time after Vladimir's disgrace over the war, banned from court for months until her husband pleaded with the tsar to forgive him, she'd not sacrificed any pride, attending other salons throughout the Season, her head indeed held high, her person adorned with enough jewels to blind every hostess. And she remained attuned as ever to current gossip.

"Everyone has heard of it by now," she said. "If Sasha hasn't, he must be deaf. Her name is Catherine Dolgorukova. Her father was a prince, a close friend of His Majesty's, and a hopeless gambler who left his family in ruin. On his deathbed, he begged the tsar to care for his children, so Alexander sent the boys to military academies and enrolled Catherine and her sister in the Smolny Institute, which, as I needn't tell you, is reserved for the nobility, founded by Catherine the Great, no less."

"Yes," I murmured. "It's very exclusive. The tsarina is its patron."

"Indeed. Yet His Majesty paid their board and tuition; upon Catherine's graduation, he acquired a suitable living arrangement for her in the city. She's still unwed, though past her thirtieth year and still ostensibly his ward, but one hardly requires a seer to deduce why his carriage has been seen coming and going from her house. Apparently, it's been going on for years. Sometimes," she said, her voice terse, "he's been known to spend the better part of the night there. Some even claim she's already borne him a child."

As my hands twisted in my lap, she added, "You can see, it's quite the scandal."

I almost told her in that moment that she was no one to cast aspersion, with Vladimir bedding ballerinas left and right while she spent his fortune embellishing their palace and her position. I held back. It wasn't the time or place. Besides, she only repeated what others said. None of it was secret, not anymore; yet still I was repulsed. She would never forgive our father-in-law for allowing Vladimir's misdeeds to be made public or the humiliation done to her as a grand duchess.

I didn't dare tell Sasha about my conversation with her. If he knew about his father's mistress, he kept quiet, attending our Sunday luncheons. Providing no one mentioned his mother, he and the tsar appeared to be mending their differences, at least on the surface.

For a visit by the tsarina's brother, the Grand Duke of Hesse, who'd been summoned to see his sister before she passed, Alexander requested that Sasha greet the grand duke at the train station and escort him to the Winter Palace. It was an overt sign of Sasha's return to favor, and he left with his entourage on that frigid February afternoon while I stayed home, getting my children to bed early so I could prepare for the banquet in the grand duke's honor. As the tsarina was too ill to leave her bed, I would receive her brother together with the tsar.

But when my troika deposited me at the Winter Palace, Sasha hadn't yet arrived.

"The train is running late," Vladimir said. "My father is not pleased. You know how he detests tardiness. He's in the Lesser Field Marshals' Salon if you wish to see him. I'll stay here and wait for Sasha."

Lifting my heavy dress train, I mounted the Jordan staircase that led to the staterooms. In the salon, I found Alexander pacing. "Where is he?" He turned to me with a scowl. "Can he not do anything as instructed? It's nearly seven. Our reception was to be at six-fifteen."

"Majesty, my husband cannot be held responsible for a train delay," I said.

Alexander's mouth thinned. When his aide-de-camp arrived to say

His Imperial Highness and our guest had arrived, he stalked from the salon, with the other grand duchesses and me behind him, including smug Miechen, who'd overheard his cutting remark about Sasha.

We had just reached the top of the staircase, looking down the steps that Sasha, Vladimir, and the grand duke were about to climb, when all of a sudden the hissing gaslights flickered.

Then the marble floor shuddered.

Miechen shot me a look of alarm. We flanked the tsar, but I'd barely reached for his arm when the enormous crystal chandelier suspended over the staircase came crashing down in an explosion of shattered glass. Shards of dislodged plaster sprayed from the ceiling. The grand duchesses reeled away, screaming; I couldn't hear them, but I saw their mouths agape and eyes flared in terror before I too was thrown off my feet, as a fiery roar burst from the dining hall down the corridor and blasted at our backs.

Darkness plunged over us. As the roiling fog of disintegrated wood, plaster, and stone billowed into the corridor, choking me, the terrifying cacophony of distant wails reached me in fragments. I groped in the thick dust for something to hold on to.

"Minnie!" Alexander's mouth was at my ear. He was yelling, but I heard him as if through a narrow tube, disorientated as he helped me up and began calling out the names of the others. As each person responded in ragged fear, I heard Miechen, and then I remembered.

My voice erupted. "*Sasha!*" I couldn't see anything below us. The entire staircase must have been destroyed, I thought in a rush of horrified panic. Sasha, Vladimir, and the Hessian grand duke had been coming up it and—

"Lights," shouted Alexander. Servants rushed out from other rooms. It seemed as if an eternity passed before they arrived bearing kerosene lanterns or candles. The weak flames scarcely illuminated, but it was enough to reveal that the staircase was intact. At its marble base, Sasha, the grand duke, and Vladimir lay in a heap. As I stumbled down to them over the crumbled plaster and glass on the steps, Sasha was the first to stagger to his feet.

He swayed, blinking, then reached down to assist the stunned grand duke. Vladimir righted himself, a bleeding gash on his temple. My court slippers crunched over the debris as I fell into my husband's arms.

He held me tight as Alexander, Miechen, and the other grand duchesses, coiffed locks in tatters and their headdresses blown off, minced down the staircase accompanied by footmen with the lanterns. We rushed outside into the square, where the palace guard had converged.

Against the snow-speckled night, nectarine flames crackled from the shattered windows of the very hall where we'd been about to dine. As we stood shivering, the tsar barked at one of his guards, "What happened?"

"An explosion, Majesty," quavered the Cossack, gazing up in bewildered horror from under his black lambskin hat at the fire-engulfed hall. "In the basement below the Finnish guard quarters." He crossed himself. "God save them. The regiment was inside."

"There must be many wounded," said the tsar. As he began to issue orders, I unclasped Sasha's hand. "They need assistance. I'm a certified nurse."

Drawing away from him, I gestured to Miechen. To her credit, despite the smudges on her powdered face and a missing slipper, she joined me at once. Together with the other grand duchesses and our ladies, we hurried across the quadrangle to the opposite wing, into the basements for sheets to use as bandages, mattresses from the servant quarters, buckets of hot water, and medicinal supplies. My Red Cross training kept me from hysteria as I ordered a makeshift infirmary set up. Once the fire in the hall was doused, the few survivors of the demolished guard quarters were hauled from the wreckage and brought to us, rescued by servants, the tsar, Sasha, Vladimir, and other grand dukes, who dug in the rubble with their bare hands.

Limbs were missing, flesh seared to clothes. Blood soaked my gown and I didn't notice it until hours later, when the doctors and nurses summoned from the city hospitals took over and Sasha arrived, bathed in grime and soot, to bring me home.

On our carriage ride to the Anichkov, I rested my head on Sasha's chest, his entire person reeking of smoke. As his arms enfolded me, Sasha uttered one word: "Assassins."

⁓

"It wasn't a gas leak." Sasha stood before me, his voice and eyes like stone. "They infiltrated the palace. Workmen were repairing the plumbing in the basement. One of them, a carpenter, brought in explosives, stick by stick. It must have taken him weeks. The officer who checked the passes remembered him coming in late on the very day of the banquet."

"A carpenter?" I echoed, unable to believe it.

"Yes. He must have lit a detonator timed to go off when we were supposed to be in the hall." Sasha showed no emotion; he might have been relating something that had no bearing on us, but I knew after years of marriage that he was never more furious than when he assumed this impassive stance. "He would have murdered us all. Instead, he killed eight Finnish guards in their quarters, twelve servants in the hall, and wounded forty-five others, some so badly burned they'll never recover."

He stared at me as I clasped my fingers together, sitting in our drawing room and feeling as if our very walls might explode at any moment. It had taken a few days for my ears to stop ringing and my hands to cease trembling, but he'd returned to the palace the very next morning to survey the ruin and involve himself in the official investigation.

"So, it was . . . ?" I finally said.

He nodded. "Nihilists. My father has ordered the arrest of every suspected dissident. This time, he vows, there will be no mercy. He cannot risk it. His Silver Jubilee celebration is coming up next month."

"Are we expected to attend?" My voice was a mere thread.

"Of course we are. We mustn't show them any fear. I forbid it. We will go and we will look them in their miserable faces so they can see how little they affect us."

"But we don't even know who they are! We don't know their faces. They could be anyone. Anyone at all. Dear God, if they hid a bomb in the palace, none of us are safe."

He placed his hand on my shoulder as I broke into tears. "Minnie," he said quietly. "If we give in to them now, we'll never stop running."

I swallowed. "Not the children. I won't risk the children."

"No," he said. "For the foreseeable future, the children must stay far from court."

THE CARPENTER WHO'D plotted our death was never found. But what did result from Sasha's urging was the tsar's establishment of a powerful branch of secret police called the Okhrana, charged with hunting down dissident groups. For every one they arrested, Sasha said, ten others eluded them. He spoke as if all of St. Petersburg teemed with them. So vehement were his avowals of retribution that I had to order him not to say another word before the children, after Nicky asked if a Nihilist could crawl over our gates to kill us while we slept. Everything I had done to preserve my children's sense of safety had been torn apart by one horrible act.

Although I couldn't admit it at the time, I already suspected that our world would never be the same.

CHAPTER SIXTEEN

Marie wept with heartrending pathos as I embraced her. She had come from England to be with her mother, and now the tsarina lay in the chapel in her coffin, wreathed in white roses. I had paid my respects, kissing her gaunt cold cheek and remembering how she'd tried to console me after Nixa and then after my baby's death. How lonely she must have been, so helpless before the blows of fate.

"She's with God," I consoled Marie, who appeared prematurely aged and overweight, nothing like the vibrant young grand duchess who'd romped after Milord in the Summer Garden. "Your mother is at peace now."

"She suffered so," whispered Marie. "Oh, Minnie, if you had seen her . . . it was dreadful. She couldn't even catch her breath at the end."

My stab of guilt that I'd not seen her—because Sasha had refused to let me return to the Winter Palace following the explosion—was stifled by Marie's sudden gasp in my arms. I half-turned to see Alexander on the threshold, glancing past the black-clad women holding mourning vigil with his daughter.

Tearing herself from me, Marie snarled at him, "How *could* you?"

Alexander went still.

"I could hear them," Marie said. "Every day, above us. Running. Playing. Laughing. While my mother, your empress, agonized on her deathbed, you brought your whore and bastards into this very palace to torment her in her last days."

"My child—" he started to say, even as I too stared at him. Marie had known for years about his mistress; she'd been the first one to tell me, but this . . . Like Marie, I thought it an unconscionable act to have installed that very woman in the palace while his wife was dying. And illegitimate children: I was shocked by the confirmation that he had them.

Marie flung up her hand. For a moment, I feared she might actually strike him. Instead, she pointed a trembling finger at the door. "You do not deserve to be here. I am ashamed of you. Whatever shame you do not have for yourself, we all carry for you."

It was an unpardonable offense, one he never would have tolerated. Yet he turned and left, his head bowed, while Marie broke into anguished sobs. The women surrounded her. I tiptoed out, thinking to lend comfort to Alexander, even if I was dismayed by his actions. But he was gone. Sasha and his four brothers brooded in the antechamber, the grim resolve on their faces warning that, for once, the Romanov sons were united against their father.

The people lined the funeral route to toss flowers and blessed medals as the tsarina was conveyed to the cathedral to be laid to rest beside Nixa. Forty days of mourning were ordained, all social activities suspended for the duration.

In the wake of his mother's death, Sasha ordered our move for the summer to the Yelagin Palace, situated on its namesake island at the mouth of the Neva. Spacious and beautiful, with a cupola-domed entryway and enfilade of staterooms, it offered peaceful vistas of the river. I missed my home, my raspberry-silk-papered study and sitting room, with all my bibelots, but under the circumstances it was preferable. At least my children could play in the gardens here without me fearing a Nihilist would toss an explosive device over the wall.

Here, I sequestered myself to write overdue letters to Alix and my parents, who'd expressed urgent concern over the situation in Russia. Alix urged me to go to Denmark for an extended stay. I planned to do just that, as soon as the period of mourning ended, yet scarcely had the tsarina been entombed, the heat of July simmering over St. Petersburg, than Sasha returned from a visit with Vladimir. He was shuddering with rage.

"We are summoned. All of us. To the Winter Palace for dinner."

"Dinner?" I recoiled. "So soon? But we're still in mourning."

"The tsar commands it. And do not pretend you don't know why."

Here it was at last: the secret, flung at my feet like a carcass.

"Yes," he said. "We are to receive Princess Catherine Yurievskaya. It's her title now, accorded by imperial decree. He has married her and legitimized their three children."

"*Three!*" I leapt to my feet, my portable desk sliding off my lap to clatter to the floor, scattering papers and startling my aged Beauty.

"Oh?" Sasha eyed me. "I thought you were fully informed. Vladimir's German cow certainly knew. She wasted no time in telling us when my father's summons came. It seems everyone knew how he bedded his ward and sowed his seed in her."

I gazed at him in dumbstruck horror, thinking of Marie, who'd departed for England as soon as she saw her mother to her grave, without speaking to her father again.

Before I could untangle my voice, Sasha went on, "I'll say this much for the German, she made quite a show of refusing to acknowledge the woman's presence. And for a Lutheran, she's not entirely ignorant. She declared the tsar has violated our Orthodox rule, as our Holy Church requires a forty-day minimum after the death of a spouse before remarriage. But Vladimir cannot ignore the summons and risk being cast back into disfavor. Nor can they afford it." He gave a sour laugh. "Without his income, how will she continue to refurbish their abode?"

I lifted my chin. "Miechen might have to attend the dinner. We do not."

"We do." My husband's jaw was set. "I'll not be deprived of the opportunity to show them exactly how we intend to receive her. You will go with me and you will dress for it. In your sapphires and cloth of silver. We apparently are no longer in mourning."

He tromped out. Beauty eyed me sadly from her cushions.

The tsar had married his mistress. God help us all.

⁓

SHE WAS FAIR and slim, painfully so. Though she and I were in fact the same age, I felt an unwitting rush of sympathy for her, her white court gown and pearl-laden *kokoshnik* making her seem like a waif in someone else's clothes. With her wide blue eyes regarding us in wary fear, she also resembled a doe among predators. No one save me cared to soften the impression.

Even the children were here, at Alexander's command. We stood grouped in order of precedence—first Sasha and me, with our sons Nicky and George, the only two I'd agreed to bring. Next were the tsar's brothers: Constantine in his red and gold uniform, beak-nosed and haughty; disgraced Nikolai, grown fat and given to sneers; and their youngest brother, gallant Mikhail, along with their respective families. The tsar's other sons—Vladimir, Alexis, Sergei, and Paul—stood together, glowering. Dressed to her teeth in blue silk and diamonds, Miechen directed her stare to the ceiling, as if only the frescoes held any interest.

Now twelve and nine respectively, Nicky and George were eager to meet their cousins, whom they didn't know. The jabbing of elbows and whispering between them and Grand Duke Mikhail's four sons, in particular handsome twelve-year-old Sandro, only added to the tension as we shushed them, for they had no idea why we were here.

Behind the tsar and his new wife stood a golden-haired boy, no older than eight, with her delicate features and his unmistakable gray-blue eyes. He was alone; their two daughters were still too young to be presented, but my sons looked amazed at this unexpected arrival. Nicky tugged at my trailing sleeve. "*Who* is that?"

Sasha glared at him. "No one."

"His Imperial Majesty the Emperor and Autocrat of All the Russias, Alexander II, and Princess Yurievskaya," proclaimed the Grand Master of the Court in a strident voice, underscoring the awkwardness. He rapped his ivory wand on the floor. We dropped into collective obeisance. But not for as long as we should have. Sasha gripped my shoulder, pulling me upright with unseemly haste as the tsar came before us. He had color in his cheeks, a startling rejuvenation for a sixty-two-year-old man who'd recently buried his wife. After returning Sasha's malignant stare as my husband ignored the woman at the tsar's side, Alexander turned to me.

"Minnie," he said, in a leaden tone, "I present Princess Catherine Yurievskaya. My wife."

I felt the barbed stares all around me. As the second lady of court now, after Catherine, my reaction was paramount. Sasha had told me not to show acceptance of her in any way, but I couldn't refuse to address her as he had. Her quivering lips betrayed that she was fighting back tears; my heart went out to her, for she wasn't to blame. A ward dependent on the tsar's mercy when she hadn't been much more than a child herself—how could she have mounted resistance?

I inclined my head, murmuring, "Your Imperial Highness."

The other grand duchesses also inclined their heads to emulate my example. Only Miechen turned her face away in disgust. With these mortifying introductions concluded, we filed into the dining room, not the one where the bomb had exploded, as it was still under repair, but the larger Pavilion Hall—a less intimate setting, where at least we'd be spaced out enough at the table to dissuade caustic asides.

Seated in the very chair once occupied by our late tsarina, the princess displayed anxious poise as she attempted to engage those around her in conversation. No one said much in return, averting their eyes at every opportunity. At the foot of the table, Sasha sat as if frozen, his massive shoulders squared under his epaulettes and his stare fixed on his father from across the vases of flowers, candelabras, and tiered food-laden platters.

I had never been so uncomfortable at court in all my time in Russia. As the desserts and coffee were served, Sasha growled, "We leave now."

I flinched. "But we've not finished. And the boys, they're so happy to be with your uncle's sons. It's not proper to depart—"

"Now." He rose like a mountain, plunging the hall into silence. The tsar, who hadn't looked at us once throughout the meal, shifted his gaze to him. "You will stay."

Sasha flung his pristine napkin onto the table. He'd not eaten a bite. "Nicholas," he called out. "George. Say goodbye to your cousins. It is past your bedtime."

As my boys hastily excused themselves, Sasha turned to me. "Are you coming, wife?"

Seated across from me, Miechen gave me a sharp-toothed smile.

"You *will* stay," thundered the tsar, but I'd already stood, fumbling for my wrap, as Sasha, with a hand on each of our sons' narrow shoulders, steered us out.

No declaration could have been more overt. Henceforth, my husband was at war with his father.

"FESTIVITIES GALORE," SAID Miechen. She'd had herself rowed out in her barge to my palace, expressing awe at my surroundings, albeit with a critical "Doesn't it get terribly damp here, so close to the Neva?" Then she looked over my latest collection of paintings—in my spare time, I'd begun acquiring Russian art—and exclaimed, "Are you never idle! And these are so different. Peasants and bazaars. Not at all what one is accustomed to, is it?"

"Sasha prefers it. He wants us to surround ourselves with works by Russian painters. He says our children should learn that not only Western art is worthy of display."

"Well. We won't see these exhibited in the Hermitage anytime soon," she replied.

Now we sat in my parlor, drinking tea as she repeated the gossip from court, for although she'd turned up her nose at the princess, evidently the tsar had chosen to ignore it. Not in our case, however. We weren't welcome, and so I'd missed the galas in Catherine's honor.

"I thought you weren't present because you had left for Denmark," said Miechen, in an offended tone. "Had I realized otherwise, I might have abstained myself."

I forced out a smile, knowing she would not have. "The imperial secretary returned word that I can visit Denmark anytime I like, but my children and Sasha are forbidden. As I won't go without them, I must endure."

"Alexander denied your family leave?" She snorted. "It's degrading, the way he carries on. One might almost admire his nerve, to put us through the shame of it." She eyed me. "I assume your absence from her receptions means you're still not speaking to him?"

"I would be, if Sasha were." I sighed, too weary from the upheaval to feign with her. "He says he'd rather be exiled to Siberia. He can't abide the insult to his mother's memory."

"Nor should he," she declared, but she didn't sound admiring. Rather, she seemed pleased that Sasha now bore the brunt of the tsar's displeasure. "It's unforgivable. A disgrace. Vladimir thinks the same, but—"

"He cannot afford it." I didn't care to ease the serrated edge in my voice. "I understand. The tsar has married her. There's nothing we can do to change it."

"And he'll crown her, too. Mark my words. This is only the beginning. By next year, we'll be summoned to her anointing in Moscow."

"Do you truly think he'll go so far?" I couldn't imagine it. Not only because Catherine was so ill-prepared but because, to me, she hadn't seemed all that willing.

Miechen said, "At the last event I attended, he had their son brought in. There was some mummery going on, an Italian juggling act"—she made a sound of repugnance—"the most vulgar form of entertainment, but what can we expect these days? In any event, he sat the boy on his lap and asked, 'How would you like to be a grand duke?' In front of everyone. Now, if that isn't a sign of things to come, I don't know what is."

I had no reply. Much as I loved Alexander, he'd gone past any justification.

"The marriage has been condemned throughout Europe," Miechen continued, munching on her fifth macaroon from my plate. "You must have heard what Victoria said? No? Oh, she was most perturbed. She declared that when emperors begin taking morganatic brides, what hope can there be for preserving the sanctity of royal bloodlines?"

"That sounds like her," I muttered. I'd received a letter from Alix, in which she'd detailed similar utterances of dismay from the queen, even if I wasn't about to admit it.

"Constantine is beside himself," added Miechen.

As she spoke, I glanced to the parlor doors, though I had told my servants to stay out, as I invariably did with her. I was never sure what she might say.

She lowered her voice. "He's been holding gatherings at his Marble Palace. To discuss the situation with his brothers and others. Vladimir has attended."

I recalled Alexander telling me that Constantine was rumored to be an occultist, in league with unsavory characters. Such persons abounded in Russia: *Strannik,* or holy wanderers, were revered by the peasantry, and *yurodiviy,* or holy fools, were common in aristocratic salons, babbling about unseen forces and fleecing or seducing—and sometimes both—the gullible. I couldn't conceive of worldly Vladimir, with his continental taste, attending such gatherings.

"Only to hear what is said," Miechen explained, taking in my silence. "He doesn't condone it; you know how he despises all that absurd mysticism. But it seems that this time, Constantine is doing more than having his cards read. Need I say more?"

"No." I sipped my tea. It had gone tepid and tasted bitter. "It is treason to speak of such things. Vladimir would be wise to avoid Constantine's gatherings henceforth."

"I advised him as much. But there we have it. The tsar's own brother plots against him. Should he go through with her coronation, well, he cannot say he wasn't warned."

I set my cup down with a hard clink on the saucer. "*Has* he been warned?" It had gone too far. Gossip was one thing, and to be honest, I'd missed it, but this was another thing altogether. This was dangerous.

"I would assume so," she said. "But if he hasn't, he certainly will be now. Won't he?"

Miechen meant it as an offering. My banishment, as she knew, was neither my doing nor my wish. I didn't approve of my father-in-law's actions, but I had my own position to consider, and wilting away on this island did not serve it. Or her. She needed her friendly rival back at court. Otherwise, with whom could she hope to compete?

She left, satiated on gossip and prodding me to action, and I returned to my sitting room to stare toward the river. I heard my children with their nanny in the garden. A horde of mosquitoes flittered over the embankment. We could not stay here through September. As lovely and safe as this palace was, Miechen was right: The seclusion was unhealthy.

By the time Sasha and I sat down to dinner that evening, I had decided. We would return to our home in the Anichkov.

And I would petition to see the tsar.

CHAPTER SEVENTEEN

Alexander kept me waiting throughout the autumn. Obeying the implicit ban from court during the Season, I attended society nevertheless, including a costume party held at Vladimir's palace, where Miechen generously had everyone line up to greet me. Wherever I went, I was warmly received, more so than I may have been had my circumstances been less sympathetic. In turn, Princess Yurievskaya was widely disparaged as a brazen adventuress and the tsar mocked for his infatuation. I did not participate in the criticism—she was his wife, after all, and he was the grandfather of my children—but I welcomed the commiseration. Word of my return to society would reach the palace, leaving Alexander with no alternative other than to receive me or make clear that he intended to disinherit Sasha.

This possibility plagued me. The succession had been altered before, albeit violently. Peter the Great had put his own son to death. Catherine the Great had deposed her husband, Peter III, who was later murdered. I didn't fear that the tsar would ever physically harm my husband, but disinheritance was almost as ruinous, and Alexander's wrath had not cooled. Times past, he'd have answered my request at once. In fact, before now there wouldn't have been any need for such a request, for his door had always stood open to family. Now he only saw those who showed his wife respect.

Swallowing my pride, for Epiphany I sent Catherine a beautiful set of blue river pearls that the late tsarina had bequeathed to me. Knowing Sasha would be enraged if he found out, I made certain he did not, replacing the pearls with an identical copy crafted by the esteemed jeweler Gustav Fabergé, whose discretion equaled his artistry.

My gift thawed the tsar. He summoned me after the New Year gala, where he inaugurated 1881 by performing the polonaise with Catherine before the court.

As I entered his study, I glanced at the empty upholstered cushion by his desk, where Milord always slept. Before I could ask, he said, "He died."

"I'm so sorry, Majesty," I said. "He was a magnificent dog."

"And a loyal friend, which is rare." Alexander stepped from his desk and the cushion, which still had red fur on it. "I had him buried in the pet cemetery at the Catherine Palace. He deserved as much."

I nodded, my gloves clutched in my hands. I didn't assume familiarity, not taking a seat until he waved me to a chair. He paced to the window overlooking the quadrangle; his study faced inward, which he must have disliked. Inward had become his entire life, without his daily strolls, with the Nihilists fomenting trouble, and his second marriage the source of widespread discontent.

"You wished to see me," he said at length. He wasn't about to make this any easier.

"I did. I wished to speak to you about . . ." My voice faltered. Now that I was here, I didn't know how to formulate the words required to spare my husband further disgrace.

"Minnie," he said, and while his voice held no tenderness, there was no recrimination, either. "We both know why you are here. This isn't something you can manage with a firm hand. Sasha will never forgive me; it is not in his nature. I would have to annul the marriage, send her and the children away. And that, I cannot do."

"I know." For I did. I realized now what so few cared to see. He was in love. His passion for the tsarina had evaporated, no doubt due to their losses, her illness and distancing from Russia, the monotony of the years together. Catherine had stoked that passion anew. To fight him would not only be futile but also self-defeating.

"You might know," he said, "but Sasha does not. Or if he does, he doesn't care. My happiness means nothing to him." He walked toward me, with a slight limp. When I expressed concern, he shook his head. "I was playing with the children and tripped. A father's mishap."

Had he ever played with Sasha or his other sons? I doubted it. Judging by what Sasha had described to me, his childhood had been austere, which was why he sought to impose the same on our sons. It was what he and his brothers had been taught.

"Constantine plots against you," I blurted out. I hadn't planned on it, not so soon. I'd meant to plead Sasha's case first, establish his restoration before setting him and the tsar together to curtail Constantine's machinations.

"Naturally." Alexander gave me a weary look. "They all plot, to one extent or another. They think I'm weak and seek to exploit it. But if they succeed, the throne they'll inherit will not be the one I occupied."

I heard the threat in his words and must have shown it on my face, for he rubbed at his mustachios in silence before he said, "The time has come. I've prepared a manifesto for constitutional assembly."

I sat still, the reality of what Sasha had long feared and railed against now upon me. Alexander returned to his desk to lift a sheet of paper. "My Catherine brought me to it. This empire cannot continue as it is, a playground for the privileged few. The people must have their say. And I will give it to them. We will still rule, only not as before. There must be a Duma of elected representatives and gradual curtailing of our autocracy. It will take time, and no doubt there'll be much dissent, your husband chief among it. But as I am tsar, Russia *will* have a constitution, because it is what we must do to survive."

I couldn't move. I couldn't even speak. It was a declaration of war against his own family; I trembled to imagine the repercussions of this act.

"Do you disapprove?" he asked.

To my surprise, I heard myself whisper, "No."

"I should think not. Your native country has a constitution, as do most monarchies in Europe. Even Queen Victoria and the kaiser answer to parliaments. Only here do we act as though Mongol hordes might break through our defenses and ravage our God-given right to do as we please. We've learned very little from history. We should have taken note of the harsh lessons imparted by the French and the Americans. When the people are denied a say in how they should be governed, they will fight, with violence if need be. Rulers can be removed. Louis XVI was guillotined. President Lincoln was assassinated. In the end, we are mortal."

"It is . . ." I met his steadfast eyes. "An honorable aspiration, Majesty." I didn't mention that President Lincoln's murder had come about from a civil war that tore America asunder, for I understood his meaning. Even a wise ruler could be brought down.

"Ah." He smiled. "There she is, at last. My Minnie. You know I speak the truth. You've seen the suffering through your work at the Red Cross. You were in this very palace when they tried to blow us apart in the hall. Their logic is crude and methods savage, but their reasons . . . If one has eyes and ears, one cannot fail to understand. It has taken me much soul-searching to comprehend it, but my Catherine isn't one of us. She understands completely. If I could," he added, "I would abdicate. But Russia isn't ready for such drastic change. It must be done slowly, in stages. We must lead her unsuspecting—"

"Like a bull to the pen," I said softly.

He chuckled. "Like a chained bear out of the pit, to be more precise."

We remained quiet for a moment. Then I said, "You must tell Sasha." I came to my feet. Now that he'd made his intention clear, I couldn't vacillate. "He must know before you issue any public announcement. He is the tsarevich. If you do not tell him first, he'll take it as the gravest of insults. He deserves as much," I echoed deliberately.

Alexander frowned. "I'm in no mood for another dinner where he throws dirt at me."

"A luncheon," I said. "Let me arrange it. You can come on a Sunday after mass to our Anichkov and tell him then. If there's to be any disagreement, let it happen in private."

"Oh, there'll most certainly be disagreement." His frown deepened. "I'll not be dissuaded, no matter what he says. I warn you now, Minnie. I'll see him, Constantine, and any other who dares oppose me thrown into the fortress or exiled."

I nodded. "I understand." Sasha would not, but he must be told, regardless.

"I'm due to leave for the Crimea," said Alexander. "I return in March. Schedule your luncheon then. And, Minnie," he added, as I turned to the door, "not a word of this to Sasha. Let me be the one to inform him. If he has something to say, he can say it first—to me."

I'D HIDDEN MY knowledge of the tsar's mistress from Sasha. I had not liked it, but I had done it for the sake of harmony within the family. But hiding this secret felt like my own infidelity; it seemed to always be lurking on the tip of my tongue, burning a hole in my mouth. To ease my conscience, I admitted over breakfast that I'd gone to see his father.

"Did you think I was unaware?" he said. "Nothing gets past the gossipmongers at court. You hadn't yet departed his study and word already reached me." He turned over his newspaper, waving to his longtime valet, Ivan, to pour more tea. "Well? What did he say? Must I abase myself, crawl on my knees, and kiss his harlot's hand in the Nicholas Hall?"

"He realizes he made a mistake." I busied myself with spreading jam on my scone to evade his stare. "He knows it was too sudden. Ill-timed. He hopes for reconciliation. He doesn't want to be at odds with you. He—" I raised my voice slightly. "He understands how difficult this has been and agrees to discuss his plans with you when he returns from the Crimea."

I felt breathless, poised on the edge of a chasm. Behind us, Ivan stood immobile. When I glanced at him, he slipped away.

"So." Sasha took up his cup. "He hopes for reconciliation. He doesn't want to be at odds. He has plans he wishes to discuss. Such as . . . ?"

"I do not know. He didn't tell me." Never again, I vowed. Never again would I lie to him. It was a terrible deception, as if I baited a trap.

"He didn't tell you because he has no plans other than to crown her as empress and live with her in sin." Sasha returned to his newspaper, his expression impassive.

"But you will see him?" I said. "You'll not be discourteous?"

He didn't look up. "The discourtesy is his. And, yes, I will see him. Providing he comes here to me."

⟶

FEBRUARY THAWED INTO March. A late snowfall powdered the city. I prepared for the luncheon, which was scheduled for Sunday the thirteenth and arranged via the tsar's private secretary. Following mass, Alexander would make his habitual inspection of the Imperial Riding Academy. Afterward, he'd let it be known that he would visit his brother

Mikhail. In truth, they'd both come to the Anichkov. To bolster the ruse, I invited my Mikhailovich nephews to go skating with my sons and purchased new skates for the occasion, giving the tsar the perfect excuse to arrive with his brother, ostensibly to fetch the boys. Instead, I'd invite them to stay for lunch.

On the scheduled day, I dressed in my fitted sable jacket and tilted cap, a calf-length skirt of blue velvet and red leather skating boots. I then went to check that Nicky and George were changing, tucking a scarf around two-year-old Misha's throat, for he had a cold, and soothing five-year-old Xenia, who cried that she wanted to go skating with us.

"But you don't know how to skate yet, darling," I said, wiping her tears as Mrs. Franklin looked on with tight-lipped reserve. She was an excellent nanny, but she disapproved of coddling. She'd decreed that children should be left to cry so they would learn that tears resolve nothing, until I retorted, "In this house, tears do," silencing her.

"Come downstairs as soon as you lace up those boots," I told Nicky and George, who were, as usual, prolonging the process by competing to see who could do it faster.

In the sitting room, Sasha sat writing at my marcasite-inlaid desk. I always found it amusing to see him hunched over it like a giant, too big for the chair; he had his own desk in his own study, but it was warmer in my sitting room, as I kept the stove lit, while his study was an ice chest because he refused to waste heat.

"We're going skating," I reminded him.

"For how long?" he asked, chewing at his pen.

"Until your father arrives, I suppose." I kissed his grizzled cheek. He'd grown out his beard again; as he began his thirty-seventh year, he'd lost most of the hair on his head and decided the beard made him resemble an "authentic Russian," as he termed it, but the bristly growth scratched my lips. I nipped at his ear instead and said, "You should shave."

"No," he replied, and I went down into the foyer to wait for my boys. As I stood there while Sophie unwrapped the boxes of new skates, I looked out the side window. Snow was drifting down, light but constant. Would it cause a cancellation? If so, where would it leave us? The only thing I dreaded more was the delivery of the court circular later in the week, with the announcement of the manifesto authorizing a

Duma. Sasha would fly into a rage, and nothing I did would stave off a pitched battle between my husband and his father.

Nicky and George came whooping down the stairs. As I turned to them with a stern look—for Sasha had told them time and time again not to race down the staircase like drunken Cossacks—a distant thud was heard. The boys didn't notice it, grabbing at their new skates, but Sophie did. She lifted her eyes to me. Moments later, Sasha emerged from my sitting room. "A gun salute at this hour?"

Before I could reply, another boom sounded, much louder this time—and so strong it rattled the windows. I heard glass crack in the drawing room, which faced the Prospekt.

Sasha met my eyes. He reached for my hand.

"No," I whispered as he pulled me to the door. He wrenched the door open. We looked out; in the snow-speckled distance, a cloud of black smoke lingered.

"Bring our troika at once," Sasha said. Sophie started to her feet. The boys, bewildered, dropped their skates in a clatter to the foyer's marble floor. I tried to smile at them, but my heart was pounding so fast, I felt ill.

Our sleigh, harnessed to two horses, was brought up outside our gates. "Fool," yelled Sasha at the stable boy. "The carriage, I said. Bring the carriage."

"You said the troika," I whispered.

He turned to me. "Did I?"

I nodded.

"Aren't we going skating, Mama?" asked George. I shook my head at him. Nicky had gone pale, as if he already knew what no one could say.

"God in heaven." Sasha stalked outside. "How long does it take to do my bidding?" He hadn't yet turned the corner to the stables in the back when a jangling of harnesses preceded the carriage drawing up to the gates. I told Sophie, "Fetch his coat," for my husband stood bareheaded in his shirt under the falling snow, staring at the carriage as if he'd forgotten why he'd called for it. After Sophie handed me his greatcoat and astrakhan hat, I gestured at the boys. "Come."

Nicky took my hand, but George inched back. Sophie said, "I'll look after him, Your Highness. Go. His Highness is waiting."

With Nicky clasping my hand, I joined Sasha, who thrust on his coat and hat as we clambered into the carriage.

"The palace," he said to the coachman.

WE SWEPT ALONG the road beside the Catherine Canal. Nicky leaned against me; I felt him shivering. I wrapped my arms around him, pulling the fur blanket over our legs when Sasha gave an alarmed intake of breath. Looking out, I caught sight of people crossing themselves, as policemen tried to detain them from dipping cloths into a crimson pool soaking the trampled snow. An overturned sleigh and dismembered horse still in its harness, its intestines spilling out, sprawled a short distance away. Dark-red smears, black in the dim light, streamed ahead of us, like bleeding grooves cut by blades.

"Don't look." I covered Nicky's eyes as he tried to lift his head.

As the carriage turned into the palace's back entrance, where the smears led, it came to a jarring halt. Sasha yanked open the door to glare at the Preobrazhensky regiment, of which he was the colonel, blocking our passage with their bayonets.

"The tsarevich!" he bellowed, and the guards hastily parted to let us pass. I caught sight of their white faces under their conical hats with the double-headed eagle emblem. With terrible certainty, I knew something catastrophic had befallen us.

The imperial troika was parked near the back door. Thick blood congealed in the snow—so much blood that my boots squished over it as I clung to Nicky and followed Sasha to the stairway. We found Grand Duke Mikhail's wife, Olga, there, with her sons, who were dressed for our skating party. When she saw me, she pitched into my arms, nearly pushing Nicky aside to the ground. My son grabbed at my jacket as she cried, "They told me my Misha was dead. A bomb, they said. God have mercy on us!"

Her son Sandro, grown tall in his fifteenth year and already showing the sculpted Romanov features, went to Nicky. I heard him whisper, "My papa is not dead. He wasn't in the same troika. But our poor grandpère . . ."

Sasha lunged past Mikhail's boys to barrel up the stairway. Blood drenched the steps. I inched up with Nicky and Olga, who wept in the crook of my arm, her boys behind us. We traversed the passage full of liveried servants on their knees toward the tsar's study.

Mikhail came out from the open doorway, still in his greatcoat, bloodstains spattered across the green wool. He murmured to Sasha. My husband thrust his head forward, flicked his hand at me, and proceeded into the study.

Olga moaned, "I cannot." Mikhail retrieved his wife, who swayed into his arms as if she were about to faint. I felt the same as I went with Nicky into the study, where only two months past I'd met with Alexander. The elegant white-paneled room, with its tables displaying the multitude of family photographs, was crammed with ministers, household officials, and members of the family. I saw Miechen in a corner among the grand duchesses. Our gazes met, collided, then I tore mine away as the crowd parted before me to reveal the couch upon which something unspeakable lay, tended by the royal physician, Dr. Botkin. The metropolitan in his cassock prayed beside it. Sasha looked down, as if stupefied.

Nicky began to cry. I pushed him back, whispering, "Go to Tante Miechen." I couldn't look away, taking one step, then another, riveted by the horror before me.

Alexander was unrecognizable. In his mutilated visage, one eye protruded; a gash with broken teeth that had once been his mouth yawned above his crushed jaw. As he agonized, blood seeped from his wounds, pooling onto the carpet. He wore the tattered remnants of his uniform, the trousers shredded above mangled stumps. He had no legs.

Rulers can be removed. . . . In the end, we are mortal.

Grief engulfed me. I reeled back toward Miechen, who had Nicky huddled at her side. She drew me away as I tried to contain my anguish.

"Two bombs," she murmured. "Two men, at the canal bridge. They hurled the first one but missed. It hit his Cossack escort. Alexander went out to attend the wounded guard and Mikhail rushed to stop him. Another man, whom no one had seen, threw the second one. It struck him directly, as you can see—"

"No." I wanted to cover Nicky's ears. His tearstained face was pinched tight, as though he was about to scream. "No more. Please."

"He cannot survive," she said. "You must prepare."

As she spoke, I looked at Sasha. He'd retreated from his father to the quadrangle window. I could discern the cries of the crowds beyond the pane, alerted to the tragedy and already congregating in the palace square.

Vladimir, dressed in his Sunday cravat and waistcoat with its fob chain, went to Sasha and put his arm about his shoulders. I saw him speak with urgency. Sasha craned his head, in that way he had when told something unexpected—or unwelcome.

"You *must*," I heard Vladimir urge, his voice, never subtle, carrying in the hush. Sasha gave curt assent. Vladimir departed the study, motioning to the ministers who hastened to follow. In the corridor, Grand Duke Constantine paced, his lean stature shrunken into itself. He flinched when Vladimir marched past him without a glance. Returning my gaze to Sasha, I saw him glaring from his post at the window at his stricken uncle.

All of a sudden a figure in a white lace gown flew, shrieking, from a side door into the study. Everyone froze as Princess Yurievskaya flung herself upon the tsar. The grand duchesses, all of whom had despised and rejected her, beheld her desperation in mute horror as she cradled Alexander's shattered head, drenching her gown with his blood.

"No, no, no," she wailed. I jerked forward without thinking, pulling her away. She crumpled in my arms, both of us on our knees on the study's bloodied floor. I felt her thin body, her very bones under her skin, quaking in despair.

"Silence, please," said Dr. Botkin. He directed his gaze at the imperial family. They drew nearer but not too much, avoiding the princess and me, their eyes fixated on the dying tsar. With a choked gurgle, Alexander went still.

Botkin checked his pulse. "The emperor is dead," he pronounced, tears in his eyes.

Catherine went silent. She seemed to dissolve against me.

Outside in the square, the palace entry barricaded by the Preobrazhensky regiment, a runner was alerted to the news. A roaring yell resounded: "God save Tsar Alexander III!"

In the study, everyone dropped to their knees to pray for the departed soul. The metropolitan, who only that morning had recited our mass, wavered in his chant for the dead. Someone took limp Catherine from my arms; she had fainted.

Rising to my feet, I went to my husband. Sasha regarded me pensively. For a heart-stopping instant, I thought I saw a smile flicker across his lips.

Then Vladimir returned, with the prefect of the police in tow.

"Has Your Imperial Majesty any orders?" asked the prefect. I almost didn't understand why he was asking a dead tsar, until I realized he directed his question at Sasha. And the poor prefect appeared shaken to his core, for his late tsar had just been murdered under his watch. Glancing past him into the corridor, I saw that Constantine had vanished.

I anticipated Sasha's immediate order to arrest his uncle. Instead, he said, "Your police are useless. You've let malefactors run loose like wolves. You are dismissed. The military will assume command for the present. I want those villains who murdered my father executed. At once." He turned to Vladimir, disregarding the prefect as the man bowed almost to the floor. "Assemble the cabinet. I will see them within the hour. And tell that metropolitan to prepare to render the Oath of Allegiance in St. George's Hall. I want everyone present. Summon priests to render the oath to the troops, as well."

"As you command, Imperial Majesty." Vladimir gave Sasha a conspiratorial look. "I will find it," he said, lowering his voice. "I will find it and bring it directly to you."

"Do so," growled Sasha. "Tear this entire palace apart if you must."

He took my hand in his before I could ask him what he'd charged Vladimir with finding. In a single moment, he transcended all expectations. As we walked toward the Jordan staircase and the servants dropped into obeisance, he did not spare them a look, his chin lifted, his bearing perfectly erect. There was no shambling now, no clumsy gestures or head thrust forward on his squat neck in awkwardness.

Sasha the Bullock was now Tsar Alexander III, Autocrat of All the Russias.

And to my stunned disbelief, I was his tsarina.

PART III

1881–1894

The Moujik Tsar

Those scarlet flowers that captivated us so much . . .
—Grand Duke Konstantin Konstantinovich

CHAPTER EIGHTEEN

"We had to kiss his forehead after mass, twice a day for seven days," I told Alix. "It was dreadful. The embalmers had done whatever they could, but he was . . . they couldn't hide the damage. And the smell—" I shuddered. "By the third day, I could smell it before I even entered the chapel."

This was the first opportunity I'd had to be alone with my sister and describe the horror of it all, as she was the only one with whom I could be completely honest. She and Bertie had arrived just in time to attend Alexander's entombment in the St. Peter and Paul Cathedral in the fortress, defying Queen Victoria's panicked warning that Russia had become a den of assassins, preying on its sovereign ruler. But Alix had not seen my father-in-law's ravaged visage as I had.

"I can't imagine it," she said. "Such savagery . . . I have no words."

"And now this." I motioned about the cramped ground-floor apartments in Gatchina Palace, located thirty miles by train outside the city. "Practically a barracks. Surrounded by a high wall and cast-iron gates." My heart sank anew as I regarded the crates of my personal belongings, which I hadn't yet unpacked. "Not even the staterooms, but here, in the Arsenal Hall, because it can be better defended if we're attacked. I wanted to stay in our Anichkov or move into the Winter Palace, but security dictated our removal from the capital. Sasha has delayed our coronation in Moscow. He will not say how long it will be before we can return to the city."

Without thinking, I took a cigarette from the silver case in my pocket and lit it with trembling fingers. Alix stared. "I can't stop trembling," I said. "The doctors tell me I have a nervous disorder. I barely sleep or eat, and—"

"Yes, you don't look well at all." She frowned. "When did you start doing that?"

"This?" I realized she stared because I was smoking. "Miechen introduced me to it. Apparently, all the princesses in Europe now smoke."

"Not in England. Minnie, it can't be good for you."

I gave her an impatient look. "It calms my nerves. I thought you said you had no words."

She pursed her mouth, watching me inhale before she said, "If Sasha thinks it's best to reside here for now, you must make do. It's not so bad," she added unconvincingly. "It needs a fresh coat of paint, but with your furnishings and some pictures on the walls—"

"Please, don't." I tipped ash into my teacup. "It's as much of a tomb as the fortress. They might as well have buried us alive." I heard my voice darken with the impotent rage that had overtaken me from the moment I realized that Alexander's murder had catapulted us into terror. "Since Peter the Great left Moscow to build St. Petersburg, never has a tsar removed himself from his capital. I understand the concern, after that awful explosion, and now this. But we're the imperial family. We can't get past the gates without an escort of Cossacks. And the secret police watch our every move. Sasha once told me that if we gave in, we'd never stop running. How is *this* not giving in to those monsters?"

"But they have been arrested?" Alix said.

"Yes." I angrily blew out smoke. "There was a woman, too. She organized it, in a cheese shop of all places. She was at the canal; she waved a handkerchief to alert the others that Alexander's sleigh approached. All four have already been executed—by hanging."

"Dear God." Alix folded her hands in her lap.

I crushed out my cigarette. I wanted to smoke another one, but she'd only scold me. "As you say, we'll have to make do until we can return to the city. Sasha has his cabinet, his officials and regiments to oversee, the entire empire to rule. He can't do it from Gatchina—"

A sudden sob caught in my voice. As Alix rose in alarm, I pressed my hand to my mouth. I had told myself not to cry anymore, that tears, as Mrs. Franklin said, resolved nothing. And still, I longed to wail in that moment, at the injustice of it, the brutal end of the tsar who had liberated the serfs and wanted so much for Russia, and the dread unleashed in its wake, from which I feared we might never escape.

"Oh, Minnie." Alix embraced me. "We cannot know why God tests us so in moments like these. But you have Sasha to protect you."

Pressed against her, I heard myself whisper, "Sasha has changed."

"He has lost his father in a horrible way. Naturally, he's changed—"

"No." I drew back from her. "It's more than that. He . . . he burned the manifesto."

"Manifesto?" she echoed, in bewilderment.

"The announcement for a constitution." I forced my confession out, the secret that haunted me almost more than my father-in-law's death. "Alexander planned to grant the right to assembly. Vladimir knew about it somehow. He found the manifesto in Alexander's desk. He ransacked the study; when he realized one of the drawers was locked, Alexander's valet told him Catherine Yurievskaya had the key. Vladimir threatened that if she didn't hand over the key, he'd throw her and her children out to beg in the streets."

Alix went pale.

"She gave him the key," I went on. "In reward, Sasha granted her and the children an annual income, providing they live abroad. Vladimir brought the manifesto here; they burned it in the hearth. It was to be published in the court circular, the day after Alexander was—" I tried in vain to control the despair in my voice. "His father's last act and he destroyed it. Alexander was going to tell him but never had the chance. All the circulars with the announcement were confiscated. Sasha has ordered any publication deemed subversive by the Okhrana to be shut down. He says Russia is unworthy of our trust."

"He does it for the country," whispered Alix. "For the future of your children."

I met her eyes. "He may believe that. But what kind of future will it be?"

~⌒~

SASHA HAD TO spend time in St. Petersburg, for while the apparatus of court might reside in Gatchina, the empire did not. So we could communicate, he had a telegraph service installed in our new residence.

I expected to miss him terribly; it disconcerted me that I did not at first. I had grown to love him, despite his gruff manner and aversion to the social activities I enjoyed. I'd attempted to attribute his reluctance and lack of graces to his upbringing, to the fact that he'd been raised to serve in the Imperial Guard, not to be the tsarevich, although neither had his brother Grand Duke Vladimir, who complemented Miechen to perfection. But the abrupt change in him, his burning of Alexander's final act, had cast me into dreadful doubt. I wondered if the man I had married was in fact still a stranger to me, despite Alix's repeated counsel that he loved me and his family, that he only acted as he must to preserve our safety, as well as the unity of the country he now ruled, following the brutal murder of his father.

Yet once Alix returned to England with Bertie and I found myself alone with my children, surrounded by legions of servants whose names I had yet to learn, I began to yearn for my husband. His familiarity, his coarse laughter at my tart remarks, our intimacy—it made me miss him more than I'd thought possible, for he was my anchor in our abrupt new existence as Emperor and Empress of Russia.

To assuage my woes, I dedicated myself to the monumental task of learning about the four hundred public institutions, including hospitals, asylums, wards, and orphanages, that I was expected to patronize as tsarina. I also concentrated on my Red Cross duties and skill-training centers for women, for which I could now establish an imperial endowment. In addition, I was the official patroness of the Smolny Institute for Girls, that educational bastion founded by Catherine the Great, and from my personal income I funded the Russian chapter of the Society for Protection of Animals, a cause very dear to me. I told myself that I mustn't forget my experiences during my father-in-law's reign. His manifesto would never see the light of day, but I resolved to do as much as I could in his memory for the people we now held charge over, even though it might never be enough: There was always far more need than my single-handed efforts could alleviate.

My children grew to love their vaulted playroom with its toys, writing desks, a billiards table, and a swing that Sasha had rigged up. They rallied around me to play hide-and-seek, racing through the curved Chesma Gallery to hide behind the magnificent tapestries or the huge jade statues and porcelain urns in the Chinese Gallery, even though I knew if we broke anything, it was irreplaceable. My younger children adapted, never asking why we now lived so far from our home in the city. They had our private gardens here, and their studies and outdoor activities to fill their time, but Nicky was more sensitive.

One night, I woke to find him standing by my bed, shivering in his shirt. When I rose to embrace him, fearing he had a fever, he whispered, "The dog. I heard it barking."

"Dog? Which one, my darling?" We had several on the palace grounds, but none right now in the family save for Sasha's hunting dogs, which he kept in kennels. My beloved Beauty had passed away at the venerable age of sixteen, and Nicky mourned her deeply with me, for he loved all animals. We'd taken her in a little casket to the pet cemetery of the Catherine Palace in Tsarskoe Selo, burying her beside his grandfather's Milord. Nicky had made me promise to erect a headstone for her.

"The ghost of Paul's dog," he said, his eyes huge in his pinched face.

For a moment I was confused, until I suddenly understood. Gatchina had been the site of Tsar Paul I's strangulation; it was said the dead tsar's mournful dog had howled in such grief over the death of its master, it had to be put down.

"No, my child." I drew him into bed with me. "It's only your imagination. There are no ghosts here. You were frightened by the sound of the wind."

"The servants say there are ghosts." He clung to me, almost thirteen years old, lanky and thin, all knees and elbows, but still so young in his heart, so easily upset.

"Well, then," I said, running my hand over his thick hair. "What can we do to banish the ghosts? Would a new puppy do?"

He lifted his face. "A borzoi?" he breathed. It was his most fervent wish; the long-haired Russian wolfhound was esteemed for its keen sight, agility, and swift pursuit of prey, but Sasha had refused, saying Nicky wasn't old enough to properly train such a valuable dog.

I hugged him. "A borzoi it is."

I inquired of a breeder. A week later, the squirming white-haired pup was delivered. Nicky was beside himself. He named her Juno, taking her everywhere with him, training her patiently and chiding her whenever she urinated on the carpet. Soon enough, he, George, and Misha were trying to turn Juno into a soldier for their games, strapping a battered shield to her back and marching her about. To my amusement, they also tried in vain to curtail her pouncing after the hares who loped across our gardens, but she caught a few anyway. I had them skinned and served for supper, telling them it was in her nature to hunt.

Our first Easter as emperor and empress was a quiet affair, coming as it did so soon after Alexander's death. Sasha canceled any official celebration in deference to our mourning and did not come back to Gatchina to spend it with us. But once he did return weeks later, tired and eager to see us, I was surprised by the noticeable change in him. With his beard fully grown now, he'd taken to wearing his baggy trousers tucked into his scuffed boots, his loose shirt, and shapeless jacket in public, eschewing the formal attire of his rank. When I asked him whether it was fitting for the emperor to go about thus, he told me it was more comfortable for him, and as the emperor, he could wear whatever he liked.

"Besides, the people like it," he said. "They call me the *Moujik* Tsar, the Little Father who dresses like a serf. They see me as someone like them, and that's how I want it."

I rolled my eyes at the motto, as he swooped in on the children, bellowing laughter when Juno leapt up to paw him and Nicky went white, rushing forth to restrain her.

Sasha gave me a look. "You disobeyed me, Manja. A borzoi now resides in our house."

"We needed a pet," I replied. "Had you been here, you might have been consulted."

I was prepared to defend my decision, as Nicky looked about to burst into tears at the mere intimation that Sasha disapproved, but my husband only gave me a sly grin.

"I doubt that," he said. "But since we didn't have a proper Easter, I've ordered a special gift for you."

Hard-boiled painted eggs were the traditional Russian gift for the holy season; on the morning months later when the package arrived, Sasha stood beside me with a satisfied look as I unraveled the perfumed tissues to expose a plain white enamel egg.

"How charming," I said, although it had no adornment, nothing on its exterior to mark it as anything other than a simple reproduction of the traditional.

Sasha chuckled. "I had it made by Fabergé. Here." He leaned over to click open the upper half of the egg. It lifted like a lid; inside, to my astonished delight, gleamed a yolk made entirely of gold. Nestled upon it was a gold hen with rubies for eyes.

I laughed in surprise. "Like the *matryoshka* doll, everything nested inside one another!"

"There's more," he said. "Open the hen."

Carefully, as it was so small and delicate, I eased apart the barely visible seam on the hen's midsection; within rested a diamond-encrusted replica of our royal crown. Looking at Sasha, who nodded, I nudged the crown open with my fingertip. George, Nicky, Misha, and Xenia crowded around me in awe as, via an unseen mechanism, a miniature painted rendition of Gatchina emerged, surmounted by tiny pearl-framed cameos of them.

Tears flooded my eyes. Holding the contraption like a jeweled bird in my palms, its open shell unfurled about it, I whispered, "It's a piece of heaven."

"My Manja is my heaven," Sasha said thickly.

The egg took pride of place in our curio cabinet, so widely admired by other family members that Fabergé was soon inundated with requests. It would become an annual Easter tradition among us. The handmade eggs were extremely costly, requiring a year or more of meticulous labor, and none ever surpassed those commissioned for me by my husband, for no one dared to spend what he did. Not even Miechen was bold enough to outdo him.

His other gifts were equally lavish: rubies and sapphires, ropes of cherry-sized pearls, brooches, earrings, and bracelets of pink diamonds set in white gold.

"Do you like your new emeralds, my Manja?" he murmured, his great body pressing against mine and creaking our entire bedstead. "You should wear them at our next reception."

"Here?" I eyed him. "In this dungeon? With you dressed like a peasant? Don't you think it would be more in keeping if I donned a kerchief and apron instead?"

He pouted. "It won't be forever."

"When exactly does forever end?" I sat upright, plumping my pillows. "It's been six months. The Season is upon us. Whatever shall we do out here? Bring our guests by train?"

I meant it flippantly, but after a moment he said, "Why not? Refurbish the palace to your liking. Hold a gala and bring them here. They should come wherever we are."

I stared at him. "Are you serious?"

"Utterly." He snaked his heavy arm about my waist, wrenching me down against him. "It's been too long," he said, nuzzling my throat as I halfheartedly fended him off. "My Manja smells of French perfume and I want to lick her."

"You hate everything French." I pushed at his chest. "No French paintings in our apartments. Only Russian art. No French spoken at the table. Only Russian. You have our poor children at their books night and day, trying to master the language."

He growled, "They must know they are Russian. There's no dishonor in it."

"There is not." I put my hands on his bearded cheeks, looking into his blue-gray eyes, which, although the same hue, were nothing like Alexander's. He'd not expressed any sentiment over his father's death, but I now knew everything he'd done since taking the throne had been to avenge Alexander and defend us. "I want to return to our Anichkov, Sasha. I miss our home. I miss our life in St. Petersburg. We were so happy there."

"Are you not happy now?" A forlorn expression crept over his face.

"Always, with you. But I could be happier."

He went quiet. Then he said, "The Okhrana tells me those malcontents are now either fleeing in droves or rotting in one of my prisons."

"So we are safe? We can go back?"

"We are never safe. But how can I refuse you? We'll reopen the Anichkov and reside there for the next Season," and as I gasped, throwing myself at him, covering him in kisses, he chuckled low in his throat. "But first, my Manja must give something in return."

I stopped kissing him, feeling his hand on my thighs, nudging up my nightdress. "Only that?" I murmured. "So easily satisfied is our *Moujik* Tsar?"

"Never satisfied." He slid his hand up farther. "But for the moment it will suffice."

That night, in our gloomy room with the vaulted plaster ceiling so low he could reach up and touch it, we conceived our last child.

CHAPTER NINETEEN

Despite my pregnancy and all my other duties, I undertook Gatchina's refurbishment. The following September, I inaugurated the palace with a splendid ball, the newly gilded halls resplendent with hothouse flowers imported from the Crimea and full of my bejeweled guests, all brought by private trains from St. Petersburg.

"Why, Minnie. How fit you are, and so soon after giving birth to your little Olga," declared Miechen, as she contemplated me in my pink silk gown with its fashionably square décolletage, the narrow layered skirts with ruffled mauve scalloping under the bustle, and a spray of pink diamond butterflies with emerald antennae poised in my coiffure. She herself was magnificently dressed as ever in French black satin; unlike me, the birth in January of her fourth child, her sole daughter, Elena, had exacerbated her naturally plump figure, though she carried the extra weight with her habitual defiance.

"Olga was born three months ago," I reminded her. "I barely gained an ounce. She's small-boned, like me." I laughed. "Though her face is entirely her father's."

"Well." Miechen's avaricious gaze roved over the splendid tapestry collection assembled by Tsar Paul I's empress, which I'd taken out of storage to display. "And you've done such wonders with this old place. I thought you'd perish of boredom here."

"It's a royal residence. Alexander used it for hunting expeditions. I've grown fond of it."

"Are you hunting?" she asked, with a surprised look. "I thought you loved all of God's creatures. Did you not establish that society to defend the animals?"

"Miechen, you know very well that hunting is not the same. And, yes, I've learned to shoot. Grouse and partridge, mostly. I also like to fish. Our Silver Lake here yields splendid trout. And, of course, we have ample grounds on the estate; the children love to run about."

She trilled laughter. "You've become a proper hausfrau, Minnie. To hear you speak, one would think you do not miss St. Petersburg at all."

I heard the barb in her mirth. I wasn't so isolated that I didn't know of her glorious receptions at her ever-expanding palace, where, in my absence, she'd set out to eclipse the court as the center of entertainment. Vladimir had benefited from Sasha's elevation; my husband had always relied on his younger brother, and Miechen reaped the rewards, for without an empress in the city to flock to, everyone flocked to her.

I took her by her arm, her wrists laden with diamond bracelets over her long gloves. "We're returning to the city for the Season."

She almost came to a halt. "So soon?"

"Sasha says it is safe enough. He has set the Nihilists on the run and agrees that we can live in the capital again for limited periods. But not the Winter Palace," I said. "Only for state occasions. He won't reside there on a permanent basis."

"He certainly has shown his teeth. To resist him is to invite arrest by the Okhrana and transport to the gallows or Siberia, from which none ever return." She spoke in the same offhanded manner she always did when imparting news that she hoped would disturb me. "We hear that any universities known for radical leanings are put under surveillance, fined, or shut down. Some dare to say our *Moujik* Tsar is becoming a tyrant."

"Do they?" I refused to show her any disquiet. "Such as whom?"

"Oh, the usual assortment of shabby intellectuals and journalists," she replied airily, pausing to examine a pair of old thrones I'd unearthed from Gatchina's basement and ordered regilded. "Are these antiques? How lovely. Anyway, many are choosing to live abroad. They claim freedom of expression is now a liability in Russia."

"A pity." I resisted a smile when I saw her eyes widen at the extraordinary miniature clocks once owned by Peter the Great, now displayed in glass cabinets. "They must not be aware that their *Moujik* Tsar is also funding exhibitions for Russian artists and sponsoring trade invest-ments in our industries, which, as you know, lag far behind those of Europe."

She gave me an amused glance. "Yes, all those quaint paintings of peasants and street bazaars now hang in the Hermitage. One can only wonder what he will do next. Be that as it may . . . well, I wouldn't wish to alarm you."

"Alarm me?" I regarded her. "How so?"

"They're not all dead, Minnie. He may have set the Nihilists on the run or forced them underground, but they're still a menace. Their pam-phlets and circulars, while considerably reduced, can still be found, if one cares to search."

At this, I couldn't curb the censure from my voice. "Do you search?"

"Me? Why would I? But one hears things. Unless one isn't in St. Petersburg, that is."

I released her arm as we neared the gaslit hall, where the guests formed in rows to greet me. "Then it's the perfect time for us to return," I said, sweeping forward and leaving her standing there. "The tsar and tsarina should hear everything their subjects say."

⁓

I WAS OVERJOYED to be back in St. Petersburg, ordering my maids to whisk off the dust tarps, open every window, and scrub every floor. The Anichkov hadn't changed inside, but outside an entire block had been demolished to build a new high wall and underground tunnel for es-cape.

The children were down in the mouth at leaving Gatchina, where they enjoyed more liberties in the enclosed citadel, but soon brightened up with visits from their Mikhailovich cousins. It amused me to see seven-year-old Xenia flush whenever handsome Sandro, who was nine years older and Nicky's best friend, came to visit. With his lean stature, dark-blue eyes, and supple mouth, Sandro was becoming a gallant youth, and he always paused to greet Xenia, telling her how pretty she looked as she gazed adoringly at him.

It was good for my children to spend time with others their age, and it was good for me to be in society—accessible and eager to dine, to attend the opera, ballet, and theater, and to show myself in public as the empress, bold in my disregard for the never-ending rumors of discontent, for, as Miechen had said, my husband had indeed shown his teeth. After years of absorbing Pobendonostev's indoctrination, Sasha now reflected it outward, his autocratic stance evident in everything he undertook. He would not be a liberal tsar like his father.

Until he caught everyone by surprise, including me.

~

WE HAD RETURNED to Gatchina. Sasha was due to depart for Moscow to prepare for our coronation, an exhaustive tradition dating back centuries and requiring endless detail. He had delayed it for almost two years, grumbling that it was a tedious and expensive affair for which he saw no use, until I reminded him that much as he might enjoy being called the *Moujik* Tsar, he was still the tsar, and tsars needed to be crowned. After a long morning of helping him look over the itinerary sent by his officials for his trip, he declared himself exhausted and shut himself in his study to nap on his shabby couch—he refused to let me change a thing in his rooms—while I contended with Olga's teething pains and a new educational arrangement for Nicky. As our tsarevich, my eldest son must be taught accordingly by new tutors, and his removal from shared lessons with his brothers had roused a storm of resentment.

"Why can't I study with Nicky?" George complained. He was my liveliest, prone to mischief despite his delicate lungs. He imitated his tutors with uncanny accuracy, sending his brothers into peals of laughter and upsetting the dignity of whichever teacher he happened to lampoon.

"Because Nicky is the heir," I said. "You will continue to take your lessons from Master Heath."

"Heath, Heath," cawed Popka, George's green parrot, an ill-advised gift from his uncle Vladimir. The creature had adopted my son's disrespect. I'd had to stifle my laughter when one afternoon Master Heath was seen fleeing the classroom, clutching at his bald head. I hadn't realized he wore a toupee until I saw it clenched in the parrot's talons.

"That's not fair. Why does he get to be the heir?" asked George.

"Because he's the firstborn son," said Xenia. She was curled on the window seat with a book. She loved to read, her nose forever buried in a tome. "Stop whining, Georgie. We'll have more fun without Nicky. He's so serious all the time."

"Xenia," I rebuked. "That's not a nice thing to say. Nicky is serious because—"

" 'He has many duties to learn,' " recited George, employing my exact tone of my voice and making Xenia grin. "We know, Mama. You tell us all the time."

"So you *do* listen. I'd begun to wonder. Now, I want your assignments completed. You can make fun all you like of Master Heath, but you will learn from him. Or there'll be no supper tonight. Again."

Georgie scowled just like Sasha as he trudged to his desk. He was not studious.

Once I left them, Tania intercepted me in the corridor. "Minnie," she said, for in our household I preferred to be addressed informally, "Grand Duke Vladimir and his wife, the grand duchess, are here. I saw them to the drawing room."

"Now? But we had no appointment. Sasha is resting, and . . ." My voice faded as I saw her expression. "What is it?" Panic surged in me, thinking another calamity had occurred.

She said quickly, "They didn't say. But the grand duke looks most displeased."

"Honestly. What now?" Passing a hand over my disheveled chignon—I was in my day gown, not ready to receive visitors, but Vladimir could be temperamental if kept waiting—I went downstairs in my dishabille.

Before I could greet them, he snarled, "Did you know?" Swathed in sable, Miechen stared at me.

"Know?" I echoed.

"About Sasha," spat out Vladimir. "What he has done. To us."

"I do not." I now showed my annoyance. I didn't mind that my brother-in-law continued to treat me with the familiarity he always had, but I found his manner most disagreeable.

"She speaks the truth," said Miechen, as if I weren't present. "Sasha never tells her anything he doesn't think she should know."

I glared at her, unable to curb my irritation.

"He has reduced our incomes." Vladimir yanked a crumpled circular from his cloak pocket. Purplish veins from too much drink stood out against his angry pallor as he read aloud: *"By decree of His Imperial Majesty, it is hereby announced that the following alterations in—"*

"Must you?" I interrupted.

Crushing the circular in his fist, he flung it to the floor.

"We are hereby limited," said Miechen, as I glanced pointedly at the ball of paper, "in who may call themselves a grand duke or duchess. Henceforth, only the sovereign's children and grandchildren through the male bloodline may carry the title of Imperial Highness. Our incomes are to be reduced accordingly. Furthermore, no member of the imperial family may wed someone already not of the Orthodox faith, with such marriages to be absolved if undertaken without royal leave." Her smile was glacial. "That is the gist of it, but if you like, Minnie," she said, emphasizing my name, "you may read it for yourself. You have it right there at your feet."

Fury sparked in me. Her supercilious tone was outrageous, but as I struggled for a response, Sasha rumbled from the doorway, "The lady before you is your empress."

Vladimir took an enraged step toward him. "How dare you do this to us?"

Sasha's voice was flat. "Don't think to play tsar with me, brother. You'll receive twenty thousand a year, which is significantly more than our uncles. I can just as easily make it five thousand."

"Constantine will not stand for it," blared Vladimir. "*We* will not stand for it. Am I, the son of an emperor, to subside on a mere pittance? Am I to forsake my wife because she is not of our faith, with three sons and a daughter to raise?"

"Stand for it," said Sasha. "Or leave Russia. As for your wife, the marriage was undertaken with our father's consent. You may count yourself fortunate on that account."

I feared Vladimir might suffer an apoplexy. His face turned crimson as his mouth worked, forming words I prayed he wouldn't say. He did not, thinking better of it and snarling instead to Miechen, "I've heard enough."

He stormed past me to the door. As I tried to catch Miechen's eyes, to demonstrate I wasn't only sympathetic but taken completely unaware, she swept past me without a word.

I reached for the back of the nearest chair, my heel crushing the circular. As I looked over at him, Sasha said, "He thinks too much of himself, as does she. It is always his own family of whom a tsar must beware. Look at how my uncles treated my father. They think they won't stand for it? *I'll* not stand for it. They defy all rules. They come and go as they please, spending fortunes in the bargain—Russia's fortune, which provides them with more than enough to live as they should yet for them is somehow never enough."

"Sasha." I had to sit down. "He's your brother. Would you have them become our enemies over money?"

He eyed me. "You think it so small a matter? The cost of our coronation alone could finance a navy. But the Muscovites must have their procession. My treasury is taxed to its limits, with all the security measures and income paid out to keep the family in diamonds, wine, and roast. They swive like hares and all want to be titled as Your Imperial Highness so they can eat at the trough. I must pay to maintain our residences, yachts, trains, and museums, our ballet, art, and music academies. Every state reception requires a ransom. In the Winter Palace alone, I've been informed, the linens are changed daily, even if no one is there. I've dismissed most of those idle servants who do nothing all day and have forbidden gold braid on uniforms and liveries."

I met his stare. "Are we so diminished that you must forbid gold braid?"

"Russia is diminished. You should know through your Red Cross work that we have hospitals and schools to build; we cannot thrive while maintaining a hundred grand dukes and their households. It's a disgrace. No court in Europe wastes as we do. I will not tolerate it. If the tsar must economize, so must everyone else."

"Does that mean me, as well?"

"You are the empress. You must set the style. Should you spend fifteen thousand rubles on a sable cloak and ten thousand on an evening gown from Paris, as your most recent dressmaker bills cite? I leave that up to you."

Stung at his unexpected rebuke, I retorted, "Not all of us care to dress like serfs."

"I never suggested we should. But that German must learn her proper place and teach Vladimir his. As for the rest," he said, turning to the door, "they'll not complain. Constantine knows he's lucky to be alive. He would have been arrested for what happened to my father, had Vladimir had his way. I refused. Our uncle might be an impossible eccentric, but he would never have dared fling a bomb at his own brother. Would that I could say the same about mine."

He left me to return to his study. I thought I should go comfort him, for in that moment I knew he'd crossed an invisible threshold. As the tsar, he was subject to all the attending preoccupations and sacrifices that his rank entailed. But this sacrifice, made by a decree that might sever accord within the family, was one only I could understand—the sacrifice for his country. None of those who bathed in imperial largesse would accept that, for him, even before the Romanovs, Russia must come first.

I admired him for it. I loved him all the more.

But I did not go to him. I sat in my chair with the crunched-up circular under my feet and realized that, henceforth, it wasn't only Nihilists whom we must guard ourselves against.

CHAPTER TWENTY

It was May but cold as February. The savage wind was seeping through my layers of ermine, freezing my toes in my gem-encrusted slippers and turning my breath to icy vapor.

All of Moscow waited, thousands gathered along the route from the Petrovsky Palace to the red-brick walls of the Kremlin and onion-domed jumble of St. Basil's Cathedral. Sasha had ridden ahead astride a white charger, in his white cap and green uniform without adornment—a huge, solitary figure among the Hussars and lancers, the Cossacks in their astrakhan kalpaks, and the Garde à Cheval in their eagle-crowned helmets—followed by the exotic line of the representatives from our Asiatic domains.

The melody of Moscow's many church bells rang in vain against the thundering gun salutes. My golden and crystal-glass coach seemed impossibly distant as I moved toward it. The diadem on my head—a Romanov crown jewel, with its silk-lace veil and twined collars of diamonds and pearls, also part of the royal collection—felt heavy as stone, the silver-brocade mantle a frozen cascade down my back.

Xenia was already inside the coach, dressed in her first court gown and *kokoshnik*. I hadn't wanted her to attend, and my sons even less so, after Sasha told me that in the new electrical lighting installed in the Kremlin—the first ever in Russia and a novelty he'd embraced for our coronation—the secret police had discovered explosive devices timed to the switches. Every inch of wiring had to be checked. Further investigation led to a Moscow garret and a heap of the high-brimmed caps favored by Muscovites, each containing nitroglycerin bombs like the one that killed Alexander. The plot was foiled, but my distress was so acute that I refused to heed Xenia's teary pleas to accompany me, until Sasha persuaded me to relent. "She's our eldest daughter. She wants to ride with you in your carriage. Let her."

By decree, no caps were allowed to be thrown in the air as we passed, lest one of those cunning bombs escape detection. We'd been assured of no further threat, all the culprits under arrest, yet I battled near-paralyzing fear as the coach brought me down the route to where the clergy, the metropolitan, and Sasha waited. The crowds cried out my name; all I could see was an endless maw of open mouths. I was trapped with my daughter in a translucent cage, which might shatter at any moment when a bomb detonated beneath us.

Only an hour later, but what seemed like years, I arrived. Taking Xenia's hand in mine, I started to descend when the coach door opened. Sasha had broken protocol to escort us himself.

"Manja." He leaned toward me. "Our jewels suit you. You're so white. Like a swan. But so sad. Smile, my love. Let the people see joy in their new empress."

I turned toward the crowds, their cheering rolling over me in waves. As I lifted my hand, I searched anxiously for that one dark face, the lone brooding figure with death at the ready, preparing to fling fire and brimstone as we stood before him.

The people roared in adulation. With Sasha's hand in mine and Xenia beaming at our side—she would later drive her brothers mad with her proud prattle about this day—we proceeded into the Uspensky Sobor, the Cathedral of the Assumption, with its five gold-painted domes and arched façades representing Christ and the four evangelists.

Within, frankincense and myrrh rose in clouds. The iconostasis glittered with a thousand icons. The metropolitan blessed and handed to Sasha the imperial crown made for Catherine the Great, with its diamond cross surmounted by a huge ruby; as the congregation knelt, Sasha set his own crown upon his head. Then I went to my knees before him. Removing his crown, he touched it to my forehead to symbolize our bond and placed upon my head the diadem of the empress consort, topped by a sapphire as blue as the sea. I had only seen my late mother-in-law wear it once, at a formal court event, and I was surprised by how light it actually felt on my brow.

In the splendor of that moment, wreathed in incense and swelling hymns, our eyes met as I stood. Clasping me in his arms, Sasha whispered, "No man has loved a woman as I love you, my tsarina."

BY TRADITION, FESTIVITIES for the populace were held in Moscow's Khodynka Field, on the outskirts of the city, where as the newly crowned emperor and empress we would distribute commemorative souvenirs of goblets and plates embossed with our insignia.

We assembled upon a canopied dais in the field three days later, after an exhaustive round of galas. A gusty wind that only Moscow could bestow flapped the canopy with loud cracking sounds, like gunshots. I tried to suppress my fear as I saw the mobs of people, come from every far-flung corner of Russia to partake of our largesse. A bomb might be concealed by any of them—hidden under an embroidered sleeve or stuffed under the peasant skirts, though the wearing of hats was strictly forbidden.

We stood cordoned off by guards, secret police disguised as tradesmen wandering among the crowds; to me, it was like a feeble fence of sticks against a swarm as the people queued up, one row for Sasha and one for me. We would not hand over the gifts ourselves, as a result of the security measures; chamberlains in bulletproof vests did it for us. Yet as each family came forth to grasp the cheap pewter plate or cup— they had little value, other than sentimental—my nails dug into my palms. I must have gone rigid, for Sasha glanced over at me, making me force out a smile. He'd shown no trepidation throughout our coronation, though he must have felt it. To all who beheld him, he was the very image of stern *Batushka,* Russia's God-appointed Little Father.

The queues seemed endless. I was growing faint with exhaustion when a mother and her child came before me. My designated chamberlain extended the plate. The mother, her kerchief removed as either a sign of respect or requirement by our strictures against headgear, lifted plaintive eyes to me, immobile on my dais. She didn't appear old, yet her dark hair was threaded with gray, betraying her origins; peasant women aged precipitously in the harsh countryside. Wisps blew in the wind, untangled from the plaits that wreathed her head. Her cheeks were hollowed by hunger and suffering.

She shook her head at the plate, issuing a babble of accented Russian I didn't understand, for she came from the provinces, her dialect unfamiliar to me. My chamberlain barked at her, thrusting out the plate, and she lifted an imploring protest, pushing the bundled child before her, as if in defense.

The wind unraveled the scarf wrapped about the child's face; as I took a step back, my fear of violence getting the better of me, I saw an eruption of boils on the child's cheeks.

The chamberlain motioned to the guards to remove the woman, whose gaze locked on me. Without realizing what I was about to do, my voice issued from the tight dryness in my throat: "Wait." I forced myself to the edge of the dais, which was low enough to make me feel completely exposed. "What is she saying?"

"Nothing, Your Highness," replied the impatient chamberlain, who must have been tired himself, on his feet for hours, handing out souvenirs. "Something about a blessing."

"Blessing?" I turned uncertainly to Sasha.

"She wants you to bless the child," he said quietly. "Some *moujik* believe the touch of the tsar or tsarina can bestow health. A superstition, Manja. You needn't oblige."

I shifted my gaze to the woman. The guards were at her side, about to turn her away. Then I looked at that pathetic child—a boy or a girl?—and I heard a voice in my mind.

Do not let yourself be overwhelmed. You are a Romanov now. You must accept your role and embrace it. There is no other way to survive.

Of all those I might have recalled in that moment, it was my mother-in-law, long dead in her tomb. I was the empress, as she'd once been. In the end she'd eschewed it, sundered by loss and her husband's infidelity. I must not do the same.

I descended the side steps, waving the baffled chamberlain aside to approach the woman. The guards tensed; I ignored the silent warning in their stares.

The child's eyes were huge, brown like its mother's, but empty, as if it had lost any capacity to feel. Reaching out my hand from my richly adorned sleeve, as if by some ancient instinct I set it on the child's head and I whispered a prayer.

The woman keened, falling to her knees, tugging the child down with her. "God save Your Majesty," I heard her say, for that much I could understand.

"No," I replied. All of a sudden, tears salted my eyes. "God save you, child of Russia." And I extended my hand to her.

She leaned to it, not touching it with her own hands but setting her chafed lips on my skin. I felt her inhale, as if I exuded a preternatural aura. Turning to the wide-eyed chamberlain, I removed the plate from his hand and gave it to her. She clutched it to her chest, tears running down her gaunt face. Then she was gone, lost in the crowds, who had received their own baubles and now waited for us to depart before the food stalls opened and the entertainment began, intended to bring them respite for the rest of the day.

When I returned to Sasha's side, he said, "Never have I been prouder of you."

I didn't feel proud. I felt freed. I no longer had to cower in abject fear of the Nihilist threat, of death by explosion or other terrible deed. It might still happen, but for today I had overcome it. I had behaved like a Romanov.

To Russia, we owed our duty. It was something I vowed never to forget.

SASHA INSISTED ON an unvaried routine. He claimed it gave him something to look forward to while he endured his interminable cabinet meetings, wrestling with the complexities of the empire and his brothers and uncles, who barged in wherever he happened to be to expound upon a problem or complaint—and they had plenty of both. None left his presence satisfied, for he'd shout at them to get out if they refused to abide by his dictates.

As a result, he started drinking too much. Never during the day, when he must attend to his duties, but often at night, when he'd disappear after supper to sequester himself in his study. I'd tiptoe in before bed to find him slumbering on his sagging couch, an empty vodka bottle at his side and his valet, Ivan, holding vigil in the corner, while his head of household, Tania's husband, Prince Obolensky, fretted in the corridor. Tucking a blanket over my oblivious husband—there was no waking him in that state—I had the bottle removed and issued my inevitable reprimand to the prince, who assured me he'd do his utmost to curb Sasha's consumption. I knew he would try and Sasha would have none of it, but it was important for me to express my displeasure.

To ease Sasha's burden, I established our routine. In the winter, we resided in the city for the Season, attending the opera and ballet and holding galas in the Winter Palace, where I reveled and he grumbled. In the spring, we went to Gatchina to enjoy outdoor activities. Early summer required a move to Peterhof by the seaside or Livadia in the Crimea to escape the heat. In autumn, we traveled to Denmark for our family reunion.

Alix and Bertie joined us, along with their children. Sasha's relief to be away from Russia was evident when we reached Copenhagen, where the reception by my parents, compared to our imperial excess, was frugal, homemade like my childhood dresses.

"At last, we are free of prison!" Sasha boomed, stomping down the platform to embrace my father and my brothers. Valdemar was still unwed, but Freddie was now married, with children of his own. And while my youngest sister's husband balked at leaving their home in Austria, so we rarely saw Thyra, my brother Willie welcomed the opportunity to leave Greece with his wife, Olga, and their brood of six children.

We, the women, assumed charge of our rambunctious offspring, mine among them. At Fredensborg, daily strolls by the lake, fishing, horseback riding, boating, and suppers on the terrace suited Sasha immensely. The boys rallied around him; he was always willing to help them bait their fishing rods or trudge into the lake up to his knees to haul out their stranded boats. In the twilit evenings, he walked the paths with my father, Bertie, and my brothers, swathed in cigar smoke, with the boys tagging right behind them like unruly martinets, for wherever Papa Sasha went, they wanted to be.

He softened in Denmark. He berated Nicky less, was abstentious in his drinking, and he smiled more—that endearing smile that crinkled his eyes. His laughter at the boys' antics as they threw socks filled with water at him and ran shrieking when he pounced after them resounded so frequently that Mama said, "I believe I hear a happy emperor."

"He is, here," I said, reclining on the wicker chaise with Alix and smoking one of my thin Russian cigarettes, a habit that neither condoned.

"And is the empress happy, too?" said Alix, with a sly look at me.

Before I could respond, Mama declared, "Of course she is. Did I not tell her as much? When two people commit, there can always be love."

And love there was: In the sun-dried sheets of our bed, fragrant with lavender, Sasha and I renewed our passion, laughing like children ourselves and bringing Mama's eyebrow up when we arrived late, disheveled, to the breakfast buffet.

As if a spell were cast in Denmark, our empire ceased to exist. Without the burden of imperial constraint, we were just husband and wife, father and mother, and eager lovers.

"If I could, I'd spend the rest of our days in peace," sighed Sasha, when the time came to leave. "Your people know how to be satisfied with the simple pleasures of life."

He was Russian to his marrow, but a bit of Denmark warmed his soul.

CHAPTER TWENTY-ONE

"Someone has lost her petticoat." Miechen gestured to a corner of the Nicholas Hall, populated by a jungle of potted trees and greenhouse flowers. "There, by that lilac bush."

When I spied the crumpled article, steps away from two grand duchesses in conversation, I clasped my hand to my mouth to stifle my giggle. "I wonder whose it is."

"Whomever it belongs to, I'm sure she too is now hiding behind a bush," Miechen said, and as her mouth twitched into a smile, I burst out laughing.

We were at the evening ball in the Winter Palace for the nuptials of Grand Duke Sergei, Sasha's twenty-seven-year-old brother, to Princess Elisabeth of Hesse and by Rhine, one of Victoria's many granddaughters.

The marriage had been my doing. Sergei had grown into his youthful promise, now over six feet tall but still extremely slim, with an intensity in his person that many mistook for malice. Following the completion of his education, he'd been appointed Commander of the Preobrazhensky Life Guards, the elite regiment founded by Peter the Great, and dedicated himself to his military career with the same exemplary standard of his childhood studies. Yet to date, he had remained unwed, so I decided to remedy the situation.

"He needs a wife," I told Sasha. "Except for Vladimir, none of your brothers are married yet, and it's my duty to arrange suitable matches for the family, as you have no desire to. Sergei is nearly thirty now. Do I have your permission? The widowed Grand Duke of Hesse and by

Rhine has four unwed daughters by his late wife, one of whom should be suitable."

Sasha frowned. "Is he the same German who married one of Victoria's daughters?"

I was surprised that he even knew, given how little interest he showed in the affairs of his own family, besides their extravagance. "Yes. Her daughter Alice, who died of diphtheria. Victoria has practically raised her granddaughters, as Alice was one of her favorite children. I realize it won't be easy to gain her approval."

"Or likely," he said. "After my poor sister Marie's disastrous marriage to that boor Alfred, I doubt Victoria will ever permit another of her family to wed a Romanov. And I doubt Sergei would be willing," he added, with a scowl.

I avoided the mention of Marie. She had fulfilled her duty, bearing five children, but her marriage had deteriorated to such a point that she'd requested a separation once her children were older, as she had inherited lands in her maternal duchy of Saxe-Coburg where she could live.

"Whyever not?" I said instead. "Your mother was a princess of Hesse and visited Hesse-Darmstadt with Nixa and your brothers; surely Sergei must have met the princesses at some point in his childhood."

"I never visited Hesse-Darmstadt with my mother," he replied stonily, "but you have my permission. It is time Sergei married. High time, indeed. I'll not have his shame upon us."

I didn't understand. Of his surviving brothers, Sergei was the most diligent, never the cause of any sordidness. The youngest brother, Grand Duke Paul, now twenty-three, had already entertained and discarded several mistresses, and older Alexis was infamous for his conquests. Only Sergei remained above reproach.

Via envoys, Louis of Hesse and by Rhine indicated that his second daughter, Elisabeth—or Ella, as she was known in the family—was the most suitable. She was nineteen years old; moreover, she and Sergei had apparently formed an attachment despite the distance between them, after she sent him heartfelt letters of condolence following the deaths of his mother and father.

Informed of her father's approval and reassurance that Louis would prevail upon Victoria for her approval, Sasha summoned Sergei from his camp at Krasnoye Selo, where he lived most of the year with his regiment. I paced anxiously in my drawing room as I awaited the outcome of their meeting in Sasha's study, anticipating his yelling as Sergei resisted.

No sound issued from the study. When Sergei came to see me afterward, he stood like a rod in his green-and-gold uniform, one hand twisting the silver ring that had belonged to his mother, which he always wore on his little finger, and intoned, "I believe congratulations are in order, Majesty. I am to marry Princess Elisabeth of Hesse and by Rhine."

"Then the congratulations are for *you!*" I exclaimed in delight, not minding that he'd addressed me by my title, for Sergei was never anything if not formal.

"No." He bowed. "The congratulations belong entirely to Your Majesty."

He left me somewhat unnerved; I couldn't tell if he was pleased or not. When I asked Sasha how Sergei had reacted, my husband grimaced. "He said, 'As Your Majesty commands.' I suggest you reserve your sympathies for the bride."

"I find his antipathy for Sergei unfathomable," I confided to Miechen one afternoon shortly before Ella's arrival, when we met for tea. While our husbands remained at odds, barely speaking to each other, we'd elected to remain friendly rivals, as sisters-in-law thrown into the gaiety and competition of the Season. "Sergei might not be as gregarious as your Vladimir, adventurous as Alexis, or accommodating as Paul, but he's a fine young man, if a bit unaffectionate and severe in his duty."

Miechen snorted. "He's not quite as unaffectionate as you imagine."

Of course, she had heard something. Yet to my surprise she was reluctant to impart it until I threatened to confront Sergei myself, as the wedding was upon us. "Oh, you mustn't," she said, more flustered than I'd ever seen her. "It's not something you should ever mention."

"*What* should I never mention? Does he have an unsuitable mistress or a vice for the roulette?" It wouldn't have taken me aback; all the Romanov men, with the exception of Sasha, and possibly Vladimir now, seemed compelled by some curse to make their wives suffer with their incurable penchant for ballerinas, gambling, and other indiscretions.

"If only it were that." Miechen inclined to me. "One of his own footmen, I'm told, and he's been known to frequent certain public bathhouses. Sympathies for the bride, indeed. The poor girl will need them."

At first, I could only stare at her in confusion. Then, as her meaning sank in, I said, "Never would I have expected you to repeat such filth about a member of our family."

"Very well." She drew back. "Ask Sasha, if you must."

She knew I wouldn't dare. Sasha would be horrified to learn I even knew of such things, much less voiced them aloud in connection with his brother. But I remembered what he'd said to me years ago: *My brother Paul has told me . . . things. Things I will not repeat,* and I didn't ask anything more. I didn't want to know. I had heard of men who preferred their own; I'd not lived in St. Petersburg for as long as I had without becoming aware of the lewd undercurrent and illicit liaisons that characterized our society as much as the veneer of refinement. But Sergei—it seemed incredible to me.

And that night during the gala after their marriage, I saw no reason to believe what Miechen had intimated. Ella was beautiful, willowy and blue-eyed, with light-brown hair, a classic oval face, and a tender mouth. Sergei seemed to visibly thaw in her presence, towering over her yet bending often to murmur in her ear, a romantic vision of what a grand duke and duchess should be.

Now they were dancing together. Once Miechen and I exhausted our mirth over the unknown lady who'd lost her petticoat, I saw my sister-in-law's gaze roving the hall in search of further diversion. Sasha had retired early, as he tended to do at court functions, but I was so pleased by my matchmaking that I'd decided to stay on without him, though it would fall upon me at some point to silence the orchestra and bid everyone good night.

"Is that Nicky I see over there?" Miechen lifted her lorgnette, which was hanging by a gold chain on her ample chest. She'd grown matronly after the births of her children, but the extra weight only made her presence more commanding. "Why, it is. He seems rather taken with Ella's mouse of a sister. What is her name again?" She clucked in annoyance. "I never remember it, though she's been presented to me twice already."

"Alexandra." I followed her gaze. "Ella calls her Alicky."

"Yes. Alicky. It shows how little impression she makes that I could forget. Not at all like her sister, I'm afraid."

I agreed. Alexandra of Hesse and by Rhine was not like her sister, but, then, she was only twelve, four years younger than my Nicky, who'd reached his sixteenth birthday, his majority of age, and received honorary rank in the Hussar regiment. He wore the uniform tonight, his slim figure suited to the red-and-black *kamzol,* with its braided gold- and fur-trimmed jacket slung across one shoulder by tasseled cords.

"Nicky is so gracious," purred Miechen. "Paying attention to a poor fräulein."

She taunted me, and I could see why. My son did appear intent, standing before seated Alicky, her solemn face upturned as he spoke with more volubility than I'd seen him display in public. Like Sasha, he was uncomfortable in social situations. Soft-spoken and reserved, he'd once confided to me that he felt his lack of stature made him appear puny beside his robust Mikhailovich cousins, who preened like bona fide Romanovs.

"And to think Sasha complains he's too shy," said Miechen. "He'd revise his opinion if he could see Nicky now. Such a shame our emperor went to bed early."

I glanced at her. She smiled. "Careful, Minnie. You might have to swallow your hatred of Prussia if you leave those two together for too long."

"If you will excuse me," I said, and I swept toward my son, who didn't notice my approach, though Alicky of Hesse did, her face turning pale. She wasn't unattractive, I found myself thinking as she rose and attempted a pathetic curtsy. Tall for her age and slender, she was thin-lipped, but her nose was regal, and she had thick coppery-gold hair. Her most arresting feature was her mercurial blue eyes, with a hint of gray; in the volatile mix of the hall's new electric sconces and gaslit chandeliers, they seemed almost violet.

A pretty girl who would be a beautiful woman, if less beautiful than her sister. In that moment I took a sudden dislike to her. A pretty German girl, to whom my son the tsarevich was paying too much attention, as Miechen had said; it rankled me. But I subdued my resentment, for surely Nicky was merely being courteous to a foreign guest in our court, the sister-in-law to his uncle Sergei. I should have been pleased to find him so engaged, rather than standing awkwardly to one side as he usually did at these functions, waiting for the hour when the gala ended, so he could return to his books.

"Your Imperial Majesty," she murmured.

I smiled, motioning her to rise. An unbecoming rash of embarrassment scalded her cheeks and throat. "Minnie," I said, trying my best to sound warm. "You are part of our family now that your sister has wed our Sergei. Everyone in the family calls me Minnie."

She lowered her gaze, without repeating my name.

"Alicky was telling me how much she likes Russia," said Nicky, with a distinct quaver in his voice. Tucking his jacket over his shoulder, as it was about to slip, I said, "Was she, my darling?" I'd not seen her doing any talking, I almost added, as I returned my gaze to her. "You've not been here for very long. There is more to Russia than St. Petersburg."

That splotchy rash crept into her spare décolletage. She was wearing an outdated gown in mauve silk, sewn by her own hands, I presumed. Despite her obsessive control over her family, Victoria was hardly generous. I should have pitied the girl. Her mother dead when she was a child and her father a penurious duke of minor importance—she might have reminded me of myself at her age, in her gauche attire. Only, to my eyes, she had none of my vitality or confidence, beset by timidity and that unbecoming rash.

"Yes, Your Majesty," she said.

Clearly I wasn't going to entice her into conversation.

"My son." I tapped him with my fan. "Don't you think you should pay some attention to your sister? Xenia might want to dance. With whom else but you?"

"Sandro," he said, to my surprise. Times past, he would have immediately excused himself to do my bidding. "She's been dancing with him all night."

"Well, he's her cousin. Go to her. I insist. It's getting late and the tsarevich should dance at least once with his sister before the night is done. The court expects it."

He looked for a moment as if he might refuse. My initial surprise turned to incredulity when he turned to Alicky. "Would you like to dance with my sister and me?"

She was going to faint, I thought. She'd gone beet red. But she gave him a shy nod and replied in a voice so low I could scarcely hear it, "If Her Majesty would permit."

"Mama?" Nicky looked at me with a resolution that made me realize my little boy wasn't so little anymore.

"Naturally." I forced out a smile.

He stepped aside to let Alicky pass. She almost forgot herself before she remembered and clumsily gave me another curtsy. She had the grace of a milkmaid. Had Victoria not taught her granddaughter the minimal requirements for attendance at court?

Yet as she and Nicky moved into the crowded hall in search of Xenia, I saw their steps move in tandem, and they leaned slightly toward each other, as if in mutual comfort.

⁓

"I THINK I might like to marry her once she is of age," Nicky said a month later, as we sat at breakfast. His siblings had already eaten and gone upstairs to their lessons. Sasha kept a strict time limit on meals, but I'd made an exception for Nicky today. He'd not been himself, more absentminded than usual. Despite Sasha's glare over his newspaper, I told Nicky to stay at the table to finish his meal.

"Marry whom, my son?" I sipped my tea, directing my gaze at the half-finished omelet on his plate. "Please, eat. You're getting too thin."

He took a bite. Looking any smaller appalled him. With his mouth full, he couldn't answer my question, so Sasha did it for him, not glancing up from his paper.

"I trust you're not talking about that Hesse girl. I heard all about how you mooned after her while she was here, going to Sergei's new palace at every opportunity to take her out for carriage rides in the Summer Garden. It's admirable to show such hospitality to the sister of your uncle's new wife, but now that she has returned to her father's realm, I expect you to put an end to any foolish attachment."

Nicky said in dismay, "You—you were *watching* me?"

Sasha chortled. "My Okhrana are charged with protecting my family. Did you think you could slip in and out of here with no one being the wiser?"

"Sasha," I said, bringing down his newspaper. "Was that necessary?"

"Yes," he said. "We are not so safe that my son and heir can gallivant about town with some chit and no escort—"

"She is not a chit." Nicky sprang to his feet. "She is a princess. And I—I was not mooning over her." His voice faltered as Sasha's eyes narrowed at him. "I was not."

"If you say so." Sasha didn't sound angry, though with Nicky, he rarely showed any tolerance. Now, he actually smiled. "Well, well. Our bear cub has fangs, after all."

"She likes me very much." Nicky drew himself erect; I felt such tenderness for him to see him puff out his slim chest. "I like her. We've promised to correspond. May I write to her without my letters being read by the Okhrana?"

"Darling, your breakfast," I said. "It's getting cold." I deliberately avoided making any comment, but I did not want my son marrying an impoverished German. It was fine for a grand duke. Not the tsarevich.

"Papa?" Nicky remained standing. "May I?"

Sasha looked back at his newspaper. "If you like. I'll post your letters myself."

"Thank you, Papa." Nicky sat down at the table to finish his omelet, then he bowed and departed, without kissing my cheek as he always did before going to his studies.

The moment he left, I turned to Sasha. "If he likes? You'll post his letters yourself?"

Sasha shrugged. "He wants to write her a few letters. Where's the harm in it?"

I reached for my cigarette case, though I made a habit of not smoking at the table. "The harm in it, as Nicky said, is that she is a princess. An unwed one of dubious prospects, I might add, whose elder sister just made a splendid marriage to an imperial grand duke."

"A marriage you arranged. Are you going to light that? I don't mind."

Just to be contrary, I set my cigarette aside. "I arranged it for Sergei."

"And I'm very grateful, Manja. Sergei seems taken with his wife, and it's a relief to see it." Folding up his newspaper, he said in a mock-indulgent tone, "Shall we have our quarrel? I'm due to inspect the riding academy today. If we must fight, we should do it now lest I'm late."

I scowled at him. "As I was saying, she's unwed, and she had Nicky wrapped about her finger. When has he ever shown interest in a girl before?" The moment I spoke, I regretted it. My words carried an unwitting echo of his fear about Sergei, which had dissipated in the wake of the marriage, to the extent that he'd granted the newlyweds use of the Beloselsky-Belozersky Palace as their city residence. With Sasha, such largesse meant he was placated. His suspicion of Sergei's inclinations had been erased by his brother's willingness to settle down and start a family.

"Nicky should show interest in girls," Sasha said. "He's a man now."

"He's shown interest in only one girl. Her. And he's sixteen. How can he possibly know whom he wants to marry yet?"

"She is . . . what? Thirteen?"

"Twelve," I said sourly.

"Too young to marry. Minnie, he must sow his oats. So, he has an infatuation with a pretty princess who lives in Hesse and wants to write her letters. Let him. It will pass. At his age, we always want to marry the first girl who catches our eye. We never do."

I nudged the cigarette on the table with my fingertips, recognizing he was right but not caring to admit it.

"If you think it more suitable," he went on, "I can ask Paul to find him a ballerina. I believe that young one who dances at the Mariinsky, Little K, is available. I hear she has a taste for grand dukes."

"For grand-duke money," I said. "The only thing little about Mathilde Kschessinka is the size of her ballet slippers. Everything else, including her taste, is oversize and vulgar."

He bent over me, kissing my lips. "Not like little Alicky of Hesse, eh, who's penniless and proper to a fault." He cupped my chin. "Are we in agreement?"

I gave reluctant assent. "Providing it is only letters. Ella resides here now and will no doubt invite her sister to visit. We might see more of Alicky of Hesse than we wish."

Sasha chuckled. "I've no doubt if we do, you'll remind her of her limitations."

As he walked out, I lit my cigarette, leaning back in my chair to smoke.

Indeed. If she made any attempt to ensnare Nicky, I would remind her.

CHAPTER TWENTY-TWO

Upon his nineteenth birthday, Nicky was appointed to the Preobrazhensky regiment under Sergei's command and went to reside at the headquarters in Krasnoye Selo. It wasn't far, just southeast of the city, but he was now gone for part of the year and I missed him terribly. I sent him weekly packages of clean linens and letters full of advice that doubtless made him cringe, for he was expected to be treated like every other soldier.

Meanwhile, my George turned sixteen, grown tall and handsome but still prone to bronchial ailments that had me in constant worry. As the second son, he was destined for a regimental career. Sasha kept saying his ailment would subside, but the doctors believed he had weak lungs, and living at a military barracks was out of the question.

At twelve, Xenia was budding into womanhood. Her infatuation with her cousin Sandro had deepened into mutual love, and they had expressed the desire to wed. Sasha and I said we would refuse our approval until Xenia reached at least her eighteenth year, and I advised my daughter that she must be mature enough before she made any commitment. She dug in her heels, which made Sasha chuckle. "Sandro or spinsterhood. She's certainly your daughter."

"Mine?" I declared. "She gets that Romanov obstinacy from you."

At eight years of age, Misha remained our most docile, not an outstanding student by any means but persistent in his efforts. Because of the disparity in my children's ages, Misha and nearly six-year-old Olga resided most of the year in Gatchina. With all my obligations, I no longer had sufficient time to devote to their upbringing. While I must ensure their preparation for adulthood, I now knew they were safe in the country, and we always returned to them once the Season ended.

Little Olga, however, was an enigma to me. She adored Misha and always ran to Sasha so he could pick her up and whirl her around. But she plucked disinterestedly at the dresses I had made for her and resisted trying them on. Instead, she retrieved the stuffed bear Sasha had given her on her second birthday, now so threadbare, while the many other stuffed toys I'd bought her over the years remained untouched.

"Darling, let me wash Poopsie and sew on his eyes. He lost his buttons. He's blind."

As I reached for the bear, she clutched it to her chest. "Poopsie's not blind. You are."

Her words made me think of my sister Alix: *Oh, Minnie. Are you so blind?* Hurt and confused, I left her. Of all my children, Olga was the one I couldn't seem to reach, but Sasha dismissed my concern. "She rarely sees you. As soon as she has to attend her first ball, you'll be her favorite person. Who else but her mother can make her look beautiful?"

I didn't think she'd ever be beautiful, not like Xenia. My eldest daughter already turned heads, with her piquant face and lithe figure. But I took solace that Olga would have her father and Misha to confide in as she grew older.

Devoted a mother as I was to all my children, I would not beg for her love.

⁓

"Five students," Sasha told me in an emotionless voice. "Carrying hollowed-out books stuffed with explosives. We took the Griboyedov Canal road, due to the church's construction, which they didn't expect. By doing so, we missed their attack. The Okhrana has them under arrest."

We rode in our carriage through Gatchina Park, having just returned from St. Petersburg for a visit to the unfinished Church of the Savior on Spilled Blood, an onion-domed church that Sasha had ordered built on the site of his father's murder.

Unable to conceive we might have died in that very same place, I started to cry. "I thought you'd rid us of this nightmare, Sasha. I thought it was over."

"Manja, don't." He awkwardly patted my hand, for our escort rode behind us and he wasn't given to public displays. "I am doing all I can, but they're like rats, breeding constantly, infecting others. Those five will be executed, but I can't predict when another five will take their place. They hate me because I won't give them what they want. But I'm prepared to die for Russia if need be. I will not stop doing my duty until they stop me."

"What *do* they want, to stalk us like this?" I wiped angrily at my tears.

He looked away. "You know. You've always known." As my blood froze, as much from the fact that we'd almost had bombs thrown at us as from his words, he said, "It was the reason for your luncheon with my father that day." He turned his gaze to me. "Am I wrong?"

"No," I whispered.

"I thought as much. I'm glad we have it out. I don't like secrets between us."

"Alexander . . . he was going to tell you. I insisted that he must."

"Only Vladimir told me, instead. He heard about it. Our father wasn't as cunning as he thought. A newspaper editor who received advance notice of the manifesto before its publication informed Vladimir. Thank God for it. I'd have been compelled to sanction something I never had intention of permitting. If the Nihilists killed the very man prepared to give them what they wanted, what might they do once they obtained it?"

I bit my lip, unwilling to admit that I'd supported Alexander's aspiration. I did not support it now, not since I'd seen what the rally for reform had cost my father-in-law and might yet cost us. As much as I endeavored through my charities to care for our people, I had to agree with my husband. Russia was not ready for such drastic change.

"I forgive you," he added. "I know you thought you were doing what was best."

His statement put an end to further discussion. I didn't broach it again, but I fell prey once more to my nerves. Seeing my distress, Sasha accepted an invitation from the governors of the Caucasus, who had expressed eagerness to show their loyalty to the tsar.

"It will do us good," he said. "The Caucasians are honest folk. A tsar hasn't visited the region in many years. We'll bring our children and our household on the imperial train. We'll have all the comforts of home and none of the poison of St. Petersburg."

"But we're supposed to go to Denmark in the autumn," I said, and then, when his jaw set, a silent reminder of what had transpired between us, I nodded. "Very well."

We might have all the comforts of home, but I wasn't comforted. The imperial train was luxurious enough, interconnected carriages containing damask-upholstered bedrooms, drawing rooms, salons, bathing facilities, servant quarters, and two kitchens. Painted in blue with the imperial double-headed eagle crest in gold on its coach doors, it was identical to a second train that was also dispatched, our route closely guarded, so that any attempt to harm us would be stymied by confusion as to which train was ours.

Under any other circumstances, I might have enjoyed it. Relieved of his regimental duties for the trip, Nicky came with us. His training in Krasnoye Selo had broadened his shoulders and prompted him to grow a luxuriant mustache. He made no mention of Alicky of Hesse, and I didn't ask. My eldest son clearly relished this time with his siblings, who laughed and teased him for his stiff posture, and he was attentive to them, particularly Olga, who cleaved to him like a clam. Even George, recovering from a bad cough, seemed improved, with color in his lean cheeks as he and Xenia read Pushkin's poetry aloud in the evenings. But I couldn't forget that we rode in a potential death trap into a remote mountainous area, with our entire staff, Okhrana agents, plainsclothes police, and Cossack guard—all the security measures I'd come to despise as indispensable reminders of our persistent danger.

Nevertheless, the visit proved delightful. The Caucasians received us with bread and salt, whirling dervishes, and the embroidered *cherkeska*. Dressed in these caftan robes, I was seated beside Sasha like an equal, for female chieftains were revered in the Caucasus.

A month later, we set out for Gatchina, the decoy train sent ahead. My younger children had grown restless, arguing over nothing, and George's cough worsened, so that I was up at night smearing medicinal ointment on his chest. Xenia was pining for Sandro, from whom she evidently couldn't be apart for too long, and I noticed that Nicky had begun penning letters, which I suspected were intended for Hesse. Tired and out of sorts, I too longed to get back to our routine, but

Sasha was in an ebullient mood, as he always was after meeting his "hardworking people, nothing like those sycophants in the city."

We rattled along in our drawing room carriage at the rear of the train, George napping on a settee as Xenia and Misha read together, Olga sketched, and Nicky wrote on the portable desk. Sasha reclined, yawning after too much vodka at lunch. Craving a cigarette, I excused myself to use the lavatory. Everyone knew I was going into the corridor to smoke, but I kept up the pretense, though Nicky had once followed me out and smoked a cigarette with me, having picked up the habit at his headquarters, to my discontent.

He did not follow me this time, intent on his letter. Pulling my shawl about me, for the corridor was chilly, I took out my case and was about to light my cigarette when the train jolted. The match singed my fingers. I dropped the cigarette; as I bent down to retrieve it, a high-pitched metallic shriek deafened me. Then a violent shake sent me sprawling. Thrown against the corridor wall, I started to crawl toward the drawing room compartment, my heart pounding in my throat.

The lights went out.

It was the night of the explosion in the Winter Palace all over again, the same mindless plunge into terror, only this time the entire train was tilting, falling off its tracks. I could hear crushing steel, a horrible grinding as brakes were applied, to no avail. Upended in the corridor with my skirts over my head, I was choking on acrid dust when the train came to a shuddering halt. Kicking against the crumpled mass of my skirts, I managed to get to my feet, emerging upon a scene of unbelievable destruction.

The drawing room carriage had buckled, part of the roof caved in, hanging like a jagged partition between me and where my family had been. I was so stunned, everything swam before me. Warmth trickled past my temple. I lifted my hand. My fingers came away bloody.

"Minnie," I heard Sasha groan. "Manja, where are you?"

"Here," I cried out. "I'm here, Sasha!" Sidling through the askew doorframe, snagging my dress, I found him buried up to his pelvis in debris, a section of the fallen roof hoisted on his shoulders. His face was contorted; he trembled as he held up the roof with all his might. "The children," he said. "Find them. I don't know where they are."

I called out their names. From above me, Nicky's frightened voice said, "Mama, here," and I looked up to see him peering from a gap in the intact portion of the ceiling, George, Misha, and Xenia beside him. Somehow, they'd managed to clamber out.

"Olga. Where is Olga?" Fear bolted through me. I thought I might vomit as Sasha gave a shuddering moan and the roof started sliding off him. I picked frantically through wreckage, lacerating my hands on shattered bric-a-brac, shouting Olga's name. I kept praying, over and over: Please, God, please let my baby be alive.

Then, to my relief, one of our Cossacks arrived, carrying Olga in his arms. She'd been thrown clear of the carriage; as I took her from him, she whimpered, "They will kill us all."

"No, no. Hush, my darling." I held her to me. The Cossack assisted me out of the wrecked carriage, which had rammed into those in front of it when the train derailed. Nicky and my other children leapt from the rooftop to gather around me.

It took over an hour to release Sasha. The Cossack, joined by other guards and the secret police, shoveled around him to free his trapped legs and lever a beam under the roof to lift it off his back, giving him only seconds to dodge before it came crashing down. Limping, his trousers torn, revealing black contusions on his left thigh, Sasha came to us as we huddled together. The children were traumatized, cut and bruised, but our hasty assessment revealed no serious injury. George was coughing from the dust, so I wrapped my soiled shawl around him. Sasha, however, worried me the most: His wounded leg needed tending. But as he turned to gaze into the smoke-filled drizzle ahead, for it had started to rain, he said quietly, "Look, Manja. God saved us."

Ahead, the disaster was unbearable. The locomotive, engine, and first six carriages had run off the tracks and overturned into the embankment. Had we been riding in any of the front carriages, we would have perished. From the crushed carriages, survivors were pulling out the dead and injured, laying out broken bodies in the mud under toppled poles tangled in wires.

"It'll take hours before anyone knows," said Sasha. "Those are the telegraph lines. We must make do until help arrives." He started limping toward the rescuers, summoning those he encountered wandering like aimless ghosts.

"My children," I told the Cossack. "Don't let them out of your sight." Xenia clung to Olga, who'd gone quiet, her eyes blank. As I made to join Sasha, who neared the area where the worst had occurred, Nicky seized my hand. "I'm going with you."

I held tight to him as we trod through the mud of the embankment, collecting random articles along the way—flung-out sheets and linens, pillowcases and towels. I labored to tear everything into strips for bandages, while he made a fire for warmth and to boil water, using his cigarette lighter and shattered wood from the train as kindling.

As Sasha ignored his swelling leg to search for survivors, Nicky and I tended to the wounded, together with the uninjured servants and our sole physician on board. We were drenched to our skin in the rain as we watched several victims die of grisly gashes, shattered bones, or shock. At one point, Nicky urgently summoned me to where he tried in vain to stanch a chest wound in a maidservant, who'd traveled with us from Gatchina and whose name I didn't even know.

"She can't breathe," he said in alarm. "Mama, how can I help—"

"It's too late," I whispered. Blood burbled from the girl's mouth as she went still.

Tears clouded Nicky's eyes. He traced the sign of the cross over her as I stood helpless, never prouder of him or more pained that he must witness such suffering.

It seemed like an eternity before the shrill whistle of the rescue train alerted us to its arrival. Our decoy had reached the town of Borki. Futile attempts by officials to telegraph us alerted them to the catastrophe. I was so exhausted, I could scarcely stand as emergency workers raced to assist us. Sasha waved them aside, shouting hoarsely that he was needed, until I went to him.

"Let the nurses and doctors assume charge," I said. "We've done all we can."

He regarded me in bewilderment, blackened by soot and grime, his hands riddled with wounds from scavenging in the wrecked carriages. "All of this," he whispered, "for what? To kill me? So much death to slay one man?"

I led him into the rescue train with our children. After our ruined train was pulled aside, we went on to Borki. There, on the station platform, in our soiled clothes, we held a service for the dead. Unabashed tears crested over Sasha's cinder-blackened features.

"Monsters," he said. "They will pay for this."

CHAPTER TWENTY-THREE

"More petitions." I deposited the bundle on Sasha's cluttered desk. Until today, I'd rarely intruded on his private time in his study. "You should read them."

"Why?" He leaned back in his creaking chair, which, like the rest of his study, was in dire need of replacement.

"Because they're from your subjects. Would you heed that ghoul Pobendonostev to our detriment? These new laws to eradicate the Nihilist cause—they go too far."

"How so?" His voice remained calm, but I knew I risked his temper. Since the train accident, he'd grown obdurate, granting the Okhrana further license to fill up our prisons and authorizing new censorship laws that prompted more of our intellectuals to flee abroad. I'd publicly supported his stance, for I knew he only sought to protect us, but I couldn't support it any longer.

"*All subjects of the empire must adhere to Russian customs and the Orthodox faith,*" I quoted aloud. "You're forbidding Jews from living outside the Pale of Settlement, extolling that they must assimilate, relocate, or leave. We have pogroms again outside the cities! Many are choosing exile. These are petitions from wealthy Jews in St. Petersburg, who've donated for years to my charities. What am I to tell them?"

"Perhaps that your husband makes the law." His tone took on a serrated edge. This wasn't my place. I did not interfere in how he ruled his realm.

"I don't like it," I said, surprising myself, for times before I had not interfered. "They are still our subjects. Would you have every Jew in Russia convert or go into exile?"

"If necessary. We must all do whatever is necessary to safeguard the empire."

"Honestly." I threw up my hands, making him blink. "And my charities and our court entertainments—must we sacrifice them as well to safeguard the empire?"

"I told you. Never again. They will never harm us again. If we must live here in Gatchina without galas or society, so be it. I'll not risk my family."

I paused. I couldn't blame him. The dining hall in the Winter Palace, his father's sleigh on the canal bridge, the thwarted attack in Moscow and then in St. Petersburg, and now, in his mind, even our private train—the dissidents had proven they would attack us anywhere, at any time, and nothing save their death or his vigilance could impede it.

"Sasha." I softened my voice. "I understand. I'm very concerned, as well. But the Nihilists weren't responsible for the accident. You read the official report. Our locomotive was in poor repair, going too fast for our overladen carriages."

"I don't believe the report. They were responsible."

"Even so, we cannot live like this, in constant fear. Nor can we blame all of Russia for it. You once told me, we mustn't ever run from them."

"We are not running." He grasped his walking cane, coming to his feet. He had a permanent limp from the accident and now couldn't walk without the cane—"like an old boyar," he griped. I knew he had back pain, too, for sometimes he'd pause and inhale sharply, cursing under his breath before he pressed on, because to admit weakness was anathema to him. "They are the ones running. And they will be run out of my realm or I'll execute the lot." He glared at me. "You can support your charities, hold your balls, and be the empress. When have I ever denied you that right? You want more money for your charities? You shall have it. But I'll not succor the enemies of our faith nor let any malcontent threaten us." He abruptly changed the subject, indicating he'd reached the end of his tolerance. "How is George?"

"Better," I said. Our son had suffered another severe bronchial attack and had recovered, though his health remained precarious. "But I don't think he'll be well enough to accompany Nicky on their grand tour next year. Imagine if he takes ill—"

"He'll never be well enough if you keep fussing over him. Let him be, woman." Sasha started toward the bookshelf where he stashed his vodka, almost revealing the bottle I knew he hid behind the volumes, then he veered away, no doubt because I'd put my foot down about that, too.

"I want to reassure those who've petitioned us," I said at length, as he stood brooding by his desk. "It's my duty. My charities depend on their contributions. If I do it discreetly, will you object?"

He grunted. "Do as you please. You always do."

"Thank you." I exited the study, knowing he'd retrieve that bottle the moment I left.

His immoderation distressed me, but its effect on my children was more troubling. Nicky had grown to fear him; as our tsarevich, he was expected to excel in everything he undertook, achieving the rank of lieutenant colonel in the Preobrazhensky, only for Sasha to jeer that he might do better were he not so preoccupied "writing sonnets to that Hesse girl."

Which led to more concern for me.

For the Season of 1889, Alicky returned to Russia to visit her sister. Ella was widely admired in the family, as Sergei wasn't an easy husband, with his propensity for conducting his household like a military establishment, wearing his uniform at all times, even at breakfast. But Ella, or Tante Titinka, as my children called her, never lifted a complaint. Whenever we were in the city, she welcomed my children at her palace across the Nevsky Prospekt, serving macaroons and hot chocolate, and not objecting when they trailed snow from their boots all over her Persian carpets.

"But no sign of a child yet," Miechen sniffed. "Either she's barren or . . ."

I sighed. "Not every woman conceives right away. For some, it takes time."

Miechen held her tongue about Sergei, though not about Ella's sister. "I hear Nicky visits the mouse every afternoon after his regimental duties. He even escorts her to all the balls and receptions. You must be beside yourself with disappointment."

"He'll be leaving soon on his grand tour. She will return to Hesse. She's devoted to her Lutheran faith. Nicky says her father has asked her to never convert while he lives, and Sasha forbids marriage to a non-Orthodox. I therefore have no reason to be disappointed."

"She may be a devout Lutheran for now, but she knows well what she's about. A tsarevich does not come around every day."

I laughed, even if I wasn't amused. I'd taken Sasha's advice to heart, hoping Nicky's interest in Alicky would fade. It hadn't, to my disconcertion. I couldn't understand what he saw in her and began to fear Miechen was wiser than I cared to admit. Was this German nobody intending to corral my son into a marriage proposal?

Matters being as they were, I couldn't dispatch Nicky on his tour soon enough. He'd visit several royal courts along the way, and I prayed another princess would set her sights on him. Variety was what he needed; as our heir, we'd make certain he had it. Saying goodbye to him and George tore at me, however, for our consultation of various physicians had failed to yield a satisfactory remedy. All agreed that my second son had weak lungs, but George refused to heed my pleas to stay home. Biting back my tears, I sent them off.

They'd not been gone two months when a telegram from Nicky arrived at Gatchina. George had fallen ill and was returning to us.

⁓

"IT IS CONSUMPTION, I'm afraid," Dr. Botkin informed us after examining George, who'd arrived looking so haggard, I was aghast. "In both lungs. He needs a warmer climate as soon as possible. He can't endure the winters here." He delivered this devastating news with profound sadness but also in some haste, for he must have feared Sasha's reaction.

My husband sat still, as if struck mute, leaving me to exclaim, "He's not yet twenty! How is it even possible? You yourself examined him many times, Doctor, as did your colleagues. Not once did any of you mention consumption."

Botkin nodded in discomfort. "I fear we are indeed at fault. He's very young for the disease, and his symptoms were inconsistent at first. But I am certain now. Forgive me, Your Majesties. I will resign my post as imperial physician at once."

Sasha said quietly, "You tended to my father in his extremis. How were you to know? You've diagnosed it now. I'll not accept your resignation." He didn't look at Botkin as he spoke, his stare fixed on some remote place.

"Majesty." Botkin bowed, gathering up his case of instruments. From his bedroom, I heard George coughing, and I started toward the door. "Our villa in the Crimea," I said absently, in a haze of disbelief. "I'll take him there to rest."

"The damp of the sea will not serve him," replied Botkin. "It must be higher. Drier. Consumptives fare much better in such climes. It can slow the disease for many years, Majesty."

"Higher?" I stared at him.

"He means the mountains." Sasha motioned Botkin out. He finally lifted his eyes to me. "The doctors advised my mother to do the same. She refused. It was Nice or the Crimea until—" He choked. "Our boy. Why does God test us so?"

I couldn't stay to console him. I had to tend to George. But as I dosed our son with the laudanum syrup Botkin had prescribed and stayed with him until he slept, I could hear Sasha's harsh weeping in the next room, as if his great heart might break.

⁓

WE COMMISSIONED A villa in Abbas-Touman, in the foothills of the Caucasus near the city of Kazbek, which had a hospital. George accepted his diagnosis without visible upset but insisted on staying in Russia rather than going abroad to a sanatorium. I organized his move, sending furnishings and chests with his belongings ahead, taking him by train and then by carriage over a goat path of a road to the villa, which wasn't luxurious by our standards but spacious enough, with a wide veranda overlooking the valley. I hired local staff to look after him. As I settled him in, making his bed myself and tucking a shawl about his shoulders, I said, "It's only until you are well. Botkin says this dry mountain air will restore you. As soon as you're improved, you can return to us."

He turned to me. "It doesn't help me to hear promises that won't come true."

Tears burned in my eyes. George embraced me, comforting me,

though he was the one now in exile. "I think I'm going to like it here," he said as I clung to him, my liveliest child, who'd always been so full of mischief, so like me in his temperament. "Not His Imperial Highness anymore. Only plain George Alexandrovich."

"Never." I cradled his face in my palms. "You will always be a grand duke."

I stayed with him for two weeks, but then I had to leave. My family couldn't be left on their own for too long. Xenia, Olga, and Misha had wept at their brother's departure, and Tania wrote to tell me that Sasha closeted himself for hours on end in his study, only to emerge for long walks through Gatchina Park with his dogs, his astrakhan cap jammed on his head and his face lowered, as if he couldn't bear to see any of the places where our children had played. His pain for George was like a pebble in my throat; it hurt whenever I breathed.

As I rode away in my carriage, down the mountain road to the imperial train awaiting me in Kazbek, George waved to me from the veranda. It was not forever, I told myself.

And yet it was. Even if I could not accept it.

⁓

"HER FATHER HAS died. Her brother Ernest is now Grand Duke of Hesse and by Rhine; in April, he'll marry Aunt Marie's daughter, Ducky. All of her family will attend, even the queen. I want to go. Alicky has invited me."

Nicky stood stalwart before us, even if his impression of steadfastness was marred by the way he kept darting his gaze at me.

"Stop making calf eyes at your mother," spat Sasha. "She's not going to intervene on your behalf this time. You are very well informed as to who is marrying whom and have had the gall to declare your intention to all and sundry without bothering to inform us first, so be a man now and look *me* in the eye."

Nicky lifted his chin. "I am informing you. I've done whatever you asked of me. I went on that grand tour and met many princesses—"

"I understand your cousin, the rake of Greece, met many princesses. You only got yourself hit on the head by a samurai for acting the fool."

"It wasn't a samurai." I gave Sasha an exasperated look. Nicky had been assaulted in Japan by an offended bystander, who'd taken umbrage at his and his cousin's antics, striking at them with a sword while they rode, laughing, in a rickshaw. The blow had glanced off Nicky's temple, missing his eye by a miracle. He had the scar now and occasional headaches even after it had healed. "He might have been killed."

"He wasn't." Sasha stared at our son. "And here he is, demanding to attend a royal wedding and pay suit to a girl who's made it clear she cannot convert because her conscience forbids it yet must now step aside for her new sister-in-law. And if my niece Ducky has anything of my sister in her, she'll put Alicky of Hesse in no doubt of where she belongs—which is not in Russia."

Nicky swallowed. I saw the movement in his throat above the starched white collar of the shirt he wore under a trim new charcoal-gray suit he'd acquired in Paris.

"Did you do anything I asked while you were in France, besides buying that dilettante's attire?" Sasha said. "Did you pay court to Princess Hélène as instructed?"

"Yes," said Nicky, and Sasha blared, "Liar. Her father the comte wrote to tell me that your cousin the rake of Greece courted her while you said as little as possible."

"She—she is not for me." I could see that Nicky was desperately trying to avoid looking at me again. I felt awful for him. But I was determined to not give in. If he went to Hesse to attend the wedding of Alicky's brother, with her family around her, who knew what might come of it? I wouldn't put it past Victoria to shove Alicky into his lap, if only to see her granddaughter become Empress of Russia one day.

"She is not." Sasha's tone oozed sarcasm. "Princess Hélène is pretty, well educated, but not for you. For any other, yes, as she's the daughter of the acknowledged heir to the French throne, but not you. Only this German girl of no account will do. Is that what we're to understand?"

Nicky said quietly, "Why are you so opposed to her? She only said she couldn't convert while her father lived. Her brother has no such objection. If I could present my case, Alix will heed me. She knows she must convert to be my wife."

"She needs more than to convert." Sasha gripped his cane and heaved himself up, stalking to Nicky. To our son's credit, he did not flinch when Sasha thundered, "She needs *my* consent. And she doesn't have it. By God, your brother George is ill, living in the foothills, and now I must contend with this tomfoolery of yours, when he'd make a better heir than you'll ever be. Go. Run off to Hesse to play suitor at her brother's wedding. But whatever you tell Alicky of Hesse, I do *not* consent."

"Papa." Nicky's voice quavered. "I don't understand. Why?"

"I have no time for your mewling." Sasha lumbered to the drawing room door. "I'm due in St. Petersburg. Minnie," he barked at me, "talk some sense into that thick head of his before I lose my patience and knock it into him."

Banging out, yelling for his valet, he left Nicky gazing after him in bewilderment.

"Shut the door and come sit by me," I told him.

Once he did, I collected my fortitude. I couldn't deny that I loved him best of my children. My firstborn, he had a special claim on me that was both his balm and bane, for he always sought my advice, and I encouraged it. I wanted him to depend on me, because it meant I'd always be first in his heart. Only I wasn't. Not anymore. She was. I had to hold myself in check, even as my dislike for her curdled into disgust. How could such a mouse, as Miechen called her, have conquered my son with a few visits and a handful of letters?

"Your father doesn't mean to be harsh," I began, for now that we were alone, his shoulders slumped in dejection. "He's very worried about George, and he loves you so. But you're the tsarevich. Your marriage is not only one of personal preference but a matter of state. Whomever you choose must be prepared to assume the duties of her rank."

Even at this moment, I couldn't bring myself to cite my other objections: her German birth, which I might have overlooked were it not for her utter paucity of court training and extreme timidity, which branded her as the minor princess she was. I couldn't say it because I knew how judgmental it was. How could I, his own mother, denigrate her for the very qualities she lacked, when I had not possessed many of them when I first arrived to Russia? But it was more than that. Penury and lack of training aside, her character alone disqualified her in my eyes. Nicky was shy enough. With her at his side, they'd be more like siblings than spouses. Neither of them understood yet how passion could fade, how much patience and effort were required to sustain a marriage over the years.

"Alicky will convert, Mama. She understands what is expected of her."

"Does she?" I tightened my hands in my lap, though I wanted to take his and somehow magically remove her taint from his heart. "Her upbringing has hardly been exemplary. She knows nothing of life here. To be the tsarevna might seem a dream come true, but believe me, it is not. I know. I once held the title myself."

"But when Papa married you, you were not rich or prepared. You've told us stories about how you and Aunt Alix made your own clothes and didn't have governesses because your father couldn't afford them. Why is she any different?"

I paused. He'd caught me by surprise, turning my own words against me.

"Our Church forbids marriage between a brother and his brother's widow, but Papa still wed you," Nicky went on. "You knew nothing of life here, but you learned. Alicky will, too. You can help her. You're my mother. I've told her you'll be a mother to her, as well."

"Nixa and I never married," I reminded him. Then, as he continued to regard me in confusion, I said gently, "I only want you to think very carefully about this. Like her, you have no experience, and we . . . we're not sure she's the right bride for you."

"For me?" he said. "Or for you?"

I drew back. He'd seen through me. Just as he could rarely hide anything from me, I couldn't hide much from him.

"Is it her?" His voice took on an edge, an anger he'd held within that now rose to the surface. "Because you don't care for her? Because she's not witty and charming or fashionable? Because she's not Ella or Miechen? Is that why?"

"Surely not. She may not be Ella, but one Miechen in our family is quite enough."

"Then why?" He reached for my hand. "Mama, I'm almost twenty-four. If I must take a wife, as you say, for myself and Russia, why shouldn't she be the woman I love? She is German, and I know that displeases you, but we've wed German brides for centuries. She'll become like you in time—a Russian. She's not what you think. You do not know her at all."

"No," I admitted. "I do not."

"Xenia will wed the man she loves," he said, lifting his voice to stave off my protest. "You can say she's too young for only so long, but you want her to marry Sandro. She'll stay here, not go abroad to wed a prince who'll make her unhappy. Don't I deserve the same?"

I couldn't speak. I gazed at his handsome face, his pleading eyes, and he was my little boy again, seeking reassurance that I'd never deny him. I found myself once more trapped between my desire to soothe him and my unfathomable mistrust of her. I couldn't understand it, why I wasn't delighted he'd found this girl to love, who surely must love him in return, as he wasn't one to give his heart away on a whim. I couldn't decipher my own objections. It was like a dark pit in my soul. All I knew but couldn't say was that while they might love each other now, love was never enough in a royal marriage. In the end, love was often the least of it.

"Yes," I finally said. "Of course you deserve the same." Before I could add that it didn't necessarily mean she would make him happy, Nicky released my hand and stood.

"Then if you think that, you must convince Papa. I will escort Ella to her brother's wedding and do my utmost to fulfill my duty as our representative. But it would cause me great shame should Papa refuse to honor my word when I propose to Alicky."

He had misinterpreted my words as approval, and I said hastily, as he went to the door, "You forget one thing. Victoria has never cared for Russia. You require your father's consent. Alicky needs her grandmother's."

"We know," he said, his next words sundering me. "I wrote to Aunt Alix. She agreed to intervene on our behalf. Victoria is very fond of Alicky, who has let our desire be known to her. The queen hasn't said yes, but she will after I propose."

He left me on my chair. Victoria had been told. He had written to my sister, even as she mourned the recent loss of her eldest son, Albert Victor, who shortly after his twenty-eighth birthday had died in the influenza epidemic sweeping Europe—an inconsolable tragedy for her.

I felt as if my right to oversee my son's fate had just been torn out from under me.

CHAPTER TWENTY-FOUR

Alix and I walked in the gardens of Peterhof, under parasols held by our attendants as the fountains cooled the stagnant air.

Xenia and Sandro had departed on their honeymoon, after having won their battle to marry. It hadn't gone easy on me. I'd balked at first, but Xenia was now nineteen, the same age as I'd been when I wed Sasha, and she staged such a scene, threatening to elope—a silly declaration, which only a silly girl in love would make, for she knew I could bar her passage out the front door—that I finally had to submit.

The palace had emptied of the wedding guests, save for immediate family. Bertie was with my husband, looking over his gun collection or stag heads or whatever they did together. My sister must have taken note of my mood, for now that we found ourselves alone, she ventured, "Sasha doesn't look well. Has he been ill?"

"His back pains him," I said. "He works constantly and worries about George."

"Is that all? Has he seen a physician?"

I came to a halt. "Do you think I neglect him? Should I let you assume charge of his care, as you've already done with my son?" As her expression faltered, I added, "Or did you not lend your approval of his proposal to Alexandra—even after she again expressed reservations about converting, this time citing Victoria's misgivings?"

"Yes, but then Victoria wanted to decide for herself when she invited Nicky to spend time in England with her and Alicky. That had nothing to do with me."

"To decide whether her granddaughter should accept," I retorted, "as if she were entertaining the proposal of a minor princeling, not the tsarevich. I'd held out hope that once Victoria came down against it, Nicky would have no recourse. I'd rather she be the one to refuse him. Instead, he came home in a Homburg hat and Scottish tweed suit to inform us that Victoria approves and we may send a chaplain to instruct Alexandra, as she's agreed to convert when the time comes—as if *our* consent is no longer of any account."

Alix glanced at our ladies, who collapsed the parasols and retreated to a distance. "Minnie," she said. "This isn't fair."

"Oh?" I wanted a cigarette. I wanted to scandalize her by lighting up in the middle of the gardens and blowing smoke in her face. "And how is it fair to connive on his behalf? I would never do that to you. I've never interfered with how you manage your family."

She sighed. "Surely you must realize Nicky never told me he lacked your consent. It was very wrong of him to imply otherwise. Had I known you didn't approve, I wouldn't have agreed to speak to the queen on his behalf."

"How could you have known when you never asked me?" Yanking out my cigarette case, before Alix's horror-struck stare, I lit one. "But now Victoria has given her consent and Nicky will have no other, so what I think is irrelevant. My George is ill. I've lost Xenia; now I'll lose Nicky, too. It's a mother's lot. We raise them; they grow up and leave us."

"Minnie, I honestly had no idea." Alix touched my arm. "You must forgive me. I know how desperately worried you are for George. I know that pain all too well. When my Eddy fell ill and died, I wanted to die, too. At least George is still with you. He is young. Strong. Providing he takes proper care, he can live for many more years with his malady."

Guilt overcame me. She'd never broken down with me over her son, whom she'd called Eddy. I had sent her many letters after his death, and her replies had always been steeped in resignation. But the loss had left its mark; she was less beautiful now, the grief obscuring her, a permanent loss from which she would never fully recover.

"Xenia and Sandro are so in love," she went on. "Like them, so are Nicky and Alicky. I saw them together in England; everyone remarked on how perfect they are for each other—even Victoria, and she's no more satisfied with their betrothal than you are."

"They're not betrothed until Sasha says so." I withdrew my arm from her, smoking as I stared toward the tumbling waters of the Grand Cascade, a gaudy fountain spraying plumes of water about a grotto with gilded lions and muscular statues.

Alix ventured, "What is it? What aren't you telling me?"

Clearing my throat, I dropped my cigarette and ground it into the path with the tip of my shoe. "You've a nerve to ask. And you know what I'm not telling you." I turned to her. "Victoria knows. The girl is unsuitable. She lacks the stamina to be tsarevna."

Alix regarded me in confusion. "Whatever makes you say that? She has occasional pain in her legs: a form of lumbago, the physicians say, from a childhood accident. She was playing in the garden at Hesse and fell into a pane of glass covering plants against frost. I saw her scars myself when we took the waters at Bath. But she's otherwise hale enough."

I knew my feelings were irrational, springing from an inexplicable core of resentment that I couldn't explain, but I tried anyway. "I mean, she speaks French with a terrible accent, is so timid she can barely speak at all in public, and she has no presence. How will she withstand the rigors of life here as the tsarevich's wife? I know too well how challenging it can be, how much one must set aside one's personal preferences to satisfy others. I rather doubt Alicky of Hesse's upbringing has prepared her in the slightest for what is required."

"Minnie, neither did yours. She will learn like you, in time," said Alix, and before I could erupt at yet another unwelcome comparison between her and me, my sister added, "Our children grow up, as you say. They must. But they don't leave us. They only leave when we make it impossible for them to stay. You cannot stand in the way of your son's happiness, no matter how well-intentioned your motives may be. It will only make him resent you. Is that what you want?"

"No." All of a sudden, I felt like a shrew. "I want him to have a loving wife, a family of his own. Just not with her. There is something about her. . . ." I avoided my sister's gaze. "You must think me unreasonable, but I know in my heart she's not right for him."

"He doesn't agree." My sister softened her voice. "Minnie, it's your nerves. You're so affected by George's illness and now Xenia's marriage, everything seems insurmountable. But Nicky knows his heart. They love each other and want to marry. Is that so terrible?"

"I don't know," I muttered. "It shouldn't be."

She hooked her arm in mine once more. "It isn't. You know that a marriage with love is a rare gift. Now, come. Let's go see what our husbands are getting up to, before they drain the cognac to its dregs. You mustn't fret so much. My impression of Nicky is that he doesn't lack for judgment. He took great care to impress Victoria." She nudged my ribs. "I needn't remind you what a grueling feat that can be."

I found myself begrudgingly smiling as she held me close and we returned to the palace, where Sasha and Bertie were indeed drinking cognac and spinning tall tales of hunting excursions.

For a time, I didn't think about it anymore. I put it out of my mind. Life was easier when I could pretend Alicky of Hesse did not exist.

⌒

"MY BOOTS DON'T fit." Sasha stood on the threshold of my sitting room at Gatchina in his stocking-clad feet, staring at me as if I were to blame.

After Alix and Bertie left, we'd taken a monthlong excursion to Finland on the *Polar Star,* our imperial yacht, bringing Olga, Misha, and George along. Our son barely coughed the entire time, although out of an abundance of caution, I wouldn't let him swim in the sea. Cheered by George's recovery, Sasha ate with his habitual gusto, taught Olga how to bait her rod with worms—she grimaced but speared them with the hook all the same—and showed Misha how to spot schools of pike and perch under the cool Finnish waters.

But he'd reverted to his moodiness once he had to bid our son goodbye, and I accompanied George back to Abbas-Touman, where he collapsed, his cough returning. For the first time, he stained his handkerchief with blood. I'd tarried in his villa for three weeks, so concerned that I wouldn't leave his side.

Now, with a frustrated sigh, I picked up my pen to resume the letter that Sasha had interrupted. "You must have gotten them wet. The leather has shrunk. You have dozens of boots. Must it be the same pair every day until the very soles fall off?"

"None of them fit."

I glanced up at him. Holding on to the doorframe, he thrust out one of his feet. "See?"

I peered. "What? I see the same big—" and he tore down his stocking. For a moment, I couldn't breathe. His toes were distended, the skin tinged with a sickly yellow hue. I went to him as he set his foot down and winced. "It hurts."

"It does? We must summon Botkin at once—"

"No." Though he'd not accepted the physician's resignation, he wanted nothing more to do with him since George's diagnosis. "I won't have him poking at me. It's probably gout."

"Sit down." I guided him to my settee. As he gingerly lowered himself, I asked, "Does your back still hurt?"

He nodded. "Since before Xenia's marriage."

"Why didn't you say so? Xenia wed over two months past!"

"I'm saying so now." He scowled. "Stop fussing. It's gout. I eat too much."

"That you do." But I told Obolensky to summon our physician. Sasha was furious as we herded him into his bedroom and Botkin closed the door behind them.

I went back to my sitting room to smoke and pace. When Botkin came through the door, I took one look at his grave expression and my heart plummeted in my chest.

"It's not gout. I believe his kidneys are severely inflamed. I've taken a urine sample for analysis. Majesty, he's lost a considerable amount of weight since I last examined him and he mentioned he has trouble with his breath. He told me he can barely walk for thirty minutes without becoming winded, when he's been accustomed to walking in the park here for three hours every day." His voice carried faint accusation. "Why wasn't I consulted earlier?"

"He never told me. He never complained of it. We went to Finland. He was fine. He fished every day. . . ." I dropped onto the settee, overcome by remorse. "I didn't notice any weight loss. I've been so preoccupied with our daughter's marriage and George . . ."

"I understand," said Botkin. "On a man of his build, weight loss can pass unnoticed. Nevertheless, I must insist he undertake a complete rest. Kidney trouble is dire. I know of an expert in such ailments, Dr. Leyden. I suggest we summon him from Berlin—"

"Berlin?" My laugh was tremulous. "Sasha won't allow it. A German. Heaven forbid."

"Your Majesty, this isn't a matter contingent on nationality. The tsar is very ill."

I heard his words. I heard them and knew Botkin wasn't prone to alarmist declarations, not after George, and particularly not where the emperor's health was concerned. But I couldn't absorb it. A bolt locked inside me, shuttering my reason, my better sense. "If I take him to Livadia, will that help?" I said.

"For the time being, providing he can rest. But no amount of sea air can cure him. He must be examined by an expert and prescribed a proper course of treatment. It is imperative. He's only forty-nine. If he follows medical advice, he can survive this."

"I will speak to him." Gripping the side of the settee, I made myself stand. "Not a word to him until I do. He mustn't be told beforehand or your Dr. Leyden will never set foot in Russia. I know my husband. He'll not submit, if he has the means to prevent it."

"Can I at least telegram his office to inform Leyden of the situation?"

"Yes," I said. "Be discreet. I don't want anyone else to know."

Botkin bowed. "You have my word, Majesty."

⁓

Sasha mounted so much resistance, I thought I'd never get him out of Gatchina.

"It's nothing," he roared, but he was in such pain, his bravado was muted. "It's gout or a kidney stone. Have you forgotten this winter is Xenia's first Season as Sandro's wife? We have responsibilities. We can't go off on holiday to the Crimea in mid-October."

"It's not a holiday," I said, buttoning up his greatcoat. It hung on him. Everything he owned now hung on him, when only six months ago he'd been bursting his clothes at the seams. "It's a rest. I've canceled our engagements. Xenia understands. We must heed Botkin's advice."

"That fool didn't know George was ill. Why should we heed him now?"

"For me." I set my hands on his chest. "Please. Do this for me. I could not bear it if—" My voice cracked. "You must do this."

"Manja. Are you crying?" He lifted my face to his. "Such a goose. You're overwrought over nothing." But he kept his palm under my chin as he kissed me softly, as he had at the start of our marriage, when he was uncertain of my love. "I've no intention of leaving you."

⁓

IT WAS STILL balmy in the Crimea, but winter neared and the imperial villa was made of wood and stone, with a jutting tile rooftop, and it could become damp when storms blew off the Black Sea. I was still in doubt as to what to do. I'd sent a telegram to my brother in Greece, requesting use of his royal villa in Corfu for the winter. He'd replied it was at our disposal. But even on our imperial yacht, the trip would be daunting for Sasha in his condition. I decided that some time in Livadia first could restore some of his strength.

Once he was settled in a room with a view of the sea, we were soon surrounded by family. It was impossible to keep Sasha's illness a secret. Word seeped out, and his brothers and their families arrived to take every empty room. Only Miechen stayed away, sending word with Vladimir that she was praying for Sasha. Xenia and Sandro cut short their honeymoon to join us with Nicky. We'd left Olga and Misha in Gatchina, but Sasha asked for them so frequently, I had to summon them. Not George, however. He was too ill and the climate too volatile. I wouldn't allow it.

And so a small but no less aggravating court revolved around us, with Sasha's decline so precipitous that his ministers could barely contain their dismay, even as he continued to harass them: He reviewed his cabinet reports daily, sitting in a great armchair with a shawl draped about his diminished frame and a scowl etched on his forehead.

Nicky hoped to marry in November, as was traditional for a tsarevich's union. I forestalled him. "Please don't bring it up with your father. Can't you see how unwell he is? The last thing he needs is more worries. Wait. Let him recover and then we can decide."

Because of his concern for Sasha, Nicky didn't persist, but I knew his plan wasn't going to pass, as I'd hoped. Despite the fact that Sasha had not granted his official consent, my son now considered himself betrothed to Alicky of Hesse.

I couldn't argue with him. I fluttered through Livadia with a cheerful demeanor and chided Xenia when I caught her crying on Sandro's shoulder. "None of that. What in heaven is wrong with you? Your father will recover. A Russian bear is not easily felled."

But at night, abandoning my daybed at his side to hold him as he murmured that it hurt, I could see he was fading. He barely ate, dribbling bilious saliva, and when he asked me for one of his cigars, as soon as I lit it and set it to his lips, he coughed and spat it out. "I can't even smoke," he groaned. "What a miserable way to end one's days."

His words plunged me into panic. I dispatched our imperial train to fetch Botkin's German expert. A fastidious man with an old-fashioned pince-nez that reminded me of Pobendonostev, Leyden endured Sasha's weak flailing and insults as he examined him. Sasha's cries as he was obliged to pass water into a cup resounded throughout Livadia.

After analyzing the sample under a microscopic instrument, Leyden came to me. "He suffers from albuminuria," he said, as if I had any idea what the ailment was.

I regarded him in silence.

The doctor continued in his perfunctory voice. "An incurable degradation of the kidneys. I regret to say, Majesty, there is no effective treatment. The tsar is dying."

Botkin led him out, back to his carriage and the train station, for I did not want him in the villa. Then I tried to collect my disintegrating composure and went to Sasha's room.

He sat on his chair, his swollen feet propped on a stool.

"Don't say it," he whispered as I clasped his hand. "Be calm. I am calm."

❧

THERE WAS NO way to hide it. Word spread fast in times of crisis, and the grand dukes were becoming agitated. Detaining me in the corridor one morning after I'd spent a terrible night tending to Sasha, Vladimir declared, "We must issue a public bulletin. Everyone is talking about my brother's imminent demise."

"Let them," I retorted, but as I made to push past him, he did something he'd never have previously dared—he grasped me by my arm. As I whirled to him, he said, "Nicky is not prepared. He told Sandro he doesn't know how to rule and never wanted to be emperor. But he knows what he *does* want. He summoned her by telegram. His bride is on her way as we speak."

I shook him away and prowled the villa, eventually locating Nicky in the colonnaded gallery with Xenia. When he caught sight of me, he froze, his cigarette at his mouth.

"How *could* you?" I said. "Is it true? Did you call for her?"

Xenia said haltingly, "Mama, he needs—" but I glared at her before I rounded back on Nicky. "Did you? Tell me this instant."

He whispered, "I asked Papa first. He gave his consent."

"When?"

"Yesterday afternoon, when he called for me." Tears sprang to his eyes, but I had no mercy or pity. I'd exhausted my reserves of both. "Mama, please don't be angry. I asked him, and he said yes because no tsar should be crowned without a wife."

"Ingrate." I was trembling. For the first time, I wanted to strike him. "He's not dead yet. And while he lives, he is still the tsar and he has a wife. Me. Your mother."

Nicky lowered his gaze. Xenia implored, "Mama, you mustn't say such things to him. He's disconsolate. We all are. He wants her with him. He thinks they should be married before Papa—before he . . ." She faltered, unable to utter the dreaded words.

"Not here," I said. "There will be no wedding here."

I marched back into the villa, storming through the dining room and startling the grand dukes, who partook of breakfast in their casual attire, as if their tsar were not dying just down the corridor. Barging into Sasha's room, I found him upright on his chair, old Ivan having managed to haul him out of bed to wash and change him.

"Did you tell Nicky he could call for her?" I asked.

Sasha let out a chuckle through his parched lips. "Vladimir wasted no time, I see." He beckoned me. All of a sudden, I fell apart. I stood there, his hand extended between us, and I wept with such gut-wrenching sorrow that I felt my knees weaken underneath me.

"No, Manja, not you. I can endure it from anyone but you," he said, and I made myself step to him, falling before his chair to set my head on his lap. He stroked me as he murmured, "Send for your sister. You need her now. Alix always gives you strength."

Alix returned word that she and Bertie would come as soon as they could and I prayed they'd reach us before Alicky did.

But God was no longer answering my prayers.

～

SHE ARRIVED CLAD in a somber gray cloak buttoned up to her chin, with mounds of luggage and three ladies-in-waiting. The villa was filled to capacity, but I had to find room. After she was brought to the bedchamber I'd prepared for her, having evicted Vladimir and sent him to the adjacent villa, Alicky said, "I am sorry to be an inconvenience."

My smile felt taut. "Nonsense, my dear. I understand we're soon to be family."

"I thought we already were." She regarded me through those cool violet eyes, which were so lovely yet also opaque, reflecting nothing of whatever she felt. "My sister Ella is Grand Duchess Sergei, Nicky's aunt-in-law."

"Yes, of course. But now you'll be family in a way we did not expect." I walked out on her, my patience tested beyond any ability to remain polite.

In the afternoon, alerted to her arrival, Sasha called for her and Nicky. His feverish gaze turned bright as they knelt before him and he made the sign of the cross over them.

"Leave me alone with my new daughter," he said, and though I was alarmed, I had no choice but to oblige. They stayed closeted together for over an hour. When she emerged, I could see moisture on her pale cheeks from her tears. Nicky took her by the hand and led her away. I never asked Sasha what he said to her, but Nicky later told me.

"He said he had an angel for his wife, and he prayed she would be the same for me."

It was done. Sasha had given them his blessing.

～

THE FIRST OF November dawned with an overcast sky and a blustering wind that made the casements rattle. Sasha was groaning. When I went to help him upright—for he could no longer recline in bed, because of the pain, and had slumped in his chair during the night—he coughed up clots of blood.

I did not leave his side. I did not eat or drink, change my clothes, or tidy my hair. I held his hand as he drifted in and out of consciousness, and the family slipped into the room with the priests, who began to chant the prayer for the dying. The children kissed him, one by one: Nicky, holding fast to Alicky, then Xenia with Sandro, followed by Olga, who was distraught, and quiet Misha, who tried to comfort Olga as she wept.

He did not seem to know they were there, but when a clock somewhere in the villa struck three, he revived. "The windows," I heard him whisper. "Open them."

Holding up my hand to detain Dr. Botkin's protest, I told Ivan to do it. The distant rumble of the sea flinging itself against the cliff and the smell of salt washed into the room, plunging me back in time to another villa on another coast, where death had awaited me.

Then Sasha said, "Minnie. My poor Minnie," and I jolted back to the present, putting my arms around him. "I am here," I whispered. "I am always here, my beloved."

His head slipped onto my shoulder. "It is not forever," he said.

Without another sound, my husband left me.

PART IV

1894–1906

Mother Dear

*Better the illusions that exalt us than
ten thousand truths.*

—Pushkin

CHAPTER TWENTY-FIVE

Black crepe caked with snow draped every lamppost, carriage, and store awning. The Neva froze solid, but the people didn't build ice hills or take to their skates. Beset by sorrow, Russia came to a halt to mourn its *Moujik* Tsar.

At the Anichkov, I secluded myself with my younger children and Nicky. As he and Alicky weren't married, she had to reside with Sergei and Ella in their palace across the street. She'd been present, however, when the Oath of Allegiance was sworn to Nicky and he was proclaimed Tsar Nicholas II. Bewildered and overcome by grief, my son had no capacity to react. It was my brother-in-law Bertie, arriving too late with Alix to say goodbye, who, with tears in his eyes, marshaled the grand dukes to oversee the funeral procession to the imperial ship and the regimental escort for Sasha's final journey home.

Alix stayed with me. She gave me Sasha's final gift, an enamel-and-ruby bracelet for our twenty-eighth anniversary, which fell a week after his death; the bracelet had been entrusted to her by a letter he'd left Bertie. I wept to see it in its Fabergé box, and I railed, blaming myself for not realizing how ill he'd been and regretting the times I doubted my love for him. My sister spoon-fed me broth, had my bath drawn, and washed me herself. She dressed me in the black weeds of my widowhood and undressed me in the evening when we returned from the daily masses and ritual kisses on his cold forehead in the Winter Palace chapel. She gathered me in her arms when I begged to die, keening that I couldn't live without him.

Only then did she say, "You have your family to live for. Your children need you. Nicky must wed and be crowned, and you must advise him. It is the way of the world, no matter how savage or unjust it may seem."

She lent me strength, as Sasha had said she would, though I didn't feel it at the time.

After the final service, with the chants still in my ears and incense permeating my skin, we witnessed his entombment in the fortress cathedral. I couldn't bear to watch his casket, draped in the imperial mantle, lowered into the vault, the marble sarcophagus then set in place to cover the last trace of him.

I couldn't believe he was gone.

Nothing in our homes could be changed. I kept his study as he'd left it, his old boots in the closet, his sun-faded hats on their pegs, his chipped walking sticks stacked wherever he'd happened to deposit them. His beloved hunting dog, Sparta, trailed me everywhere, whining when the hour for their walk came and Sasha failed to appear. Like me, everything seemed suspended in time, waiting for him to arrive, to stomp his boots to shed the snow and grumble that his cabinet was comprised of idiots and cowards.

I heard him sometimes, too. I'd be smoking in my sitting room, not bothering to crack a window, and through the drifting pall I'd hear him say, "Manja. You smoke too much." I'd bolt to my feet, stumbling over my black skirts to throw open the door, only to find Tania or Sophie in the corridor, my constant guardians, worried I wasn't eating as much as I should or I might set the house or myself on fire with my incessant cigarettes.

Eventually, numbness set in. It was better than the talons of grief. I could at least exist if I felt nothing. Alix and Bertie stayed with me, and all the dignitaries and members of royal houses who'd come to Russia to pay their respects also lingered, despite the onset of winter. I knew why they stayed. My parents, both aged now, hadn't attended the funeral, at my insistence, as Papa's arthritis was too debilitating to withstand travel. But they replied that they hoped to attend Nicky's wedding—which drove an invisible knife into me, reminding me why everyone tarried. Although I detested the pitying looks and sympathetic whispers behind my back—*poor Minnie*—what lay ahead felt worse.

To keep busy, I sat down with Olga to compose thank-you cards to the avalanche of condolences I'd received. Olga had loved her father more than she did anyone else in our family except Misha, but she was only twelve and had spent herself on such paroxysms of tears that she eventually cried her eyes dry.

She now frowned as I instructed her what to write on my embossed stationery. "Must we? So many cards. Who are all these people?"

"People kind enough to write to us. And, yes, we must. It's the polite thing to do."

"They wrote to you." She squared her jaw in that way she had, which now pierced me with its uncanny resemblance to Sasha. "They don't care about me."

"They most certainly do. They care about all of us." I heard exasperation in my voice; she never ceased to try me, and for once I welcomed it as a small sign that life might resume. "Now, write. I'll sign each card after you finish."

When we finished, she had ink smears on her hands, her dress, and the tip of her pert nose. I smiled, wetting my finger to wipe it off—an unexpected maternal gesture that made her squirm. Then she said abruptly, "When is Nicky going to marry?"

"Certainly not before our period of mourning is over. Why do you ask?"

"No reason," she said, too quickly. I knew she'd accompanied Nicky on his daily visits to the Serge Palace, as Ella and Sergei's residence was known, so I held her gaze until she added, "Alicky says he's the tsar now and she doesn't think it proper they're still unwed."

"Does she think it more proper to wed after his father has just been laid in his tomb?" I retorted, and Olga, who wasn't afraid of my occasional outbursts, replied, "I'm just telling you what I heard. You did ask."

I wished I hadn't. "Go wash your face and hands."

As she scampered out, I sat at my desk with the piles of cards and envelopes to seal before me. Anguish thick as a storm cloud fell over me.

My son must marry her. And I'd have to feign my joy.

⁓

THE WEDDING TOOK place on November 26, the day of my forty-seventh birthday. In Russia, a birthday wasn't celebrated; instead, we celebrated Name Days, based on the name of one's saint, so no one thought it amiss. I didn't, either. I thought the entire situation amiss, so whichever day it happened to fall upon was irrelevant. His uncles the grand dukes and his ministers had pressed upon Nicky the vital importance of marrying soon, and he capitulated. Or that's what he told me when he came to ask my permission. I nodded and agreed, telling myself that no matter what I felt about his bride, he had made his decision and I must accept it. Perhaps I was being too overprotective as his mother. Perhaps in time she would prove herself fully capable of assuming my rank and duties.

I put on the same compliant face as I accompanied Alicky to the Winter Palace for her ceremonial bridal robing. I could see how anxious she was. She looked beautiful but so pale, her profile like an ivory icon as she confided, without prompting from me, that she wasn't sleeping well.

"The change in climate," I said. "The long nights. It takes time to grow accustomed."

"I suppose that must be it." She sighed, looking out the carriage window toward the palace. "But I also know how terribly difficult this must be for you, so soon after . . ." She shifted her gaze to me. "I wish with all my heart that it were not so. I love Nicky so much, but I never expected any of this. I feel terrible for you, Mother dear."

It was her first endearment to me, the first time she'd revealed an emotion. It touched me, revealing her vulnerability and reminding me of how disconcerting my own marriage to Sasha had been, how strange and demanding the etiquette, the endless duties and people I had to please. Only I'd been tsarevna first, with years to learn what was required of me before I was crowned. She had no time. About to be flung into an existence she was completely unprepared for, she was being honest with me in this moment. She had indeed never desired any of this.

I reached across the seat to take her hand in mine. I held it lightly yet could feel how cold her fingers were through her gloves. "You need fur."

She gave me a blank look.

"In your gloves," I explained. "Fine leather is lovely for the spring, but your hands will freeze in January without any fur. Frostbite can be very painful."

She almost smiled. "I must seem so inexperienced to you."

I squeezed her hand. "We all are, at your age."

We did not speak more, but as we entered the palace she kept hold of my hand, like a child who feared she might get lost.

THE WEDDING WASN'T lavish. Under the circumstances, it couldn't be. Yet she wore the silver tissue gown, the side locks and crushing mantle, and the bridal diadem on her head. She moved with grace as she mounted the dais in the chapel. After their vows, she and Nicky turned to me and I kissed them, tears spilling down my cheeks.

Nicky whispered, "Mama, please don't cry," not because he was embarrassed but because he could see my sorrow overwhelming me, the memories of my own wedding day crowding around me in that chapel, thrusting home the realization that I'd never be a wife or an empress again.

Alexandra Feodorovna, her adopted Orthodox name, was the wife and tsarina now.

As they proceeded out to the clarion of trumpets, I followed with Alix, Bertie, and my other children behind me. I had to surrender. What had once been mine was hers. She had my rank and my son. God willing, she'd bear my grandchildren. I must resign myself. Though as dowager empress I would hold precedence by court tradition, she was now the first lady of the empire. I must not interfere. I must sacrifice my pride for Russia.

But promising to forsake my past and actually doing it was not so simple.

⁓

OUR GUESTS DEPARTED before they were buried in snow. Alix made me promise to be patient with Alexandra. "Remember, she's still new to Russia. You must be a mother to her."

I hated to say goodbye, but she and Bertie had tarried too long, enduring Victoria's irate requests for their return. The queen had sent me a letter of condolence and a book of Tennyson's poems; she considered herself an expert in mourning, and her words and gift were heart-felt, reaching out to me as a fellow widow, so I wrote back to her in gratitude.

Because the Winter Palace had stood unoccupied for years, the state apartments required updating. The cabinet issued its demand that Nicky reside there for the sake of continuity; while the refurbishments took place, Nicky and Alexandra moved into my palace, after their five-day honeymoon at Tsarskoe Selo. They inhabited the suite of four small rooms below mine that had been his bachelor apartments.

Xenia and Sandro also moved in with me. Except for George, I had all my children back under my roof, and the loving familiarity subdued my ghosts. Nicky came to breakfast with me every morning in my din-ing room; afterward, we went into my study, where I began to impart everything I'd learned. His coronation date wasn't set; in the meantime, he needed to grasp the complexities he now faced as tsar.

"A constitution," I advised. "Your grandfather told me it was the only way to safeguard Russia and our dynasty, bringing us into the modern age. You must do it for our people. It is time for us to set aside the autocracy and allow a Duma to guide the state."

"Papa never wanted that," he said. He had lost weight, the strain of the past months showing in his angular face. "Autocracy, nationality, and orthodoxy. That was Papa's motto. My uncles tell me I must abide by it."

"Our situation was different," I replied, realizing as I spoke that while I'd always upheld Sasha, now that he was gone I'd reverted to my previous trust in my late father-in-law's policies. I had experienced enough tumult to recognize that, prepared or not, we could not go on as we were. Reform was necessary for Russia, for much as I loved my son, he was not his father. He lacked Sasha's force of will; he'd never had it, save for his desire to wed Alexandra. "You cannot rule as your father did. We saw your grandfather murdered. Sasha acted as he did to rid us of the Nihilists and crush their movement. They're no longer a threat, and yours is a new regime. You must move forward with your grandfa-ther's plan to allow the right to assembly. Your uncles may not agree, but if you do not put a rein on them now, they will run roughshod over you."

"I will consider it," he promised.

He didn't say another word about it. One morning, he failed to appear for breakfast. I waited and waited. Pregnant with her first child and suffering from morning sickness, Xenia watched me warily from across the table as I tapped my plate with my fork, until the meal ended and Nicky hadn't sent up a note to explain his absence.

"Where can he be?" I pushed back my chair.

"Mama," said Xenia. "Perhaps he and Alicky need some private time—"

"Private time?" I regarded her in astonishment. "It's eight-thirty in the morning. We have the cabinet reports to review, letters to write, and then he must go to the Winter Palace to check on their apartments. When one is emperor, there is no private time."

I went downstairs. The door was ajar; their suite wasn't spacious, and Nicky had set up his study in the front room, so he could receive his ministers without leading them into the rest of the apartments. He and Alexandra were in his study now. I heard their voices, lifted in dissent. Even as I knew I shouldn't eavesdrop, I paused behind the door.

"I must go," Nicky was saying. "I missed breakfast. Mama will be worried."

"Let her wait," said Alexandra. "She has you at her beck and call every minute of every day. She goes over your reports and correspondence; she must state her opinion on everything. She didn't allow us to move into the Winter Palace, though these rooms are impossibly small. And we could only stay at Tsarskoe Selo for five days because she wanted us back, although it's far more comfortable there."

"Sunny," he said. It was his nickname for her, though I found nothing sunny about her now. "She's in mourning for my father. She needs us with her."

"She needs *you* with her. She needs you to do as she says, when she says. If I want to receive anyone, I must ask permission to use her drawing room. Her servants are everywhere, prying into our affairs. We need privacy, a home of our own so we can start our family."

Frozen behind the door, I now heard what I believed was the true character of this supposedly reluctant and timid young woman. It welded me to my spot. I had been right all along; moreover, Miechen had been right. Alexandra knew exactly what she was about. Had Nicky known all along that she was as demanding, as *imperious,* as she now sounded?

My son's weary sigh seemed to confirm he did, indicating they'd had this argument before. "Our apartments at the Winter Palace aren't yet ready. Mama only wants what is best for us. I don't know how to rule and—"

"She will rule for you. She'll be dowager empress, tsarina, and tsar, if you let her."

He remained silent as she added, "Did she not tell you to authorize a Duma, though it undermines everything you represent? And at the farewell banquet for Alix and Bertie, did she not put her hand on your arm and proceed first into the hall? She left me to follow behind like a servant—"

"That is the rule here," he cut in. "You know she holds precedence as dowager empress."

"She doesn't need to abide by the rule! I am the empress now. If she truly wants what is best for us, as you say, then she must realize that by not allowing me to enter first with you, my husband, the tsar, she sets an example. I will *not* be ignored."

I'd heard enough. Pushing the door open, I walked in. Nicky swiveled around, his face draining of color. I had to admire Alexandra's composure, for she didn't betray a hint of surprise. She looked as if she'd known all along I'd been lurking behind the door.

My gaze passed over them to her German ladies, seated in the foreground. It was time to send them away and appoint Russian women to attend her, so she could learn that it was not only unwise to criticize me with servants nearby but also in very poor taste.

I sweetened my voice. "You didn't come up to breakfast, Nicky, and we have those cabinet reports to address. Did they arrive?"

He bolted to his cluttered desk, searching for the folder.

Alexandra met my stare with icy calm. "You must forgive us, Mother dear. I was feeling ill. I asked Nicky to stay and have breakfast with me this morning."

Indeed, upon the table was the tray with their crumb-filled dishes and teacups. She must have instructed my staff to serve it here. I'd have a word with Obolensky, who'd stayed on after Sasha's death to oversee my household. I gave the orders in my palace.

"You are always welcome at my table," I told her. "I trust you're feeling better. Would it be premature to hope your malaise might be the first sign of a joyous event?"

Her mouth thinned. Though she'd never concede it, she knew I'd overheard their conversation and aimed my remark at her with deliberate malice.

"After a mere month of marriage?" she demurred. "We can indeed hope. And, yes, I feel much better. Thank you." She retrieved her embroidery hoop, threading her needle as Nicky brandished the folder.

"I found it," he quavered.

"Very good. When you are ready, come upstairs so we can talk." Casting another smile at Alexandra—"I hope you continue to improve, my dear—" I swept out.

No doubt she had more to say to him, but I didn't care to hear it.

CHAPTER TWENTY-SIX

"She's unfathomable." I lit a cigarette in Miechen's drawing room. "The paint in their new apartments in the Winter Palace was scarcely dry before she had them leave my house. Yet now she sits in those refurbished rooms and refuses to host a single gala. She won't do any social rounds, either, so I'm told the Season—her first here—was a disaster."

Spring was upon us. The forty days of mourning mandated by our Orthodox Church had passed, but I still wore black, and until now I'd refrained from social engagements, even as I started to chafe at my seclusion. Visiting Miechen for tea was hardly a sign of disrespect for my dead husband, I convinced myself. She'd kept her distance. At first it pained me, as regardless of Sasha and Vladimir's quarrels, she and I had remained friends, at least on the surface. As time wore on, I began to suspect she stayed away for another reason, so I finally had myself driven to her palace.

She expressed delight to see me, corpulent now yet dressed as always to perfection in a silk day gown and jeweled hair combs. As we sat over her Limoges tea set, her samovar steeping with a fresh brew, she said, "Oh, it was. Everyone spoke of how our new empress is too proud to mix with boyars. I suppose she doesn't feel the need to prove herself. She has what she set out to achieve: Nicky in her bed and your crown on her head."

I should have heeded the bite in her tone. Since both were German princesses—only Alexandra was younger and ostensibly in a more influential position—it was to be expected that Miechen would denigrate her. But I was too flown with my own frustration. "She doesn't have my crown yet. And if only for Nicky's sake, she must make the effort. I certainly did when I was in her position and long before, as tsarevna. Her duty is to ensure that society accepts her. Hiding away in her apartments isn't going to win over anyone."

I exhaled smoke in exasperation, my anger tumbling out, for now that the dam had been breached, my outpour was unstoppable. "She resents me. She resents that he seeks my advice and that his ministers defer to me. She resents that I have my own income and that the imperial standard flies over my palace when I'm in residence, that I have full command over Gatchina, my cottage at Peterhof, as well as the *Polar Star* and my own train. She might even be perusing my dressmaker bills as we speak to tally how much I spend."

Miechen made a moue of distaste. "And in all this, no sign of a child yet?"

"No." I crushed out my cigarette and lit another. "I replaced her attendants, of course. They report that while she's often ill with various indispositions, she shows no indication of pregnancy. I hardly think Nicky is at fault."

"Indeed. Now you know why I didn't visit you while she was there in your palace."

"Need I remind you that I lost my husband? A visit from you would have been welcome."

"You must forgive me, Minnie." She clasped my hand. "Sasha and I had our differences over the years, and I fear he never liked me, but you were in my thoughts every day. I was very affected by his passing. It grieves me to hear you so upset, but . . ."

"But?" I fixed my stare on her.

"Well." She withdrew her hand. "Despite your terrible loss, you're still in an enviable position. Nicky relies on you to approve his household and cabinet appointments. Your own selection of ladies attend her, and your estate is intact. Such influence is hardly negligible."

"I don't approve his appointments. He asks, and I give my opinion."

"Nevertheless, as dowager empress, you remain above her in rank."

"Yes, and she resents that most of all," I said, recalling what I'd overheard at my palace. "Were it up to her, I would retire, as any self-respecting widow ought to do."

"She may despise it, but she cannot change it. I realize you will always grieve Sasha and may wish to wear mourning for the entire year, but, given the circumstances, perhaps you should entreat Nicky to hold a court ball as the new tsar. Then you can demonstrate by example how a tsarina ought to comport herself."

I considered this, for while I should indeed remain in mourning for the year, the idea appealed. "I can't," I said at length. "Xenia is due to give birth in July, and I'm leaving for Abbas-Touman next month. George wrote to say he's much better. I must pay him a visit. I wouldn't allow him to go to the Crimea to see Sasha, so he's been grieving by himself."

Miechen made a commiserative sound. "Not to mention, he's now our tsarevich apparent."

"He may be well enough to return to St. Petersburg," I retorted, stung by her implication. A sick heir to the throne was also hardly reassuring.

"I pray he is. All the more reason to hold a ball, yes? To reassure the court and the aristocracy that everything is as it should be."

Everything was not as it should be, but in this instance, I thought she was right.

———

GEORGE WAS SO improved, I could scarcely believe it. His respite in the foothills had put color in his cheeks; he'd grown out his beard and gained some flesh on his lean frame. He was bicycling daily along the narrow pathways outside his villa, and though he was smoking—which concerned me with his malady, but who was I to reproach him for a habit I indulged—he barely coughed during the entire two weeks I spent with him.

I also found signs he wasn't lonely—nothing overt, but subtle indications in the way his clothes were arranged and a telltale trace of a feminine touch in the vase of sunflowers on his bedside table. A local woman, I suspected, but I didn't pry. What he did was his own affair, providing he didn't create a scandal. A dalliance here, so far from St. Petersburg, was of no account in any event, as he wasn't married. I did impress upon him, however, that as our tsarevich apparent, he'd be expected to assume his duties once he returned to the city.

He chuckled. "I still have consumption, Mama. I'm not cured."

"People can live for many years with it. Look at you, the very portrait of health."

"Here. I'm healthier here. I can't assume any official duties. Hopefully it won't be a concern for much longer. Nicky wrote to tell me that Alexandra is with child." As he lit his cigarette, I sat frozen on my chair. "Didn't he tell you?"

"He did not."

"Perhaps it's a recent development."

"Perhaps."

I cut short my stay. Xenia was due for her confinement and George appeared content. As he kissed me goodbye, he said, "Be kind to Alexandra. Nicky mentioned that you and she are not, shall we say, on the best of terms. You mustn't make her feel less than you."

His words took me aback. Nicky had confided in him but not in me? They'd always been close, yet I felt a clench in my insides, as if I were being denied something I'd not known I was missing. "She thinks rather less of me," I said.

George smiled. "Mama. You don't realize how forceful you can be. If she thinks less of you, make her think more. Do it for Nicky. He has enough burdens as it is."

On the train ride back, I had plenty of time to think. Once I disembarked in St. Petersburg, I went directly to the Winter Palace.

"Why didn't you tell me?" I sat in Nicky's new study as he smoked and avoided my gaze. "I had to hear the news from your brother, who resides in the Caucasus. Does everyone in Russia know except me?"

"George knows because I wrote to tell him," he replied. "He mustn't think because he's my heir apparent for now that we expect anything of him. We wanted to wait until a certain time had passed for Botkin to confirm it."

I detected caution in his voice. "Confirm it? Women know these things; our bodies tell us. The doctor's confirmation may be required, but it's superfluous."

He set his cigarette in his ashtray. Passing a hand over his beard, he paced to the window. He'd had this study built, refusing to employ the one where his grandfather had died. It overlooked the Neva; as he gazed out toward the river, which glistened like a wide green-blue ribbon in the June sunlight, he said quietly, "She lost one before."

I found myself stunned. Again. "When?"

"Shortly after we moved here. It was very sudden. That's why when she became pregnant this time, Botkin advised us to wait before we announced it. To be sure."

"Is there any danger?" I was overcome by the news.

"He tells us it's unlikely. She's nearing her fourth month."

Her fourth month. All this time, I'd been left unaware.

"I wish you had confided in me. How can I be of any help if you will not trust me?"

He turned around. "I do trust you. With my life."

"I see. But she does not."

"Mama, this is very difficult for her. To many, you are still the empress. She feels . . . unwelcome. Her miscarriage was a humiliation for her; she didn't want anyone to know."

"Especially me."

He sighed. "I don't know what else to say."

"You've said quite enough." I came to my feet. "I must go to her."

SHE WAS ON her chaise in her beautiful new pale-blue apartments, where the fresh gilt and wide windows were overcome by a plethora of overladen tables, cushioned armchairs, and fringed footstools. She'd filled every nook and cranny. One entire wall glimmered like a cathedral iconostasis, covered in blessed icons. For a former Lutheran who'd first balked at conversion, she'd taken to our faith with startling fervor.

"I hear you're with child," I said, as she drew her shawl about her shoulders and tinkled a porcelain bell at her side for tea. There had been no preemptive niceties between us. I was too tired from my travels and the disturbing news to engage in small talk.

She nodded. "I am, praise be to God."

"It's wonderful." I thought I should embrace and kiss her, but her expression was so reserved, I couldn't bring myself to it. "I'm so very happy for you and Nicky. A child is a gift that changes our lives forever."

I wondered if she knew I had lost a baby, my second son. It should have brought us closer, for I understood her pain, even if her child hadn't been born. But she gave no indication that she knew, and I'd come to make amends, not stir up past tragedies.

"I pray daily for a son," she said, as her maidservant poured us tea. Not one of my appointed ladies, I noted. Had she cleared her ranks while I was away?

"You mustn't pray too much—" I stopped. No advice. She hadn't asked for it. "Whatever it is, your child will be deeply loved."

She didn't touch her tea, letting it grow cold while I sipped mine. She preferred bland English brews, not the pungent Asian blends of Russia, which I'd learned to savor.

"We must celebrate," I said after another lengthy silence, in which she gazed off into the distance, seeming to forget I was there. I'd never seen an expectant mother behave thus, as though she'd fallen into a trance. "Xenia will give birth soon. We'll make it a dual occasion— a magnificent gala, where I can personally introduce you to the court."

She started to attention, turning narrowed eyes to me. "Isn't it too soon?"

I knew what she referred to, and I refused to let it hinder me. "My husband is gone. I needn't hide myself away to prove my grief. My son is now emperor, and you are his empress, about to bear his first child. It's the perfect time to display you." I gave a slight laugh that sounded forced in my ears. "Surely you don't expect to stay in these rooms until the birth."

"I hadn't expected to stay here at all. I want to move to the Alexander Palace in Tsarskoe Selo. It's very peaceful. I feel quite at home there."

"But it's too far from the city." In that instant, I forgot my intention for coming to her. "It's a summer residence. You can move there for your confinement, if you like; I did when I gave birth to Nicky, but for now you must remain here. Let yourself be seen and admired."

"I hardly think I'll be admired." She did not take her gaze from mine, her leaden tone sinking into me. "Mother dear, I know you mean well, but you don't seem to realize that I can never be you. I do not say this to offend. You were an exemplary empress, one to emulate, only I don't wish to emulate anyone. And I know what is said of me: *The Funeral Bride,* the newspapers call me, who married the tsar too soon after his father's death. The court and society think the same."

"You exaggerate," I said, both because I was caught off guard that her apparent reclusiveness hadn't shielded her from malicious gossip and because the situation careened into the very brambles I sought to avoid. "Society does not know you yet. To refine their impression, you must let them."

"Why?" A frown knit her forehead. "As you say, I'm the empress. I will bear Russia an heir. Must I be liked, as well?"

I was dumbstruck. *How* was I supposed to answer?

"It would make it easier on you," I finally said.

"Would it?" She tugged at her shawl once more, as if she felt a chill. "I think they should respect me regardless. Nicky chose me as his wife, but God willed it. Would they question our tsar and the Almighty because I'm not who they expect?"

"They shouldn't." I couldn't argue her point, even if I disagreed. "But you might hasten their respect if you made an effort." Without warning, for I hadn't planned on doing it, I reached over to take her hand, as I had done on the day of her wedding. "If you'll allow me the honor of presenting you, I can assure you of their respect and approval. The former is required, but the latter must be earned. I had to earn it myself when I first came here."

She withdrew her hand. I had the unsettling sense she wanted to wipe it on her shawl. "If you think it so important," she murmured.

It was as close to a capitulation as I was likely to achieve. I smiled again, finishing my tea. "I must leave you to rest. I've only just returned from Abbas-Touman, and look at me, in my dusty cloak. I'll see to everything. I'll send you the guest list to look over once I've compiled it. It'll be a splendid occasion. I know you'll impress everyone."

She nodded, inclining to me to let me kiss her cheek. I resisted again the temptation to advise her not to spend her entire pregnancy on that chaise. It wasn't healthy. Restorative seclusion to protect the babe might be the norm in Britain but not in Russia. I'd danced my way through all of my pregnancies, and none of my children had suffered for it.

I refrained. And as I left, she did not say another word.

⁓

I BUSIED MYSELF with the gala, reassured by my Orthodox priest that I could return to society if I wished, providing I honored the requisite masses for Sasha's departed soul. I sat with Tania for hours on end to draw up the guest list, which grew immense because I couldn't bring myself to exclude anyone of importance.

Miechen chuckled when I showed it to her. "She'll have an apoplexy. Over six hundred people. She can barely contend with tea for three."

Undaunted, I sent the list to Alexandra. Nicky had told me she was becoming more comfortable with my idea and had expressed eagerness to see who was invited. When he arrived for our morning meeting—we still met daily to review his reports and discuss pertinent business—he divested himself of his hat, lit his cigarette, and handed me the list.

"Sunny wishes to amend it," he said.

I perused the list. Scores of names, scored through by her pen. "But it's more than half the guests." I looked up at him. "She cannot be serious. Why? It'll only give insult to deny these members of the aristocracy the opportunity to greet her."

He wet his dry lips. He was smoking too much, and his eyes were rimmed in dark circles that betrayed sleepless nights. "She's been informed those guests lead dissolute lives. She doesn't believe they warrant the privilege of greeting their empress."

I laughed shortly. "If we're to exclude everyone who's led a dissolute life, we might as well cancel the gala. It's St. Petersburg. Everyone hides a sin or two."

He cleared his throat. "There is more."

"Oh?" I sat back in my chair, bracing myself.

"She wants to wear the crown jewels on that night."

I waved a hand. "She can petition for them. They're in the vault, I presume."

"Not all." He met my stare. "She had the inventory sent to her for review. The pink-diamond tiara, the pearl-and-sapphire necklace, and several other pieces are missing. What is in the vault is the older collection and the tsarevna jewels."

Recalling the day of my coronation, Sasha complimenting me on my display of the jewels, and all the other state occasions when I'd worn them so proudly, my voice sharpened. "Those pieces aren't missing. They're here with me, as she well knows."

He shifted his stance, without speaking.

"Does she expect me to surrender the jewels I wore for many years as your father's wife?" I added, unable to stanch my resentment. "She has that entire vault at her disposal."

"Mama." His cigarette smoldered between his fingers. "Papa bought you many personal jewels to wear. The crown ones belong to the empress."

"I see." My fist curled on the table. "Perhaps as she hasn't been crowned yet, she should be concerned with cultivating favor rather than with how she will adorn herself."

He stubbed his cigarette out in the ashtray on my desk. "She wants to be presented according to her rank. The jewels in the vault are outdated or belong to a tsarevich's wife. You kept the best pieces because they're easier to wear. Can you not accommodate her?"

"And this list? Should I accommodate this, too? Shall we hold your first court gala in my drawing room? Because we hardly need the Nicholas Hall if we're going to entertain a few elderly nobles and their sinless matrons."

His expression hardened. Seizing up his hat and coat, he strode to the door. I called out after him, "We still have your reports to review."

"Then review them," he said. "You'll do whatever you like, regardless of what I say."

❧

I RETURNED THE amended list and scheduled an appointment with Madame Bulbenkova, the St. Petersburg couturiere who held official license to make our court gowns. She'd dressed me on numerous occasions before; in her refined atelier, we designed my new gown for the gala. When I asked if Alexandra had consulted her, she sniffed. "Perhaps our empress prefers a German dressmaker, Your Majesty."

"Is there such a thing?" I replied.

Seeing as the official period of mourning had ended, I was no longer precluded from being fashionable. Still, I kept my attire a secret until the night of the gala, when I arrived early to review the hall and ensure my décor had been completed to my specifications. As I inspected the profusion of fresh flowers arranged in the window alcoves, the saffron gaslight refracting against the gleam of the polished mirrors in the hall, I felt like myself again, excited to be in a new gown and about to receive guests. Somewhere along the way, I'd ceased to feel the aching void Sasha had left. I felt guilty, for he'd not been dead a year, but I reminded myself that to grieve him wasn't an act I must indulge like a penitent. He would never want me to be unhappy. I hoped that from heaven he was looking down at me and smiling at my nerve.

Even if Alexandra would not.

Her face was glacial when she and Nicky arrived to welcome the guests. She'd chosen a traditional court dress of gold tissue, with a purple and gold-embroidered mantle, although she'd swelter in it. She also wore her bridal diadem and a dense antique necklace of diamonds from the vault. The jewels shone dull against her splotchy skin; now in her sixth month of pregnancy, she'd been afflicted by that discoloration that made her look as if she had rubella.

"Mama," said Nicky, in audible surprise.

I twirled for him, allowing my sculpted dress to flow at my heels, a confection of black satin and tulle overlaid with glass beads that adhered to my slim figure, with ruffled dark-crimson chiffon at my shoulders and fitted sleeves, not the overhanging ones customary for a court gown. "Do you like it?"

"It's . . ." Nicky was at a loss for words, which I took as a compliment. I wore no jewels save for onyx-and-ruby combs in my upswept hair—as Alexandra must have noticed, her gaze passing over me and turning virulent. I'd not sent over the jewels she requested but had disdained them tonight, to prove one didn't need diamonds to shine.

"How lovely you look." I leaned to kiss her so she could smell my expensive Rallet rose attar. "All that gold and purple. So imperial."

She recoiled.

As the guests queued up to be presented, bowing first before Nicky, handsome in his dark-blue Life Guards uniform, then before Alexandra and me, I whispered each name in her ear, along with the corresponding titles from memory. After she thrust out her hand to be kissed and gave a wooden nod, making no attempt to engage in discourse, the guests proceeded to congratulate Sandro and Xenia on the recent birth of their daughter, Irina. I saw a drop of sweat creep down Alexandra's neck from under her side locks, which must have taken her hairdresser pains to create. She stood stiff as an effigy, her belly hidden under her stomacher and the folds of that monumental gown. Rather than exalt her fertility, she disguised it as if it were shameful.

And every guest whom she'd struck from the list was present, at my invitation.

She danced only once, after walking the polonaise with Nicky to open the gala. Then she retreated to her throne on the dais, Nicky anxious by her side. I went to him, holding out my hand. "Come dance the mazurka, my son." He glanced at her, uncertain, until she nodded and he escorted me onto the floor.

Under the chandeliers, the court made room for us, gathering around to clap and stomp their feet as the gypsy-inspired dance had me swirling in Nicky's arms, and he, a fine dancer himself, broke into an exuberant grin as he reveled in the moment.

When we finished, managing to break through the crowd, many of whom clasped my hands in theirs and told me how marvelous it was to see me looking so vibrant, I caught sight of Miechen with Vladimir, red-faced and stout in his tight uniform.

With a conspiratorial smile, Miechen arched her plucked eyebrow at me.

Turning to the dais, I saw Nicky standing there, disconcerted. Alexandra's chair was empty. She had abandoned us in mid-gala, and only Miechen had noticed.

⌒

"You humiliated her on purpose," said Xenia, as I oversaw the packing of my luggage with Sophie. "She left the gala in tears. I saw her. I almost went after her. Mama, how could you? It was to be her introduction at court, and you made sure everyone laughed at her."

"I did not." I gestured to Sophie to take the luggage downstairs for loading onto my carriage. "She elected to behave as if the honor was all theirs. She didn't speak to anyone, sitting on that dais like a statue. She left of her own account. No one hounded her away."

Xenia glared. "You are impossible. I am ashamed of you."

I paused. Like Nicky and Misha, my eldest daughter tended toward conformity, so her outburst surprised me. But she was perceptive; I had deliberately ignored Alexandra's request to amend the list and return the jewels, contriving to outdo her at the gala to prove she had much to learn. In my mind, she only had herself to blame. Had she behaved as befitted a tsarina, she would have won much-needed approval. Instead, she had shown herself to be arrogant and aloof.

As Sophie hastened out of the room to allow us privacy, I returned Xenia's stare. "How dare you speak to me in that tone before my maid-servant?"

"Because it's the only way you will listen. What would Papa say if he were alive? You must ask her forgiveness. She is Nicky's wife."

"Papa never wanted her to be Nicky's wife. And she has left for Tsar-skoe Selo. Do you imagine I should go all that way to be disdained? Absolutely not. Your grandmother in Denmark is ill. I must visit her. Olga and Misha are already on the yacht, waiting for me. I've tried my best, but I've gone as far as I will for her."

Xenia made an impatient gesture. "Is this your best? Ignoring the fact that she's our empress and about to bear you a grandchild? Grand-mère Louise is not ill; you are only leaving for Denmark out of spite. You always call her Alexandra, too, not Alicky, as if to emphasize she's not part of our family and must do as you, the dowager empress, say."

"I never said she's not family," I replied. "And she *should* do as I say. This dowager empress was beside her emperor for thirteen years and has lived here for many more."

"Mama, she's about to give birth—"

"In November. It's August. I won't stay here in this heat or take up residence in the Alexander Palace to watch her rest on her couch. Now, please step aside. I'm late, and I believe I hear Irina crying. Go tend to your child."

She blocked the door. "If you force Nicky to choose, you won't like his choice."

I almost pushed her aside. "When she's ready to deliver, I'll return."

Xenia stepped aside. As I made to march past her, she said, "She will never forgive you if you refuse to make an attempt."

"Has *she* made an attempt?" I retorted, and when Xenia pursed her lips, I nodded. "She has not. Nor does she have any intention of doing so."

I left my daughter staring after me in disbelief. As I rode in my carriage to the harbor, I knew that while I was abroad, she and Sandro would seek another residence. They wouldn't stay under my roof. Xenia was loyal to Nicky; I couldn't fault her for it.

As for me, I wanted to spend time in my native land, without any talk of Alexandra.

Much as Sasha had often declared, Russia was starting to feel like a prison to me.

CHAPTER TWENTY-SEVEN

I found my mother forgetful, chastising me for neglecting to bring her shawl when it was draped across her chair. Papa's arthritis had worsened, but nothing impeded his daily stroll in the gardens at Fredensborg, his cigar in hand. At sixteen and thirteen respectively, Misha and Olga relished the lack of etiquette, boating together and reading with their heads bent over the same book, as they had done since they were children.

Alix came to visit us, alone this time. She was quiet, somewhat withdrawn, but when Mama asked what ailed her, she murmured, "Nothing. I'm just a little tired."

I knew it was more than fatigue. Her grief for her dead son was still overwhelming, she'd had a serious fever that left her with a stiff leg, and she now complained of increasing deafness. But I read the foreign newspapers in St. Petersburg; I'd seen scandal items in the London *Daily News* about how His Highness the Prince of Wales escorted notable actresses about town. Recalling my mother's warning years before to never mention it, I kept silent, but I also made sure to give Alix my affection.

We took afternoon promenades by the lake, Alix's arm wrapped about mine as she gingerly trod the path with her cane, which she'd made such a fashion staple in England that hundreds of women employed one to resemble their princess. I asked her about her son George, who'd wed his late brother's proposed bride, Princess Mary of Teck, known in the family as May.

"They are so happy together," she said. "As you know, May is of German descent, but as she was born and raised in England, she knows how to behave. And my George looks so much like Nicky, they might be twins. But Victoria isn't well. The rebellions in India and strife in Ireland weigh on her. It's not easy to rule as long as she has. She's enjoyed very little of her life and abides no disobedience to her will."

She made an irritated moue, looking for a brief moment like her younger self, my wily sister who'd refused a tsarevich to marry the British heir. "She was touched by your letter thanking her for the book of poetry and kind words after Sasha's death. She still remembers when you went riding without a hat." She paused. "Do you miss it?"

"Riding?" I said.

She nudged my side. "Being tsarina. It cannot have been easy to surrender it."

"It wasn't. I took pride in thinking I'd bear the title until the day I died. But after Sasha left me, it didn't seem so important anymore." I looked toward the lake, not wanting her to see how her question had stirred both the pain of the past and my frustration with the present. "Without him, I'd rather be as I am. I find it less strenuous."

"And Nicky? He fares well?"

I forced out a smile. "Very well. He's overjoyed about the upcoming birth of his child. But being tsar," I said, quickening my voice so as not to fall into the trap of having to talk about his wife, "isn't easy on him. I fear we didn't have time to prepare him well, in that respect. But he will learn. He must."

She regarded me. I assumed she must have heard something about the situation in Russia. Alexandra wrote regularly to Victoria, and I doubted she had anything laudatory to say about me. Or perhaps she didn't mention me at all. That alone would be enough. To my relief, however, Alix didn't probe further.

"You're looking so well, Minnie," she said at length. "To lose a son is terrible enough, but to lose a husband . . ." Her voice faded. In losing her beloved Eddy, she had also lost Bertie. I loved them both; it hurt me that their mourning had cast them further apart, but I didn't want to oblige her to confess what she didn't wish to reveal.

"We must go on," I said. "That is what you told me. We must live for our children."

She sighed. "You learned more than that. You've also learned to live for yourself."

ALEXANDRA HAD THE forethought to ban all bystanders from her chamber at the Alexander Palace, so although I returned as promised, I wasn't present to witness my grandchild's birth. Only Nicky was allowed to stand by as her pangs lengthened into fourteen agonizing hours.

Word came to me via the Winter Palace that Her Imperial Majesty was delivered of a child. Before I could count the traditional gun salutes from the fortress—three hundred for a boy, one hundred and one for a girl—I'd boarded my train for Tsarskoe Selo. As soon as I reached the Alexander Palace and entered Nicky's study, I knew.

"A daughter," he said as I kissed him, wrinkling my nose at the pungent stink of tobacco on his breath. "Botkin tells us she's perfectly healthy. A girl now, but a boy next time. Alicky and I are still young. We've plenty of time."

He spoke as if rehearsed, as if he'd uttered these words before, no doubt to her. He also had the disjointed movements of a man who'd been on his feet too long, his fingers twitching at his sides, fiddling with items on his desk before he reached for his cigarettes.

"Give me one," I said.

He gave me a startled glance. I shrugged. "Why not? We're alone." He lit and passed the cigarette to me. "How is she?" I asked, inhaling deeply.

"As you can imagine."

"I cannot. Enlighten me. And, please, sit down."

He sank into his leather armchair, his hand curled at his face, the smoke from his cigarette diffusing through his beard. His pale eyes were red-rimmed, watery from lack of rest. "She is very tired. She's sleeping now."

"Yes. Well, I can imagine that much, after fourteen hours to deliver a babe."

He was so tired himself, he failed to notice the sarcasm in my voice. Nothing was easy with her, not even the most natural of functions. Even her first delivery had to be epic.

"I'm not sure how she feels about it," he suddenly said. "When the midwife handed Olga to her—we've decided to name her Olga, as Sunny loves that character in *Onegin*—she seemed . . . disinterested."

Or disappointed. She had much to prove, as my gala had thrust home. A son and heir would have gone a long way toward achieving that respect she lacked.

"As you said, she's tired. Once she recovers, she'll fall in love. The first child is always very special." I smiled at him. "You were, and still are, to me."

"I think so, too." He didn't sound convinced. "It was so terrifying, Mama. She looked as if she might die; there was more blood than I expected. Everyone kept saying it was normal, but I had to leave the room. I was starting to feel ill."

"It's not a man's business. No man except the doctor should be allowed. Your father hated watching me give birth. After you, he refused to be in the same chamber."

He smiled weakly. "That sounds like him."

"But the child is well formed and healthy, yes? Then there's no reason for concern. Give her time. She'll be an excellent mother. I know she will."

It was all she had, I nearly added. If she failed as a mother, she would fail utterly.

"You should go see her," said Nicky. Ash tumbled from the tip of his cigarette onto his chest. He brushed at it, smearing it over his lapel.

"You should wash and get some sleep," I replied. "I'll not disturb her. The last thing a newly delivered woman needs is her mother-in-law poking her nose in to wake her."

"Not Alicky," he said. "Little Olga. I think she looks like you."

SHE WAS CHUBBY, kicking and howling, battling with her wet nurse to clamp onto the nipple. The moment I saw and heard her, I felt as though my legs might give way under me. I hadn't realized until now how much I'd dreaded a weak example of Alexandra's blood, but my first granddaughter by her and Nicky had a pair of defiant lungs like Sasha's.

"Like a Romanov," I heard myself say.

The wet nurse gave a weary nod. "She's always hungry, Majesty. From the hour of her birth, she's done nothing but demand."

"Good for her." I took the wiggling bundle in my arms; as my granddaughter beat small, surprisingly strong fists at my chest, I kissed her still-misshapen crown and smelled the milky scent of her—of hope and possibility, of life before the years take their toll.

She went quiet all of a sudden. Her eyes were slits but appeared to be blue-gray, like Nicky's, though most babes' eyes were that color before they matured.

The wet nurse smiled. "She certainly knows who her grandmother is."

"She should." I held her close. "Welcome, Grand Duchess Olga Nikolaevna."

⁓

As I'd predicted, once she recovered from the birth, Alexandra showed intense interest in her daughter. She seized the opportunity to persuade Nicky to take permanent residence in the Alexander Palace, where she devised an intimate familial environment, importing a British nanny recommended by Victoria to assist her with Olga's rearing.

I protested to Nicky. "Tsarskoe Selo is too far away. You must let yourself be seen."

"It's only an hour or so to the city by private train," he pointed out. "Papa moved us to Gatchina, which is farther, and the government adapted."

"*We* adapted," I replied. "Nicky, it was done for our safety, and I never liked it. How will you know if a threat arises until it's too late? Your place as our tsar is in the capital."

"Sunny doesn't want to live in the city. She thinks it's too insalubrious, with the overcrowding and outbreaks of disease. She wants to keep Olga safe."

"I don't understand. We've all raised children in the city—" Then I paused, recalling the death of my babe, little Alexander. Seeing Nicky's expression turn inward, as it invariably did when confronted by my frustration with his wife's unfathomable need to isolate herself, I forced myself to say nothing more. Regardless of the distance between the Alexander Palace and St. Petersburg, we both knew that she wasn't motivated solely by concern for her child. Alexandra had never wanted to assume the social obligations required of her, and now she had the perfect excuse not to do so.

"I was thinking of commissioning an Érard pianoforte for her as my gift for Olga's christening," I said instead. "Do you think she'll like that?"

"Oh, yes," he said eagerly, grasping at any effort toward reconciliation on my part.

And she did like it. She expressed delight and promptly set pots of violets all over the expensive satinwood lid, proceeding to play the piano, Nicky told me, every evening. Again, I stifled my resentment. Providing she was content in her new abode, let her care for her daughter and get with child again. We needed a tsarevich.

⌒

SIX MONTHS LATER, the May sky over Moscow gleamed like steel, crows circling with raucous caws as Nicky and Alexandra proceeded to their coronation.

Judging by her countenance as she suffered through the ceremony, she was counting the minutes until she could return to her palace. As I watched Nicky set the diadem on her head—the same one Sasha had bestowed on me—emotion welled inside me. I excused myself from attending the gala held in the Kremlin that evening, telling Xenia to assume my place.

My daughter didn't rebuke me when I said that just hearing the music made me feel as if Sasha's tomb were being plundered. I stayed in my drafty apartments—the Kremlin needed updating—and then retired to bed to cover my head with my pillows. Not even my cruel envisioning of Alexandra in her finery, forced to greet thousands of well-wishers, assuaged me. For the first time since my husband's death, I couldn't abide not being the tsarina.

To oversee his coronation, Nicky appointed his uncle Sergei as Governor General of Moscow. The city's burgeoning industrialization and resultant miseries had attracted its share of radicals, for while the Nihilist movement was no more, its ideals still thrived. Sergei had enforced the arrests of demonstrating students, of which Moscow apparently had hundreds, and evicted the Jews, making himself widely unpopular. And poor Ella had wept to leave St. Petersburg for Moscow. Having no children of her own, she'd become a devoted aunt to her Romanov nephews and nieces, especially Maria and Dmitri, the children of Sasha and Sergei's youngest brother, Grand Duke Paul; Paul's wife—my niece by my brother Willie—had died giving birth to Dmitri.

When Nicky invited me to participate in the ceremonial gift distribution at Khodynka Field the day after the coronation, I had to agree because I'd not attended the other events, though I dreaded the reminder of my own time there with Sasha. On the appointed day, I was still dressing when Tania rushed into my rooms in a panic.

I turned to her so precipitously that the bonnet Sophie had affixed to my head flew off. "What is it? Dear God, tell me nothing has happened to my son!"

"No, not His Majesty," said Tania hastily. "He is safe, but we've just received word from His Highness Grand Duke Sergei. There's been a calamity at the field."

Seizing my shawl, I started for the door. Sophie cried out, "Majesty, your bonnet!" and flung it at me as I hurried with Tania to my carriage. Though it was springtime, there was a nip in the air. Tania fussed over me, fastening my bonnet and pulling down its veil, covering my legs with a blanket as I gave the order to depart. Not until we were jolting upon the route to the field did Tania breathlessly relate what had occurred.

Rumor had spread among the populace that there weren't enough souvenir goblets and plates. In a spontaneous rush, the crowd had broken through the fences to ransack the pavilions by the dais. Used as a military training ground, the field was pitted with trenches barely covered in loose earth. As people plunged into these, shattering bones, others trampled them in their zeal to reach our largesse. Cossacks on horseback, armed with their *nagaikas*—a short, thick whip—slashed through the upheaval to curtail the looting, rousing a terrified stampede.

I couldn't breathe as my carriage drew to a halt on the road, blockades curtailing my passage. Tarp-covered wagons lumbered past, with a dangling foot in a crushed red boot here or an arm in a blood-spattered peasant blouse there. Wagon after wagon trundled past me as I sat, horrified, in my carriage, clutching Tania's cold, gloveless hand.

Someone must have recognized me and sent word, for Sergei came cantering to us on his black steed, erect in his uniform, his sharp face with its incised cheekbones over his groomed dark-gold beard set like stone. Only his narrow green eyes showed any sign of life as he swept his gaze over me—and it was icy life I saw, removed from the devastation that had occurred under his authority.

"Majesty." He inclined in his saddle. "You must turn back. The festivities have been canceled. It was my understanding you'd been informed."

I gaped at him. Struggling for my voice, I said, "How many?"

"It hasn't yet been determined. Under the circumstances, we may assume the casualties are substantial." He grimaced. "With such a crowd, these things happen. Rebels and malcontents, spreading chaos wherever they infest."

"Has Nicky been told?" I swallowed my ire. I'd always liked Sergei, perhaps because so few did, but now I felt actual revulsion as I heard his pejorative explanation for this public tragedy that should have been a celebration of my son's coronation.

"I went at once to inform him. Now, Your Majesty, I must insist. It is not safe here." He started to order my coachman to turn the carriage around when I lifted my voice. "He is coming in person? He and Alexandra will come to console the survivors?"

Sergei did not reply. Kicking his spurs against his mount, he charged away. My carriage made the awkward maneuver to turn about and return me to the Kremlin. By now I was trembling. As I met Tania's eyes, she said, "I did inform you, as soon as he sent word."

I nodded. "Coming here was my doing. One of us had to."

For I already knew Nicky would not.

CHANGING INTO MY black mourning, I went to the Moscow hospital where they'd transported the injured. I didn't attempt to see Nicky, knowing he'd be besieged by his ministers and officials and, no doubt, outcries against Sergei for not erecting stronger barriers to impede the populace. The carnage at the hospital resembled a battleground; every available cot contained a broken body—men, women, and children, come from all over Russia to partake of the entertainment and crushed or flayed to the bone by the whirling *nagaikas* as the Cossacks savagely determined to restore order. Many would later die of their wounds. The official estimate would cite over a thousand dead, making Nicky weep.

Sergei had not informed him of the gravity, and his pronouncement to me that "with such a crowd, these things happen" was overheard—and maliciously misinterpreted. It made its way throughout the empire and abroad like an ominous prophecy, attributed to Nicky, who was condemned for his indifference.

When summoned to explain himself, Sergei intoned that he'd had no idea of the gravity, for he'd gone first to the tsar before proceeding to the field to assess the damage. He shifted the guilt to his Moscow subordinates charged with overseeing the event.

"He offered to resign as governor general," Nicky told me, his face pale when he came to me that evening. He wore his white uniform with its black sable trim, his diamond emblems and imperial sash. "I refused. Sandro and his brothers demanded it, saying Sergei was at fault. But Vladimir, Alexis, and Paul shouted at them that they were acolytes of Robespierre, for how could Sergei have foreseen it?"

"No one could have," I said, relieved I'd elected not to go to him and bear witness to the grand dukes tearing into one another. I thought he'd be wise to accept Sergei's resignation, if only to calm the storm yet to erupt in the newspapers. But I was too exhausted from my vigil at the hospital to argue, and when he remarked, "You're not dressed," I must have looked bewildered.

"Mama, the ball in our honor at the French embassy. We're expected to attend."

"After this?" I stared at him in disbelief. "Cancel it. We have dead subjects to bury."

"France is our ally. Sunny says we must go, for diplomacy's sake."

"Since when has she cared about diplomacy? She'll not be appreciated for it, dancing in Catherine the Great's tiara with our people's blood still wet on that field."

He turned to the door.

"Nicky," I said, and he paused. "Please." My voice caught. "Your people need you. You must listen to me. Cancel the engagement at the embassy and issue a proclamation of national mourning. We cannot appear indifferent at a time like this. Alexandra may not understand it, but she's not one of us."

"She understands me," he replied.

Wrenching open the door, he walked out.

CHAPTER TWENTY-EIGHT

O n June 10, 1897, the fortress cannon thundered. One hundred and one salutes: My second granddaughter by Nicky, christened Tatiana, also in homage to Pushkin, had been born. Another beautiful and healthy child, two years after the first, but not a son.

I wasn't present. I'd been summoned urgently by my father. At almost eighty years old, Mama was failing. When I arrived in Fredensborg, where Alix awaited, I found our mother crooked and brittle as a twig, confined to a wheeled chair. She'd suffered a stroke, her twisted figure with her chin bobbing against her shriveled chest a specter of the stalwart mother we'd known. When she passed away in her sleep the following year, Alix and I returned for her funeral. We were disconsolate, even if we knew it was better this way. Mama would have despised her own frailty.

Papa took to his chamber and refused to come out.

"Next year," Alix whispered when we said goodbye. There was no feigning that we'd ever enjoy another family reunion, the gardens and palace bustling with our children. As crown prince, Freddie would assume most of Papa's duties. Papa himself wouldn't last long without Mama, but until he was gone, Alix and I must return every year to see him.

"Sisters forever," I said, holding her close.

"Forever," she said, but as she went to her ship, I wondered how long forever would be. I was nearly fifty-one, not so young anymore. And with each loss, death was dismantling the world I had known, leaving me anxious about what might arise in its stead.

"WHAT A LOVELY gesture." I tried to muster a smile as Nicky stood before me in my Anichkov. He had come to the city on state business, after Alexandra had given birth to their third daughter two years after Tatiana, as if on an immutable timetable. "Is it truly her idea?"

He nodded, discomfited. "We realize you're only just out of mourning for Grandmère Louise, but Sunny says it would be an honor to christen our new daughter with your name."

"My name is Dagmar," I reminded him, trying to keep judgment from my tone. "Maria is my Orthodox name, not the one with which I was christened." Then, as I saw his eyes dim, I said, "But tell her I'm indeed honored. As I said, it's a lovely gesture." I did not add that seeing as his daughter had been born two months ago, what I thought was of no importance; they had already decided on the child's name and only now elected to inform me.

A fleeting smile crossed his face, then we heard the clatter of the telegraph machine in Sasha's old study. It was a new contraption, recently installed in my palace, as Nicky had one in Tsarskoe Selo, but I disliked its static sound and had it set up in a room I never used. After a moment, as we both strained to hear if Obolensky had retrieved whatever message came through, Nicky said, "It might be from Sunny," and he strode out.

I sat, clenching my hands. Another daughter. It now seemed unlikely she'd ever bear a son. The silence extended, until I wondered where on earth Nicky had gone. Had Alexandra sent a message that prompted him to leave without saying goodbye? As I moved to my sitting room doors, I detected urgent susurration in the corridor, Nicky's voice saying to my steward, "Let me prepare her first. She—"

I stepped into the corridor. "What is it?"

Nicky turned from Obolensky, who averted his eyes. My son's face was deathly pale, his eyes full of tears. In his hand, he clutched the telegram. "Mama . . . George, he—he's . . ."

I heard his voice. I heard what he couldn't say aloud. And yet I couldn't hear it. A dull roar filled my head and I felt a vast void, unaware that my knees were giving way until Nicky rushed to prevent me from crumpling to the floor. He held me as his pent-up sobs gushed out. I couldn't cry. Not a single tear.

My sorrow was so profound, I had nothing inside me to shed.

. . .

HE'D BEEN FOUND in a ditch, his bicycle toppled beside him. Most likely a massive hemorrhage, said the local doctor, who came from Kazbek to Abbas-Touman to examine my son's body. But in order to be certain, he'd have to perform an autopsy.

I refused. I already knew what had killed my son. I bathed his cold flesh and dressed him in his uniform, his stricken staff conveying me to my train with his casket for the journey to St. Petersburg. Only when I saw his coffin strapped into the storage compartment of my train did I recall my impression that he'd not lived alone, that he'd kept a woman in his house with him. I hadn't thought to ask, so overcome by the loss of him that I'd barely been able to address the immediate concerns, for he must be interred with the obsequies of a grand duke.

Now I'd never know. He'd taken his secret with him. Burying my face in my hands, I waited for grief to overwhelm me, sundering what remained of my fractured heart. Instead, I heard him as if he sat beside me:

Not His Imperial Highness anymore. Only plain George Alexandrovich.

Of all of us, he alone had lived and died unfettered by our invisible chains.

⁓

MY THREE GRANDDAUGHTERS by Nicky were ethereally beautiful, their seclusion at Tsarskoe Selo gracing them with angelic innocence. I did not see them as often as I would have liked. Though I didn't await an invitation, I always sent word in advance, so Alexandra could prepare. I also never overstayed my welcome. If she never stated directly that she had wearied of my company, she made it apparent by retreating to her mauve boudoir, because to her, whatever she found intolerable must be ignored, even if she couldn't ignore that our need for an heir had become pressing since George's death.

Nothing made this more apparent than when she dispatched frantic word by telegraph to my palace that Nicky had fallen ill in the Crimea.

I raced immediately on my private train to the very villa where Sasha had died. It was already half-demolished, Nicky having ordered the old structure razed to build a new summer palace. He had come to oversee its construction so we could visit in the summer.

In my panic, I barely paid heed to the gloomy surroundings that held such terrible reminders of Sasha's final days. Our imperial physician, Botkin, waited for me.

"Typhoid, Your Majesty," he said. "His fever is very high. You shouldn't have come. It's very contagious. It's not safe at your age."

Typhoid. The same malady that nearly killed my sister Alix's surviving son. Swallowing my anguish, I said, "I will not lose another son. If someone must die next, let it be me. Send word to the empress. Tell her under no circumstance is she to come here. She mustn't put herself at risk or, God forbid, bring the illness to their palace and endanger their daughters."

Nicky was delirious. Botkin and I assiduously tended to him as rose-colored spots spread over his body and he drenched his sheets with sweat. I bathed him, changed his linens, and prayed for his life. Once the fever broke nearly a week later, he was so gaunt and weak he couldn't lift his head. I'd taken to sleeping in a chair at his side, despite Botkin's fear that I'd catch the disease. As I heard him stir, I bent to his parched lips and he whispered, "Promise me."

"Anything, my beloved boy." I caressed his veined hand.

"Sunny. My girls . . ." He struggled for his voice. "Promise you will care for them."

"You're going to be well. Your fever has broken. Rest. I am here. I'll not leave you."

"Promise." He gazed at me, imploring.

I nodded. "I promise. Now, please rest."

It took another three weeks for him to recover enough to travel; by then, in counsel with his finance minister, Count Witte, we decided he should name Misha as tsarevich apparent. Nicky gave reluctant consent, with the caveat that Misha would renounce the title once Nicky had a son. Now twenty-one and in the Horse Guards regiment, Misha expressed dismay; we assured him it was for expediency alone. Nicky's illness had opened our eyes to what might befall us should he die without a declared heir to succeed him.

Everyone understood the urgency, save for Alexandra. As Nicky convalesced in the Alexander Palace, her devotion for him was undeniable, as was her fury toward me.

"And will our new tsarevich be seeking a tsarevna soon?" she asked, as we sat in her mauve boudoir, with my daughters, Xenia and Olga. They'd come to the palace at my behest to keep company with the girls while I assisted in caring for Nicky.

"I haven't given the matter any thought," I said, for I hadn't, and I wondered how, with Nicky still barely able to walk from his bed to his study, she would.

She turned to Xenia. "Well, if he does, I fear I shall have to appear in public without any jewels at all. Misha's bride will get all of mine, as it belongs to the tsarevna, and the dowager empress cannot spare the rest."

I loathed her in that moment with such intensity that had my daughters not been present, I would have informed her as much. Instead, I lit a cigarette. As she narrowed her eyes, for she hated smoking in her private room—though I'd smelled tobacco in the air more than once, betraying she had the occasional cigarette herself—I said brightly, "Once you bear a son, it will set the matter to rights. *His* bride won't require jewels for years."

Her face blanched, except for two bright spots of rage scalding her cheeks.

I left for Gatchina the next day with my daughters, assured that Nicky was on the mend. On my train, Xenia said, "Did you have to insult her? Your comment and having Misha declared tsarevich imply she might never bear a son."

"She hasn't yet," I said, and Olga sniggered. Not fond of Alexandra, either, she concealed it much better, for she loved her nieces and knew earning their mother's wrath would not serve her. Unlike me, the tsar's sister could be banned from future visits.

Xenia shook her head. "You defy reason, Mama. If you didn't make an enemy of her before, you certainly will now."

I looked forward to it. I wanted to confront her, tell her everything I thought about her abhorrent manner and bourgeois mentality. I was outraged that she could launch a petty quarrel over jewelry after my son, her husband, had narrowly escaped death. To emphasize my disgust, I returned the crown jewels in my possession to the vault and had a letter sent to inform her.

As far as I was concerned, she could drown in them.

TALL AND ELEGANT, with his long Romanov features and indolent smile, Misha attracted his share of female attention and warned me he had no desire to settle down. But with the turn of the century, my Olga reached her eighteenth birthday, without showing any interest in marriage, either. I decided she must have her debut. She'd not grown into a beauty, but she was comely enough, especially her dark expressive eyes, though she remained entirely Sasha's child.

"A debut?" she said. "Whatever for? I detest parties."

"You think you do, but how will you know if you don't try?"

"No." She clenched her jaw.

"Yes," I replied. "And you will smile while you do it."

She made the fittings for her gown such a torment and complained so loudly that her slippers pinched her toes during the gala that I cringed to see the gentlemen braving her grimace to ask her to dance. After the night ended, she spun to me and yanked off her diadem. "There. I had my debut. I still hate parties."

As she stalked out, I gave Tania a frustrated look. "How will I find her a husband?"

"With a great degree of caution," replied my lady. "And forbearance."

OLGA'S DEBUT LAUNCHED the Season, my first out of official mourning for George. I'd splurged on a new rose velvet gown, with cream satin appliqués and lace-trimmed sleeves. As I entered her palace and removed my wrap, Miechen exclaimed, "Why, Minnie, how can it be you refuse to age! If I were as gullible as our Mère Gigogne, I'd suspect you've taken up with miracle workers to detain the years."

She'd dubbed Alexandra with that nickname, based on the French marionette character of a reclusive woman who surrounds herself with children. Amusing and malicious, it was telling how fast it had spread among the other grand duchesses, eliciting an outraged gasp from Xenia, who berated me for repeating it. I didn't like it, but it was apt.

Still, Miechen's remark unsettled me as she swept me into her sweltering pantheon to declare that only at Grand Duchess Pavlovna's soirees did Her Imperial Majesty the Dowager Empress see fit to appear. An exaggeration, of course, as I planned to appear everywhere I was invited, but I allowed her the conceit to impress her guests.

Later, as we stood in her salon, surrounded by her guests, she asked me about Alexandra's recently announced fourth pregnancy.

"She rests constantly," I said. "If her couch could produce a son, she'd have a dozen by now. I sincerely pray this time it will."

"It certainly will, if she has anything to do with it." Miechen nodded to a passing countess, the emeralds about her plump neck flashing opulent defiance against the countess's meek opals. Again, I heard that undertone in her voice, a telltale sign she had a secret she was eager to impart—but not without some effort from me. Miechen always liked to feel as if she held the better hand, and one must first outwit her to win the round.

"She can hardly order God." I didn't care to mind my words. I was still enraged by Alexandra's behavior, for once she'd received my letter about the jewels, she returned word she no longer found them suitable and would commission new ones. She'd forced my concession out of spite, then had her pregnancy announced to render herself inviolate. I did not travel to the Alexander Palace to congratulate her. I saw Nicky whenever he came to the city to meet with his cabinet, but henceforth I refused to indulge her whims.

"God is superfluous," said Miechen, "when one has Dr. Philippe." She raised her wineglass to her lips, pretending to sip—an artful maneuver that made it appear as if we discussed inconsequential matters. She slid her gaze to me. "Did you not know? She truly has left you out in the cold."

I smiled to soften the stinging effect of her words. "If I'm not mistaken, I believe you're about to light the stove for me."

With a chuckle, Miechen set her cards on the table. "They met through a mutual friend, Anna Vyrubova—a lady-in-waiting of hers of no particular merit. Yet our Gigogne saw fit to grant her a cottage on the palace estate; they sew and play the piano together like the best of friends. It seems Vyrubova introduced her to this Philippe from Paris. I'm not clear on what his credentials are, if any, but among his purported talents is the ability to communicate with a child in the womb and persuade it—or does he command it?—to change its sex. Gigogne consults with him at Vyrubova's cottage."

She paused as if she'd relayed a minor peccadillo, though there was nothing casual about her revelation. The hall swam before my eyes, a nauseating parade of peacock-colored figures and hors d'oeuvres heaped on gold trays. When I failed to speak, she went on, "If God will not oblige her, she must do something, yes?"

I sharpened my voice. "This had best not be idle gossip."

She pouted. "See? The stove can be very hot if you get too close. And I heard it from a reliable source who knows these things and informed Vladimir."

"Has Vladimir told Nicky?" Though I assumed if my son already knew, he'd surely not appreciate hearing that his wife's strange proclivities were public knowledge.

Miechen might have rolled her eyes had we not been in company. "You know very well how Vladimir feels about—well, all of it. He knows better than to say anything to Nicky. As for me, my lips are sealed. I also know to guard myself where our tsarina is concerned."

I WENT THROUGH the Season with my habitual gaiety, pleased to find myself as warmly received as ever. From salon to opera house to theater and gala, I whirled my way through society and tried to put out of my mind what Miechen had relayed.

Until I heard it again, this time from Princess Zenaida Nikolayevna Yusupova, a premier figure in society and heiress of the largest private fortune in Russia. She laughed about it in mid-gala, while I stood only steps away. Before I could blink, Zenaida was fending off an avalanche of avid queries from the other ladies. I knew that before the Neva thawed, everyone who was anyone, and many who were not, would hear that our empress delved into mysticism.

I asked the French ambassador to investigate, requesting the strictest confidence. The report he returned was worse than anticipated. Armed with it, I could barely wait out the days until Nicky arrived at the Winter Palace to conclude his business before the advent of Christmas.

Like his father before him, my son couldn't restrain the family. His uncles often barged in on him without warning, bellowing about this or that. He must have had one such visit already, for when I entered his study, he said wearily, "Mama, if you've come to complain, please don't. I've heard enough today to want to abdicate and live out my days tending sheep."

"Do not say that even in jest. You are anointed by God to rule."

"So I keep hearing. Even if my uncles apparently have not." He lit a cigarette, eyeing me over his stack of papers. "What is it?"

"Nothing. Can a mother not pay an overdue visit to her son?"

He motioned to a chair. "Tell me."

From my cloak's inner pocket, I removed the leather folder. Then I sat and adjusted my skirts, as if the report were of no consequence. I wanted to gauge his reaction and was satisfied to see his forehead furrow as he read it. He lifted troubled eyes. "Who else knows?"

"Everyone, I assume. I heard it first from Miechen, then at a ball held by Princess Yusupova. Such matters cannot be kept secret, even in Tsarskoe Selo."

Without comment he closed the folder, about to hand it back to me when I said, "I had it prepared for her. She should know her Dr. Philippe has no license to practice medicine. In fact, he was arrested in Paris for larceny."

"I read the report. I saw why he was arrested."

"He's a fraud. Will you allow such a man to visit your wife at the Alexander Palace?"

"Not only her. I've also consulted with him. He does have powers. He can communicate with the dead. He summoned Papa for me at a séance."

The revelation was so shocking that at first I thought he was making a joke at my expense, and in very poor taste. But when he regarded me as if he hadn't uttered such a preposterous notion, my equilibrium fractured. "Are you insane?" I leapt to my feet. I was almost in tears. "How—how can you say such a thing to me, your mother and his widow?"

He rounded the desk in alarm. "Mama, Dr. Philippe is our friend. I feel more confident when he advises me. He tells me Papa watches over me." He reached for my hands, which I snatched away. "You don't understand what I endure. This wheat crisis has caused a regional revolt; at Witte's advice, I had the peasants sell their crop at a reduced price, in exchange for a lesser tax. Now they suffer widespread famine. Agitators clamor throughout Moscow—Sergei has arrested dozens of malefactors—and word has come that Sunny's brother's marriage is in ruins. Ducky left him after she found—"

"I'm well informed about the state of our country," I interrupted, staring at him, "and also of Ducky's marriage. She found her husband in bed with his page. Or was it his valet? It's horrid. Mortifying. Let Victoria sort it out. Ducky is her granddaughter, after all."

"Victoria is dying." His voice was pained. "Sunny is grief-stricken. She wants to see her grandmother one last time, but as she's with child, we cannot travel to England."

I was astounded. Séances with a charlatan, and now this incomprehensible sorrow over a monarch who'd turned his aunt Marie's existence into a purgatory, let alone been no friend to Russia—had he lost all sense of who he was?

"She saw her grandmother three years ago." I refused to express regret over Victoria's imminent death. "When you both visited England during your grand tour."

He stood quiet, as if uncertain. I had to be firm. I sympathized with him too much; I understood more than he thought. I'd lived in Russia for over thirty years. I knew all too well what he endured. I had seen his grandfather and his father endure it before him.

"You must see the man dismissed," I told him. "If the newspapers catch wind of this, they'll turn it into a farce. She cannot be seen to consult false seers in hope of bearing a son. Only God can grant what you both so fervently desire."

He retreated to his desk to light another cigarette, though a cloud of smoke hung thick in the air, as he couldn't open a window in the freezing cold.

"Well?" I longed to stomp my foot and shout at him, as his uncles did. "Show her the report. She detests scandal. When she reads the truth, she'll send him away herself."

"I cannot," he said quietly. "I'd rather abide a thousand charlatans telling Sunny whatever she wants to hear than her tantrums."

Clutching the back of the chair, I swallowed against a lump in my throat. Here it was at last, the moment I had long dreaded—his confession that he'd married the wrong woman. But then he said, "She only

wants to be respected as the empress. She started her own charity—
a guild for aristocratic women to lend their skills at needlework, making garments for peasant children. She hoped to expand the enterprise
to orphanages. But the women who joined her guild submitted lists of
appointments for their sons in the regiments and posts for their daughters at court. When she refused, saying helping the poor should be
recompense enough, they withdrew. Her enterprise failed."

I tried to sound conciliatory, though it was the last thing I felt.
"Had she asked, I would have told her as much. No one does anything
for free. It's how these matters go, unless one is very firm, as I have been
with my state charities—"

"State charities you will not surrender." His voice hardened. "Mama,
must you deny her at every turn? First the jewels. Then that disastrous
court gala, followed by Misha being named tsarevich. I realize we had
no choice after George's death, but Sunny took it as a grave insult—and
now you want me to tell her you had our friend investigated?" He
crushed out his half-smoked cigarette in his overflowing ashtray, muttering, "I hear enough already about how everyone thinks you're the
one who rules Russia."

He might as well have struck me. I stood with my hand gripping the
chair, and before I began to cry or yell, I raised my chin. "You needn't
concern yourself. Destroy the report. I will never interfere in your affairs again."

I made myself turn to his study door, expecting his apology. It was
the first time we'd had such a quarrel. He didn't move. I left his study
and he said nothing to detain me.

I now understood she was more than a thorn in my side. She was
poisonous to my relationship with Nicky, whom I'd raised to respect
and admire me. She could not oust me from my rightful place, but she
could do worse. She could banish me from my son's affections.

If only not to lose him, I had to submit.

CHAPTER TWENTY-NINE

Walking into my sitting room at Gatchina in her oversize travel bonnet and rumpled coat, my daughter Olga announced, "I think I am engaged."

I paid her no mind. I was writing overdue letters to my family, having repaired to Gatchina to escape a very difficult start to the year. Queen Victoria had died in late January, with Alexandra turning the end of our Epiphany into an interminable litany of funeral masses. With Bertie now King Edward VII and my sister Alix his queen consort, I had to suffer through it, residing in the Alexander Palace and entertaining my granddaughters while Alexandra grieved. To distract her, I offered up a few of my charities for her to oversee, which she accepted graciously enough but subsequently ignored, so that the directors of those institutions continued to issue their requests to me. She was too preoccupied with mourning her grandmother and safeguarding her pregnancy for good deeds now. In her mind—indeed, in all of our minds—the only duty she must fulfill was to bear a male heir.

Now here was my Olga, whom I'd left in the city with Xenia and Sandro in their new palace on the Moika embankment, as my daughter preferred to attend the spring concerts and receptions without me standing guard over her.

"Darling, how lovely," I said, without glancing up. "Did you have a nice time?"

"Pay attention." The tenor of her voice lifted my gaze to hers. "I attended a gala at the Oldenburg Palace. Princess Eugenie invited me, so I felt I had to go."

"Naturally. The Oldenburgs are a very distinguished family, and Princess Eugenie Maximilianovna is so charming. Was she pleasant with you?"

Olga said flatly, "Very pleasant, so much that I had no idea what she was about. Her son, Peter, had escorted Xenia and me to a ballet at the Mariinsky; I thought nothing of it. But the night of the gala, the princess led me into another room, where Peter was waiting. He proposed to me. I could hardly believe it."

A burst of laughter escaped me. "You jest! Peter is past thirty and a confirmed bachelor." Not to mention a hopeless gambler, I almost added, who'd caused his mother no end of despair.

"He is thirty-two. He told me that until now he'd never met a woman he wanted to marry. He was desperate for my reply. I finally said, 'Thank you.'"

I could see she wasn't teasing. She didn't have the wit. "That is all?"

"That is not all. When I returned to the salon, everyone congratulated us. Xenia was dismayed." From her pocket, Olga extracted a letter. "From Peter. He believes we are engaged. He requests your permission to announce it."

I snatched the letter from her and read it. "He says you consented to his proposal!"

"I said, 'Thank you.' Does that mean I gave my consent?"

I reviewed the letter again. "He seems to think so." I returned my gaze to Olga, standing there in her coat, with that hideous bonnet on her head. Not quite nineteen and she was already dowdy as a spinster, I found myself thinking; as guilt overcame me, I asked sharply, "Do you favor him at all?"

"Not particularly. But I suppose he's better than someone I don't know."

I found it impossible to untangle my emotions. Peter Oldenburg was suitable enough, related to the Romanovs through his maternal grandmother, a daughter of Nicholas I. But he wasn't someone I'd ever have selected for her, although as I thought this, I recalled my words to Tania: *How will I find her a husband?*

Perhaps Olga had blundered into the solution on her own.

"I have given it some thought," she went on. "I wouldn't have to marry abroad. I could stay here. That is what you want."

"Yes," I said. "I would prefer it if you stayed here, but you obviously don't love him."

She shrugged. "I never expected to love the man I marry. I'm not Xenia."

She certainly was not. An accomplished pianist and painter, she'd expressed only one aspiration thus far: to open an art studio. Though I had tried as best I could to inculcate her with the graces required of an imperial grand duchess, Olga dwelled in a private world that I found impenetrable. She lacked Xenia's vivacity or domesticity, but I appreciated her sensibility. A grand duchess must indeed wed. As she said, few found love in the process.

"Then we must write to Nicky," I said at length. "If you're quite certain."

"I am. I want to marry as soon as possible."

NICKY RETURNED WORD that, while surprised, he'd not refuse if Olga was decided. I queried her again, for I was growing increasingly concerned by the strange haste of it. Even if I'd failed to establish the closeness with my youngest daughter that I sought, I didn't want Olga to make a terrible mistake she might regret for the rest of her days.

"Must we discuss it?" she said impatiently. "I've already told you, why not him? He'll not trouble me for the most part, which is how I prefer it."

Seeing as there was no changing her mind—like Sasha when he'd made a decision—I took consolation that at least she'd remain in St. Petersburg, where I could try to keep an eye on the situation. She was formally engaged to Peter in May 1901; upon their marriage in August, she would move into the Oldenburg Palace on the Field of Mars. Misha was very sad to see her go and I knew he'd miss seeing her every day; of all my children, only he remained unwed, and as our tsarevich apparent, his bride must be well considered.

I left for Denmark after Olga's engagement to see my father and spend time with Alix before returning to Russia for the birth of Alexandra's fourth child.

THEY NAMED HER Anastasia—a beautiful name for a beautiful daughter; cherubic, with red-gold ringlets and startling violet-blue eyes like

her mother's. I had to admit that, her faults aside, Alexandra bred perfect children. My four granddaughters by her were enchanting and
healthy, without a serious defect among them. Nevertheless, this time,
Alexandra's disappointment was palpable. She wept in despair, Nicky
told me, saying she'd failed. Russia had no tsarevich borne by her. She
was now frantic to give him a son.

I wondered if it was possible, let alone safe. Now twenty-nine and
approaching the age when fertility became compromised, Alexandra
risked her life in childbed every time, as birthing taxed her. Her health
suffered for it, her lumbago confining her to bed for weeks on end, her
beauty fading into her thickened figure and exhausted air. Raising four
girls wasn't easy on any mother, much less one like her, as she ran her
palace on an infrangible schedule that a general would envy.

But I'd learned my lesson. I did not interfere—a choice I'd soon
come to regret.

⁓

THAT SEASON, THE salons of St. Petersburg were awash in gossip as
word spread anew that Her Imperial Majesty consulted mystics. Alexandra's fervency, coupled with her disregard for the consequences, had
always disturbed me; now I found myself fending off pointed questions
about Dr. Philippe and about my daughter-in-law's mysterious friendship with Anna Vyrubova. That England had achieved a détente with
France and urged us to join an alliance aimed at curtailing Prussia, or
that Japan threatened hostility over our holdings in Manchuria, was of
no importance. The only topic anyone cared to discuss was whether the
tsarina's bizarre associations would yield fruit.

"She'll make a laughingstock of us," I said to Miechen. "After her
brother's marriage fiasco, you'd think she'd refrain from exposing herself
to further ridicule."

"You would think. Did I tell you Ducky sent me a letter? Oh, the
things she told me. From stable hand to kitchen help, none was safe
from her husband."

I grimaced, already apprised of the sordid details surrounding the
collapse of Alexandra's brother's marriage. "Be that as it may, the marriage has been dissolved. Ducky has returned to Saxe-Coburg to reside
with her mother." I eyed Miechen. "I trust you're not encouraging her."

She plucked at her latest emerald bracelet. "Whatever do you mean?"

"You know very well. Didn't Ducky once express a desire to wed your Cyril?"

She sniffed. "They formed an attachment at one time, yes, years ago, when he went on his grand tour. She chose to marry that degenerate instead."

"Well, it's impossible now. She is divorced. And you know that members of our family are forbidden from wedding divorcées. She and Cyril are also first cousins. They'd require a dispensation from the Church, which only Nicky can request—and he will not."

"I am well aware. I told Cyril if he's still inclined, he should take her as a mistress," and when I stared at her, aghast, she laughed. "Imagine Gigogne's reaction, though the shame of it is on her brother. At least my Cyril doesn't fancy kitchen boys."

I could envision Alexandra's dismay—while she'd reluctantly supported her brother's divorce, she avoided any mention of his part in it—and it soured my precarious confidence in Miechen, whose antipathy toward my daughter-in-law surpassed even mine.

The Season ended on a bitter note.

Alexandra declared herself again with child, but when Botkin examined her and pronounced she wasn't pregnant at all, she broke into sobs and secluded herself, with Nicky dancing helpless attendance on her as his ministers besieged me with grievances that he was letting the business of the empire fall astray.

It took all of my strength to not charge to Tsarskoe Selo and box his ears, with incinerating words flung in her direction. My suspicion, confided to my sister years ago, was coming true: Alexandra was unsuitable and she was affecting my son's ability to rule.

⟳

"I MADE A mistake. All Peter wanted was my money, and he's spending it." Olga pushed her hand through her hair; to my dismay, strands of it peeled away in her fingers. "I'm going to need a wig. Look at me. He'll be my death. I should never have agreed to marry him."

"But I thought you wanted a husband who let you alone," I said helplessly, for she was near tears—a first for her.

"On our wedding night?" she cried. "And every night thereafter, to go out gambling at his men's club? He's having affairs. I want to separate from him. And don't tell me to try. I'm miserable. My marriage is *not* going to improve."

What could I do? My daughter left her husband and returned home, an intolerable scandal for me. Misha took her under his care, escorting her about town and accompanying her to St. Petersburg's 1903 bicentenary celebration.

For the occasion, I entreated Nicky to hold a court ball. I proposed having our guests don seventeenth-century Russian costumes to exalt our heritage. We mustn't neglect our obligations, and we'd had enough family disgrace that we needed to put on a show. Once he agreed, everyone adopted my idea, plunging into secret fittings and teasing others with telling details so no one would arrive in the same raiment.

I undertook the responsibility of dispatching the embossed invitations to our three hundred and ninety guests, as Alexandra had made it clear that she would prefer to stay in Tsarskoe Selo. But she had no choice other than to appear at the ball, solemn-faced in antique silver brocade and a magnificent emerald replica of a seventeenth-century crown, crafted for her by Fabergé. At her side, Nicky wore a caftan of gold silk and curled-tip boots. In her inimitable style, Miechen donned a feudal noblewoman's costume, replete with a *kokoshnik* of dangling pearls that swathed her head like a turban. I selected a diamond-and-sapphire-tiered crown with a veil (smaller than Miechen's, which pleased her) and a gold-and-white sable-trimmed brocade gown worn by Peter the Great's consort, unearthed from storage in the Kremlin. Princess Zenaida Yusupova, clad in a stunning pearl-studded *boyarina* sundress, performed a solo dance, to everyone's delight.

It was a magnificent evening, harkening back to my time as empress and lasting well into the next day. We posed for many photographs; stirred to emotion despite herself, Alexandra offered to curate the pictures and have them published in a limited edition as a memento. She signed each copy herself, sending them with a handwritten note to each of the guests. I thought it a considerate, and rare, gesture of appreciation on her part.

At the ball, Misha introduced Olga to a fellow officer in his Blue

Cuirassiers regiment stationed at Gatchina, to which my son had transferred. This Officer Kulikovsky and Olga were soon seen driving about in a carriage and dining together, until word reached me.

"You've only just separated from your husband and now you're consorting with a common officer. Everyone is talking about it. Have you no sense of decency?"

"His family has served in our military for many years," she replied. "They were invited to the ball, so he's hardly indecent. And before you say another word, I want a divorce. Peter must give it to me. He's the one with secrets to hide. I have none."

"Apparently not," I said through my clenched teeth. "But even if Nicky grants you a divorce, you can never marry this officer. He has no rank. Have you forgotten that your great-uncle Grand Duke Paul was a widower when he wed that common woman last year? Nicky stripped him of his income and title. He had to go abroad with her, leaving his children permanently with Sergei and Ella. Is that what you want?"

"Like secrets, I have no children," she said.

She continued to see Kulikovsky. As I could do nothing to deter her, gossip spread that Olga had taken a lover. I bore the brunt of it. I couldn't control my own daughter's behavior, just as I couldn't control Alexandra's thrall over Nicky.

In the late fall of 1903, Botkin confirmed that Alexandra was now indeed pregnant. Doctor Philippe assured her that she'd bear a son, but no one save her and Nicky believed it. I certainly did not. And as I prepared for the birth of yet another granddaughter, who, while welcome, would not secure our succession, we were suddenly confronted by the outbreak of war with Japan.

I was beside myself. Nicky had been repeatedly advised by his chief minister Witte and other moderates in his cabinet that he must negotiate to avert hostilities in Manchuria. Even Bertie had written to him, warning that since Britain had signed an alliance with Japan, it would put the British at odds with us should we end up at war. Nicky sided instead with his bellicose grand duke uncles, who dared to quip that a brief war was just what we needed to rouse patriotism. All we had to do was throw our caps at them and the Japanese would cower like "yellow-bellied dogs."

In February 1904, Japan launched a surprise attack on our Port Arthur in Manchuria. Miechen's son Cyril, serving as first officer, had to leap into the sea to save his life. As our ill-prepared men waged battle from the fortified hilltops, the Japanese employed long-range artillery lent to them by Prussia, destroying our Pacific battleships. Nicky had to commandeer our Baltic fleet as reinforcement, mobilizing our army to travel hundreds of miles across the still-incomplete Trans-Siberian Railway—costing us time, as temporary tracks were laid down, and paving the way to our unthinkable defeat.

My son's reputation plummeted. Corrupt indolence, the bane of our commanders, obliged him to enact sanctions and further harsh measures after one of his war ministers was shot to death in Moscow.

As word of the assassination raced through St. Petersburg, my blood froze. The murderers, whose identities were unknown, had sent a grim warning to the newspapers, proclaiming themselves members of a new revolutionary movement called the Social Democrats, inspired by the socialist fervor of the German philosopher Marx. As I'd warned Nicky, a new threat had risen to take the place of the vanquished Nihilists while he'd been tending to Alexandra. In response, he granted Sergei as Governor General of Moscow license to hunt down these new revolutionary groups, raid their meeting places, and arrest their adherents. But our war with Japan only fueled more recruits to their cause, as hundreds of unwilling men were conscripted into service and sent to perish on foreign battlegrounds.

Despite my repeated behests, Nicky refused to come to St. Petersburg to contend with the furor. To bolster flagging morale, I went to work with my charities, organizing my Red Cross to provide supplies, nurses, and doctors at the front. But the battles were taking place halfway across the world, with casualties mounting by the day.

Alexandra went into labor in August. Awaiting the outcome at Peterhof, I prayed with all my might that this time, surely her last, she would not fail, even if I had given up on her. A tsarevich born to the ruling tsar would ensure the continuance of our dynasty and give cause for celebration, distracting the people from this ruinous war with Japan.

Only three hours later, as I sat anxiously in the anteroom with Xenia and Olga, Nicky arrived. He looked as if he'd given birth himself, his hair plastered with sweat, his shirtsleeves rolled to his elbows, having discarded his jacket during Alexandra's ordeal.

His tired smile could have lit up St. Petersburg.

"Praise be to God," he said, as we staggered to our feet in disbelief. "I have a son."

CHAPTER THIRTY

He was God's gift to Russia—a robust boy with his father's gray-blue eyes, tufts of fair curls, and an eager smile, his little hands grabbing curiously at everything he saw.

As his godmother, I stood by the gold font in the royal chapel of Peterhof while he was christened as Alexei Nikolaevich. Nicky and Alexandra weren't present, by tradition; their four daughters, dressed in miniature court dresses and small pearl-studded *kokoshniks,* stood wide-eyed behind me as their brother was baptized. At the touch of the cool water on his forehead, he let out a wail. Anastasia giggled. Tatiana hushed her. Olga and Maria smiled as I glanced at them, lifting my finger to my lips to demand silence.

I wasn't displeased. He should be baptized in laughter. He was our future.

The fortress fired three hundred cannon salutes; throughout Russia, people rejoiced, the Japanese war forgotten for the moment. On her daybed in Peterhof, Alexandra received a steady queue of well-wishers; it was even reported that she smiled. She'd fulfilled what few thought possible, but she did not attend the gala in her honor, still recovering from labor. I went in her stead, beaming at Nicky's side.

Following the celebrations, Nicky returned with his family to Tsarskoe Selo and I resumed my charity efforts. After a long month of visiting wards and shipping boxes of medicines to the front, I entered my palace to find Obolensky at the gates.

Nicky had sent me an urgent summons.

"WHY DOESN'T THE bleeding stop? The stump has fallen off. The opening should be healed by now. Is there nothing else we can do?" I stood by the lemonwood cradle as Alexei kicked his bound legs, which had been fastened to an evil-looking device to curtail his movement. He cried piteously; he was hungry, not having nursed in days. To me, he looked extremely pale, his skin almost colorless. Botkin adjusted a fresh bandage about his navel, over the seeping wound where the umbilical cord had been clamped. Fresh blood wet the gauze within moments, as Alexei writhed feebly.

Eugene Botkin passed his hand over his balding pate. To my eyes, he appeared very troubled. He turned to Nicky, whose features were taut as he watched his nine-week-old son. In the corner, the nursemaid was praying. At a curt gesture from Nicky, she exited the room, letting in a draft of cool air.

"It's like an oven in here. Can't we open—" I stopped. There were no windows.

Nicky murmured, "Sunny worries that air from the outside might sicken him."

"No one is asking her to throw open every pane as Victoria did at her castles. But surely it's not healthy for him to be shut in like this." I looked to Botkin for confirmation. He gave a weary sigh. He'd not slept in three days, never leaving Alexei's side. Not even Alexandra had displayed such fortitude; after nearly fainting from her vigil, Nicky had led her away to rest, against her protests.

"Fresh air isn't the problem," said Botkin. "If this bleeding doesn't cease . . ." He met Nicky's eyes. "Your Majesty, we must consider the possibility."

My son shook his head. "No."

"What do you mean?" I rounded on him. "What possibility?"

"*No.*" Nicky's voice rang out, piercing in that shuttered room. For a second, the child went quiet. Then Alexei began to cry again, and Botkin returned to his ministrations.

My son led me into the corridor. At his order, the passage had been cleared of servants. Only his turbaned Abyssinians stood at the far doors, to prevent an intrusion.

"You mustn't speak of it," he said, a tremor in his voice. "Never before Sunny. Promise me."

"There was no one else in the room but us," I replied, but my own voice faded as I recalled the nursemaid he'd sent out. My anger evaporated, leaving an icy core in its wake. "Nicky, for the love of God, what possibility does Botkin think we must consider?"

My son stood so immobile, I thought he'd fallen into a stupor. Then he said, "He believes Alexei has the *bolezn gessenskikh*."

I frowned. "Is that German?"

"The Hesse curse," he clarified. "It causes uncontrolled bleeding."

I gazed at him in bewilderment. "But . . . it's an English disease. It runs in Victoria's family. How can he—" I went quiet. Alexandra was Victoria's granddaughter.

He lit a cigarette with a trembling hand. "The queen's son Prince Leopold died of it. Sunny's sister Irene bore a son Heinrich, who died of it in his fourth year. And Sunny's youngest brother, Frittie—she believes he had it, too. He died after a fall from a first-story window, but she says the fall didn't kill him, as he barely had a scratch. He bled to death from within."

I felt as though the entire palace had gone so quiet, so still, that the very gilded eaves above us were listening, the structure crouched like a beast, waiting to pounce.

"Can it be cured?" I whispered.

He coughed, smoke trailing from his nose. "No."

I feared I might be sick. I turned for a chair, a stool, anything to sit upon.

"Mama." His voice wrenched my gaze back to him. "Sunny is distraught. If the bleeding stops, there's hope. Botkin says Swiss experts are studying the malady. Sometimes, the patient recovers. Other times, a hemorrhage develops. We must—" He drew in a shuddering breath. "We must watch Alexei very closely. If he has any bruising or swelling, if the pain increases, it could be a sign of an internal hemorrhage."

"But how can we know for certain if he even has this sickness? He might not," I said, but my denial sounded too shrill, as though saying it aloud could make it true.

"Only time can tell." Nicky's shoulders sagged. His very person seemed to cave into itself. "The experts claim the disease is passed through the maternal line; when Botkin mentioned it before you arrived, Sunny made such a sound—like an animal caught in a snare. But Botkin says the symptoms are consistent. A minor wound, a fall, a stumble: Anything can cause the bleeding. It can turn severe. In order to know how severe—"

"Yes." I reached for him, my hand groping at his sleeve. "I understand."

"We must never discover how severe it can be." He struggled for his composure, his joy in his new son turned to cinders. "No matter what, Alexei must be kept safe."

I folded my arms about him. Setting his head on my shoulder, he wept. But then he drew back abruptly, already looking down the corridor to her boudoir. "I must go to her."

"Go." I straightened his collar. "I'll see to the girls. They must be worried."

As I started away, he said, "Remember: Say nothing. They're too young to understand. Children repeat whatever they hear. Sunny doesn't want anyone else to know."

"Of course," I said, but as I hastened to the girls' apartments, I wondered what he intended to do. If Alexei had this terrifying disorder, how could we hide such a calamity in the very heart of our family, much less conceal it from the world?

ALEXANDRA HAD FURNISHED her daughters' rooms with ordinary maple furniture, with chintz drapery that echoed her own staid upbringing, set alongside military cots on cast-iron bedsteads like those Sasha had insisted upon for our children. Each set of girls shared a bedroom: Nine-year-old Olga and seven-year-old Tatiana, known as the "Big Pair," had a stenciled frieze of flowers and dragonflies on their walls, with matching dressing tables and blessed icons above their beds. Five-year-old Maria and the youngest, Anastasia, the "Small Pair," had roses and butterflies and the same interchangeable décor.

Olga had gathered her sisters in her room, pushing together the two narrow beds, their little dogs on the floor, though the moment I entered, the dogs yipped and sniffed my skirts. Anastasia was asleep, her chubby arms wrapped around the stuffed Danish teddy bear I'd given her as a present for her Name Day. The others were awake. Their eyes, varying in hue from Olga's mellow blue-gray to Maria's deep blue, turned in unison to me.

They already had distinct personalities, despite Alexandra's grouping of them in pairs. As the eldest, Olga was the leader—and my favorite, because I knew her best. Like my daughter, her namesake, she was unconcerned with appearances, her chestnut hair often disarrayed and her frocks rumpled. She liked to paint, too, and was also a gifted pianist.

Now, as Maria nestled in the crook of her arm, Olga said warily to me, "Will he die?"

"Oh, no." I made myself smile. "Babes often suffer from colic."

"Is that all?" asked Olga. Had she overheard something? Their nanny had been seated at their apartment entrance and given me a suspicious look. I didn't like the woman and had motioned her to stay put, lest she follow me inside to overhear everything I said.

"Yes." Hiking up my skirts and wishing I could loosen my corset, I perched on the bedside and smoothed Anastasia's tumble of golden hair. She was perspiring; the palace was overheated tonight. "That is all. A bad colic."

Maria blinked sleepily. She was very pretty, if too plump. Tatiana sat erect. Though still quite young, she would be the beauty of the quartet, with her almond-shaped blue-gray eyes that, like her mother's, could appear violet, and Alexandra's coppery hair, a wide-lipped mouth, and Nicky's aquiline nose. She was also tall for her age, with supple limbs, like a ballerina.

"We heard Mama crying," Maria ventured. "She told Papa she had cursed Alexei. Why would she say that? Mama is good. She never sins."

"Your mother is upset. There's no curse," I said. "He'll recover. But babes are delicate, so you must be very careful with him. You mustn't play too roughly with him."

As the truth was out of the question, I was saying whatever I could to prepare them. Even if they weren't told, they'd suspect, Olga especially. She was inquisitive, unlike Tatiana, who often appeared lost in reverie, having inherited Alexandra's detachment. Anastasia would also notice; in time, she and Alexei would bond as younger siblings did. Despite her youth, she'd proven keen-eyed and boisterous. One night at dinner, when she was allowed because of my visit to sit with us at the adult table, she'd made me laugh under my breath by eating her peas with her hands, ignoring Alexandra's reprimands.

"The child is too willful," Alexandra had remarked, after Anastasia was marched out by the nanny, green smears all over her face. My daughter-in-law looked directly at me as she spoke, as if I were to blame. Her implication was clear: My youngest granddaughter had my character, contrary and determined to thwart.

"So," I said, passing my gaze over them. I loved them so much, these beautiful grand duchesses who were also our future. "Will you be tender with your little brother?"

Olga and Maria assented. Tatiana gave me a pensive look. "We're not allowed yet to play with him," she said. "When we are, we'll be careful." She spoke as if he were made of Sèvres china, a fragile teacup. Which, I realized, he was. He could fall and crack.

I leaned over Anastasia, who grumbled, her flushed face buried against her teddy bear. She smelled of chocolates; I espied the telltale stains on her fingers.

"Eating bonbons in bed?" I asked, and Maria giggled. Olga averted her eyes, abashed, while Tatiana demurred, "Not me. I don't like sweets."

"I won't tell. But don't eat too many." I pinched Maria's side, making her squeal. "Or you'll grow fat as Tante Miechen."

The girls' laughter woke Anastasia. Her groggy gaze warmed at the sight of me. "Amama!" she cried, citing her nickname for me, and she flung herself into my arms. She was the most impulsive. No matter how often she was chided for it, Anastasia showed no distinction, lavishing her affection on her pets, servants, and any others she liked. If she disliked someone—such as the nanny—she ignored them. And that, I thought as I kissed her cheeks sticky from the bonbons, was indeed like me.

I stayed with them, heaped together like puppies. Anastasia pulled up her French bulldog, Shvybzik, and tucked him between us, his snuffles making Olga and Maria shake with laughter.

Eventually, they all fell asleep, save Tatiana. She sat quiet, gazing into the distance; when I touched her hand, she said without turning to me, "It's not a colic."

Not a question. A statement—one that I couldn't bring myself to refute.

"No," I said. "It is not."

She nodded. "Then we must be very tender with him."

⸻

THE LOSS OF Port Arthur, along with twenty thousand of our men, was decried in Russia. Newspapers printed scathing editorials of the tsar's mismanagement, and agitators took to the streets. His cabinet warned Nicky that talk of revolution, spurred by the insidious Social Democrats, spread, further damaging his reputation, with jubilation over Alexei's birth now subsumed by unrest.

Due to the massive casualties in Port Arthur, the 1904 Season in St. Petersburg was suspended. Our family Christmas at Tsarskoe Selo was tense, overlaid by unvoiced concern for Alexei. The bleeding from his navel had been stanched, causing immense relief, but Botkin believed Alexei had the disease and suggested a protocol to safeguard him in the future, including restraints and a leash-like device to hold him in check once he began to crawl. While Alexandra betrayed none of the terror she must have felt, I wanted to say that all children bumped and scraped themselves. They stumbled and fell. He was a babe now, but as Alexei grew older, how could we detain his curiosity, his natural desire to explore the world around him? Yet not even the beloved family dogs were allowed near him, as if a sniff from a gentle pet might harm him. When told her Shvybzik mustn't enter the nursery, Anastasia gave puzzled voice to what no one else dared say: "Why not? Shvy won't bite Sunbeam."

"Sunbeam" was Alexandra's endearment for her son, but she herself wasn't sunny now. I watched her throughout Christmas as she closed into herself like that room that now served as her babe's cage, eschewing anything that might touch on Alexei's condition.

"You mustn't allow it," I finally told Nicky in a fit of despair when he came to St. Petersburg with Alexandra for Epiphany and the Blessing of the Waters, leaving the children behind. "We cannot hide it. You must tell the family; already they ask why the boy is hidden away. Issue a public bulletin. It's a disease, not a curse. She might blame herself, and God knows how terribly I feel for her, but your plight will engender sympathy. After the loss of Port Arthur, all of Russia will rally to you once they hear your son is ill."

He looked as if I'd asked him to expose his soul. "Mama, our son's health is a private matter. We'll not make a spectacle of it for political gain. How can you ask such a thing? Since when are we, the imperial family, obliged to divulge our personal pain to the world?"

"Our pain is evident," I replied, hearing Alexandra in his words. "Our soldiers are retreating through Siberia. Bertie, the American president Roosevelt, and the kaiser himself are calling for a cease-fire. We've lost our standing in the Orient. You must amend your policies. Grant the concessions espoused by your grandfather, dismiss everyone who counseled you otherwise, and tell your people your son is unwell. You must do whatever is necessary to protect your throne."

His hand curled into a fist on his desk. "Absolutely not. There will be no cease-fire. I've kept Witte on my cabinet, as you advised, though his liberal stance displeases me, and I sanctioned those who lost us Port Arthur. But I am still the tsar. I will rule as my ancestors before me. Papa never wanted our autocracy abolished. If I permit a constitution and Duma, we will rule in name alone, if we're allowed to rule at all. Never, whilst I live."

"Nicky—"

He held up his hand, still in a fist. "Say nothing more on the subject."

For the moment I obliged, reasoning that the ongoing burden of the war, the shock of Alexei's illness, and Alexandra's distress were an impossible combination. Let time ease the brunt of it. Once it did, I'd try again. I'd not cease until Nicky accepted that in this modern age, our autocracy was already doomed. No tsar could rule as his ancestors had.

If he didn't concede, they would force him to it.

With the grand duchesses and Alexandra, rigid in her court finery, I stood at the Winter Palace balcony overlooking the Neva for the Blessing of the Waters. The grand dukes and Nicky, bearing lit tapers, were out on the frozen river, assembled under the canopy as the metropolitan dipped his gem-studded crucifix into the hole cut in the ice.

It was one of those perfect January days that polished everything to brilliance, the people assembled at the distant cordons, wreathed in the vapor of their own breath, bearing pails to gather the blessed water.

Alexandra was taut beside me, anxious for the ceremony to end; I wanted to chide her. Miechen and the other grand duchesses were eyeing her; I wasn't the only one who could see how unwilling she was to be here. By now rumors ran amok that something awful ailed her son and he wouldn't survive his first year. When Miechen confronted me, I said nothing was wrong save for the usual babe's ailments.

She laughed. "Minnie, do you want everyone to think you're a liar? No one hides the tsarevich away for a colic."

Concluding his prayers, the metropolitan turned with the chalice to Nicky, in tandem to booming gun salutes from the fortress.

A sudden explosion shattered the balcony window. As the grand duchesses shrieked, flinging themselves back to avoid the shards of glass, I stood as if paralyzed, slivers showering me. Pandemonium ensued. Guards raced out from the palace to haul Nicky and his uncles inside. Alexandra bolted away, shoving aside the grand duchesses to hasten down the corridor, surrounded by Cossacks assigned to her protection.

Like me, Miechen was bathed in broken glass. A cut on her cheek seeped blood. She stepped forward on the balcony, peering out into the cloud of dust dissipating in the frigid air.

"A shell has hit the wall below us." She turned to me. "I thought the cannons only fired blanks for the ceremony."

"They do." I was breathless, fighting my own panic, memories of the detonation in the dining hall and the train derailment assaulting me with visceral force. The terror of the Nihilists had been crushed by Sasha, but their shadow remained, their zeal to destroy us taken up by this new revolutionary cause. We'd had no word from the Okhrana of any threat and no one was seriously hurt, but I felt a deep foreboding as Miechen took me by my arm to lead me away.

"Well," she said, our thin-soled court slippers crunching over the debris on the floor. "That was *not* a blank."

CHAPTER THIRTY-ONE

PROTESTERS TO MARCH ON WINTER PALACE.
LEAVE AT ONCE.

"I will not," I told Obolensky, dictating my reply to Nicky's urgent telegram. "Inform my son that I will stay right here and prove everything is as it should be."

But it was not as it should be, as Miechen emphasized when she arrived to see me that evening, having fearlessly crossed the city in her troika with its distinct insignia, as if she dared anyone to throw a bomb at her. She still had the nick on her cheek, for it was only two days since that mysterious shell had hit below our balcony at the Winter Palace. None of the guards in the fortress responsible for the cannon had confessed they'd armed one with an actual shell, even by mistake, so all Nicky could do was dismiss those on duty that day and issue a decree that henceforth no cannon would be fired for state events.

"Have you heard?" she asked, unhooking her sable mantle in my sitting room.

"Yes," I said. "Nicky has ordered me to depart for Gatchina. He says there's to be a massive protest tomorrow."

She let out an exasperated breath. "He's also ordered Vladimir to contend with the mob, should they approach the palace. Vladimir doesn't know what to do; he says the Okhrana has infiltrated their ranks. There are revolutionaries among them, of course, but most are factory workers out on strike because of the war and their working conditions. They plan to march with a priest at their head, with their wives and children, to present a petition. They say the tsar has always—"

"Met with his subjects in person." I sank into my chair. "But not since Alexander was assassinated. Is Vladimir certain they will march in peace?"

She met my stare. "Nicky is prepared to act as if they won't."

I sent another telegram to Nicky, imploring him to come at once to the city. Again, he issued the order for me to leave. Again, I refused.

The next morning, January 22, I sent for Xenia. Olga was already here, and Miechen came, as well. A household of women, we huddled in my drawing room as the demonstrators proceeded down the Nevsky Prospekt toward the Palace Square, singing "God Save the Tsar" and carrying placards with Nicky's likeness.

"Do they know he isn't here?" I said, casting a worried look at Miechen.

She gave a grim nod. "Vladimir informed them. They didn't believe him. They said their Little Father would not abandon them in their time of need."

When we heard the sudden rattle of gunfire, I lunged to the window facing the Prospekt. People came staggering back down the road, bleeding, holding others crumpled between them. I issued my command: "Fetch the carriages. We must leave at once."

"Now?" Xenia said in horror.

Miechen shook her head. "Minnie, now is not the time. If we try to leave . . ." She left her conclusion unvoiced. "We must stay inside until it is safe."

I had Obolensky set extra guards at my gates. My palace wasn't disturbed, but he was, returning inside with a sickened expression from the carnage he'd witnessed. By nightfall, Vladimir arrived, perspiring despite the cold, as if he'd been through battle.

"The guards' commander, Vasilchikov." He collapsed onto my couch as Miechen thrust a cognac at him. "That old fool ordered his regiment to open fire. Right there in the square! They were singing hymns and he shot at them. Then he had the Cossacks ride in with their sabers and whips." He drank the cognac in a gulp. "Hundreds. Slaughtered by us."

"Dear God." I pressed my hands together so tightly that my rings cut into my palms. Our subjects, killed by us in the Palace Square. It was that field in Moscow after Nicky's coronation again; it would rain more calumny upon our heads, add more cause to the grievances piling up against us. I should have admitted as much, but I only whispered, "Nicky will be beside himself. He—"

"Ordered it," Vladimir bellowed. "Nicky *ordered* it. He told us under no circumstances were we to let the mob near the palace, and now they'll tear us apart."

"He didn't know," I said desperately.

"He knew." Vladimir hauled himself to his feet. "You wired him. I begged him to come to attend to the matter in person. He refused to listen."

I regarded him, seeing my brother-in-law for the first time for who he was, no longer the charming rogue of our youth but a fifty-seven-year-old man, overweight and in poor health, enraged by circumstances that had denied him his superiority, as he believed he would have made a better tsar. "He knew, and now we'll be blamed for it. Because he's a weakling who should never have taken the throne. Sasha would be ashamed of him. He *was* ashamed. My brother died too young and left Russia to a mewling coward who lives only for his wife's approval and cannot make a decision on his own."

"You forget yourself," I said. "I am the tsar's mother. I suggest you leave, before you say something you'll regret and I cannot forgive."

Miechen took him by his arm. Her eyes bored into me as she murmured, "Vladimir, come. We'll not be thrown out, even by the tsar's mother."

He shook her away. As he tromped past me, he said, "You know I speak the truth, Minnie. I've always respected you, but I'll not be his lackey any longer. Your son is unfit. If he doesn't recognize it, we will all pay for his mistakes."

I stood immobile. Xenia was so upset she was crying, and Olga patted her hand as she might a disconsolate child. I couldn't speak. I couldn't admit it.

Yet I too feared that this time, Nicky had gone too far.

⟿

ST. PETERSBURG AND MOSCOW erupted in riots, with mass demonstrations in the streets over the massacre dubbed "Bloody Sunday." Martial law was declared. As armed soldiers corralled the city, factory workers went on strike by the thousands, bringing our industries to a standstill, though we needed supplies for our unresolved war with Japan. Anyone who wasn't outside, hoisting inflammatory banners or inciting turmoil, stayed indoors to pray that a worse cataclysm would not befall us.

Aristocrats closed up their palaces to take extended vacations abroad, "as if the guillotine were being mounted at the Narva Gate," sneered Miechen, when we met at her palace for tea. To me, her indifference was further evidence that to those of us in the ruling class, the discontent must be ignored or disdained.

Riding in my unmarked carriage back to my Anichkov, I forced myself to lift the blinds at the window. I saw beggars huddled in the cold by the bridges, while women in tattered shawls trudged with their baskets to market stalls stripped bare by the war. I felt despair claw at me like a talon. The vibrant city I had known was gone, replaced by the specter of revolution, by the insidious scarcity and resentment that crept in like thieves in the night.

I wanted to leave to visit my father in Denmark but wasn't certain if I should under the circumstances, so I boarded my private train for Tsarskoe Selo to consult with Nicky. The railway to the Alexander Palace, used exclusively by family or provisions for the estate, was heavily monitored. I had to endure guards boarding my carriage to inspect my luggage until I exclaimed, "That box contains chocolates for my grandchildren, not a bomb!"

In the palace, I found Alexandra confined to her rooms with an attack of her lumbago. The girls, studying under their tutors, were happy to see me. Alexei was plump and content, watched over by Derevenko, his devoted sailor *dyadka,* a constant bodyguard lest he injure himself. He cooed when I bent over him, yanking a jet bead from my sleeve and trying to stuff it into his mouth. I caught him by his wrist to pry it from him. He pouted and then howled at me. Seized by fear, I checked his wrist for bruising. He had no mark. He was merely upset that I'd deprived him of something sparkly to chew.

As soon as I entered his study, Nicky looked up from his desk, his face haggard from the aftermath of the massacre. He lifted a sheaf. "A twenty-page letter from the kaiser. He says he wrote the same one to you. Did you receive it?"

"Yes." I lit a cigarette. "I haven't read it yet. I assume it's a lecture?"

"It's a warning," said Nicky. "He dares advise me to avert revolution and defeat by Japan. He chastises me for not acting sooner in Moscow after that unfortunate incident at the field and for not averting this recent one in St. Petersburg. He says I must strip Sergei of his governor generalship of Moscow, as my uncle is too reactionary, and declare my intent to establish a parliament. I must rouse my countrymen to patriotism, as clearly Russians have lost their sense of duty." He tossed the voluminous letter back onto his desk. "According to him, the Japanese will die for their cause to a man, unlike our sailors, who mutiny in mid-battle, and our soldiers, who sing out revolutionary slogans."

"Well. The kaiser certainly thinks much of himself, like every German." As soon as I spoke, I bit my lip; my anti-Prussian sentiment, while well known, wasn't welcome here, with his German-born wife, but Nicky seemed not to hear me, too engrossed in his travails.

"Perhaps he has a point," I ventured. "Defeat after defeat can only cause more discontent. And Moscow and St. Petersburg under martial law, while factory workers call for our heads, is hardly conducive to stability."

"You *agree* with the kaiser?"

"Never. But the advice is sound. About Sergei, at least. Your uncle has made himself the most despised Romanov—"

"After me," Nicky said bitterly.

"You are not despised. You're blamed. As the tsar, you can still put matters to right. But Sergei has exceeded his authority, sentencing thousands to imprisonment or the gallows. By his very actions as our representative, he abets this fury against us. You should ask him to resign as a conciliatory move, to prove you intend to make amends."

"He already has," Nicky said, to my surprise. "He had no choice. He received a death threat. Ella is distraught. She has Paul's children with them and fears for their safety. She implored Sergei to resign his post. I'll have to appoint another in his stead."

I watched him pace to his window, his perennial cigarette in hand. "I know it's my fault," he said at length. "You advised me to go to the city and deal with the protesters in person, as did Vladimir. Now he too has resigned. He came here in person to rip the medals from his uniform and upbraid me, saying he'll not serve in my cabinet because I'm now called the Bloody Tsar, even after his own son Cyril went abroad to marry Ducky without my consent."

I felt on more solid footing when it came to family matters. "I told Miechen it wouldn't be tolerated. She knew perfectly well what would ensue if her son went ahead and married Ducky."

Nicky returned to his desk. "Yes, but I cannot go through with it." He lifted another letter off the stack. "From Aunt Marie. She's incensed that I've deprived Cyril of his title and income, leaving him and Ducky without recourse. She says I'm a traitor to the family. And I need Vladimir back at court. He alone tried to keep the guard from opening fire on the people. He was right; I should have listened to him. And to you."

What could I say? He should have. We both knew it.

"Will you restore Cyril?" I asked, thinking of Miechen, who, since the incident at my palace with Vladimir, had turned her back on me. I missed her, even if I wondered why. Nothing was ever easy where she was concerned. I suspected she'd incited Cyril to wed Ducky on purpose. Gaining Alexandra's former sister-in-law as her new daughter-in-law was a slap to our tsarina's pride that Miechen couldn't resist.

Nicky sighed. "What else can I do? I don't approve of their marriage and Sunny is outraged, but with the situation as it stands, I cannot have us at one another's throats."

It was perhaps the wisest thing I'd heard him say since he took the throne, and it made me more confident to tell him, "This impossible war with Japan is also at our throats. If it requires humiliation for the sake of peace, so be it. Send Witte to negotiate. You must act now, before it gets any worse."

He gave me an exhausted nod. "Yes. This time, I promise to do as you say."

ALEXANDRA BESTIRRED HERSELF from her couch to sup with us and listen to Olga and Tatiana play a duet on the piano. In the isolation of the estate, I slept better than I had in weeks, without the nightmares I'd suffered in St. Petersburg, running down corridors pursued by a mob I couldn't see but could clearly hear, baying at my heels.

When I woke and went down to the dining room—breakfasts were informal at the palace, as Nicky rose much earlier than Alexandra, and the girls ate in their apartments—I found my son waiting, his eyes red, as if he'd been crying.

"No." I came to a frightened halt. "Not again. Is Alexei . . . ?"

"Not Alexei." He took my hands in his. "Sergei. A bomb, as he went out in his carriage from the Kremlin." His voice snagged in his throat. "They murdered him."

"Murdered? It's not possible. . . ." I couldn't draw in a full breath. "Didn't he resign his governorship? We were only speaking of him yesterday."

"They blew him apart, like Grandpère Alexander." Nicky's voice quavered as he fought back tears. "Ella telegraphed us; she went out to retrieve his remains. She and Paul's children were supposed to go out with Sergei, but Dmitri had a stomachache, so they stayed behind. They would have been killed, too. The explosion was so powerful, it shattered a spire on the cathedral."

I swayed, gripping his hands, recalling Sergei's lean grace, those green eyes and erect carriage on horseback when he'd stopped me on the road to Khodynka. They had never forgiven him for that day. They'd waited for the hour to exact their revenge.

"Ella says there's hardly anything left of him for the funeral. I've ordered the malefactors arrested, but Moscow is a cesspool. Who knows if they'll be found." Nicky swallowed, summoning fortitude for what awaited him. "Sunny doesn't know yet. She's still asleep. Alexei had a restless night. He's starting to teethe. She stayed up to rub his gums."

"We must attend the funeral—" I started to say.

He gripped my hands tighter. "No. Other threats were sent to the police, saying Sergei was the first but not the last. I forbid it. None of us can set foot in Moscow. I'll ensure he's laid to rest with full honors, but I forbid anyone of the family to attend."

"But Ella is caring for the children because Paul is in exile abroad. What shall they do without Sergei?" I searched his face, feeling in that moment as aimless as he did, adrift on this storm of violence, where the next wave, exploding out of nowhere, might submerge us.

"I will provide whatever they need." He kissed my cheek. "You must leave as soon as possible, Mama. Go to Denmark. Visit Aunt Alix in England. Don't return until I call for you."

He strode away to inform Alexandra that her sister's husband was dead. He left me in the dining room with the servants tiptoeing about me, setting out coffee and pastries; when I heard Alexandra's cry of despair, I pressed my hands to my mouth and turned away.

⁓

UPON MY ARRIVAL in Denmark, Nicky fulfilled his promise and dispatched Count Witte to the United States, where he persuaded President Roosevelt to support our refusal to pay indemnities, in exchange for our immediate evacuation of Manchuria. Witte was heralded for bringing about the end of a war that had cost thousands of lives and plunged us into revolution, and Nicky rewarded the count by entrusting him with devising the Manifesto for the Improvement of State Order—my son's first step toward a constitution.

Witte wrote to tell me the announcement of pending reforms had quieted the rioters. Okhrana agents, working as moles in Social Democratic groups, reported grave concern among the agitators that should we grant constitutional liberties, their revolution would be squashed. These agents had intercepted messages from anarchic leaders in Geneva, who encouraged relentless defiance. One of these revolutionary leaders in particular, Witte warned, posed a significant threat. Born in Russia to a wealthy but untitled family, his name was Vladimir Lenin. He'd become a proponent of Marxism after his elder brother was executed as a terrorist under Sasha's regime. Arrested for sedition twice, he fled abroad, where he became the head of a radical Marxist faction called Bolsheviks, who advocated seizure of power by the proletariat and abolishing imperial rule. Unlike the Nihilists, who'd never possessed unity of leadership, these Bolsheviks were united under Lenin. What Witte did not say explicitly but I inferred was that my son had reached a perilous crossroads. Unless he ceased to defend the autocracy, Nicky risked the loss of his throne.

I wrote to Nicky at once: *Better to give up something than regret everything.*

My father was now eighty-seven, his court calcified since Mama's death. Alix could not join me due to her own duties as queen, but my sister Thyra did. After years of not seeing each other, Thyra and I reveled in our reunion, taking residence at the Amalienborg and shopping in Copenhagen, to the Danish people's delight. Thyra was sorely tried

THE ROMANOV EMPRESS 279

in her marriage, but we shared memories of our childhood, when life had been less complicated. When she left, I promised to visit her in Austria.

I was still in Denmark when word came that our broken soldiers straggled home to discover no provision made for them. With the economy in tatters from the war, uproar surged anew, paralyzing the country with another general strike and more violent demonstrations. The revolutionaries were organizing in Moscow, demanding the assembly of local "soviets," or regional advisory councils, whose members were of the working class. They underscored their intent by assassinating several government officials and planting bombs. Again, Witte wrote to me, requesting my support. Despite the disruption in the telegram services, I managed to cable back my response, urging Nicky to move forward as quickly as possible to sanction civil liberties.

By October, it was done. My son declared Russia under a semiconstitutional monarchy. A State Duma, or parliament, would be established, as well as an expanded state council to consult with the soviets, with restrictions on freedom of conscience, speech, and assembly rescinded. What my father-in-law had planned all those years ago was now a reality, yet when I wrote to tell Nicky I was coming home, he replied that I must wait.

Celebrating Christmas so far from my children was dismal for me. I tried to enjoy the holidays with my father and brothers, who rallied around me to make me feel at home, but Denmark no longer felt that way to me. Russia was where my heart belonged.

After the New Year celebrations of 1906, Papa complained of chest pain. As I sat holding his gnarled hand, he left us as Mama had, without any fuss. Alix made haste to attend the funeral. Watching our father's coffin lowered into the vault in Roskilde Cathedral beside our mother, my sister slipped her hand in mine.

"Now we are truly orphans," she whispered.

⁓

With my return to Russia delayed, I decided that Alix and I should fulfill our childhood dream of purchasing our own house in Denmark. Our sixty-two-year-old brother, now King Frederick VIII, moved with his family into Amalienborg to resuscitate the court. Freddie had waited patiently in the wings for more than forty years, and while he assured Alix and me that we were always welcome, a sister, much like a mother-in-law, could overstay her visit. Instead, I hauled Alix with me to visit several available properties, until we found Hvidøre House, a manor on the Øresund coast.

The house reminded me with a pang of Sasha, for he would have found it as charming as I did, with its Italianate clock tower, unkempt rose garden, orchard of herbs and fruit trees, and a private beach just across the road. It had plenty of space—a study for Alix and me, five bedrooms and two drawing rooms, as well as ample servant quarters—but no working bathroom, to my sister's dismay.

"The owner can't maintain the upkeep," I said. "The asking price is absurd. We'll offer less and use the savings to renovate."

I had to practically shout in Alix's ear, as her deafness had worsened, but she agreed, so I undertook the purchase. I commissioned modern-izations like electricity, central heating, and new plumbing, as well as a tunnel to provide access to the beach without crossing the road. Alix suggested a British firm for interior décor; we submerged ourselves in sampling wallpapers and furniture catalogs until she had to return to England.

"Next year in September," I said, "we'll come here by yacht and not be a bother to anyone. Won't it be lovely, a place of our own. We can be orphans together."

She smiled. "You always find a way to live."

We hugged each other, vowing as always when we said goodbye, "Sisters forever."

In April, Nicky sent word that he wanted me present for the Duma's inauguration. Boarding my train with my retinue, dogs, and enough luggage to fill six carriages, as I'd spent lavishly on myself and gifts for the family, I returned to Russia. I'd been gone nearly a year. But I wasn't sad to leave Denmark. I now had a house to which I could return.

Little did I suspect how much of a refuge Hvidøre would become.

PART V

1906–1914

The Tsarina's Mystic

Pray, Tsar of Russia. Pray.

—Rasputin

CHAPTER THIRTY-TWO

I surveyed the newly elected members of the Duma on the left-hand side of St. George's Hall in the Winter Palace, dressed in worker blouses and *moujik* trousers, their caps doffed out of respect but with the odious revolutionary scarlet kerchief at their throats. Their expressions varied between insolence and hatred, with one in particular catching my eye with his sneer.

"*Who* is that?" I hissed to Miechen at my side.

"One of them," she said in my ear. "Vladimir says he takes orders directly from Lenin. A Bolshevik to his marrow. I'd not be surprised if he threw the bomb that killed Sergei."

My throat constricted. I tried to remain impassive as I stood with my daughters, Alexandra a short distance away, dressed like us in her white court gown and pearl-and-diamond headdress. Under the canopy over the dais, Nicky prepared to give his opening speech, dressed in his Preobrazhensky uniform.

But my gaze kept darting to the elected representatives opposite us. I'd been shocked to learn upon my arrival that Witte had been dismissed, the post of prime minister given over to Goremykin, a sixty-six-year-old cabinet member without significant accomplishments. When I queried Nicky, he said, "Witte wanted more concessions than I was willing to make. I asked him to resign. I no longer trusted him to do what's best for us."

I'd found his reason inexplicable until now, seeing these sullen men who would participate in our government, a stark contrast to the right-hand side of the hall, where our ministers and officials had donned formal uniforms or court dress.

Nicky lifted his voice. "The welfare of Russia's sovereign cannot be separated from the welfare of our people, and their sorrows are our sorrows. We call upon you, loyal sons of Russia, to remember your duty to our country, to assist in ending this unprecedented turmoil and, together with us, make every effort to restore tranquility."

As he expounded on his intention to rule in concert with the Duma but to never alienate his son the tsarevich from the inheritance due to him, I glanced at Alexandra. Her face had gone as hard as the diamonds about her throat. Sensing my eyes on her, she shifted her gaze. For a heart-stopping moment, her virulent stare drove into me.

"She blames you," Miechen whispered. "She thinks you and Witte devised this humiliation, depriving Alexei of the autocracy when his time comes." Her smile was shallow. "If she could, she'd throw the next bomb. At you."

"It was necessary." I trembled in sudden rage. I had supported this reform for Russia and my son's welfare, but all of a sudden I couldn't abide it, our submission to these uncouth rebels who sought to abolish what God had bestowed upon nearly three hundred years of Romanov rule. It was a travesty, brought about by thugs and murderers. Sasha would have roared to see us reach such a pass. Had he lived, we never would have. He'd have seen them garroted in the Palace Square by those red scarves.

"That remains to be seen," Miechen replied.

Applause rose as Nicky finished his speech and turned to us. We wept openly, although my tears were mostly of relief. It was finished. Done. We had submitted. It might be a travesty, but at least now we could resume our lives without fear of evildoing.

Only Alexandra remained dry-eyed, as if carved of stone.

⁓

"WE LOVE EACH other," Misha said. "We didn't mean for it to happen, and I realize it's complicated, as Natalia still has a husband, but we want to marry."

I regarded my youngest son in dismay. I'd returned only weeks before to Gatchina from my annual trip abroad. Three years had passed since the inauguration of our Duma, but nothing had gone as expected, with Duma members at odds with one another and with Goremykin (who'd proven as ineffective as I'd feared, prompting me to implore Nicky to replace him), while the revolutionaries continued to agitate and gnaw at our heels. Seeing as I could only advise my son and often found my advice appreciated but ignored, I'd elected to spend as much time as I could abroad, going away every year to visit family and friends. This year, I had gone to Paris for a monthlong stay with my brother-in-law Alexis, then to the south of France, and finally to Denmark to see my brother, after which Alix had joined me in Hvidøre for three weeks, during which we'd cooked our own meals and read together at night. I always missed Russia when I was away, but as soon as I returned, I realized that what I missed was the memory of a past that no longer existed. In its place was turmoil and the unexpected—and the unwelcome, like now.

"You cannot be serious," I exclaimed. "If she has a husband, she's already married."

"She's also been previously divorced. She has a daughter by Wulfert, her second husband—"

"Who is your fellow officer! God in heaven, what is amiss in the Cuirassiers? I'm ashamed to be its honorary colonel in chief. First Olga with Kulikovsky, now you with another officer's wife. Does your commander exercise no control over how his regiment behaves?"

Misha's eyes hardened, although I showed restraint. He'd always been the most pliant of my children, dedicated to duty and mindful of scandal, despite his share of lovers. I'd practically given up on Olga, who, still denied her divorce, continued to parade about with Kulikovsky, but I counted on Misha to remain steadfast. While no longer our tsarevich, he was vital to the dynasty; after Alexei, he stood next in line to the throne. I'd suggested various brides for him—princesses of Great Britain and Sweden—and he'd showed no interest, so he had caught me by surprise.

"Wulfert has agreed to grant Natalia a divorce," he said.

Despite my effort to remain calm, I rapped my hand on my desk. "Out of the question. Misha, how can you do this to us? Are you not aware of what is happening? Prime Minister Goremykin was useless; your brother had to dismiss him and appoint another in his place. The

Duma is a disaster, with no one able to agree on anything, and daily protests in the streets. Those revolutionaries dare to demand your brother's abdication. If we fail, they win. You must marry to bring us advantage. The twice-divorced wife of a common officer brings quite the opposite."

He returned my stare. Then, to my horror, he said, "Perhaps Nicky should abdicate. He never wanted to rule. All he need do is see how our people live, their hunger and lack of work, their constant struggle to survive. Many no longer believe the tsar can save them."

I bolted to my feet. "It is our dynasty. Would you disregard centuries of tradition, the sacrifices made by your grandfather and father, for us to be who we are?"

He met my infuriated gaze. "Mama, Russia no longer needs us to be who we are. I never wanted any of this, either. I want to marry whom I choose." He paused for a moment before he said, "Natalia is with child. It is mine."

I felt short of breath. "How . . . how can you even know? She still has a husband."

"With whom she doesn't sleep." He ran a hand through his thinning hair; his premature loss of hair plagued him, like his father before him. I thought it accentuated his noble forehead and gentle features, his sculpted nose with his trim mustache, and soulful eyes, even if I now began to recognize that, much like Olga, he was a child of mine that I didn't know well at all. "I see no reason why Nicky should deny me. He has Alexei as his heir. Olga loves someone else but cannot divorce her husband. Xenia and Sandro have separated. Does my brother want me to be equally unhappy?"

"Do not mention Xenia to me," I cried. "Must you break my heart as she has? Marriage is for life. One doesn't leave a spouse over a misunderstanding."

"Mama, you know it's more than a misunderstanding. Sandro has been keeping a mistress in Nice. He asked for a divorce and Nicky took him to task, rupturing their years of friendship. And for what? Xenia told me she's suspected for some time and merely waited for Sandro to confess. She may be content to remain as they are, with her residing most of the year with the boys and Irina in the Crimea while Sandro comes and goes from France, but that isn't the arrangement I desire for myself."

"Nicky will never permit it," I repeated, but I was starting to panic. Misha might appear pliant, but he could be as stubborn as Sasha when he set his mind to something. "You're his brother. A grand duke. Natalia Wulfert has no position. No title. She is nobody."

"She is somebody to me." He drew himself to full height, his plumed helmet tucked under his arm. "I'm prepared to resign my rank and title. I'll follow Uncle Alexis's example and move abroad. He likes Paris well enough. At least there, he can do as he pleases."

"Alexis has always traveled extensively, and he moved to Paris after the fall of Port Arthur and Sergei's assassination. Moreover, he's not in succession to the throne."

"He moved to Paris because his mistress is still married to her husband," Misha countered. "As Nicky would never have tolerated their liaison here, Alexis left to be with the woman he loves. I admire him for it. Why shouldn't I do the same?"

I stumbled over my hem in my haste to reach him, to touch his shoulder and somehow restrain him. "Alexis chose to leave. But your other uncle Grand Duke Paul was stripped of his title and income, banished for marrying that common woman. Misha, you are the tsar's brother. We cannot afford another scandal. Promise me you'll not do anything precipitous. Give it time. Resign from the Cuirassiers and take another military assignment away from here. If you're still determined to marry her after a year, I'll speak to Nicky on your behalf."

Misha raised his chin, so that I had to crane my gaze to his. "You think time will resolve it? You want me to go away and wait, in case she miscarries or dies in childbirth?"

I recoiled. "How can you say such a dreadful thing to me?"

"Because I've seen how Olga is treated." He paused, considering me. "I'll request a transfer to the Chernigov Hussars at Orel, outside Moscow. But I warn you now: I'll not abandon Natalia. I've rented an apartment for her in St. Petersburg and she has separated from her husband. Let her be. That is my condition for waiting until you think the time is right. If she's intimidated in any way, I'll marry her at once. I'm not afraid of leaving Russia. In fact, I think I might welcome it."

Before I could say another word, he turned on his heel and departed.

I had to press my hands to my mouth to keep from screaming.

"A DISASTER!" I cried at Miechen as soon as I entered her drawing room. "What am I to do? Misha claims he *loves* her—a married woman of no rank, who's already divorced once and is carrying his child. Another family disgrace, in the midst of everything else."

She made a commiserative sound. "I do feel for you, Minnie. When our sons refuse to heed our counsel, it can be very trying. As you know, Cyril's marriage to Ducky did not go easy on me. Sometimes, much as it pains us, we must let our sons make their own beds. Only then will they learn we only want clean sheets for them."

"At least Ducky is a princess! This Wulfert woman is a commoner. When Nicky hears of it, he'll be furious. And Alexandra will rub my face in it, though she has no right, ensconced in Tsarskoe Selo while the country falls apart and all she can think about is protecting—" I curbed my outburst.

"Yes?" said Miechen, with an arch of her eyebrow. "Please don't hesitate on my account. Whatever ails the boy must be serious, indeed. Does she intend to hide our tsarevich away until he reaches his majority of age?"

I wished I'd kept quiet. Rumors persisted about my grandson, although Alexei had just turned five, sturdy and mischievous, doted on by his family. I couldn't tell Miechen that he'd suffered no further episodes of prolonged bleeding, even if he'd had a few persistent bruises whenever he managed to evade his *dyadka* and bump hard against a table or chair. That he'd inherited the dreaded ailment was evident, but I wasn't convinced it required such overbearing seclusion, even if I dared not breathe a word against it to Alexandra.

"She won't let any of the children be seen," I said. "She fears assassins might lurk behind every bush. Were it up to her, none of them would leave Tsarskoe Selo save for their summer excursions to Finland."

"Apparently, it is up to her." Miechen motioned. "Minnie, sit. Have a cigarette." She extended her case. "Turkish tobacco. I was nearly fined for importing it without a permit. Goremykin may have been useless, but he had our customs officials working overtime to find any contraband upon which to levy a fine." She snorted. "I sent some to Nicky for his Name Day. He liked them so much, he asked the Turkish ambassador to provide him with an annual supply. So much for contraband, if the tsar himself allows it."

After lighting the aromatic cigarette and gulping down my tea, I blurted out, "Nicky dismissed Goremykin on my advice. I first suggested we bring back Witte, who can manage the Duma, but Nicky wouldn't hear of it, so we agreed on Stolypin instead. Stolypin proposed that the Duma hold new elections; now, he wants to increase state funds for the peasants to acquire farmland. Keeping them content in the country, he claims, will deprive the revolutionaries of fodder."

"Ah." She reclined in her chair. "That must explain the bomb that went off at his house, after he barred the Duma from assembly to force them to these new elections."

My cigarette wavered as I lifted it to my lips, as much from the memory as from her callous recollection of it. "Miechen, you mustn't make light of it. Twenty-eight of his guests were killed by that bomb. His own daughter's legs were crushed when the balcony fell on her."

"Yes. It was terrible." She dropped four lumps of sugar into her cup. She didn't seem perturbed; no matter what happened, she never seemed perturbed.

"How can you be so calm?" I said in despair. "Look at me. My nerves . . . Misha and Olga are determined to send me to an early grave, and we'll have no peace until those monstrous revolutionaries are destroyed. They want us all on our knees."

"Or shot in the head. Minnie, I'm rational. We're not dead yet." She sipped her tea before she said, "As for Stolypin's daughter, she is walking again. Her injury mustn't have been as severe as you were led to believe. Or perhaps this friend of Gigogne's is truly what they say."

"Friend?" A sudden pit yawned in my stomach. "Dr. Philippe died four years ago."

"Not Philippe." She savored the moment of catching me off guard. "Haven't you heard? I understand this latest one is right out of Dostoyevsky. When that bomb went off at Stolypin's house, Gigogne dispatched her new friend there at once. Apparently, he healed the girl. The doctors were preparing to amputate her legs, and he prayed over her. Lo and behold, by the next week she'd risen to her feet like Lazarus. Wherever do they find these miracle workers? Whenever I have a pain in my back, there's nary one to be found."

Resisting my barrage of questions, I drew on my cigarette. It had gone out; as I reached for her gold-plated lighter, she added, "His name is Rasputin," in a tone that implied the name should mean something to me.

I now let the moment get the better of her. "Is that so?" I said.

"It is. And he's no fraud from Paris, though he too was introduced to Gigogne through her lady Vyrubova," she replied tartly. "A Siberian peasant, who claims he had a vision of our Lady of Kazan and became a *strannik,* making pilgrimage to all the holy sites—barefoot, naturally. Vyrubova heard of his allegedly miraculous healing powers, traveled all the way to his home village to consult with him, then invited him to the Alexander Palace to meet with Gigogne. From what I hear, she's very taken with him." Miechen paused, gauging me. "He now resides here, in St. Petersburg, and was invited again to Tsarskoe Selo as recently as last week, to what purpose is anyone's guess—which, as you can expect, everyone is doing. A man of such ill repute, visiting the empress at her own palace . . ."

"Ill repute?" I shed my feigned disinterest. "How can I not know any of this? I was only abroad for four months this year!"

"I'm only telling you what I heard, Minnie."

"Yes, and *how* did you happen to hear it?" I retorted.

"At a luncheon at the Yusupov Palace," she said, as if it were to be assumed. "By the way, I saw your granddaughter Irina there. Such a beauty she's become. All that time away in the Crimea must agree with her, though it's a shame we don't see more of Sandro and Xenia these days. I forget, how old is their daughter now?"

"Almost fourteen." I found myself gripping her Limoges teacup so hard, I feared I might shatter it. I wasn't about to discuss Xenia with her. She was no doubt already fully apprised of the disintegration of my eldest daughter's marriage.

"Only that? She appears older. You must keep close watch over her. She and Prince Felix Yusupov seemed rather fond of each other, and he's already twenty-one."

"What harm is there in it?" I replied. "Felix is heir to one of the largest fortunes in Russia. We've both known his mother, Princess Zenaida, for many years; our circle isn't so large that we can forbid their acquaintance. Irina could do worse."

She smiled. "You might not be so amenable if you knew more about Felix than his worth. Suffice to say, he suffers from the same vice as our late Sergei. Only Felix doesn't care to hide it. And he prefers to *dress* for the occasion, if you understand my meaning."

I did. And I'd rather not have known. All of a sudden, as often happened, I wished I hadn't come to her to spill out my troubles. From my upset over Misha and Olga to my fear that Russia careened again toward revolution, we'd come full circle to sordid gossip. Inevitably, I would leave her feeling as if I'd confided more than intended.

But I did not leave. Instead, I said testily, "You were saying about this new friend?"

"Oh, yes. Well. It seems Felix has developed an interest in mysticism, as indolent rich young men are apt to do. Zenaida told me he made a trip to Moscow to visit Ella. The poor dear's grief over Sergei has unhinged her." She grimaced. "Madness must run in their Hesse blood. Ella showed Felix one of Sergei's fingers. It was found on the Kremlin's rooftop after his funeral, and she keeps it in a reliquary. She also spoke to Felix at length about renouncing her worldly goods to endow a convent. A Romanov grand duchess, serving gruel to the poor!" Miechen started to laugh, until she saw the look on my face.

"It's not cause for derision," I said. "I know how it feels to lose a husband." I abruptly came to my feet in disgust and was reaching for my shawl when she said hastily, "Zenaida was the one who mentioned to me that Gigogne has this new friend. Just by coincidence, her son Felix is acquainted with Anna Vyrubova. Apparently he either heard of Rasputin through her or met the man in person at one of the usual assortment of salons."

I stared at her. "Did Zenaida say anything else I should know?"

Miechen waved her hand. "Only that Gigogne's favor has made Rasputin exceedingly popular. Entertaining enough for some, I suppose, but I never attend such gatherings. Felix Yusupov does, however. Perhaps you should pay a visit to Zenaida? She told me she hasn't received you in over two years and fears she may have done something to offend."

"She has not. What of his ill repute?"

She hesitated, making me clench my teeth. "He's amassed quite the following," she said. "All women, naturally, and of all sorts. He's known to frequent gypsy taverns and brothels on the islands . . . I don't wish to be indelicate, Minnie. Must I spell it out?"

Since when had *she* not wished to be indelicate?

"Yes," I said. "If you don't, someone else will."

I could see her aversion wasn't pretense. Were it the habitual peccadilloes, she'd have had no reluctance in describing them. She never had in the past.

"A lecher," she said. "Orgies. Public drunkenness. He seduces his acolytes, telling them God wants us to sin because only then can we be forgiven. A harem at his disposal, yet he has a wife and children in Siberia. Is that enough? As I said, Felix Yusupov might know more. How much more do you need? An uncouth peasant who abandons his family to come to St. Petersburg and frolic like a satyr is hardly suitable company for our tsarina."

Having heard enough, I abruptly changed the subject. "Alexis took me to Louis Cartier's establishment in Paris. Such beautiful things. I purchased several brooches. Monsieur Cartier told me you're a favored customer and maintain an open account with him."

Her face immediately brightened, gossip tossed aside for her favorite passion: jewels. She had her maidservant bring down her coffer, spreading out for me her latest acquisitions—a ransom of diamonds in white gold, rubies, emeralds, sapphires, and topaz, embedded in filigree settings depicting insects and animals, all delicately wrought as lace.

"You'll never be able to wear all of it," I remarked sourly, thinking that even in the midst of chaos, she never ceased to indulge herself.

"I most certainly will. Just as soon as we're rid of these tiresome revolutionaries and can hold a proper Season again. Here, take this." She handed me an enamel-and-gold cigarette case edged in pink diamonds, monogrammed with an M. "Isn't it convenient that we share the same initial? You must put some of my Turkish cigarettes in it for Nicky."

To no avail, I protested against her generosity, leaving her palace with a new bauble and an inescapable trepidation. I refused to ask the Yusupovs about my own family.

Instead, I would go to Tsarskoe Selo and find out for myself.

CHAPTER THIRTY-THREE

The estate, enclosed by its wrought-iron palisade and patrolled at all hours, was quiet, the miniature Chinese hamlet built for the children like an exotic mirage in the morning mist. Though the morning was still mild for late November, frost sparkled on the grounds; the chill in the air meant the palace would be icy. Alexandra shared her late grandmother's notion that cold environments were healthy, even if on a whim, she'd suddenly decide to order the stoves lit and have us sweltering.

Footmen unloaded my luggage from the carriage that had conveyed me across the park from the private train station. While the trip was only a little over an hour by train, coming here was never a daylong event. I had to pack for a week's stay, as I could never be certain of what I might find. If Alexandra was ill, as she often was, I'd have to tarry before I saw her.

In the palace vestibule, I paused. It was a dark space with a black-and-white marble floor and glazed cloth on the walls, the repository for gifts from officials—symbolic keys to cities in the empire and other items no one knew what to do with, its mélange of bazaar-like offerings propped in niches and curio cabinets. Unhooking my ermine mantle—today the palace was heated, and it hit me like a blast—I wondered if Nicky was in his study or with Alexandra in her apartments on the east side that overlooked the lake and the gardens.

Around me, the footmen bustled, nodding at my request to have my bags taken to my suite of apartments. I was about to inquire why no one was here to greet me when I caught sight of two figures hastening toward me down the corridor.

I immediately recognized Prince Vladimir Obolensky, Nicky's *gof marschal* and one of his few trusted intimates. Obolensky was regal in his bearing, with perfectly waxed mustachios and a mournfully aristocratic face. Impeccable in his red-and-gold uniform, a cousin of my own head steward, he'd mastered centuries of convoluted court etiquette to fulfill his exacting position.

He quickened his pace at the sight of me. Beside him loped an unfamiliar figure with a straggling black beard and shoulder-length hair, dressed in loose trousers tucked into his boots like a *moujik* and a cassock-like linen peasant shirt. A vagrant caught wandering inside the palace? I wondered as Obolensky bowed before me.

"Your Majesty, we were not expecting you," he said, with evident dismay that I'd been left to attend to myself.

I glanced at the stranger at his side. He did not bow. He was shorter than the prince and no vagrant, either, despite his disheveled appearance. In fact, he looked well fed, a working man, his legs strong, his broad shoulders straining his cassock, and his large, veined hands with tapered fingers clasped at his midriff. A plain wood crucifix hung on a leather cord about his neck. His eyes were arresting—almost sulfuric in their pale-blue intensity, like glazed ice. He regarded me with undisguised interest.

"Didn't you receive my telegram?" I asked the prince, having to tear my gaze away as the man's thick lips under his unkempt beard parted in a leer.

"We did." Obolensky sounded agitated, highly unusual for him. "But we thought you would arrive later this afternoon." He was upset that he'd not been informed of my train's arrival; someone's head would roll for the lapse, if I knew the prince. "I must beg Your Majesty's forgiveness. It is inexcusable of me to have left you waiting."

"I've not been waiting long." I was starting to feel uneasy. *Who* was this stranger staring at me? The moment I thought this, I realized: Alexandra's new friend, Rasputin.

"I'll only be a moment, Majesty." Obolensky turned toward the entryway, about to escort the friend out. The friend didn't follow. He continued to regard me as if he could see my discomfort under my skin. He made a sudden, almost predatory move. Thinking he sought to embrace me with the traditional Russian hug and triple kiss, I stepped back. In a rough-gravel voice, he said sadly, "*Matushka,* why do you fear me? I wish you no harm."

"Fear you?" I echoed. "I certainly do not."

He inclined his head, greasy hair cascading over his face and hooked nose. He followed Obolensky out. I felt as if I should take a bath. The man surely had fleas. He had left in his wake an unpleasant odor, of sour sweat and dirty clothing. This was the friend with whom Alexandra was so taken? Had she lost her mind? He was nothing but a common serf, evidently unaware of St. Petersburg's numerous public bathhouses.

Moments later, Obolensky returned. With murmured apologies as I reassured him again that I was fine, he led me past the Abyssinian guard posted at Nicky's study door.

It was my favorite room in the palace: masculine, with polished walnut cabinets and high paneling, above which ran a strip of red damask wallpaper. He'd filled the room with personal articles, a globe on a brass tripod and shelves lined with his leather-bound books. His desk was orderly, for he liked to keep his papers tidy, populated by silver- and enamel-framed family photographs, many taken by Alexandra and the girls with their box Brownies. The air smelled of tobacco and linseed oil, of paper and ink—redolent of Nicky himself, reminding me of his devotion to literature and need for solitude.

"Her Imperial Majesty the Dowager Empress," announced the prince, before he bowed to me and retreated.

Nicky had been dozing in his green leather armchair, a book on his lap. When he heard my entry, he came so suddenly to his feet, he tipped the book to the floor. "Mama."

I peeled off my gloves. "It seems no one was expecting me. You must reassure Obolensky that I don't hold him responsible. I can handle my own reception, if need be."

He lit a cigarette, still in his dressing gown, a tasseled velvet bedcap on his head. His breakfast tray sat untouched on his desk. Had he overslept? He always rose hours before Alexandra. Surely he should have eaten and dressed by now.

"Did you spend the night here?" I asked, in concern.

He nodded. "Alexandra is exhausted. I let her have our bed to herself."

I knew from my visits that, unlike most married couples, they still shared a bed despite maintaining separate apartments—proof of their devotion to each other and of mutual tolerance. But the manner in which he spoke increased my concern.

"Is she unwell?" I said, wondering how long I'd be required to stay here.

He nodded, motioning me to the matching armchair beside his. "She's been caring for Alexei. He had an accident."

I went still. Then I made myself sit, scavenging in my wrist bag for my new cigarette case. "Is it serious?" I couldn't stanch the accusation in my voice. "I had no word of it."

Nicky sighed. "He fell while playing with the girls. At first we thought it was just a contusion, but his knee swelled up—" His voice caught; he smoked nervously for a few moments, reaching for his silver lighter and handing it to me. "It was twice its normal size. The pain, Mama . . . Nothing eased it. Alexandra followed Botkin's advice and gave him the salicylic acid, which she takes for her lumbago. It didn't help. He developed a fever. We didn't know what to do."

I was horrified by the news. "Why didn't you tell me? I would have come at once."

"He's much better now." Nicky finished his cigarette; in the awkward silence, I extended my case to him. "The Turkish ones, from Miechen. She tells me you like them."

"Did she?" He extracted a cigarette from the case, turning the Cartier object over in his hands as if he were admiring it. He wasn't. He was prolonging the moment, loath to admit that he would have sent for me, only Alexandra wouldn't allow it.

"I am his grandmother," I said. "I'd rather be informed by you. Miechen mentioned to me that a new friend has been visiting here. Is Alexei the reason why?"

His eyes narrowed. "Does Miechen know about my son?"

"Of course not," I replied, my voice sharpening at the suspicion in his tone. "I've told no one, as you requested. But she suspects something grave ails the child. They all do. What can we expect? If they don't know the truth, they speculate." I paused, drawing on my cigarette. "Was that the new friend just now, leaving the palace?"

"Yes. Father Grigori. He's been a godsend to us."

I found it difficult to believe. "How so?"

"He has a power—" Nicky paused, amending his words, for he knew I didn't believe in such things. "A way with Alexei. He calms him. He sits with him, prays, and talks to him. He stops the bleeding. He came when it was at its worst. Alexandra was in such despair, I didn't have the heart to refuse her, though I'd barely met the man. But he did the impossible." His sleep-deprived eyes were full of relief. "Within a day, the swelling started to abate. No hemorrhage. Alexei is still abed, but Father Grigori has assured us he'll recover. He never says more. He never promises, but he gives us such hope."

"I see." I did not, but I'd take him at his word. What did it matter if an unwashed self-proclaimed holy man mumbled a few prayers and offered solace, if he did no other harm? I might not like it, but it wasn't anything I could reasonably object to, no matter how disturbing it might be. Hope was essential for a sick child, even if with an illness like Alexei's, it could be dangerous to hope too much. The disappointment would be all the more difficult to bear.

"Can I see him?"

"Father Grigori left. You did see him. He never stays here. I wouldn't allow it—"

"No." I touched his hand to reassure him. "Alexei."

"Yes, of course. He's in his room. I'll take you to him."

HE WAS ASLEEP, his elfin face pallid but without visible pain, his leg hoisted up by a sling so the trapped blood could drain from his knee, which was very discolored and, it seemed to me, still horribly inflamed. As I glanced at Derevenko standing vigil in the corner, I pulled up a stool by my grandson's bedside and watched as he slept, his eyelids fluttering. Biting back tears, I brushed his fine gold-brown hair from his forehead as I whispered, "Our precious boy." His skin was warm to the touch but not feverish.

His gray-blue eyes opened. Nicky's eyes. "Grandmère."

I smiled. "I came as soon as I could. How do you feel?"

He paused, as if taking stock of his body. "It doesn't hurt anymore."

"That's a good sign. A very good sign. Before you know it, you'll be up and running again." I wouldn't chastise him for behaving like any boy. Alexandra did that enough, seeking to instill in him constant awareness that he stood apart, not only by rank but because he was ill.

"I was running," he said. "That's why I slipped. Is Mama very upset with me?"

"No, no." I caressed his cheek. "She's worried. Not upset. Never with you. Rest now. Your papa is here. See?" I shifted away as Nicky stepped in. He'd been tarrying in the corridor.

"My son." He spoke with such composure, I had to avert my face. Nicky's concern for Alexei ran so deep, I knew it was all he could feel. Yet he never showed it, stalwart as he sat upon the stool I vacated to take up a book from the bedside table. "Shall I read to you?"

I tiptoed out. Though his knee looked awful, Alexei didn't appear to be in discomfort. Nicky stayed with him while I went to see the girls. I found their apartments empty, a maid changing the sheets. She suggested I wait in the drawing room, as Their Highnesses took their dogs outside for a walk at this hour.

In the drawing room, I found Anastasia on the window seat with her scrapbook.

At eight years of age, my youngest granddaughter had grown, though she would be short, taking after my side of the family. And very pretty, too—not ethereal like Tatiana or as arresting as Olga, but with a liveliness to her wide-spaced blue eyes and with tousled ringlets of red-gold hair like her mother's, drawn back from her round face with a crumpled bow. Her simple white frock with its lace hem was stained with what looked like plum jam from breakfast. The moment she saw me, she leapt up to embrace me, then proceeded to show me her scrapbook, in which she'd pressed dried petals, scraps of leaves, and a crow's feather, all surrounded by her determined scrawl.

"What does this say, Malankara?" I asked, using my nickname for her as I peered at her indecipherable writing. I had to resist my sorrow, comparing Anastasia's robust bloom to Alexei upstairs.

"A prayer," she said.

"In Cyrillic? No? But it's not French, either."

"English," she said with pride, as she should. She was still quite young to attempt the language, which both her parents spoke fluently.

"An English prayer." I smiled. "For what do you pray, my child?"

"For whom." Anastasia's chin lifted in uncanny resemblance to Alexandra when she heard something she didn't like. "For my brother.

Our friend tells us that prayers can heal him. Writing our prayers down is the best way for God to hear us."

"Oh?" My stomach plummeted. "Does your friend often give you advice?" I tried to keep my voice placid, for Anastasia was sensitive, despite her youth, and after the suffering Alexei had endured, she'd be even more attuned to any undercurrents.

"He's our friend, Amama," she said, as if puzzled by my ignorance.

"Yes, but I do not know him," I reminded her, recalling his leering smile and how his strange gaze had lingered on me. "Therefore, he's not yet my friend."

"Oh." Her frown cleared. This made sense to her, but she'd forgotten my question. I set her scrapbook aside, taking her hands in mine. Looking at her little fingers, marred from playing with the family dogs, the palace cats, and other mishaps, I was taken aback to see how thin and spotted my own were under my rings. The weight of the years seemed to fall upon me as I gazed into her eyes. "What else does your friend tell you?"

I wasn't sure why I was so concerned. Miechen had relayed that the man was hardly a paragon of virtue, but it was impossible to conceive he'd done anything untoward here. Alexandra had never tolerated the slightest infraction at court; she'd not abide it in her own abode. Yet he'd evidently met my granddaughters. He'd been allowed to visit Tsarskoe Selo not only to tend to Alexei but also to see the girls.

"His name is Father Grigori. He says prayers are how we can help Alexei." She hesitated. "He says God will heed us because He loves us so."

It was the expected childish response, but something in her voice, a slight quaver, made me ask, "Has he ever said anything else to you or your sisters?"

She didn't reply. I saw it then, a secret in her wary eyes, and when I said sharply, "Answer me," she whispered, "Mama says we mustn't speak of our friend to—"

Her voice cut off. She pulled away, looking toward the drawing room doors, which stood ajar, as though she anticipated someone lurking there. The stiffening of her shoulders sent a wave of anger through me. I started to my feet, about to demand that whoever was hiding come out, when Anastasia said, "Mama."

And as I strained to listen past the thud of my heart in my ears, I heard what she already had: the approaching creak of wheels.

Anastasia snatched the notebook from the window seat and tugged at her bow, which only tangled more in her hair. Before I could reach out to straighten it, Alexandra rolled in through the doors.

She sat in a wheeled chair like the one my mother had used in her final days, her mauve shawl draped over her shoulders, and one of her ladies pushing the chair from behind. In the sudden hush at her entrance, Alexandra's gaze swept immediately to me, standing by the window, with her daughter.

Alexandra pursed her lips. "Nastya, why aren't you outside with your sisters? It is the hour for exercise, not for dawdling indoors."

As if on cue, distant laughter and excited barking were heard through the window. Olga, Tatiana, and Maria strolled past on the outside terrace, swathed in matching blue coats, with their dogs straining at the leashes. Anastasia stood as if petrified.

"I asked her to stay." I set a hand on my granddaughter's shoulder. She was trembling. "I wanted to hear about everything she's been studying."

Alexandra waved her lady out, without taking her gaze from me. Her appearance disturbed but did not surprise me. The quiet beauty that first won Nicky's heart was no more, submerged by her poor health and cares; I hadn't known, however, that her lumbago had grown so debilitating, she required that chair. Had she nursed Alexei until she collapsed? Again, anger surged in me. How could she abandon herself so completely? Did she have no sense to take proper rest, to remain strong for Nicky and her daughters? The hostility between us must have been noticeable, for Anastasia kissed me quickly and, after an obligatory peck on her mother's cheek, bolted out the doors.

"Please walk," Alexandra called after her. "Do not run." It was probably an admonishment she uttered every hour of every day, intended to restrain Alexei, and futile in Anastasia's case, as the pounding of my granddaughter's retreating feet demonstrated.

I did not move as Alexandra staked her place by the gilded table, cluttered with framed photographs and assorted knickknacks, including an incongruous porcelain thimble. Looking at her as she settled into the space cleared to accommodate her chair, I had to resist the impulse to berate her.

"You're unwell," I said, moving to a chair opposite her. "I didn't know."

"You've been away." As she rang a bell on the table, I wanted to retort that my annual trips abroad were no reason to keep important family business from me. Instead, I sat, my outrage knotting my throat.

Never uncomfortable with silence, Alexandra waited, plucking stray threads in her shawl. Her reddish hair was coiled in a chignon, and, I noted, tarnished with gray. She looked ten years older than her thirty-seven. At her age, I'd been dancing all night till dawn, clad in my splendid gowns—a whirlwind in my zest for life. Again, I quelled the aggravation that beset me whenever I was with her. I hadn't endured the circumstances that she did.

"Did Anastasia show you everything she's studying?" she abruptly said. "She cannot have," she went on, preempting my reply. "She had that one notebook with her, and if I'm not mistaken, it wasn't one of her grammar lessons. An ideal student, alas, she is not."

She missed nothing. This, too, had not changed.

"Anastasia showed me enough," I said, and she glanced away.

Her lady arrived with the tea service and set it before us. Alexandra said, "We'll let it steep." Her lady curtsied and left. Once the requisite time passed, I waited for my daughter-in-law to check the pot. When she leaned forward, a spasm crossed her face, and I had to assume the duty, though I couldn't recall the last time I'd served anyone.

She sighed. "It is better now."

I understood. Everything was better now that her son was on the mend. I should have agreed; she must have been frantic. Instead, I recalled her friend's rude stare and probing question, the hot tea scalding my tongue. Finally, after another lengthy silence, I could abide no more.

"She told me about *your* friend," I said, making certain she heard my emphasis. "It seems he's been teaching a child how prayers are the only way to help her brother."

Alexandra paused, her cup at her lips. "I assume you came here for a purpose. Say what you must, Maria."

Not Mother dear. Not Minnie. Maria: my adopted Russian name. Something about the way she uttered it vanquished my pity, my understanding that she'd been fighting for Alexei and was confined to that chair because of it. In that moment, my anxiety for my grandson, the residue of my upset over my own children, and my talk with Miechen surged to the surface. All of a sudden it bothered me very much that this holy man of hers would have free rein over a place to which I must send advance word of my arrival.

"How can you permit it? *Who* is he to enjoy such liberties? There is talk of how he flaunts his association with you, pandering your name to all and sundry. Would you allow this friend to do and say whatever he likes?"

Though I was braced for it, she didn't launch into indignant denial. "I do not take kindly to gossip," she said. "I never have. And what he does is cure my son the tsarevich."

God help me, I wanted to fling my tea in her face.

"He does not. He cannot." I heard the fissure in my voice, betraying my eroding composure. "What the child has is incurable."

Her tone was flat. "What did they tell you?"

"You know already. Don't ask me to repeat it."

"It doesn't matter. God sent Father Grigori to guide me in my trials."

"Did God also send him to guide your daughters?"

"Never." Her hands constricted on her chair arms, as if she might rise to her feet. "He has never done anything improper here. I am always present when he visits," she said, confirming that, as usual, she knew far more of the gossip than she let on.

"Tell that to St. Petersburg," I replied. "Tell that to Miechen, who claims he's—"

"I don't care what Grand Duchess Pavlovna claims. I don't care and I will not hear it." Her stare bored through me. I found her fervor frightening, as if she were daring me to say aloud what she claimed she wouldn't hear.

"You cannot ignore society and think people won't talk," I said, repressing the urge to toss out into the open what Miechen had cited. "They will always talk, regardless."

"How is that my concern? Father Grigori saved Alexei. It is all I need to know."

Another burst of laughter echoed from the gardens. The girls trotted past the window again, going the other way, the wind billowing their scarves.

"Hurry up, Nastya," I heard Olga chide Anastasia, and I realized then what Alexandra must see—her girls, partaking of the morning air, mocking her with their exuberance, while her son, the one she felt most deserving, would never enjoy a carefree youth.

"You cannot know what it is to suffer as I do," she murmured.

It was a stab to my heart. "I lost my son George. Have you forgotten?"

"No." She returned her violet gaze to me. Violet, the color of her gown and shawl—a melancholic taint that clung to her, seeping into her pores, like smoke from a lavender pyre, quenching all joy. "I will never forget. Neither can you. Would you wish the same upon me?"

My tears crested. I forced them back. I would not weep before her.

"I would have died for my son," I whispered.

She looked away again, back to the window, where her daughters had passed.

"I wish I could," she said.

⁓

UPON MY RETURN to St. Petersburg, my brother-in-law Vladimir, Miechen's husband, died of a cerebral hemorrhage. Though disconsolate at his loss, in a typical display of her courage Miechen refused to vent her grief, seeming almost impervious as she dressed her husband's corpse in his uniform—he'd died over lunch, smoking a cigar—and oversaw the funeral arrangements. All of us were in attendance as Vladimir was entombed beside his parents and brothers in the St. Peter and Paul Cathedral.

For me, it felt like the end of an era. I recalled Vladimir's embrace of me after Nixa died, his ebullient charisma. Even when contentious, he'd been a loving brother-in-law and, in spite of his occasional dalliances, a devoted husband to Miechen. I knew widowhood wouldn't change her, but it would redefine her, as it had redefined me. And his death resurrected my grief for Sasha, so that one morning I ordered my coachman to take me over the frozen Neva to the fortress and the cathedral.

Under the painted vaults, I knelt before Sasha's tomb. I'd avoided visiting as often I should, his marble sarcophagus, so solid and impartial, too stark a reminder that I would never again see him in this life. It was too painful, all the tombs of those I loved—my husband, my infant boy, my George, Nixa, my father-in-law and his long-suffering wife, and now Vladimir. It served as evidence like nothing else could of how fleeting time was, of how we moved through our days without knowing which hour might be our last.

"I miss you," I whispered. "I miss you even when I'm not thinking of you. I miss your voice, your appetite. Your smile. Russia misses you, Sasha, so very much. Russia needs you, and you're not here. Our children are like strangers to me. Nicky is lost. He doesn't know what to do, how to stand up to the revolutionaries, to his ministers or his uncles. To his own wife. He tries so very hard. I see him struggling, but I cannot help him. And his son, his beautiful boy—" I lowered my face, a tear slipping down my cheek. "He is not well, Sasha. He suffers so. They are crushed by sadness over him, with worry and fear. So much fear. What will become of him? What will happen to Russia if he dies? What will happen to us?"

The tomb reproached me with its silence. We were taught that the dead watch over us, that even after the body decays, the soul endures. They never truly leave us, alive in our hearts and in heaven above. I believed it. But I never felt him near. I never had the sense he protected me. He was a memory, already fading, so that I found myself forgetting his favorite sayings, the things he loved. Other times, an image of him came rushing into me like a deluge, and I tried to hold on to it, to retain him with me, but it was like grasping at water—he slipped through me and vanished, back into the pool of the past.

"Where are you now?" I said. "Where are you when we need you so?"

I heard Tania behind me. "Majesty, the time . . . Your train for Gatchina is waiting."

Wincing at the crick in my back, I rose, handing her the little velvet pillow she carried for me in her bag, for there were no worldly comforts provided here in God's mansion. God did not want us to feel at ease, lest we forget the vale of thorns outside.

On the train ride to Gatchina, Tania left me alone in my compartment to smoke, gazing out my narrow window at the landscape. Pressing my hand to the glass, I felt impending winter's chill like flame on my fingertips, without heat.

By the time I reached Gatchina, I decided to go abroad again in the early spring. Ahead of me stretched months of winter, a subdued Christmas because of Vladimir's death and Alexei's recovery, his leg encased in an iron brace to keep him from bending his knee. He'd be confined to sedate activities, watched always by Alexandra and his sailor. The girls would read to him, draw and paint with him in his playroom, but they'd also treat him as if he were made of spun glass—recruits in the conspiracy of silence that now smothered Tsarskoe Selo, never asking what they already knew.

Their brother might die from a simple fall. And Russia could die with him.

I had no sense of what lay ahead. No premonition. Perhaps I would have, had I been like Alexandra and taken up with seers. But she did not sense it, either. We existed in a dream, enclosed in our lacquered splendor like the varnished miniatures of our fabled Easter eggs, even as the world beyond our gates began to crumble.

CHAPTER THIRTY-FOUR

"No, it can't be. It can't. Not again." I clutched at Olga as Tania retrieved the telegram that had dropped from my fingers.

"He died over a week ago," said Tania, reading it. She lifted her sorrow-filled eyes to me. "Your nephew asks you to come to England as soon as you can. I'm so very sorry, Minnie. I know how fond you were of him. Your poor sister must be disconsolate."

I gulped, suddenly starved for air. "I can't breathe."

Olga unlaced my dress at the back, tearing apart my corset stays. As the whalebone contraption enclosing my ribs loosened, I fell onto my chair and sobbed into my hands.

Bertie—charming, gallant Bertie—dead. Like my Sasha.

"How is it possible?" I whispered after I spent myself, Olga patting my shoulder helplessly as Tania sent Sophie out to fetch me tea. "He was only sixty-eight. He traveled often, always content. . . . He wasn't ill. No one told me he was ill."

Olga took the telegram from Tania. "It doesn't say how he died, just that they want you there as soon as possible." She paused, trying to lend comfort, although she wasn't very good with me in the best of times, let alone in a crisis. "Shall I go with you?"

"No," I said immediately, and when she flinched, I added, "George hasn't asked for anyone else; he must want me there for Alix. But surely he'll request that the family attend the funeral. I must reply to him." I dragged myself up, leaning on Olga's arm. In only a moment, I felt like an old woman. "Nicky should be informed at once."

"I'll telegram the palace." Olga saw me to my desk and made for the door. No matter what my nephew George responded, she was definitely not accompanying me. She couldn't wait to exit the room. What use would she be to me as I comforted my sister?

She returned while I was in the midst of penning my letter to assure my nephew that I'd arrive as quickly as I could on my private yacht.

"Nicky already knows. He too received word. . . . He cannot attend the funeral."

I shed my despair in that instant. "I'll not hear of it. If she must stay here for the children's sake, let her. He can go alone. The King of Great Britain, his aunt's husband, has died. Every monarch in Europe will be there to pay their respects."

"Don't fault her for it," said Olga. "George requested that only you attend, because his parliament says they cannot have the tsar present, given the circumstances."

As I stared at her, baffled, she clarified: "They can't provide the extra security, Mama. There's to be a public viewing. Too many people to ensure Nicky's safety."

"Dear God." I looked down at my unfinished letter. "Then there's no need to post this. If only I'm to attend, I might as well depart at once."

"I can accompany you," Olga offered again. "I don't want you to be alone."

"Alix is there. The last thing you need worry about is my loneliness."

———

"SHE REFUSED TO let us remove Papa's body," my nephew George told me as he escorted me to Sandringham House in Norfolk, where Alix had been taken. "After weeks of severe bronchitis, Papa had a heart attack. Mama veiled his body for eight days; when we tried to persuade her to let the embalmers do their work, she screamed at us. We had to force her away. She didn't seem to understand. She kept behaving as if he might wake up."

He searched my eyes, looking so much like Nicky that it was like seeing my son in a mirror, down to the same trim build, luxuriant beard, and tranquil manner. "I know she's going deaf, Aunt Minnie, but could her mind also be affected by her hearing loss?"

"Her mind is affected by the loss of her husband," I said. "It has nothing to do with her hearing. She knew he was dead. She simply couldn't bear to admit it."

"The lying-in-state at Westminster is for her. We thought a public paying of respects might help ease her grief." He rubbed at his beard, reminding me again of Nicky. "I hope you can be of solace to her. She won't let anyone near her. She just sits in that room. . . ."

I gave him a reassuring smile. "I will do everything I can. She'll be ready when the time comes. See to your realm and your family now. They need you."

Sandringham's stately façade, with its multitude of bay windows and turrets, belied its interior. The main rooms were airy enough, if overstuffed, but the living quarters of the royal family were cramped and dark, like the apartments Sasha had allocated for us at Gatchina. Yet here in this rural estate, Alix had raised her children, retreating to escape the gossip in London about Bertie's indiscretions.

In her apartments, her ladies-in-waiting—many of whom had been with her for many years, since her extensive tenure as Princess of Wales—wore mourning and came hastily to their feet. Inscrutably British, their hair in identical buns and faces bearing the same stiff miens, they reminded me of that funereal assembly Victoria had kept about her. I did not know their names, never bothering to remember any when Alix mentioned them. I didn't attempt to remedy my lack of knowledge now.

"Where is Her Majesty the Queen?" I demanded.

"Her Majesty Queen Mary is at Buckingham Palace," replied a sharp-nosed woman in neck-to-toe black. "Her Majesty the Queen Mother is presently in her bedchamber and—"

As I marched past her, I heard her stifled gasp. Pulling open the bedroom door, I stepped into a room so dark, it was like a cave.

I had to pause, blink to adjust my eyes. The room came into focus—a chintz-laden sitting area, with bulky valance drapes shuttering the windows.

"I said I'm not hungry. Leave me alone." Alix's disembodied voice reached me from somewhere to my left. As I edged farther inside, avoiding a top-heavy table, every inch of its surface littered with framed photographs, I said warily, "Alix. Where are you?"

Silence. Then a dog barked, and I saw her rise from a winged armchair by the hearth, her hair disheveled about her face. She hadn't heard me but the dog had alerted her; as she peered toward me, she said in disbelief, "Minnie?" Then she staggered to me. "Oh, Minnie! They stole away my Bertie."

As she fell into my arms, and the scruffy white terrier accompanying her sniffed warily at my feet, I wondered for a paralyzing second if my sister had indeed gone mad. After what her son had told me, it wasn't entirely out of the question. But as she clung to me, weeping, and I led her back to her chair, I saw she wasn't mad—only so bewildered by the sudden twist of fate that deprived her of her husband, she hadn't yet fully accepted it. I knew this because she lifted her hand to her hair in a weak gesture of vanity, trying to smooth its disarray. The terrier, having determined I wasn't a threat, settled on a cushion by her chair and watched me with its sad brown eyes.

"His name is Caesar," she said, as I returned the dog's mournful regard. "Bertie adored him. See there on his collar: It says he belongs to the king. He had no affection for me before. But he kept wandering the palace, whining, so I brought him here with me. He's not left me for a second." She tried to smile. "He doesn't mind that I must look a fright."

I desperately wanted to smoke but resisted the temptation, as Alix had never liked it. "Everyone is very concerned for you," I said, raising my voice so she could hear me.

"Are they?" Her eyes were like bruises in her face. "They'll forget me soon enough."

"Come now." I looked about for a bell to ring for tea. "You mustn't say such things. Remember what you told me after Sasha. The loss is terrible; I know it too well. But you have your family to care for. George is king and you must advise him. It's the way of the world," I said, returning her own words to me. "No matter how savage or unjust it may seem."

"It's not the same. George has his prime minister and parliament to advise him. May is now the queen. Here, a dowager is expected to retire."

At least she was talking sense. My fear that she'd forsaken her reason waned.

"You shouldn't retire unless that is your inclination," I said. Locating a pull cord on the wall, I rang it. When no one came, I started toward the door. It abruptly opened, the unctuous sharp-nosed lady peering in as if she expected something to be flung at her. Caesar barked again. The woman recoiled. The dog had been keeping the ravens at bay.

"Hot tea," I told her. "Make it strong. And biscuits. Or scones with plenty of butter."

"Minnie, I'm not hungry—" Alix protested, but I held up my hand, motioning the woman out. "You will eat," I said, returning to her chair. "I will not see you turn into a wraith. You were there for me in my time of grief. Now I am here for you."

Tears spilled over her cheeks. "What am I going to do?"

I embraced her, keeping an eye on Caesar, who growled. "You will live," I said. "You can do nothing else."

She cried for a time, but not even she had an endless supply of tears. Once the worst of it subsided, her raw sorrow given vent by my proximity, she let me brush and arrange her hair. Then she sipped the tea served by her wary lady, nibbling listlessly on the toast with jam but giving most of it to Caesar. Apparently there were no biscuits or scones available, though I'd have thought such staples essential in a British household.

"Have you considered where you'll live?" I ventured, after she wiped the crumbs off Caesar's snout. With some nourishment in her stomach, she began to look more like herself.

"I want to stay here. It's my home; Bertie allocated it to me. George may not be pleased, as he was raised here and thinks he must do the same with his children, but I cannot be expected to reside in London, with all the memories. I never liked it there."

"You can go to Hvidøre whenever you wish. If you're expected to retire, you might as well travel." I deliberately avoided any mention of Bertie. I saw no point. I knew how much she'd suffered in her marriage. While she'd grown to love him and he'd been a benevolent husband, she must have felt as if she'd never been good enough, no match for the actresses and other exciting women he'd chased with the same exuberance he'd displayed for hunting and diplomacy.

She let out a shallow sigh. "I cannot think of it now, Minnie. I'm so very tired."

"Then you must rest. There'll be time enough to sort it out." Bringing her to the adjoining chamber, I tucked her into bed and sat by her side. Caesar, whom Bertie had apparently taught to disregard any limitations imposed on pets, leapt onto the bed and nestled beside her. She fell asleep moments after she set her head on the pillow.

"I am here," I whispered. "I will never leave you. We are sisters forever."

WHILE THE POPULACE lined up for hours outside Westminster to view the king in his casket, I did my best to restore Alix to presentable dignity. She cooperated, to my relief, but when we returned to Buckingham Palace in advance of the state funeral, I caught her sorting through her jewels, dividing the pieces and painstakingly labeling them.

"What on earth are you doing?" I asked.

"These aren't mine." She pointed to the largest grouping. "They belong to the crown. May must wear them now."

I looked over the assortment. Nothing as dazzling as the jewels I'd worn as tsarina or even some of my personal ones, but a considerable treasure, in particular the diadem, which Alix had worn to openings of parliament, and a silver-and-diamond butterfly brooch.

"You must keep them. You've worn them all these years. Let May wear whatever they store in the vault. Or that tower of theirs in London. Or wherever they keep their crown jewels."

"Minnie, these are the crown jewels. I can't keep them. There's a protocol."

"Is someone going to demand you surrender them?" As I spoke, I had an unwelcome recollection of when Nicky had come to me on behalf of Alexandra. "I never gave up mine," I went on, omitting that in the end I had. "I kept them and I wore them."

"You had the right. Here, I must return the jewels that Bertie didn't acquire for me and renounce my precedence. It is expected. George told me I must walk behind May at the funeral."

"You most certainly will not," I retorted, and I went directly to George, bypassing his astonished attendants to enter his study.

"No matter what the protocol is," I said, wagging my finger at him, "surely you don't intend to relegate her to second place. May has her entire life ahead of her to be queen. This will be your mother's last appearance beside her husband, your father. In his coffin."

He mumbled that it was highly unusual, he'd have to consult the officials in charge, but in the end I had my way. Alix preceded May, and my sister had the pluck to insist that Caesar head the procession, led on a leash by a highlander behind the carriage bearing the coffin and before every head of state, including George and eight other monarchs—an outrage to which Kaiser Wilhelm II vehemently objected.

"Bertie doted on Caesar more than on our children," Alix said after the funeral, as I laughed, recalling the kaiser's scowl. "Why shouldn't his dog be the first to say goodbye?"

With those words, she reassured me that in time she'd accept the loss of her beloved husband and her rank as queen. She wouldn't undergo the tumult that I did in my widowhood in Russia, for May, while strong-willed, wasn't Alexandra. She made a point of adapting herself to Alix's presence and refrained from excessive hauteur.

After the burial in St. George's Chapel at Windsor, I persuaded Alix to travel with me to our house in Denmark, where Caesar delighted in the sea and left wet sand all over the sofas and beds, for no matter how much I rebuked him, he never listened.

Then my sister and I had to part.

"I don't know when we'll see each other again," she said, her arms about me as Caesar whined. "I feel as if I can bear almost anything as long as you are with me."

"I'll visit you every year. I'll come first to England and then we can travel together to Hvidøre. I promise, you'll never be alone in this world whilst I live."

I only realized as I set sail back to Russia on my yacht that our positions had reversed. From being the older sister, whom I'd idolized and envied, who married first and left me behind, Alix was now dependent on me. She needed my company more than ever, for her son's kingdom was stable on its island, and she was the queen mother, who must be content with her gardens, her grandchildren, and occasional visitors to her rural estate.

I did not enjoy the same luxury. At my age, I should have found myself in the same position as her, free to retire and grow bored in my dotage. But Russia needed me; my children, while grown and resistant to my advice, could not do without me.

While much may have changed between Alix and me, I still envied her.

⁓

HIS NAME WAS everywhere when I returned to St. Petersburg. In the salons, where society ladies clamored to receive him; in the taverns and riverside stalls, where he communed with all sorts of riffraff; and in the newspapers, where speculation was rife over this mysterious *starets* who'd become so intimate with the imperial family.

The journalists were mistaken. He was not a *starets*. Holy elders meditated in monasteries, seeking divine truth in solitude and silence. A *starets* did not entertain avid matrons in palaces or accept the invitations of female disciples into their homes; he did not spend the nights swilling vodka or carousing on the island encampments of Novaya Derevnya, nor did he proclaim that sin was the sole path to redemption.

And while no one had deduced exactly why Rasputin visited Tsarskoe Selo, I feared it would be only a matter of time, as he didn't seem to have much use for discretion. For the moment, however, he remained silent. He might advertise his association with Tsar *Batushka* and Tsarina *Matushka,* denoting his origins by referring to them as any devoted peasant would, but he said nothing of Alexei. He'd become part of the conspiracy, if unlike the rest of us.

Eventually, curiosity overcame me. I couldn't receive him, that would be unthinkable, but I told myself it behooved me to find out as much as I could. A common man like him, so close to the throne . . . he might harbor ambitions beyond the obvious.

Bowing to the inevitable, I paid a long-overdue visit to Princess Zenaida Yusupova.

Thin and beautiful, with crystalline light-green eyes and blue-black hair like raven plumage, Zenaida had been an indispensable guest at our galas when Sasha was alive. Having inherited immense wealth, she and her husband oversaw one hundred thousand acres and thirty palatial estates. Her jewelry collection surpassed even the imperial one, containing the *Peregrina* pearl, a royal Spanish heirloom, and a pair of

Marie Antoinette's diamond earrings. In the city, she resided in her saffron-hued palace on the Moika, near my daughter Xenia's residence—a classical edifice, with a private theater and vast galleries housing thousands of priceless works of art.

She welcomed me in her immense red salon with its rococo plaster moldings and frescoes on the ceiling. Dressed in elegant black, she had strong Turkish coffee served and, with her gracious smile, offered her condolences on the deaths of Bertie and of Vladimir, the latter of whom she'd known well.

"Such a tragedy to bury a husband," she said. "Which, sadly, you know, Minnie."

"I suppose it depends on the wife." I tasted her pungent coffee before adding another lump of sugar to the thick brew.

"Or the husband." She laughed. She had a subtle laugh, perfected in salons; she knew all eyes were upon her, so she had no need to attract attention. "How does Her Majesty your sister fare?" she said, referring to Alix by her title. Zenaida never assumed familiarity.

"As well as can be expected. Apparently they have no provision in England for a dowager queen. Alix had to surrender her jewels."

"All of them?" She knew better than to display shock, but I could see by the lift of her plucked eyebrow that she felt it.

"All her royal ones," I said. "The misfortune of a husband's death reaches even to one's adornment when one's husband happens to be a king."

She made a tut-tutting sound. Then she motioned to my bag with her long-nailed white hand. "Let us smoke, Minnie, in honor of the occasion. It's been so long since you visited me."

I took out my case.

"Cartier." She nodded in approval, though she hadn't seen the insignia. "How charming. He does make such innovative objets d'art. I understand our Grand Duchess Pavlovna is one of his greatest sponsors here."

"And no doubt he has the unpaid bills to show for it," I said, extracting two cigarettes and offering her my lighter.

She smiled; society-born and bred, gossip was her pastime. "Grand Duke Vladimir must have rued the day he said 'I do,' as far as access to his fortune was concerned."

We laughed together, two women smoking over coffee in a salon that could accommodate five hundred. Tapping her cigarette ash into a porcelain Fabergé plate on her table, she asked, "Have I done anything to offend?"

"No, no. I'm the one who's been remiss. My schedule these days . . ." I sighed. "It seems I do nothing but rush abroad, return, and rush abroad again. This must be the price of longevity. Those we love leave us, and we're left to wonder when our time will come."

"Come now. You haven't aged a day since I met you. Unlike another whom I'll refrain from mentioning, so as not to spoil our afternoon."

I understood. She and Miechen shared antipathy of Alexandra, whose inability to conduct herself as an empress had put a damper on the very lifeblood of St. Petersburg—entertainment. The empty halls of the Winter Palace, once ablaze with glamour, were proof enough. Where I'd once reigned supreme, Alexandra left only vacancy.

"I actually have a reason for coming to see you," I began, suddenly ashamed of my self-interest, having been so engrossed in my travails that I'd neglected my social obligations. "Miechen mentioned something to me about Felix."

She made a gesture. The maidservant in a distant corner, out of earshot but not out of sight, came forward to pour us more coffee and replenish the platter of petit fours. Then Zenaida dismissed her. "Please, speak openly. If I can be of assistance, I'm at your disposal."

I gave her a grateful smile. "You'll think it rather silly, I'm afraid."

"Not at all. Irina is your granddaughter. I've been most firm with Felix on her account. He cannot entertain proposing to her until she's reached her eighteenth year."

I belatedly remembered what Miechen had also said about my granddaughter and the Yusupov prince. "Has it gone so far?"

She might have appeared unsettled, had she been any other. "I thought you wished to discuss the matter on Xenia's behalf? I realize my son might not be the spouse that she and Sandro would desire for Irina."

I swallowed. Zenaida must have also heard of my daughter's separation from her husband, so there wasn't a way to avoid it. "Xenia hasn't said anything about it. She . . . she's often in the Crimea now, so perhaps she's unaware of Felix's affection for Irina. But, yes, it would be her and Sandro's decision; Irina is their child."

"I see." To my relief, she sat attentive, until I said in a voice that sounded more conspiratorial than justified for the situation, "I'm actually here about Grigori Rasputin."

She didn't react in a visible manner, yet I sensed a sudden tension emanating from her, as if an unidentifiable foul scent had leached into the room. Then she took a delicate inhale of her cigarette, saying through smoke trailing between her lips, "Alas, in that matter, I cannot be of any assistance. Whatever Miechen told you is all I know."

"Miechen thought Felix may have met him, as your son has an interest in mysticism and even paid a visit to Ella at her convent in Moscow. I thought perhaps . . ."

"Dearest Minnie, you too have grown sons. How often do they inform you of their interests or acquaintances?"

"Rarely." I forced out a smile in return. "As I said, it's rather silly of me."

"Not at all. If I were in your shoes, I'd be concerned myself. May I speak freely?" When I assented, she said, "Her Imperial Majesty does not endear herself. For our empress to entertain such a man in her palace, with four young daughters and a son who will one day inherit the throne: It's not only unseemly but also quite dangerous. I needn't remind you of how difficult our situation is. The Duma in disarray; the secret police on a rampage; the revolutionaries planting bombs and threatening annihilation—she has no idea of what she might be inviting inside. A wolf is still a wolf, even in holy guise."

A chill crept through me. "You think he is a wolf."

"I do. I've never met him, but one doesn't need to meet the wolf to know when to bolt the door." She crushed her cigarette out on the plate. "I can say that Felix did visit Ella and found her an inspiration, raising Grand Duke Paul's children after Sergei was appointed their guardian, then, upon Sergei's death, seeing young Maria betrothed to the Prince of Sweden and insisting her brother, Dmitri, complete his education before he was installed in his palace here. Only then did she sell off her possessions to endow her convent. Such piety is exemplary. Felix was so impressed, he vows to do the same. I owe Ella a debt of gratitude for opening my son's eyes to the suffering in this world."

I nearly laughed aloud. "He wishes to endow a convent?"

"For the moment," she said dryly. "I assured him that as my sole surviving son, his first duty is to continue our family line. He can marry and give me grandchildren, and then, by all means, he may dedicate himself to charity. I daresay it'll be a relief once he does, for his aimlessness has not come without a price."

"I sympathize more than you can imagine," I muttered, thinking of Misha, whose mistress, Natalia, had given birth to a son while I'd been abroad, precipitating his urgency to marry her, even as I'd begged him for more time.

She regarded me pensively. "If you wish to speak to Felix in person, I'll have him call on you as soon as he returns. He's not in Russia at the moment; I sent him to study fine arts at Oxford. I insisted he must cultivate interests beyond racehorses and clothes if he hopes to wed Irina. However, I don't think he's ever met the man, either. My son has his eccentricities, but I believe I would have heard of it. This city isn't so vast that Felix can go unperceived, particularly given Rasputin's reputation. I will, of course, inform you should I discover anything more before Felix's return."

"Thank you," I said, finishing my coffee. I felt dejected, having embarrassed myself to no purpose, other than to learn what I already knew. "In any case, I suppose I should speak with him. Xenia will want my opinion on him, should he propose to my granddaughter."

"Yes, I think you must. I want to be quite certain you'll have no objection. Felix can be determined when he wants to be, and he's determined to wed Irina. As I've said, he's attempting to mend his ways, but he still has a past to contend with."

For the sake of propriety, I stayed with her for another hour or so, inquiring about our acquaintances and catching up on the latest intrigues. None of it gave me solace. Times past, I'd have reveled in the betrayals and affairs, the petty lies and competitions, but now it felt as though that world in which I'd once excelled had left me far behind. Society continued to outspend and outdo one another, mounted on a lavish carousel spinning round and round, without any thought for the future.

Zenaida was wise, but, unlike her, most of those we knew were not. They did not see the wolf prowling outside, and their doors remained wide open.

CHAPTER THIRTY-FIVE

"Nicky refused me," cried Olga, as I sat in my study in Gatchina and avoided Misha's stare, wishing I could set sail for Denmark this instant. They had come to me as a united front, with Olga launching a tirade. "Peter can continue to enjoy the privilege of calling himself a grand duke, while I'm seen as the wayward adulteress."

"Peter cannot call himself a grand duke," I said. "Nicky knows you are separated and will not allow him the imperial title."

"As if that matters," Olga replied.

We'd been through the argument so many times—albeit without my younger son present to add fuel to the fire—that I didn't know what to say, repeating the same advice that even to my ears sounded unconvincing.

"We face too much upheaval. Our new Duma has barely opened and already there's dissent. Prime Minister Stolypin threatens to resign, and revolutionaries plot our downfall at every turn. To allow his own sister to divorce is a disgrace Nicky cannot allow."

"The disgrace is in his own palace." Olga rarely minced words now, not where her Kulikovsky was concerned. "He should look first to his wife, who's letting that *starets* dictate who should be appointed to this or that office."

I started in my chair. Olga glared at me. "It would be on all the front pages, were the Okhrana not arresting every editor who cites his name. Perhaps I should petition Rasputin instead for my divorce."

"He is not a *starets*," I said wearily.

"Whatever he is, he exerts more influence than we do." She turned to Misha. "I told you she wouldn't listen. Maybe you can present a better case. I'm going back to Xenia's house. I cannot abide it here another moment." Before I could respond to her harsh judgment, my daughter stormed out, slamming doors.

"This cannot go on," I said, meeting Misha's gaze. "Olga cannot parade about the city with her lover while still married. What kind of example does it set?"

He tossed his hat onto a chair. "Perhaps you should ask Nicky about examples. He'll not hear of Olga divorcing so she can marry Kulikovsky because he's not of noble birth, nor of me marrying Natalia, though we have a son. Yet he allows this Rasputin free rein."

"I . . . I didn't know," I said, wishing I'd taken the matter in hand after my visit to Zenaida and confronted Nicky. "Is it true he counsels Alexandra on political issues?"

"That is the rumor," replied Misha. "Whatever Nicky does in his palace is his own affair. I only wish he'd allow us the same. Instead, he has left Olga in misery, and my Natalia must live like a prisoner because no one in society will receive her."

"I did warn you. She has no position."

"You told me you'd speak on my behalf." He was controlling his tone of voice, but I could tell that, like Olga, he'd reached his limit. "Have you?"

"What would you have me say? Nicky cannot permit you to throw away your life on a woman who is not of noble birth."

I saw his entire being congeal, like Sasha had when he found himself faced with a compromise he couldn't tolerate. "I will marry her, regardless. Even if we must go abroad and live in exile."

"Misha. Please wait awhile longer. Transfer back to the Chevaliers at Gatchina," I said. "My villa on the grounds is unoccupied. She can live on my estate with your son. Once society hears I've accepted her, doors will open. When the time is right—"

"The time will never be right," he interrupted. He didn't attempt to engage me further, taking up his hat and leaving me, though he refrained from slamming any doors.

A month later, he moved Natalia to Gatchina. Having not met her until now, I found her a surprise. At thirty-one, she wasn't particularly beautiful, in my opinion, certainly not the brazen adventuress I'd expected. I found her rather timid and plain, in fact, but her and Misha's love for each other was also undeniable; I saw it in the way they looked at each other, those quick reassuring glances that made me feel invisible.

And when I beheld their sturdy little boy, christened George in honor of my late son, with his lopsided smile and ferocious appetite, I couldn't help but think that here was a Romanov. I felt ashamed to compare him to the sickly heir Alexandra had borne, which was the reason we found ourselves in this untenable position. Had Alexei not inherited her Hesse curse, there would be no Rasputin or familial discord. Divorce might still be contentious, but it may have been less so had we a healthy tsarevich.

Meeting my new grandson lent me fortitude, even if my relationships with my children were anything but congenial. Still, it took an unexpected visit from Prime Minister Stolypin himself to prompt me to action.

A thickset man, bald as an egg and with a manicured beard and steel-gray eyes, he warned me that the new Duma muttered of "dark forces" near the throne.

"They've finally endorsed my bill to reform the provincial soviets and provide land grants for the peasantry," he said. "But the state council refuses to approve it. Rasputin is blamed for adversely influencing the council through his contact with Her Majesty."

I sat in troubled silence. What I had feared was true. The mystic did harbor ambitions, and Alexandra was encouraging him.

"Our metropolitan has disavowed him after hearing of his vices," Stolypin went on. "And I prepared a report for His Majesty, detailing everything I could compile. His Majesty suggested that before I defamed him, I should meet with Father Grigori in person. Which I did."

"And . . . ?" I recalled the report I'd had prepared on Dr. Philippe and Nicky's adverse reaction to it. I didn't want Stolypin to fall into disfavor, for he'd proven to be the effective overseer of the Duma that we desperately needed.

"There can be no doubt he believes he has great power," Stolypin said. "He tried to mesmerize me with those strange eyes of his, muttering inarticulate words and making odd movements with his hands. When I told him I wasn't susceptible to trickery, he made no attempt to justify himself. Never have I felt such loathing for any man."

I sank deeper into my chair. "Is he so dangerous?"

Seeing my distress, Stolypin softened his tone. "He's not a revolutionary, Majesty. If anything, he's overly ardent in his devotion to the tsar and tsarina. But he's still a peasant to whom they give too much credence. He's become inviolate because they permit it."

"Dear God." I forced myself to sit up straight. "What can I do?"

"I fear not much. There are also letters to contend with. He was drunk and the letters were stolen from him, then sold to one of the newspapers. We have the Okhrana searching for them, but we don't know which newspaper has them."

I regarded him, aghast. "Letters? From whom?"

"From Her Majesty, and their Highnesses the Grand Duchesses."

As I let out a horrified gasp, Stolypin paused, as if considering how candid he should be. When I did not avert my eyes, he said, "As Your Majesty must be aware, letters can be misinterpreted to highlight an agenda, and many of our journalists have become secret revolutionary sympathizers. We cannot shut down every newspaper in the city. We've done our utmost to enforce His Majesty's mandate against printed criticism of Rasputin by arresting the most egregious offenders, but a free press is considered essential to constitutional liberties, as set forth in the tsar's own manifesto. He can retain the privilege of some of his powers, but in censoring the press to this extent, all he accomplishes is to incite the Duma's fear that he has no intention of honoring his promised reforms."

"Then I shall speak to my son," I said. "That much, at least, I can do."

"Majesty." He inclined his head in gratitude.

"In the meantime, see that the Duma doesn't fall apart again over this land bill of yours," I told him. "If the peasants can acquire their own land, perhaps it will help end the unrest."

"I'm due to address the state council next month in Kiev. The bill must be passed. However, some new council members were recommended by Rasputin; as they're in the man's debt, they will vote as he tells them."

"Or as the empress tells them. He carries no weight on his own."

"I appreciate Your Majesty's wisdom," he said, implying he found too little of it elsewhere.

⁓

THE FOLLOWING MONTH, Stolypin traveled to Kiev to address the state council. Afterward, he attended a performance of Rimsky-Korsakov's *The Tale of Tsar Saltan* at the Kiev Opera, in the presence of Nicky, Olga, and Tatiana. At my urging, my son had gone to Kiev as a gesture of support for his beleaguered prime minister. Despite the security posted throughout the opera house, as Stolypin conversed with a general during intermission, he was shot by a revolutionary. The assassin was apprehended; when the wounded Stolypin caught sight of Nicky rising in alarm from his imperial box, he raised his hands to ward my son away. Nicky had to herd his terrified daughters out amid the uproar.

Stolypin died that very night.

Only days after his funeral, the newspapers published Alexandra's letter to Rasputin via hectograph and distributed illicit copies throughout St. Petersburg.

⁓

"HOW MUCH MORE do you need?" I sat in the Alexander Palace, brandishing the hectograph copy delivered to my doorstep. "They're passing these out everywhere, like confetti. Everyone is reading it. You must banish him before he casts her reputation into further ruin."

I'd waited until the afternoon tea had concluded, until my granddaughters had visited with me, Olga and Tatiana still pale from the events in Kiev. I'd admired Alexei's latest drawing of a horse and covertly assessed his thin but otherwise unbruised leg in its brace. I'd smiled and made polite conversation with Alexandra, who was out of her chair and appeared less fretful, perhaps because she believed Stolypin's murder had served her well. Our late prime minister had attacked her mystic, but she needn't fear a dead man. However, Nicky showed integrity by appointing Kokovtsov, Stolypin's well-respected associate and a senior cabinet member, as his new prime minister. Kokovtsov wasted no time in offering Rasputin a substantial sum to disappear—an offer the mystic rejected.

The moment Alexandra accompanied her daughters outside for a stroll in the September sunshine, I turned to Nicky, who gazed at me over his cigarette with a forlorn expression.

"She will not hear of it," he said. "He made a prophecy to her, that should he be harmed by anyone in our family, it would be the end of our dynasty. She believes him."

"Do you? A debauched peasant, who let her own letter be made public, prophesying our end to suit himself?"

"Father Grigori did not intend for any letter to—"

"I don't care what he intended. I care only for what *you* intend to do about it."

Before he could respond, Alexandra said from the sitting room doorway, "If you have anything to say about my affairs, Mother dear, please do so. To me."

I shifted in my chair as she walked past me to her settee. "It's too cold for a walk," she explained. "I left the girls with Alexei and their servants upstairs." She pulled her coverlet over her legs with a resigned air, as if preparing for an unavoidable assault.

"It is not your affair any longer," I said. "It is Russia's affair now."

"Not that it matters to those who reside there, but St. Petersburg is not all of Russia."

I held up her letter. "Shall I read it to you so we can see whose affair it is?"

"I wrote it. I am perfectly aware of what it says."

"Are you?" I recited aloud: *"My beloved redeemer and mentor, how tiresome it is without you! My soul is quiet and I relax only when you, my teacher, are sitting beside me. I kiss your hands and lean my head on your blessed shoulder. Oh, how light, how light do I feel then. I wish for only one thing: to fall asleep forever in your arms. What happiness to feel your presence near me. Come quickly, I am waiting for you and I am tormenting myself for you. I am asking for your holy blessing and I am kissing your blessed hands. I love you forever."*

I watched her face tighten. Glancing at Nicky, who sat cross-legged, his cigarette smoldering to ash between his fingers, I saw he was horrified, but I couldn't tell if it was with dismay at his wife's words or at my effrontery for reading those words aloud.

"'Fall asleep forever in your arms'?" I echoed. "Would you have us ridiculed before the entire world and sow the seeds of our destruction with that unholy profligate?"

She did not speak. Nicky cleared his throat. "It's an intolerable violation of our privacy. Kokovtsov ordered that our name not be associated with—"

"Your name isn't associated. The letter is signed 'M.' For *Matushka*. It is her privacy that has been intolerably violated. And by her own hand, no less."

With glacial calm, Alexandra said, "Are you finished? I am tired and wish to rest."

"I am not finished." Enraged by her disregard for her own humiliation and Nicky's evident unwillingness to speak up in my defense, I came to my feet, waving the letter like a flag. "You think you can ignore this and it will blow over like so much else to which you turn a blind eye? Stolypin told me there are other letters, from your own daughters. I dread to think what they wrote, for they only follow your example. As long as you continue to let him advise you and rest your head on his blessed shoulder, our entire family will dwell in this storm, until they've had enough and storm our gates! He must be banished. I *demand* it."

Alexandra's jawbones clenched under her skin. "You demand it?" she whispered, and in that moment, the brittle veneer of cordiality we'd maintained for Nicky and the children's sake disintegrated like the false façade it was. "I appreciate you bringing this appalling breach of decency to our attention, but your demand is inexcusable."

"What is inexcusable is this!" I flung the letter aside. "What is inexcusable is how you refuse to see what is before your very nose." I whirled to Nicky. "He has been disavowed by the metropolitan. Use it as your excuse and exile him."

Nicky's cigarette crumbled into dust. Wincing, he went to the cabinet by the wall, extracting a new package. As he opened it, Alexandra said to him in a honeyed voice that harbored a hidden blade, "Please tell Mother dear that she needn't worry. The other letters were found and returned to us. Tell her, Nicky."

He didn't look at me as he muttered, "It's true. We have them in our possession."

"Were copies made before they were found?" I said, unable to comprehend how they could pretend to be so indifferent. I knew they were not. Alexandra's letter alone was damning enough. Had I not known her as well as I did, with her disapproving sensibilities, I'd almost have believed she was in love with that filthy peasant.

When Nicky didn't reply, I added, "Of course, you don't know. But you'll send the Okhrana baying after them, so they'll not dare publish any copies even if they have them. We might thank God Almighty the newspapers still fear something, if not you."

He looked up abruptly then, his pride touched. I noted with satisfaction how he squared his shoulders, turning to Alexandra. "Perhaps it is time to send him away."

She went still, her face blank save for angry splotches reddening her cheeks. "And what shall we do then? How will we protect our son? When has anyone in Russia thought well of me? *When?*" She leveled her gaze at me. "Let them say whatever they like. Without Father Grigori, we have no hope. Only he can heal my son."

As I returned her stare, I understood. Before the Duma, before the people, before the family or Russia, Rasputin came first. She *was* in love with him, I realized with a sickening twist in my stomach. She was in love with the illusion he pandered, an offering wrapped in a mystical promise that while he was there, whispering in her ear, Alexei would survive. To defend that tenuous hope, she'd fight for the very man whose drunken carelessness had permitted her letter to fall into the wrong hands and dragged her name through the mire. She had gone beyond reason. Her guilt and fear for her son had indeed blinded her.

"Some time away," Nicky finally said into the chasm between us. "We'll send him to visit his family in Siberia. Only for a time, Sunny," he added, lifting his voice against her protest. "Alexei hasn't had another incident. We'll keep close watch over him, as we always do. We have the upcoming events in Moscow, then we're due to depart for Livadia and on to Spala for the hunting season. A few months apart will do no harm. We mustn't ignore how this looks."

"How does it look?" Alexandra drew her shawl about her, as if to enclose herself in a cocoon. "He never asks for anything. He seeks only to serve and spread God's word, to ease suffering in Christ's name. No one with any sense would believe such foul things of him."

"Everyone already believes it, sense or not," I said. "Unless you do something about it, they'll continue to believe it—and more."

I wasn't happy with Nicky's suggestion. Exile was preferable, but at least he'd stated an opinion, making me think that under his passive exterior, he shared my condemnation. He may not believe there was anything more here than an anxious mother's unseemly gratitude to the mystic she believed could heal their son, but he couldn't have heard that letter without it wounding deeper than his royal pride. His pride of manhood must smart, too, for when had this woman he'd married ever shown such passion for anyone but him?

"I think it would be best." He tried to smile. "Let me see to it."

She turned away, from him and from me. "If you think it best," she murmured.

Nicky led me out to his study. In a mere hour, he seemed to have aged years beyond his forty-three. "Will you stay?" he asked. "Your apartments are always ready for you."

"No. My train is waiting at the station. I must return to Gatchina. She will want time without me now, and I intend to give it to her. As much time as she needs."

"Mama," he said, as I turned to the door. "I know how difficult this was for you. You were right to speak as you did. Rest assured, he'll be sent away. You will still come with us to Livadia? The children are look-ing forward to it. I want you with us."

I made myself nod, though I wasn't sure I should. "Yes, of course."

How I'd be expected to endure a months-long vacation with Alex-andra, however, wasn't something I cared to contemplate.

❧

I DIDN'T HAVE to contemplate it. As we prepared to embark on our trip to Livadia, word came that after ruling Denmark for only six years, my brother Freddie had died from a paralysis attack. Accompanying me to his funeral in Roskilde Cathedral were Olga, who was in a state of nervous collapse over the frustration with her estranged husband, as well as Misha, Natalia, and their son. Alix came from England. Soon after the funeral, Freddie's eldest son was crowned Christian X.

Misha and Natalia proceeded to Nice for a holiday. Olga, Alix, and I went to Hvidøre. The loss of Freddie was compounded by news from Greece, where my other brother Willie had been evicted due to an up-rising that plunged his realm into violent conflict with Turkey. Willie, his wife, and their seven children had fled to Italy, from where they were negotiating their return by agreeing to strict terms.

As Olga embarked on aimless walks along the beach, reminding me of Sasha's perambulations after our George was diagnosed and sent away, I railed in my drawing room with Alix.

"The entire world is turning against us," I said, undone by the successive blows.

Alix gave sorrowful assent, barely hearing me, for I couldn't bellow at her with a staff of thirty servants now attending us at the house.

A few days later, I received a telegram, summoning me to Spala.

My grandson Alexei was dying.

CHAPTER THIRTY-SIX

I'd been to the Bialowieza Royal Hunting Lodge of Spala in Poland with Sasha many times; each evening, the carcasses of the slaughtered animals were laid out on the ground for the guests to admire, the hunters proudly pointing out their prey as the ladies pressed perfumed handkerchiefs to their noses to ward off the smell.

I arrived at the remote stone-and-wood-paneled lodge after a week of travel, bruised to my bones from jolting carriages over unpaved roads. The air stank of charnel as I dismounted, limping from my sore back to the lodge with Olga lending me her arm.

In the main hall, festooned with antlers and mounted stag heads, the invited guests enjoyed aperitifs and discussed the morning's stalking as if nothing were amiss. Surprised by my entrance in my cloak and veiled hat, they surrounded me with greetings and condolences on my brother's death, as I tried to fend off their solicitous onslaught to inquire where my son the tsar was.

Finally, just as I thought I might have to gulp a cognac and take up a shooting rifle, Alexandra's newest lady, Anna Demidova, hastened down the main staircase. In a shrill voice, she declared, "Your rooms are prepared, Majesty. Their Imperial Majesties wait to receive you. Come, come." She gestured at Olga, who stood dazed among our pile of luggage in the entryway. "Leave your bags. A footman can bring them up."

I scowled at her. Of course a footman must bring them up. Did she expect us to lug our bags up a flight of stairs by ourselves? But Demidova was like that other Anna who'd befriended Alexandra and introduced her to Rasputin: not what I'd have deemed a superlative example of intelligence. Hefty and blond, resembling the daughter of a prosperous merchant that she was, she'd earned favor for her unstinting loyalty and shrinking disposition. Alexandra preferred her servants as docile as possible, and Demidova fit her requirements.

As soon as we reached the landing, the conversations of the guests below muted, I snapped, "What is the meaning of this? My son sent a telegram. I was told the child is—"

Olga gripped my arm, propelling me about. At the far end of the corridor, Nicky was standing by an open door. He had a finger to his lips.

"You stay here," I said to Olga, realizing that in my anger, I'd almost let the secret slip out. All those people downstairs, the ambiance of genial comradery before the afternoon killing started—it had seemed to me as though I'd been lured all this way on false pretext.

"I know," Olga whispered in my ear. I froze. "Alicky told me. I know about Alexei."

I couldn't even look at her.

"Xenia does, too. I told her. Now, go." Putting her hand at the small of my back, Olga pushed me forward. The passageway seemed to stretch before me. As I neared, I saw that Nicky was like a specter, his countenance hollow and his eyes rimmed in pockets of shadow.

"Be very quiet," he said. "He's finally asleep. He's been given laudanum, but the effect . . . it wears off too fast. The pain, it—" He turned aside, allowing me to step into the room.

Derevenko stood in the corner, as Alexandra sat on a stool by the narrow bedstead. Spala was hardly luxurious by our standards. Only recently equipped with electricity, the dim lighting did little to relieve its rustic décor, intended to enhance the pretense that we, accustomed to luxury, could live like ordinary people. She didn't turn to me as I approached. She didn't have to. I already knew she too must resemble a ghost, for Alexei appeared already dead.

He was so thin and colorless, bluish veins could be traced under his skin—those weak veins that were his purgatory. His left leg, the same from his previous hemorrhage, was elevated on a stack of pillows, his nightshirt hiked past his stomach, his undergarments drooping about his genitals. The exposure was obscene, but it paled in comparison to the monstrous swelling in his groin, like a fist pushing against inflamed skin.

His sleep was restless. He made piteous mewling sounds, a film of sweat beading his limbs. Alexandra had a cloth on his brow and a basin by her chair. When she removed the cloth to wring it out, I half-expected to see blood dripping from it.

"He will not die," I heard her say. "He cannot. He cannot. He cannot . . ."

I reeled away, my cry scraping at my throat. I could hear the guests tromping outside for the hunt, marshaled by the steward to adhere to the schedule. After Livadia, the girls had returned to Tsarskoe Selo under the care of their servants, as hunting wasn't a suitable pastime for them. Otherwise, everything must proceed as normal. No one in that party leaving for the slaughter had any idea of what was happening right over their heads.

"How?" I said, as Nicky took me to my room at the opposite end of the corridor.

"Boating in Livadia. He hit his leg on the oar." My son's voice had no emotion; he was drained of the capacity to express it. "Botkin examined him and confined him to bed for two weeks. But the bruise faded. He balked at the inactivity. He kept saying he wanted to go outside, that we were on holiday and he felt fine. It didn't hurt, he said. He kept telling us it didn't hurt." Nicky fished in his pocket for his cigarette case. "It's my fault. I insisted we keep to our itinerary. Alexei was so excited to come here, I never thought . . ." He faltered. Tears filled his eyes. "Botkin says there's a severe risk of peritonitis from the inflammation. He's advised me to issue a public bulletin to prepare the people. He believes Alexei will not survive it."

"Can't he operate?" I burst out, and then I realized my folly. An operation would unleash a deluge of blood. My grandson would die from the surgery itself.

"Nothing can be done," said Nicky. "Nothing now, save pray."

"I will pray. Later." Pulling off my hat, I tossed it onto my bed; Olga stood by the bed opposite mine, our luggage having been brought up. She was helping Demidova to unpack. Both acted if they didn't hear a word being said. "But first I must relieve Alexandra. She cannot sit there for—how long has it been?"

"Nearly twenty-one days," he replied.

"Blessed Savior have mercy. She must rest. Eat. Change her clothes. You have guests. What are they saying?"

"I view the kill every evening and dine with them every night. I went out hunting with them yesterday but sent down my excuses today that I was indisposed. They don't know. Sunny hasn't appeared, and no one has asked after her."

They wouldn't. They knew she didn't like to appear if she could avoid it. She might not appear until they left, and no one would think anything of it.

"I will assume her place at his bedside, if only for an hour or so." As I started to step past him, he said quietly, "She's waiting."

I met his eyes. "For what? The priest?" Last Rites must be administered; she'd of course want to be there when Alexei drew his last breath.

"For a message from Siberia. She believes our friend will send word."

"How? By carrier pigeon? We're miles from the nearest telegraph station."

"She says he will know. He will sense it. He knew about Stolypin; he saw him in a dream, in his carriage in Kiev driving to the opera house. He woke up shouting that death pursued the minister." Nicky sighed. "So, it came to pass."

I didn't know what to reply. Traversing the passage to Alexei's room, I set my hand on Alexandra's shoulder. "Let me watch over him. I promise to call for you when he wakes."

To my surprise, she didn't hesitate. Coming clumsily to her feet, her eyes—dull as blue chips—locked on mine. "He will not die," she said. "I know he will not."

He woke up screaming. The fever spiked so high that he raved he wanted to be "buried under the sky." This time, there was no hiding the tragedy unfolding in the lodge. Nicky sent the guests away, their kill strapped to the tops of their carriages, carrying with them the news that the tsarevich had been heard wailing upstairs.

Nicky had the bulletin prepared after Alexei lapsed into a silence so profound, Alexandra cried out and pressed her ear to his narrow chest.

"He's still breathing! I can feel it. Send word to our friend. He will come; he'll know how to save him."

As Nicky gathered her in his arms, she beat her fists against his chest—"Send word, I beg you!"—and Botkin prepared another laudanum-laced tonic for Alexei.

Alexandra flew at the doctor, knocking the cup from his hand and spraying the infusion against the wall. *"Don't touch my son."*

Olga started to cry and had to leave the room. Alexei might still be breathing, but when I touched his wrist with my fingertips, he was shockingly cold, death already laying claim to his helpless body. While Nicky escorted Alexandra back to their bedroom, his arm around her waist as she moaned in despair, I sat beside my grandson.

Before Derevenko's impassive presence, I lowered my head and prayed.

I didn't beg for a miracle. I didn't implore God to spare him. I prayed that He take him swiftly, release him from this unbearable burden he'd been forced to endure. I asked for an end to his suffering, for angels to swoop down and carry him aloft in their wings.

"Now," I whispered. "Take him now. Don't let him agonize. He is an innocent."

Hours later, as I mopped his forehead of that persistent sweat and he didn't make a sound, I heard a cry from down the passageway that sounded like desperation. I jumped up, so startled that I clutched the cloth at my chest, drenching my bodice. Derevenko shifted to me, holding out his hand for the cloth. "Majesty, I will tend to him if you must go."

I paused. Should I leave? What if Alexei . . . ?

Olga appeared at the door, breathless. "It's arrived. A telegram, brought all the way from Warsaw. Come quickly."

She assumed my post by the bed as I went to Nicky and Alexandra's room. The lodge was so quiet now, I could discern the wind in the forest beyond the walls. Nearing their room, where candles flickered before the icons, I saw Demidova on her knees in the doorway, her head bowed to her clasped hands. I stepped around her onto the threshold to find Alexandra also on her knees, with Nicky.

Alexandra crossed herself, stood up, and pushed past me, hastening back to Alexei.

I looked at Nicky. He said softly, "Father Grigori says the malady isn't as dangerous as we fear. We mustn't bother Alexei too much."

ALEXANDRA BOLTED THE door. Henceforth, only she and Nicky, with Derevenko and Botkin, would keep watch over her son. Together with a maidservant, Demidova prepared us a meal; as Olga and I sat at the long wood table in the hall, now devoid of guests, the clatter of our spoons against the soup bowls was so jarring that I abruptly said, "Why didn't you tell me you knew about Alexei?"

She glanced up. "You never told me."

"Nicky swore me to secrecy. You said Alexandra herself told you. Why?"

"She knew Stolypin had compiled a report on Father Grigori. She summoned me to explain that he is a man of God. He helps Alexei and gives her comfort."

"I'm well aware of the comfort Father Grigori gives her. I daresay, so is all of St. Petersburg. And if there were any doubt, we're now fully informed. A mere telegram from Siberia and she bars us from the room. My grandson will die without us to say goodbye."

"He won't die," said Olga. "Father Grigori says he'll recover. Alicky believes him, and she makes Alexei believe. Faith is very powerful, Mama. When did you lose yours?"

"I have *not* lost my faith." Seeing Demidova pause at the sideboard, where she was slicing up a roast-something for us, I shoved back my chair. "I find it intolerable that my own daughter should see fit to lecture me. I'm going out for a walk; I need some fresh air."

"It's almost dark. You can't go out alone," said Olga.

"Why not? They've killed every animal within a hundred miles by now." Taking up my mantle, I marched out.

The fenced paddocks wavered under mist, melting into night. At the rear of the lodge, pine trees swayed, soughing nettles mixing with the gurgle of the river. Past the lodge, the forest deepened—a wild place where it was said wolves roamed. I'd never seen a wolf in Spala, nor had anyone I'd known ever killed one here. Tucking my mantle over my head, I paced down the main driveway to stare up at the sky.

A few stars glittered in the dusk-laden sky, like diamond shards. I took a deep breath, trying to invoke that sense of peace that the lodge, despite its purpose, had always instilled in me. I'd learned to enjoy hunting as Sasha's wife, though there was always that moment of remorse when the stag or doe, run to lathered exhaustion, went still, trembling, as I waited now for death to strike. Sasha had scoffed at my sentimentality. Animals did not have feelings, he'd said. But he'd adored his dogs. He must have known that when he rebuked them for some mischief, they cowered, then crept to him with their ears laid back in apology. They knew pain, fear, and love. Why shouldn't the beasts in the field feel the same?

Now I wasn't sure anymore what I should feel. While deeply saddened by Alexei's illness, I must resign myself. He couldn't survive what he had. No man, even one of Rasputin's alleged abilities, could heal a dying child from across the distance. A telegram sent to console was only that. I had to prepare for my grandson's death.

When I heard footsteps coming down the path behind me, I tensed, not turning until Nicky said, "Mama, you shouldn't be out here alone."

I looked over my shoulder, drawing back my mantle. In the fading light, he appeared sketched in charcoal. "Is it over?" I asked quietly.

"He's still very weak." A match flared as Nicky lit a cigarette. He smoked too much, I thought absently. It couldn't be good for him. "But the fever has subsided. Botkin is baffled. Alexei is resting now, without laudanum. Sunny insisted on stopping all medicine."

I knew that sometimes just before death, the person rallied. I'd seen it with Sasha in Livadia, when he ordered the windows opened to the sea. But no one had thought he was going to live. All of us in that room had known he neared the end.

"His fever is gone?" I said.

Nicky gazed toward the tree-lined horizon. "And the inflammation is lessening. We can't know for certain yet, but the signs are there. A miracle."

"From one telegram?"

He turned to me. I couldn't decipher his expression. "You still do not believe."

"Olga just accused me of the same. I suppose I have no reason to believe."

His cigarette crackled, glowing briefly as he drew on it. The scent of burning tobacco reached me. "Sunny has enough faith for all of us." He turned back to the lodge. "Don't stay out too long. Those lamps by the entryway aren't working properly; they should be lit by now, and as you can see, they're not. I wouldn't want you to lose your way."

He retreated. Silence again enfolded me, the night unfurling its mystery.

Sunny has enough faith for all of us.

From this hour forward, should her son live, her faith would be unassailable. She would never lose her way, while I had to wonder if I'd already lost mine.

CHAPTER THIRTY-SEVEN

Spala changed everything. Who were we to argue it, Olga declared. We'd seen the miracle with our own eyes: the fever fading away, clarity returning to Alexei's wan face, his whispered request for food and drink. How he'd survived wasn't anything we could explain. No one could, except Alexandra. As Alexei was taken to recover in Tsarskoe Selo, the brace with its straps affixed to his leg once more, she was now even more zealous in her belief that Father Grigori had saved her son by divine power. And when I heard that Rasputin was again visiting the palace, I knew I couldn't dare protest. I'd done what I could. For a time, Nicky heeded me. He had sent the mystic away. But now my son would never again deny his wife.

A month before Christmas, Nicky came to see me at Gatchina. In a terse voice, he said, "Misha sent me a letter. He's married that woman Natalia in France. He asks me to officially recognize her as his wife and a grand duchess. Did you know?"

"No, of course not." I was stunned by the news. After everything that had happened, it was the last thing I expected, though I should have. Unaware of Alexei's illness and weary of waiting, Misha had finally done what he'd often threatened.

"How can he do this to us?" demanded Nicky. "I will never recognize her, nor can anyone in the family. If he doesn't repent at once of his folly and have the marriage annulled, I'll deprive him of his rank and income. He'll never set foot in Russia again."

"He's your brother," I said, but he was beyond forgiveness.

"If he wishes to remain my brother, see that he does as I command."

Despite the advent of the holidays, I arranged to meet Misha in England, calling upon Alix to bolster my appeal. He arrived with Natalia and their son, refusing to admit he'd done anything wrong. "The time would never have been right," he told me. "I haven't divorced. I've taken a wife. I was unaware Alexei had been so ill, but he's well now, yes?"

I had the distinct sense that Misha knew more about Alexei than he let on, but I refrained from saying as much because it wouldn't change his mind. Instead, I wept bitter tears. Nicky refused to let Misha return to Russia. My surviving sons were now estranged and both of my daughters were deeply unhappy.

Before the holidays, I went to Hvidøre with Alix, where I ignored my sixty-fifth birthday.

⁓

IN THE NICHOLAS Hall of the Winter Palace, I sat with Nicky on the dais as my seventeen-year-old granddaughter, Olga, radiant in her first adult court gown and diamond-studded *kokoshnik,* opened the gala marking the 1913 tercentenary of our dynasty.

"How lovely she is," I said to my son, who smiled in return, deep brackets at his eyes and mouth. I was worried to see him so aged; his refusal to forgive Misha weighed on him, and the nearly nineteen years since he'd assumed the throne had taken their toll, as well. His hair had gone mostly silver, he was too thin, and his skin was parched from his incessant smoking. Yet at my insistence, he had donned his green-and-gold uniform to attend the gala, leaving Alexandra in Tsarskoe Selo and heeding my appeal to bring Olga with him.

"She reminds me of you, Mama," he said, as Olga laughed at the young prince accompanying her. In his fluster to be dancing with the tsar's eldest daughter, the prince had forgotten to remove his hat, until it slipped over his brow to drop at his feet.

"Does she?" I blinked back sudden tears. I could no longer remember when I'd been so gay, as I saw Olga toe the offending hat aside, then whirl across the floor in the prince's arms, to the ardent violins of the mazurka.

"She has your spirit." Nicky reached across the short span between our thrones to take my hand. "Thank you for insisting that I bring her.

And for trying your best with Misha. I know it couldn't have been easy on you, and now with poor Uncle Willie . . ."

As his fingers squeezed mine, I averted my gaze, again fighting the onslaught of tears that never seemed far from my eyes these days.

My brother Willie, George I of Greece, had been shot to death by a Turkish partisan. He'd been sixty-seven years old; devastated by his death but unable to attend his funeral due to the instability in Greece, I had mourned him in Russia and sent long letters of condolence to his grieving wife and their children.

"You must stay with us this summer at Tsarskoe Selo," Nicky said. "The girls and Alexei miss you. Sunny has suggested we can go from there to Livadia, if you like."

"Yes," I murmured. "I would like that very much."

An invitation from my daughter-in-law or an impulsive gesture of affection from my son, after such a trying end to the past year and start of the new one? It shouldn't matter, I told myself. I'd avoided the Alexander Palace as assiduously as Alexandra did public receptions, knowing that as far as she was concerned, I must remember my place. Rasputin had become a persistent, if unseen, obstacle between us. She would never forget or forgive how I'd made Nicky send him away, so that he'd been in Siberia when Alexei almost died. That I'd been invited at all to spend time with my grandchildren since then was a victory.

The mazurka ended. After the prince bowed to Olga amid the court's burst of applause, she came back to us, her cheeks flushed, her auburn hair, more the hue of Nicky's in his youth than mine, escaping its net under her headdress.

"Papa," she said eagerly, "will you dance with me next?"

"What?" He motioned to the queue of eager young aristocrats lining up behind her. "And deprive all those fine gentlemen of the chance to enjoy your company?"

Olga looked over her shoulder. Her eyes widened.

I heard myself laugh—an unexpected, welcome release. "You're only young once, my dear. Your papa says you remind him of me. I would never disdain such admiration."

Olga hesitated, then quickly stepped on the dais to kiss my cheek, the warm smell of her youth, of the heat in the hall bringing out the touch of perfume borrowed from my own vial, washing over me as she whispered, "I love you, Amama. Thank you for inviting me."

She returned to the floor, a smile on her lips as she accepted the next offer to dance.

"Yes," I whispered to Nicky. "She is like me, isn't she?"

⁓

IN THE SUMMER, the Alexander Palace estate was idyllic, never too hot like the city, which emptied of the aristocracy as everyone fled to the seaside. We had not gone to Livadia; Alexandra had a flare-up of her lumbago and was restricted again to her chair. She seemed to prefer it this way, even if her gaze remained forever sharp as the children rallied around her, pushing her down the paths to the artificial lake to feed the swans or reading aloud to her as she did her interminable needlework.

Today, however, only Alexei was at her side, his devoted spaniel, Joy, at his feet. He'd been given the dog as a pup to raise, to keep him occupied, and he trained the animal with such diligence that Joy became his constant shadow, attuned to his every move. My grandson wore his white sailor shirt and short blue pants, because the brace chafed him under trousers. With his straight brown hair, thick-lashed gray eyes, and pert mouth, he reminded me of an imp, but his frown as he watched his sisters while he sat ensconced in a special chair that allowed him to stretch out his braced leg was anything but amused.

From the terrace overlooking the gardens, my granddaughters— clad in identical high-necked white frocks that had gone out of fashion with the new century yet in which Alexandra had dressed them since childhood—chased polished wood hoops, tapping them with wands and attempting to trip one another up. As the youngest, Anastasia was relentless, even though she was caught more frequently and fell with an abandon that made her mother's lips purse. Alexandra didn't seem to notice that Olga had a visible bosom or that sixteen-year-old Tatiana moved with a fawn-like grace that would be captivating in silver tissue. Even fourteen-year-old Maria, with her dimpled smile and warm blue eyes, was now an adolescent. Nevertheless, Alexandra called out peevishly, "Do be more careful. You'll stain your dresses," as if they were little girls with nothing else to wear.

"I want to play with the hoops." Alexei slapped his book down on the table between him and Alexandra, rattling her Wedgwood teapot. She never used the Russian samovar.

"Alexei. Must you?" She glanced pointedly at his book, which had nearly sent her precious English pot and matching teacup crashing to the terrace flagstones.

"Yes. I must. Why should they have all the fun?" His frown deepened into a scowl; he was quite imperious, expecting every guard on the estate to salute him when he passed and glaring at them if they failed to render the proper homage.

"Do you see what we must put up with?" Alexandra gave me a look of resignation. "Not yet nine and already an autocrat."

"I am going to be *the* autocrat," asserted Alexei, looking past her to me. "Aren't I, Amama? Autocrat of All the Russias. Like Papa."

I chuckled. "That you will. If you don't start chasing hoops like a girl."

He pouted. It wasn't the hoops he necessarily wanted to chase; he wanted to romp with his sisters without fear that he'd precipitate an emergency.

"You can read to us," said Alexandra. "Go on. You know how much I like it."

"No." He crossed his thin arms at his chest, a gesture that reminded me of Nicky. "I'm bored with reading. I'm bored with books and drawing and trains and toys. I want to—"

"We know what you want." Alexandra set her hand on his knee. "We want the same for you. Always. Please be patient, my Sunbeam. Botkin says you're doing so very well; if you continue to improve, the brace can come off next month."

His dejected exhalation indicated that for him, like any child, a month was a lifetime.

"Girls." Alexandra motioned to her daughters. "Come. Your brother is bored."

Hoops and wands were immediately abandoned on the lawn as the perspiring grand duchesses flocked to the terrace, pulling up wicker chairs to engage Alexei, whose ill-tempered monotone conveyed he was still not amused.

Alexandra winced, setting her embroidery aside, a near-imperceptible sign that another of her incapacitating headaches was upon her. "I wonder where Nicky can be?" She lifted a hand to her brow to shield the sun, though she sat under an enormous parasol that had us all in shade. "He went out riding hours ago with his officers."

"He loves to ride," I said, thinking it was the only time my son had to himself. "It does him good to get some exercise." To brighten her sour expression, for the only thing she disliked more than being asked about Rasputin was the reminder her husband might entertain interests that excluded her, I added, "Let's plan a coming-out ball for Olga and Tatiana, shall we?"

Olga started in her chair. Even Tatiana, the most reserved of the sisters and therefore most like her mother, looked taken aback.

"A ball?" echoed Alexandra. "Absolutely not. The Winter Palace is hardly safe for—"

"Not at the Winter Palace." I felt my own imp inside me, needling her. "We can hold it at my Anichkov. A small affair, only family and a select guest list. Olga had such a nice time during the tercentenary gala, and Tatiana is of age."

The girls seemed to hold their collective breaths as Alexandra met my eyes. She knew exactly what I was about, but I'd inadvertently sprung my trap to perfection. She might want her daughters to remain virginal princesses forever, trapped in her fairy tale, but Olga had no doubt returned from St. Petersburg full of stories of her evening at court. Reclusive as a hermit though she was, Alexandra was still royal. She couldn't avoid the fact that her daughters must be presented to society. It was required to launch them into the marriage arena.

"Oh, please say yes, Mama," Olga finally breathed, unable to contain herself.

Alexandra prolonged her silence. She wouldn't be coerced; as I snuck a glance at Tatiana, she leaned to her mother's ear to whisper. Whatever she said eased the tetchy line between Alexandra's eyebrows. She sighed. "I suppose it can do no harm."

Olga clapped her hands in glee. "Whatever shall we wear?"

"New dresses, I presume." Alexandra looked at me. "I'm quite sure your grandmother can arrange those, as well."

"I can, indeed. I'll pay a call to Madame Bulbenkova once I return to St. Petersburg. But you must come early for the fittings," I told the girls. "I'll provide your measurements, but a dress cannot be completed until it's been fitted in person. And you mustn't eat too much until you are fitted; it's very time-consuming to let out a bodice or widen a skirt."

"Bulbenkova?" said Olga in disappointment. "Not a Parisian couturiere?"

"No," replied Alexandra. "You will wear a Russian gown. If that does not suffice, you needn't go at all. Do not try me. I've had my arm twisted enough as it is." But to my relief, she didn't sound angry— merely annoyed that I'd somehow managed to have her persuaded.

That evening before dinner, I drew Tatiana aside. "What did you say to Mama?"

She smiled with insouciance. "That we'll ignore every boy you invite, of course."

I laughed as she glided into the dining hall. Alexandra's favorite daughter she might be, but, like Olga, she had a touch of me, too.

⁓

I LOVED HAVING them to myself in the city. I ordered my entire palace aired, dusted, and cleaned; I prepared for them the apartments that Nicky and Alexandra had occupied after their marriage and put lavender sachets in their bureaus and under their pillows.

To reach Madame Bulbenkova's establishment proved an ordeal. Tatiana and Olga arrived with an Okhrana security detail; separate daily routes to the dressmaker's address had to be established, so we never knew which way the carriage would take us, with decoy carriages sent ahead to confound a would-be assassin. It saddened me that my granddaughters should dwell under constant vigilance, but unlike me, they'd been born into a world where fear of violence was so frequent, they did not question it.

I decided they should not wear white. While customary for an unwed girl—and I myself had worn white to scintillating effect in my youth—they'd been denied any other color for so long, they wilted at the suggestion. Instead, Madame fashioned a carnation-pink satin gown for Olga, which brought out her blue eyes and fresh complexion, and an olive-green one for Tatiana, highlighting her feline gaze and slightly sallow skin. Décolletages were high, as befitted their age, but the gowns were scooped low at the shoulders, which made Olga wiggle in delight and Tatiana to primly request a fichu.

Still, they were both ravishing. To inaugurate their arrival in society, I took them to the Mariinsky to see a ballet from the imperial box, together with their aunt Olga, whom they adored. My daughter was so fond of them in return that she deigned to have a new gown made for herself in russet taffeta, which she accessorized with my black pearls.

I had to blink back tears when the audience came to its feet as we entered the box. The orchestra struck up "God Save the Tsar" and I waved, while the girls, still traumatized by Stolypin's murder in Kiev, held back.

"Come forth and greet them," I said. "It's the Mariinsky. You're perfectly safe."

The timid lift of their gloved hands resulted in thunderous applause, reminding me that despite the tumult in the streets, in some places we were still revered. Both of them had bright smiles on their faces as we sat. The curtain lifted. I'd sent word in advance of my granddaughters' presence and my expectation of an appropriate evening. The previous Season, the dancer Nijinsky had scandalized society by performing in tights with nothing on underneath; for weeks afterward, matrons had swooned over the indecency of it. Tonight, the ballet was a Mariinsky-choreographed presentation of *Le Talisman,* with costumes of regulation length.

For intermission, I ordered the traditional private tea table, so I could have tea served to those who came to the box to greet me. I soon discovered that Miechen had her own tea table set up in her opposing box, so I gathered up Olga and Tatiana and, with my daughter shaking her head behind us, went off to confront my longtime rival.

Miechen went pale when she saw us—not an easy feat, for she'd taken to powdering her face to alabaster pallor and donning so many jewels against her widow's attire (which she might have discarded by now) that she resembled an overwrought concierge.

"Minnie!" she exclaimed. "And Olga and Tatiana. And your Olga, too. *Quelle surprise.*"

"Surprising is this performance of yours," I remarked, after she kissed my granddaughters and admired my pearls on Olga. "Nijinsky himself couldn't dance his way out of it. A private tea table, when I myself am present. Whatever were you thinking?"

"I didn't know you were here," she protested.

"Did the applause at our entrance not alert you? You wouldn't have done anything differently." I pinched her corseted side so hard, she flinched. "You've contrived to put me to shame before my own grand-daughters and half the city."

"Surely you know I never intended it," she said.

"Didn't you?" I accepted the tea glass in its elaborate silver *pod-stakannik* from her servitor as she indignantly declared, "And did you only come here tonight to upstage me, Minnie?"

I lifted my glass. "Naturally. Did you think *I* would do anything differently?"

It was almost like old times again. Miechen compressed her mouth to stop her guffaw and we sat in her box for the rest of the ballet, where she whispered intrigue in my granddaughters' ears. Olga hissed at me, "Mama, what will Alicky say when she hears you let them near Miechen? You know how much they detest each other."

"By the time she hears of it, the girls will be back in Tsarskoe Selo," I replied. "Say what you will of Miechen, she commands respect in society. Let my granddaughters learn now that respect is something we all must earn."

⌐

THE BALL AT my palace was sublime. My select guest list of two hundred filled my hall to capacity, with attendees spilling over into the drawing room. Despite their promise to their mother, Tatiana and Olga did not ignore the gallant sons of princes or their grand duke cousins who came to dance with them. Olga's feet were so sore by the conclusion of the ball at four-thirty in the morning that she could scarcely walk the next day, and Tatiana charmed everyone, her elegant indifference belied by the tantalizing gleam in her eyes. Both were besieged with calling cards and invitations to tea.

Unfortunately, they couldn't accept. Alexandra had been adamant: Once the ball ended, her daughters must return home. Before they left, they made me promise to visit them soon, their wilted corsages tucked into their bags and new gowns wrapped in the tissue-lined boxes for the journey by private train to Tsarskoe Selo.

I accompanied them to the station. As the train pulled out, I saw them lean out the window of their carriage, ignoring their *dyadkas'* remonstrations, to wave at me. Swathed in Hussar-inspired fur hats, their faces were suffused with joy.

The brittle casing around my heart from years of disillusionment and loss fractured. While I was aware that my end was closer than my beginning, I had my granddaughters to keep me young. They must all be introduced into society, escorted through the pitfalls and heartaches of young adulthood, until they met the right husband, married, and started families of their own. A new generation of Romanovs waited inside them to be born.

I wanted to be present to welcome every one.

CHAPTER THIRTY-EIGHT

"Move out of my way. How dare you refuse me admittance?" I brandished my umbrella at the impervious Abyssinian detaining my entry into my newlywed granddaughter Irina's residence in London. Behind me, the horrid English rain pounded on my carriage at the curb.

The guard didn't blink. Why on earth my grandson-in-law Felix Yusupov had elected to import an imperial guard on his honeymoon was baffling enough, but I was getting drenched and losing my composure. I might have stabbed the guard with my umbrella had Felix not drawled from inside, "Let her inside. She's the dowager empress."

I pushed past the guard, irate as I shook my umbrella on the carpeting of the foyer, thrust it into the receptacle by the hat rack, and glared up at Felix. He stood on the staircase, dressed in a Turkish robe, cigarette in hand, though it was midafternoon.

"What is the meaning of this absurdity?" I said. "We're in London, not Sarajevo."

"Ah." He smiled in his laconic way. "You've heard the news."

"Everyone in Europe has heard the news. The talk is of nothing else." Unbuttoning my wet coat, I shrugged it off. Seeing as there was no footman present, I let it fall to the floor as I took the stairs, wincing at the recurrent ache in my knee. Felix descended to assist me. "This dreadful damp," I muttered, accepting his arm. "I loathe it. I hurt everywhere."

He led me into the upstairs drawing room, which was large enough to host a banquet, his youthful desire to give away his worldly possessions and endow a religious house evidently discarded in his zeal to impress Irina. They were in the midst of a grand tour for their nuptials, consisting of the finest rented homes and hotel suites, first-class travel accommodations, and shopping excursions that his fortune could buy. As I stood in my rain-spattered skirts, covertly assessing the price of their stay here, he paced to the buffet laid out on the sideboard and poured me a cup of tea.

"Where are your servants?" I took the cup from him. "Surely you don't expect my granddaughter to serve herself."

He chuckled. "Never. But we were otherwise occupied, so I told the servants to stay belowstairs. I had the guard at the door; I thought it was enough."

With his dark hair impeccably groomed and a white scarf tucked about his throat under his outlandish robe, I wondered how they'd been occupied. But his inference wasn't one I cared to question; as I'd promised his mother, Zenaida, once he proposed to Irina I'd summoned him personally to question him. After Olga's disastrous marriage, I was determined that no other woman in my family should wed into dishonor.

Slim and elegant, with Zenaida's cut-glass eyes and fine features, in my opinion he was almost too attractive. He also proved disconcertingly candid, admitting that while his youth had been spent in unsavory pursuits—"Whatever you've heard is likely true," he confessed—he had recently earned his degree in Oxford; he loved Irina and intended to be a loyal husband. In truth, by the end of our meeting, I'd been charmed by him myself and saw no reason to object. Felix was rich enough to provide Irina with everything she might need, and while the marriage would be morganatic, requiring Irina to renounce her distant claim in the succession for any sons she might bear, Xenia expressed weary approval, stating her daughter had made it clear she'd not have anyone else.

"I've heard such avowals before," I said sourly, still smarting over Xenia and Sandro's estrangement. Nevertheless, my granddaughter's marriage to the Yusupov prince went ahead with due pomp in the chapel of the Winter Palace. During the reception at the Yusupov Palace, Zenaida embraced me. "Now we can be mothers-in-law together," she said, forgetting that Xenia was the bride's mother. Still, I was pleased by her acknowledgment—she knew the marriage wouldn't have transpired without me—and now I sat to drink my tea as Felix settled opposite me.

"Irina will be down in a moment," he said. "She was still in bed."

"You needn't remind me; I'm aware you're on your honeymoon. But it's past midday. And the news is terrible. Not only have Austria's heir, Archduke Franz Ferdinand, and his wife been assassinated in Bosnia, but Austria has declared war and Germany is supporting it."

"Yes. Such a dreadful inconvenience," he said cavalierly.

I pursed my lips, pulling out my cigarette case from my bag. Felix immediately leaned forward with his gold-and-enamel Cartier lighter. "Alix hates me smoking in Marlborough House," I told him, exhaling smoke. "She caught me at my bedroom window the other day like a charwoman, seeing as she refuses to let me smoke inside, and chided me as if I might set the city on fire. Honestly, she grows more British every time I see her."

Felix chuckled. "And harder of hearing, which must be quite a trial, as you can't yell at her in her own house to mind her business."

Normally, I'd never have allowed anyone to make such a remark about my sister. Yet somehow he managed to make even the most caustic comments sound amusing, so that I found myself smiling even as I rebuked, "One day, you'll really go too far."

"No doubt." He rose to serve me more tea, obviously in no hurry to call for a servant. His lackadaisical attitude eased my nerves. He didn't seem overly alarmed by the news that had swept London and me into a panic.

"Nicky sent me a telegram," I said, when he returned with my cup. "He thinks the situation will grow dire very soon and we should return home at once. He says none of us should be abroad at a time like this."

Felix arched one of his eyebrows. "Did Rasputin tell him that?"

"Now, that is enough," I said, curbing my laughter. "We're obliged to support Serbia. A lone assassin killed the archduke and his wife, but the kaiser has seen fit to make it a point of contention and blame the entire nation. Nicky is about to mobilize our troops. Yet surely there won't be a great war over this, as the newspapers claim. How can we throw our agreements aside over a murder, outrageous as it may be?"

"I'm not so confident," he said, betraying he was not so cavalier about it and undoing my tenuous calm. "I think there may indeed be a great war over it. The kaiser has been waiting for just such an opportunity."

I froze, my cup in my hand. But whatever I was about to say was stifled by my granddaughter's entrance, her beautiful face flushed with content as she kissed my cheeks. "Grandmama, how wonderful to see you. I didn't know you were coming so early."

"It's not early," I grumbled. "Must I send word in advance?"

"Never with us," said Felix, as Irina drifted to the sideboard for tea. I could see by the way his gaze followed her that whatever his penchants may have been in the past, he was enraptured by her. How could he resist? My granddaughter by Xenia was as enticing as Nicky's daughter Tatiana, with the same sphinx-like tilt to her eyes, though hers were dark. Her dark hair had been cut short in a new style to frame her face. Under any other circumstances, I should have been appalled, catching them abed with the day half gone and Irina in her lace peignoir as if she were still in her bedchamber. Yet I was not. Their disregard for propriety was alluring—they were like two sleek, self-indulgent cats.

"Well?" I said, once Irina sat beside Felix and drowsily regarded me. "What are we to do? Nicky has asked us to return as soon as possible, lest the borders close."

"Must we?" Irina turned in dismay to Felix. "We're scheduled to travel to Nice next week to visit Mama. . . ." She sighed. "Is it truly as serious as all that?"

"I'm afraid so, my love." Felix caressed her arm. "I'll defend you."

Her pout was precocious, as only a girl of nineteen could be with a dashing older husband. I doubted his assurance. His wealth might protect her, but if I knew anything about Zenaida, her only surviving son would not be entering military service.

"How tedious," she said. "I don't want to leave."

"None of us do," I replied, but I lied. I did want to leave England. I'd been here for over a month, visiting Alix, and my patience had reached its end. Between my sister's deafness, the unvarying routine of tea and crumpets at Marlborough House, and now this new crisis, I was looking forward to vacating this dismal island, although I'd hoped to join Irina and Felix on their trip to see Xenia. "But your uncle the tsar says it's imperative we return to Russia."

"How?" said Felix. "It's not wise to sail, with German ships prowling the waters."

"Why shouldn't we go by land? We're not at war yet. I'll arrange for my train to meet us in Calais."

"If we're returning by train, we'll have to go by way of Berlin to Warsaw," he reminded me. "We should send word to Xenia about any change of plans."

"Such a nuisance. Only the Germans could contrive to make everything impossible." Yet under my irritation, I was increasingly worried. It was midsummer; we were scattered across Europe on our annual vacations. Should war break out, how would any of us return home, if Berlin shut down the sole international railway to St. Petersburg?

"I could wire Princess Cecilie of Prussia," Irina suggested. "She can petition her father-in-law. I can't believe he would refuse us passage. We didn't kill the archduke."

"Of course the kaiser won't refuse us." I avoided Felix's mordant regard. It was well known that for years I'd avoided passing through Germany while on the Continent. "Do so," I told Irina. "I'll cable Xenia to meet us in Calais. How soon can you be ready?"

"Is tomorrow soon enough?" said Felix.

I nodded. "I'll send my carriage for you. Alix will be most unhappy."

~

MY SISTER WAS more than unhappy. She started crying the moment I instructed Tania and Sophie to pack my luggage. "But you'll be perfectly safe with us. Why must you cross Europe when there's a war about to explode? I don't understand."

"I must." I raised my voice so she could hear me, trying to stem my impatience. "Nicky needs me. The Red Cross. Provisions for our soldiers: Alexandra won't attend to any of it. Alix, will you please stop crying? You'll make me cry, too, and I can't be a bawling old woman if I must contend with the kaiser."

Alix moaned. She'd done her best to adapt to her limitations as queen mother, but she was lonely, always wanting me to stay longer than I could. I'd thought of inviting her to go to France with us and perhaps on to Hvidøre in Denmark. Now it was impossible.

"George thinks it very ill-advised of Nicky to oblige your return. You could stay here as long as required, until this awful situation is sorted out."

"Yes, he told me the same," I said as she craned her head to hear me. "He doesn't want war any more than Nicky, but we mustn't let the kaiser dictate the terms of peace, either. Let's not make this any harder than it has to be. We'll see each other again soon. My son needs me. You would do the same if you were in my position."

I was frantic by the time I departed London. Overnight, Austria had begun to mobilize, and Germany had declared war on Russia for supporting Serbia. As I waited to board the train to Dover, pandemonium reigned in the station, with Felix and Irina failing to appear, though I'd sent my carriage for them. I had to depart with them; it was only as I boarded the ship for the channel crossing that they finally arrived, rushing on board with their little dogs and complaining about some trouble with their luggage. Once we reached Calais, my train was waiting, as instructed. Xenia was not. She'd sent a telegram, saying she'd meet us in Berlin. Irina assured me Princess Cecilie had agreed to intervene on our behalf, but their missing luggage was another matter. Felix left instructions for the luggage to be forwarded, and we went on, forewarned that Germany was about to close its borders.

My blood was up. We had to travel for three exhausting days, obliged to stop at regular intervals to allow German soldiers to board my train and conduct "inspections." When we arrived in Berlin, we were brought to a halt at the station platform.

Stranded on the train as a jeering mob surrounded us outside, I ordered the curtains drawn on the carriage windows, but the insignia on my doors announced my occupancy, and the horde flung whatever they could find, splattering my carriage with mud and stones, chipping the paint and gilding until soldiers with bayonets stepped in to cordon the area. For hours, we sat like prisoners in the sweltering carriage with our panting dogs, hearing the Germans deride us, one well-aimed stone cracking a window and frightening Irina into tears. Finally, the Russian ambassador, accompanied by an official of the kaiser's Ministry of Foreign Affairs, arrived to inform us that we could proceed no further.

I forgot my manners, pointing my finger in the official's face. "How dare you issue directives to me? I am the Dowager Empress of Russia."

"Yes, and your country has declared war on Germany—" he started to say.

"That is a lie. *You* declared war on us. I demand to see the kaiser this instant."

"His Majesty is unavailable. Your Majesty may return to England or travel on to Denmark, but not through Germany."

"But my daughter is supposed to meet us here," I cried out as he clicked his heels and turned to depart. The Russian ambassador stepped close to me. "I will wait for Her Imperial Highness. Your Majesty must leave. Now."

"Now?" I gazed at him in disbelief.

Felix stood, holding out his hand to Irina. "We will wait for Xenia here. We'll not depart until she's with us." He gave me a sardonic smile. "We might be at war and unable to agree on who declared it first, but the kaiser will not arrest us."

I didn't want to leave without them, but Felix waved aside my protests, entrusting their dogs to me and taking Irina by the hand, following the Russian ambassador out.

Two hours later, my train left Berlin. I had waited as long as I dared and Xenia had still not arrived, though other Russians had, aristocrats forced to cut short their vacations abroad. I accepted all of them on my train, unable to watch them cowering on the platform, subjected to derision. Surrounded by strangers, the dogs at my feet, I traveled through the night to Denmark. I had no idea if my granddaughter, her husband, or my daughter were safe, until I arrived and was informed they'd made it out by the skin of their teeth, boarding the last overcrowded train from Berlin to Copenhagen. Irina had taken ill from the fright, and Xenia was enraged by the long delay she'd endured at the German border, her bags confiscated and searched.

"Perhaps it was best that our luggage went missing," remarked Felix. "I suppose I'll have to buy some things here while Irina recovers."

They were staying in a suite in Copenhagen's finest hotel. After I visited my granddaughter to ascertain she mostly suffered from exhaustion—I suspected she might be pregnant, as it turned out she was—I decided to continue to Russia with Xenia, leaving Irina and Felix behind. My daughter fretted over Sandro, from whom she had no word, as he'd been in Cannes with his mistress. In no mood for her woes, I berated her. "He can find his way home on his own," I said. "Seeing as you've let him do everything else as he pleases."

Xenia shut her mouth, brooding as we departed Denmark for Finland, where the Finnish people rallied to us, alerted by the newspapers to our harrowing experience in Berlin.

"You cannot imagine my satisfaction that after disguising my feelings for fifty years, at last I'm free to say how much I detest the Germans," I announced to the journalists. My comment was printed in every edition, making me hope it would reach the kaiser.

Not that anything I said mattered. Hungary pledged forces to Austria. Germany declared war on France and invaded Flanders. By the time we reached St. Petersburg, Great Britain had entered the fray. Felix had been right. A great war had broken out.

The murder of one archduke had unleashed damnation upon us all.

PART VI

1914–1918

The Seeds of Destruction

Our happiest and serenest times are now over.

—MARIA FEODOROVNA

CHAPTER THIRTY-NINE

St. Petersburg was awash in patriotic fervor that failed to impress me. I'd seen similar sentiment before during other conflicts and knew how quickly it could turn. My nephew King George V was in urgent communication with Nicky, warning that the kaiser's aggressive militarization had amassed a powerful force, against which none of us were prepared—least of all Russia, where we barely had electricity outside our cities, our people toiling in candlelit isolation, unaware of the modern horrors about to march across Europe.

At my insistence, Nicky appointed Sasha's first cousin, Grand Duke Nikolai, known in the family as Nikolasha, as commander in chief of military operations. Fifty-seven years old and a career officer, Nikolasha had never led an army in the field, so the strategic planning was entrusted to our generals. Yet as I warned Nicky, as the tsar he must delegate, lest the unpredictability of war affect his reputation, which hadn't improved since our last disastrous engagement with Japan.

Although nearly fifty-four and in exile for twelve years due to his unapproved morganatic marriage, his children having been raised by Ella, my brother-in-law Grand Duke Paul begged Nicky to forgive him and grant him a military appointment. I lent my voice in support of Paul's return, and he reclaimed his status when Nicky appointed him to lead the First Corps of the Imperial Guard. Likewise, after much urging on my part, Nicky gave Misha leave to return from his own exile in England to serve as major general in the newly formed Caucasian Native Cavalry. As a gesture of reconciliation, Nicky accorded Misha's four-year-old son George the title of Count Brasov. Natalia was thus free to style herself as Countess Brasova, even if she wasn't acknowledged as Misha's wife. Misha housed Natalia and his son in the city, where Natalia took to her imperial duty, founding two hospitals. Hearing of them, I went to tour the wards, chuckling under my breath when I saw the blank space over the entryway where Natalia's portrait had been temporarily removed, so as not to cause me any offense.

I had no patience for such trivialities. We must all do our part. Germany posed a threat unlike any before, dividing nations and families, including mine. Due to her husband's penurious position and residence in Austria, my sister Thyra was obliged to side with the kaiser, while my nephew in Denmark, if outwardly neutral, lent covert support to the allied nations, installing defensive cannon on my beach at Hvidøre.

However, when I said everyone must contribute, I didn't include Alexandra, who I was certain would remain out of sight, a German-born empress hardly conducive to public appeal. Waves of anti-Prussian loathing had resulted in the smashing of German storefronts throughout St. Petersburg, prompting the renaming of the city as Petrograd to eliminate the German "burg."

But to my astonishment, Nicky informed me that Alexandra, Olga, and Tatiana were training to become nurses, following my example. Alexandra had even installed a hospital ward in the Catherine Palace, which she would oversee. Despite my surprise, I found it commendable. My schedule was filled to capacity with my Red Cross duties; at my age, I couldn't be expected to work in the wards. Olga and Xenia assumed that task for me in the Winter Palace, while I organized charity events to collect funds and dispatch medical supplies for the front. I called upon all my society contacts. Miechen threw open her palace for a charity gala, her famous cut-crystal bowls, once filled with gemstones for her guests, now serving as receptacles for rubles to support our war effort.

My relief work was the only means I had to keep fear at bay. We'd barely recovered from our 1905 revolution, and the Duma was not a success. War brought out the beast in man. I lived daily with the terror that should the Germans prove victorious, we'd turn on one another like Zenaida's proverbial wolf. And while I was tireless in my endeavors, not even I could overcome the entrenched corruption in our bureaucracy. Unscrupulous ministers had no compunction in siphoning funds, sending our soldiers into battle without basic supplies. I had to tele-gram Nikolasha in outrage to request his personal leave for my Red Cross convoys to pass, as they were deemed unauthorized and returned to St. Petersburg, at the expense of a situation that grew more terrible by the hour.

The end of 1914 came and went in a tide of grief. Battle upon bat-tle, each mind-numbing in its magnitude, plunged Russia into mourn-ing, the lists of casualties so immense that the newspapers devoted separate editions to publish them. From the various fronts, injured sol-diers were delivered to us on cattle-car trains after weeks of jarring travel, laid out on piles of rags, infested with lice, suffering from putrid wounds, dysentery, and barbaric battlefield amputations. Every hospi-tal overflowed. Any palace not occupied—and many that were—was requisitioned as a ward, where society ladies who'd never fastened a but-ton by themselves toiled under ghastly conditions until they fainted from the screams of the dying or the stench of gangrene.

Germany was relentless, foraging like a dragon through the mud and blood of the trenches, unloosing monstrous modern weapons of gas and artillery. I began to think any peace accord would be preferable to this horrid waste of life, with so many dying for a cause that few understood. I thought nothing could be worse than a war waged in the name of vengeance, but I hadn't begun to realize what lay ahead.

⁓

"Are you planning to stay here forever?" Miechen demanded, hav-ing arrived in Kiev in a fury, on her private train. I'd repaired to the southern city in the Ukrainian region with my daughter Olga to estab-lish a triage infirmary, after another terrible series of battles throughout the spring had resulted in Poland's fall to the Germans and the decima-tion of our forces. Those of our men who'd managed to survive and claw their way back home had arrived in tatters, emaciated, frostbitten, and gravely wounded, with Polish refugees flooding in behind them, literally carrying whatever they could salvage.

"You know I'm here to assist Olga," I said, bringing Miechen to the upstairs drawing room of Kiev's Mariinsky Palace. The room was filled with furnishings that had been lugged up from the lower level, now oc-cupied by our infirmary. "We had no place to put any of the wounded.

Every hospital in the city is filled beyond capacity. Because Kiev is closer to the front lines, Olga thought it the ideal place to set up a new ward and refugee center. How could I begrudge her? She's been tireless, training staff and spending sixteen hours a day on her feet as a nurse."

Watching Miechen's gaze narrow as she took in the extra chairs, tables, paintings, and statues heaped about us, sheets tossed over them like forgotten artifacts, I didn't add that my youngest daughter's lover, Kulikovsky, a colonel in active service, had suffered a head wound in Poland, which partly motivated Olga's determination to remain here.

"I must commend Olga for her dedication," Miechen said, "but this hardly looks comfortable for a dowager empress, Minnie."

"I can assure you, our soldiers have far less comforts," I retorted. I signaled Sophie for tea, resigned to receive Miechen with the social niceties she required. "You needn't have come all this way. I'm well enough, under the circumstances."

"I didn't come to see if you are well. I came to tell you that mystic of hers is more of a menace than ever." Before I could reply, she went on, "He's *advising* her. He's telling her which ministers to favor and which to dismiss. The Duma protested in mid-session, recommending she be shut away in a convent. The city is in an uproar; we have shortages of everything. As you surely know, our army is so poorly supplied they couldn't keep out a pack of dogs, much less the kaiser. Yet she sends prayer books to German prisoners of war and forwards her mystic's political recommendations to Nicky, clogging up his private line at his *stavka*. The talk everywhere is that Rasputin now rules Russia and that Nicky will dismiss Nikolasha to assume his post as commander in chief, with Alexandra overseeing the state."

I remained silent as Sophie brought in the tea, served us, and retreated.

Miechen glared at me. "Are you going to say anything? Or better yet, *do* something?"

"What would you have me do?" I met her stare. "She has made it clear she'll broach no interference where the mystic is concerned. We are at war. I cannot fight her when Russians are dying by the thousands."

"Even more will die if you don't. She's hated by everyone. They call her *Nemka,* the German spy, and say that foul man is her lover. She may hide the truth for her dependence on him, but I know." When I recoiled, she said, "The boy is ill. Is it the bleeding disorder?"

Though I tried to resist, I glanced over my shoulder, to the ajar doors through which Sophie had disappeared. Other servants wandered the halls; there were ears everywhere.

"Minnie." Miechen's firm voice wrenched my gaze back to her. "Answer me."

I swallowed. The admission stuck in my throat, but my lack of response was enough.

"As I thought." Miechen dumped too much sugar into her cup, as usual. I wondered why she didn't just clamp a cube between her teeth like the peasants and drink her tea through it. "She thinks her miracle worker can heal the child, so she'll tear down Russia to defend him. You must intervene. No one but you can persuade Nicky to reason."

"Nicky promised me that he'll not assume military command. He appointed Nikolasha to that purpose and will not—"

"Nikolasha is losing the war. *We* are losing. The Germans are sending zeppelin raids over London! She thinks Nicky must assert himself as supreme commander because Rasputin told her so. My Cyril informed me Nicky said he'll consider relieving Nikolasha of command once he returns to the city to review the new Chevalier Guard, though what he intends to review is beyond me. Will he dispatch riderless horses into battle to confound the Germans? We have no men to recruit. You know it better than anyone. You're setting up wards in every nook and cranny. At this rate, by Epiphany we'll be performing surgeries on our dining room tables."

I picked up my cup but was so upset I could barely hold it.

Miechen made a contrite sound. "I understand your predicament. He's not only our emperor, he's your son. He chose her, though you knew she was unsuitable, and her son is ill, so how can you set yourself against her when, as a mother, you know how she suffers? But she must be stopped. This is not the time for her to assert her delusions of grandeur. She must keep her nose out of our affairs, and her mystic must be eliminated."

"Eliminated?" A vise closed about my chest.

She shrugged. "Contrary to her belief, he's not touched by God. He's as mortal as any other. It's a matter of survival. Should Nicky allow her to oversee the government and she keeps Rasputin at her side, how long will it be before we have another revolution on our hands?"

"We cannot." I was aghast. "We are Romanovs. We do not condone murder."

She chuckled. "Since when? Romanovs have been eliminating opponents for centuries, including our own flesh and blood. Do you think Peter or Catherine the Great would have abided an uncouth peasant telling them what to do? He'd be dead already."

I lunged for her hand so abruptly that I knocked her cup aside. "No," I whispered. "You mustn't contemplate such a horror."

She looked down at my tea-spattered hand gripping hers. "I'm not the one you need be concerned about. Will you speak to Nicky?"

"Yes," I said. "I'll return to St. Petersburg for the review. I'll do whatever I can to keep him from assuming military command, but you must never suggest this again. To harm Rasputin would be a catastrophe for us. You have no idea of what she might do. He made a prophecy to her that should any of us seek to harm him, the entire dynasty would fall. She told Nicky. She believes it utterly."

"Naturally. It's a very convenient way to safeguard him." Miechen poured herself more tea. "As I said, he's only a man. And with thousands of men dying, what's one more?"

⁓

RED WAS NO longer the color of Russia. Black was our new color, the hue of war, of festering entrails spilled across Europe. In St. Petersburg, I saw mourning armbands on everyone walking the streets; black crepe slung across doorways, balconies, and storefronts; black streamers twined about lampposts; and black like a film of oil darkening the river, as the city, muted by loss, shrank into itself like a maimed animal. Yet to my disbelief I also saw officers in uniform on leave, in the cafés and strolling down the avenues with their sweethearts—men who should have been fighting at the front yet for some unfathomable reason had obtained passes to return to the city, as if nothing were amiss.

At the Winter Palace, my son Nicky reviewed the procession of our new troops—the latest recruits, destined to fight in the Carpathians. In his blue uniform with its gold-fringed epaulettes, he mounted his horse and rode before the lines of men, with Alexei beside him in a matching uniform, on a specially trained pony. Nicky maintained a stern demeanor, offering no encouragement. He was the emperor and they were his subjects, who must obey their Little Father. It was a somber moment as, together with his son, he confronted the flesh he was willing to sacrifice, his countenance emotionless.

I held a luncheon for him at my Anichkov. It had been months since I'd seen him, and I hoped he'd come alone as in the past, although Alexandra and their daughters were here from Tsarskoe Selo to lend their support. I had the meal served outside on my terrace and waited until the girls and Alexei went for a walk, overseen by their *dyadkas,* before I broached the subject.

"I'm told you are considering relieving Nikolasha of his command."

Nicky didn't respond, smoking his cigarette and gazing moodily outward, but I saw Alexandra's expression tighten. She did not look well. Her service in her ward at the Catherine Palace was commendable, but as always she'd taken it to such an extreme that she'd suffered one of her lumbago attacks, confined to bed for weeks. I was shocked by how much weight she'd put on. She appeared almost bloated.

"Are you?" I said, waving my servants into the house and leaving the used plates and cutlery on the table, not wanting anything to interrupt our confrontation. For I already knew that a confrontation it would be. The grim line of Alexandra's jaw confirmed it.

"He's not won a single battle so far," she suddenly said. "He let Poland fall. Would you have him drag us into perdition? He may be a Romanov, but he's no commander in chief. We need someone else at the helm if we're to turn the tide."

"That someone being Nicky, I suppose?" I said.

My son still hadn't spoken, crushing out his cigarette in the ashtray and lighting another. In the cruel sunlight, the edges of his eyes were seamed with lines and his bearded mouth thinned to a sullen crevice. He too had aged, only in contrast to her, he had lost too much weight, so that his uniform hung on him as if his shoulders were pegs.

"Who else?" Alexandra lifted her chin. "An emperor must lead by example."

Miechen had warned me, but to hear it directly from my daughter-in-law was altogether different. I had to remain poised. I mustn't show how much my hatred toward her surged, how I longed to lambast her for being blind as ever when it came to Russia.

"If we are in so precarious a position, the last thing he should do is assume command of our military," I said. "He'll be blamed for everything that goes wrong. It would be wiser to have Nikolasha continue to assume the responsibility and assign other generals to advise him, as despite his lack of accomplishments, our troops still respect him."

At this, Nicky reacted. His bruised eyes met mine. "And am I to be the coward who stays behind while my soldiers die for his cause?"

"*Our* cause," I said. "Russia's cause. You did not start this war. You did not—"

"Enough." His voice was low. "Nikolasha will lose us half the empire."

"If you remove him, you might lose it all."

Alexandra gripped her cane, starting to rise. "It's late. We must return to—"

"You will stay." Though I did not raise my voice, she went still, staring at me as if I'd barked at her. "You obviously have an opinion, and I'm prepared to listen. To reason, not fantasy. To informed remarks, not the ravings of that mystic you keep about you, against my advice. Rasputin," I said, causing her to glower, "is not anyone to me."

"Do you see?" She turned to Nicky. "How she speaks to me? How she *disdains* me?"

"Not you," I said, preempting him. "I never disdain you. But you've let this situation career past any logical explanation. Miechen knows," I added, seeing her flinch. "She told me. How long before the others find out?" When she lowered herself back into her chair, stiff with anger, I went on: "The news that our tsarevich is ill will not serve us now. It might have in the beginning, but with this horrendous war at our doorstep, it will be interpreted as another sign of our inability to rule. The people could turn against us."

"I will not hear this." Alexandra was rigid. "You've wanted him exiled from the moment you heard about him, but you know nothing. *Nothing.* Alexei had a nosebleed last month when we went to Nicky's base camp at Mogilev to visit. It started on the train; by the time we arrived, he was faint. We couldn't stop it—" Her voice caught, those ready tears of hers moistening her eyes. "We thought he would die. But our friend came when I summoned him, and the bleeding ceased. Would you still condemn him when you know what we suffer? Will you deny us the only solace we have left in this wretched world?"

I lowered my gaze. I mustn't let her draw me in. It was her inevitable tactic, to fling at me another episode of near death that I'd been unaware of, to force me to admit she was right, Rasputin was our only hope, because we were helpless victims of fate.

"I am very sorry to hear it," I said at length. "But he meddles in state affairs. He gives you advice, to the Duma's outrage, though I cannot for the life of me comprehend how a Siberian peasant knows the first thing about governing this empire."

Her ringed fingers twisted about the tip of her cane. "He does not seek any power. He merely tells us God's truth. He counseled us against this war and believes the tsar alone can bring us back to peace, by assuming supreme command. Nicky believes it, too."

She flung these words at me across the table, returning my stare to my son. "Is this true? Would you heed a man reviled throughout Russia?"

Nicky stood, brushing cigarette ash from his cuff. "Mama, we should continue this conversation in private. The children could return at any moment." Before Alexandra could protest, he lifted his hand. "Sunny, please wait for them. I'll only be a moment."

Her face turned icy as he went into the palace. As I pushed back my chair to follow him inside, she hissed, "You've always smothered him, made him think he's useless, that he cannot make a decision without you. But he is our tsar. He must prove himself now."

I gave her a taut look before I turned away. I would not dignify her outburst with a response. She'd trespassed beyond any shred of sympathy I had retained for her.

As soon as I entered my drawing room, Nicky said, "There will be no discussion. I will assume military command. Nikolasha has proven unworthy of his charge."

"You cannot." I stood immobile in the doorway. Hearing the flat tone in his voice, I knew he'd made his decision before he'd come to St. Petersburg. Had I not brought it up, he wouldn't have informed me. Somehow, in the chaos, I had forsaken his trust. "It would be a terrible mistake, Nicky. We are losing the war. You'll bear the blame for it." I made myself take a step toward him. "Consult with the Duma first. Let them advise you."

His gaze did not falter. "I've had enough of their counsel. I'm suspending the Duma; they've done nothing but whittle away at my rights, pushing me into a corner so they can have their say over me. With Russia in peril, my duty is to lead. I'll not shirk it anymore."

"You are not shirking it by allowing experienced men to guide you!" I exclaimed, trying in vain to subdue my panic. "Your cousin George in England, even the kaiser himself—they rely on able counselors, not their wives or friends. It's what a ruler must do."

He drew on his cigarette, blowing out the smoke. "I must act as my conscience dictates. Sunny has no part in it. Mama, please do not persist. It is already done."

"Done? What do you mean, it is already done?"

"Nikolasha has been relieved. I will assume command at Mogilev next week."

He didn't explain, didn't make an attempt to help me understand. He faced me with such an undiscernible expression, I felt as though I stood before a stranger.

"And Alexandra?" I managed to say. "Will she continue to keep her mystic in her counsel, dismissing whomever she pleases without oversight?"

"She has our best interests at heart. You give her too little credit. You always have."

I regarded him, incredulous. Before I could curb my temper, I said, "You are indeed a fool if you believe that. The only interest she has at heart is her own. That man Rasputin—he'll bring us to ruin because of her. You want to be seen as the tsar? Behave like one. Exile the mystic and bridle your wife. Otherwise, you'll indeed be pushed into a corner."

He remained impassive, but I saw the flare in his eyes, the compression of his lean frame under his uniform. "You mustn't say such things to me. It is beneath us both."

"No," I said. "What is beneath us is to continue as we have. Too long have I shielded you from the truth. You must hear it now. To declare yourself commander in chief is the worst error you can commit. You know nothing of managing a war."

"Neither did Nikolasha. Unlike him, I can learn." He looked past me toward the terrace, where the children's laughter could be heard as they approached.

Anastasia burst into the room, her face bright with color. She came to a halt, sensing the tension between us before she said, "Alexei fell into Amama's pond."

Nicky bolted past me; as I turned after him, Anastasia said sheepishly, "He only got his trousers wet. The pond isn't deep."

"No." I forced out a smile. "It's not deep at all."

Outside, Alexandra was fussing over Alexei, who appeared embarrassed. Olga, Tatiana, and Maria anxiously clutched their parasols, for as she daubed Alexei's pants with a napkin Alexandra scolded, "You're supposed to be watching him at all times. Where was Derevenko? How can you have let such a mishap occur?"

"It was Joy." Alexei pointed at his spaniel. "His leash caught around my legs. I only stepped into the pond. I'm not bruised at all. See?" He tried to yank up his soaked trouser leg, but Alexandra was already gesturing to her daughters and the contrite *dyadkas*.

"Fetch our belongings," she said. "He'll catch cold. We must get him to the Winter Palace at once."

"I have extra towels and a robe here," I said. "He can take a warm bath in my tub."

She ignored me, her smile razor-thin as she marshaled the girls. Within moments they were walking out of my gates with their dogs and guards to the waiting motorcars, a novelty Nicky had brought to Russia and I thought very unsafe.

He kissed me goodbye. I didn't have a moment to beseech him, and he didn't allow it. As they drove away toward the Winter Palace, I had to restrain my wail of anguish, my sudden realization that Alexandra was right: We were helpless victims of fate.

Her fate. A fate she was determined to thrust upon all of us.

CHAPTER FORTY

I closed up Anichkov, leaving a small staff to oversee its upkeep, and went back to Kiev. Olga needed me, and I needed something to occupy my time. The capital might bustle in the evenings with concerts and theater engagements, society still dining and dancing as if the war were an inconvenience, but I had no heart for any of it. I sent Miechen a brief missive, advising her of my departure. I couldn't look her in the eye and admit that I'd failed, that my son no longer solicited or heeded my advice.

In Kiev, I busied myself with the ward and refugee center, having brought blankets, clothes, and other necessities from my palace. Miechen sent me a letter: Nicky's proroguing of the Duma, followed by the public announcement that he'd assumed supreme command of our forces, had finally shaken society out of its ignorant whirlwind.

Gigogne rules entirely. When informed of the Duma's suspension, a senior member spoke out in full session against her and R., blaming them for our setbacks. Ella herself left her convent to plead with G. She was shown the door. G. will hear nothing against R.

I burned the letter. If Alexandra's own sister, a true acolyte of God, couldn't convince her to rid herself of Rasputin, there was indeed nothing any of us could do.

The war continued on its nightmarish course, consuming lives and upending the world. November 1916 marked my sixth-ninth birthday and the fiftieth anniversary of my arrival in Russia; I wasn't of any mind to celebrate the occasion, but the family gathered in Kiev at the behest of Nicky, who came with Alexei to present me with a medal of honor, depicting the number 50 etched in diamonds. Miechen gave me a precious icon, inscribed by all the grand dukes and duchesses. We attended a concert together, then held a luncheon the next day, during which Nicky, though visibly careworn, took time to converse with everyone present. Misha had come, as well; having my two sons at my side that day, without Alexandra to spoil our reunion, was joyous for me. But the mood soon soured when Misha petitioned Nicky for a transfer to an administrative post in Mogilev. After serving valiantly with his corps, he'd fallen ill with diphtheria. He had recovered but now had an ulcer, aggravated by the poor diet at his base camp. Natalia had begged him not to risk his life further; now stationed in Kiev with our Imperial Air Force, my son-in-law Sandro added his voice in appeal for Misha.

Nicky frowned, to my disbelief. I knew Alexandra had not forgiven Misha for his morganatic marriage or proximity to the throne; to her, he remained a threat. But I was stricken by Misha's downcast expression when Nicky, with habitual evasion, replied that he'd "consider a transfer at a later date." Not one to curb her tongue anymore, Miechen erupted in anger, declaring, "Would you sacrifice your own brother to please that madwoman you married?" nearly causing an open rift as Nicky glared at her.

Before Nicky left, I again implored him. "Please transfer Misha to Mogilev. He can support you better there, as he's been ill. And return full command to Nikolasha. Do it now, for the sake of the country."

"I cannot," he said curtly, and he boarded his train with his son. At the last moment, Alexei ran back to hug me. Now twelve, he'd grown tall, very slim like his father; though his leg often pained him, requiring the odious brace, he did not let it deter him. "Don't worry, Grand-mère," he said. "I'll ask Papa to transfer Uncle Misha."

He did not succeed, but perhaps in remorse, Nicky unexpectedly approved Olga's long-contested divorce, though officially it was called an annulment, as Olga claimed her marriage had never been consummated. Finally freed of her husband, my daughter wed her colonel in a quiet ceremony in Kiev. I fretted over whether to attend, fearing my presence would be interpreted as my sanctioning of yet another morganatic union among my children. When Misha arrived from his camp to give Olga away at the altar, he said, "She's your daughter. How can you not be there?"

I agreed but insisted on a strictly private affair. I needn't have worried; as the war continued to devour lives, few paid any notice to Olga's new matrimony.

The winter snows were less harsh in Kiev, but the cold was not. By Christmas, we lacked sufficient fuel for the stoves, relying on smoky kerosene lamps and charcoal braziers in the infirmary. But soldiers still died under our care, our supplies so depleted that Olga resorted to tearing up her own sheets for dressings.

"We must return to Gatchina," I told her when she came to see me, her nursing uniform bloodstained, her entire person limp with exhaustion. "My estate is better equipped. At least we'll not freeze to death there."

She removed her soiled coif. "We are at war," she said, making me realize I always underestimated her fortitude. "My patients can't be moved and my nurses are under my supervision. If you must leave for Gatchina, do so. I will not."

I would not leave her, so I sent to my estate for provisions. While she and Kulikovsky kept residence in the palace, I went to live on my train, which was more easily heated and would allow me to survive the winter. At my age, I felt the cold more keenly than ever. As my equally aged Sophie and Tania attended me, swathed in shawls and wearing bulky mittens, I had to laugh. "Look at us, like three beggar women. Who would have thought we'd reach such a pass?"

I laughed to conceal the pain of it, the humiliation that I, who'd graced the grandest court in the world, had been reduced to bedding on my train. As determined as I was to be of service, I'd be no use to anyone dead. I telegrammed my staff at the Anichkov to inform them that I was planning to return soon, then sent another telegram to Miechen.

I was preparing for departure when an urgent letter from Miechen arrived. She warned me to stay put. The situation in Petrograd was deteriorating. Bread shortages had provoked violent riots; factory workers were on strike again, with daily demonstrations and irate speeches in the squares, denouncing both the war and our tsarina, as word spread that more than half of Nicky's cabinet had resigned, forced out by her. At Rasputin's recommendation, she'd filled the empty posts with sycophants indebted to the mystic, who told her only what she wanted to hear. Popular hatred had fallen upon her with such spleen, it astonished me that she could still think her mystic was worth all the uproar he caused.

Still, I did not expect it when on New Year's Day 1917, Xenia's husband, Sandro, whom I'd thought still on leave in Petrograd visiting his family, arrived unannounced at Mariinsky Palace as I was breakfasting with Olga.

"Rasputin," Sandro said breathlessly. "He's dead."

We sat frozen, staring at him. The dreadful silence extended until I managed to whisper, "How . . . ?"

Sandro glanced at Olga, who didn't budge from her chair. His very reluctance to impart before her what must be grisly details made me brace myself.

"Felix, and Paul's son, Dmitri," he finally said. "They killed him."

"What?" I half-rose to my feet in incredulous horror.

"According to Felix, he conceived the entire plot. He enlisted Dmitri and a senior member of the Duma who'd spoken out against Rasputin. They lured the mystic to the Yusupov Palace, on the pretext that Irina and Felix required spiritual advice, where they served him cyanide-laced cakes."

"They *poisoned* him?" The revulsion in my voice caused Sandro to flinch.

"Poisoning was the least of it," he said, looking more discomfited with every word he uttered. "Hours later, he still hadn't died, so Felix took up Dmitri's pistol and shot him repeatedly. Then they dumped him in the Neva. They must have been desperate. They were seen; witnesses came forth after Rasputin went missing and Alexandra demanded an investigation. The police dragged the river. The mystic had water in his lungs." He shuddered. "After all the poison and bullets, he drowned instead. He was still alive when they threw him under the ice. Can you imagine it?"

"I cannot," I whispered. But I could imagine the grief in Tsarskoe Selo, Alexandra's wails for vengeance. Remembering my one and only sight of him in the Alexander Palace vestibule, those piercing eyes and craggy reproach—*Matushka, why do you fear me? I wish you no harm*—I gripped the edge of the table. "God help us, we're in for greater trouble now." I met Olga's stare. "She will clamor for their heads."

"She already has." Sandro's voice wrenched my gaze back to him.

"Alexandra wanted Felix and Dmitri arrested and shot. The Duma accomplice fled the city, and Felix fled to his estate in Kursk. But poor Dmitri has been conscripted for duty at the Persian front."

"Not to mention poor Zenaida," said Olga. Her remark, the first she'd made, was emotionless, as if Rasputin's demise was inconsequential. "She must be beside herself." My daughter stood, folding her napkin and setting it aside. "I must go to work."

"You will not," I said sharply. "This is a family crisis we must attend to."

She paused, regarding me. "It's not my affair, Mama. I feel for Dmitri, but Felix? He took advantage of some archaic law that an only-son in a family is exempt from military service, though only-sons without his wealth are indeed serving. Now at least he has bestirred himself to serve, unpleasant as it may be."

"How can you . . . ?" I returned her steady gaze in utter dismay. "You are Irina's aunt. Felix is her husband. They have an infant daughter. Should Alexandra—"

"She will not," interrupted Sandro hastily. "I've spoken to Miechen, Cyril, and others in the family. We will sign a joint letter to Nicky, requesting leniency. Nicky must grant it. He cannot afford to harm our own while we're at war."

"You should sign the letter, too," Olga said to me. "I don't like that the mystic was murdered, but they indeed did us a service." Without another word or awaiting my leave, she walked out to return to her infirmary.

I turned to Sandro. "We don't expect you to sign it," he said. "We know that for Nicky's sake, if not Alexandra's, you mustn't appear to condone this."

I met his blue eyes, this still-handsome but now war-weary man I'd known since he was a boy, Nicky's best friend, whom Xenia had loved and fought to marry. I'd nursed fury toward him for taking a mistress and causing my daughter pain, but as he stood before me in his uniform, obviously distraught by what had occurred yet with our duty foremost in his mind, a solution already at hand, I couldn't do anything but nod.

"I will sign it," I said quietly. "For Felix and Irina, and for Dmitri, whom Ella raised. But it is a horror. I never wished such a fate upon anyone, not even Rasputin."

Sandro lowered his eyes and said nothing more.

⁓

SANDRO ACCOMPANIED ME to the Yusupov estate in the countryside of Kursk, south of Moscow, a long trip on my train that left me in no better temper. I found Zenaida indeed beside herself. After having avoided overt scandal all her life, she was now submerged in it. But Felix, while visibly perturbed, was also defiant when I questioned him.

"He was a devil," Felix declared. "A blight on Russia. Someone had to act. I only did what no one else dared to do." He glanced at his mother, who was mute with despair. "If we must, Irina and I can go abroad and live in exile. My fortune is my own. They cannot touch it."

"Did you have to involve Dmitri?" The anger in my voice turned him paler than he already was. "*What* were you thinking? He's been dispatched to Persia, on military duty in one of the most inhospitable posts on earth. He is a Romanov. He doesn't have your recourse." And to make sure he understood, I added, "The worst is death. The law is clear. A murderer can be tried and executed."

"No," cried Irina. "You must stop it! Talk to Nicky. Tell him—"

"We're sending him a letter," I said, easing the bite in my tone. Irina had to keep her wits about her; she couldn't afford to become hysterical. "We've all signed it. None of us want to see Felix or Dmitri harmed."

Sandro gave grim assent. "I'll take our letter to Nicky in person. I will get down on my knees if I must to persuade him."

"But until then Felix must remain out of sight." I stared directly at my grandson-in-law, wanting to berate him, to shout and slap him as I might an errant child caught in a mischief, for it was clear to me that he'd acted on impulse, without thinking of what he might unleash in its wake. "No boasting. No running about claiming you killed the mystic to free us from his tyranny. Nicky will not want a trial, for Dmitri's sake, but . . ."

"She will." Felix bowed his head. "Yes," he muttered. "I never meant to cause trouble."

Had I felt any mirth, I might have laughed in disbelief. He spoke as if he had no idea that murdering the tsarina's mystic would bring her wrath down upon him. Looking at his slim fingers caressing my granddaughter's hand, it was almost impossible to believe he'd taken Rasputin's life. How had he found the courage?

"It's done now," I said. "Stay here and do nothing. Let Sandro see to the rest."

⸺

BACK IN KIEV, I busied myself with Olga. For once I was grateful for her reticence; she did not ask about my visit to Felix, and I did not offer. The mystic who once loomed like an inescapable shadow in our lives was no more, yet his shadow remained, prompting me to send a personal letter to Nicky, telling him I'd signed the family appeal for leniency because it was how we must behave. To strike against one of us would be a strike against all of us. While I did not approve of the deed, I assured my son, neither could I allow a grand duke and my granddaughter's husband to be arrested and shot at Alexandra's behest.

When Sandro returned from Tsarskoe Selo, he was so tired and drawn that he dropped onto the nearest chair before me, shaking his head.

"No?" I said in alarm. "He will have them brought to trial?"

"No trial. There will be no charges. But Dmitri must remain in Persia and Felix is banished. He can never reside in Petrograd again." Sandro lit a cigarette, swallowing smoke and coughing, avoiding my gaze. "It took me three days to convince Nicky. He was so . . . strange. I've never seen him like that; he told me that because we had all signed the letter, he would not proceed further. He's under so much strain, I fear he might be suffering a nervous collapse. Alexandra is giving him herbal tonics to restore his health, but he looks terrible."

"Is he ill?" I lifted my hand to my throat, my collar suddenly cutting off my breath. I didn't want to get anywhere near Tsarskoe Selo; it was the last place I wanted to tread while she mourned her mystic, but if Nicky had fallen sick over this . . .

"In his mind, perhaps." Sandro hesitated before he said, "I reminded him that he bears the blame for what's happened, as he allowed her to encourage the mystic. I also advised him to send her away, to Livadia or somewhere else, remove her from influence and reinstate the Duma. He refused. And she knew it."

"Was she there?" As much as I'd come to admire Sandro for his stalwart defense of Felix and Dmitri, I couldn't conceive of him suggesting Alexandra's banishment from Nicky's side while she herself was present.

"She wasn't, but she has spies everywhere in the palace. The new telephone line in her mauve room—she listens in on every call Nicky receives. She allows him no privacy."

I shuddered. "Did she say anything to you?"

"Not a word. But the next morning, Nicky refused to receive me. They left me to wander the palace alone. I visited with Alexei and the girls, who, as you can imagine, are very upset. The atmosphere there—it's thick. Like ash in the air. She has them in constant dread of her moods." He finally lifted his eyes to me. "She buried Rasputin on the grounds of the palace. Alexei told me that he and his sisters go out every day to pray at the grave site, as though that cretin were a saint. She is mad. There's no other explanation. She sends her own children out in the cold to honor her dead mystic. I left the following afternoon. Nicky didn't say goodbye; he had closeted himself in his study. Only Alexei came to see me off. The poor boy—he kept asking me why his friend had been killed. What could I say to him?"

"God have mercy on him." All of a sudden, I started to cry. At the awkward touch of Sandro's hand on my shoulder, I swallowed my grief, my outrage that my grandchildren and my son had been plunged into this tragedy because of Alexandra.

Sandro murmured, "God have mercy on us all. Should Nicky not bestir himself and assume control while he still can, I fear we'll lose more than this war."

CHAPTER FORTY-ONE

The end came suddenly. Or so it seemed to me.

In Kiev, we underwent another lethal winter. We found some of our soldiers frozen to death in the infirmary, while outside our doors crowds of women, clutching frostbitten children, lined up for hours in front of the bakeries for crusts. Across the rest of Russia, it was far worse: By March 1917, shortages of food, fuel, and other necessities had become endemic. Inflation reached such an incredible level that the entire economy, brought to the brink by the war, collapsed. As a result, the people staged mass demonstrations in Petrograd and Moscow. There was no dissimulation now. As word reached me of furious marchers pouring down the avenues, waving the red flag and bellowing, "Down with the tsar!" I knew that what we'd long feared, that unthinkable possibility foretold by both Miechen and Sandro, was again upon us.

Revolution.

The glacial winds and snows had toppled wire lines and cut off telephone services; communication was sporadic at best, yet I barraged Nicky at Mogilev with cabled entreaties to return to the capital to restore order. He must make a personal appearance, reassure his subjects that he would fight for their survival. Instead, he sent Nikolasha to clear the streets by force. When the news reached me that open shooting in the city had killed over two hundred civilians, I broke down, sobbing; Olga went white, and Sandro frantically telephoned Xenia, demanding she leave Petrograd with their sons to take refuge in Kursk with the Yusupovs.

On March 12, our fall began. Our elite regiments, now comprised of factory workers and others not fighting on the battlefield, defected, shooting their commanding officers and joining the mobs. In the barracks and fleets, where over sixty thousand awaited deployment, mutinies ensued. Those slated for the front killed whomever tried to detain them, to march in solidarity with their "fellow comrades," as they styled themselves.

"Moscow and Petrograd are in chaos," Sandro told me, having been in contact with our beleaguered prime minister, even if the news he managed to obtain was days old. "Government buildings are being ransacked and set ablaze. The Duma has assembled for an emergency session and agreed to a provisional government with the Soviet of Workers' and Soldiers' Deputies, ostensibly to limit the Soviet power and curtail the revolt."

I gazed at Sandro, my senses dulled by sleepless nights. "Nicky prorogued the Duma because of the war. They cannot make any changes to the government if the tsar suspended them. And who is this Soviet to reach arrangements with the Duma?"

He went silent for a moment. "The Soviet is the representative body of the people, Minnie. They call themselves Bolsheviks. They are demanding Nicky's abdication."

I felt the word like a thrust in my gut. Bolsheviks, those adherents of Lenin whom Witte had warned me about years ago.

"Abdication?" I said. "For what? To give them free rein over us?"

"The abdication would be in Alexei's favor. But they'll require a regent until he reaches his majority of age. From what I hear, Nicky hasn't yet responded."

I had no doubt. My son must remain unaware of how dire the situation was. He'd barely known the extent of the massacre in Moscow's Khodynka Field after his coronation and he'd been less than an hour's carriage drive away. Separated by frozen distance, under the weight of his command as the Germans pummeled our troops, how could he know his throne was about to be ripped out from under him?

"And if he agrees? Whom do they propose as regent for Alexei?"

When Sandro replied, "Misha," I moaned in despair. "But they have to summon Misha to accept the charge," he tried to reassure me. "He's on duty with his corps. There's still time." He pressed my hands in his, though mine were so numb that I barely felt his grip. "You must go to

Nicky, tell him to negotiate an honorable agreement. The Duma has placed Alexandra and the children under house arrest in Tsarskoe Selo, for their protection. They'll not be harmed for now, but should the Bolsheviks overrule the Duma and gain control of the state . . ."

"Yes, I know. I will go." But I hesitated, unsure of how to proceed, and then Olga said in an enraged tone to Sandro, "Are you mad? You cannot send her into the jaws of the wolf."

I turned to her, my blood chilled by her words. I heard Zenaida in my mind.

One doesn't need to meet the wolf to know when to bolt the door.

"You cannot." Olga turned to me. "Nicky hasn't been seen since this started. Where are you supposed to speak with him?" She glared again at Sandro. "Tell her."

"Tell me what?" I felt faint, my legs weakening under my skirts.

"He left Mogilev," said Sandro. "To pay a visit to Tsarskoe Selo. But revolutionary soldiers are blocking the tracks, so he couldn't have gone there. We don't know where he is."

I dropped onto my chair. "You must find out," I whispered. I couldn't lift my voice.

He nodded. "I am trying. I'm doing everything I can."

～

NICKY HAD BEEN taken back to Mogilev. Apprehended by the Petrograd Soviet, he'd been allowed to return to his base camp to collect his personal effects and bid farewell to his troops. When we received official confirmation by a week-old telegram smuggled to us, my son had already been served with the fait accompli: The provisional Duma and Soviet government had assumed charge of his state. Left with no choice, my son abdicated, in both his and Alexei's names, giving over his throne to his brother. Yet when Misha was located and summoned to Petrograd, he refused the charge, declaring he wasn't the rightful emperor and would only accept if elected by constitutional assembly. To me, it was a double stab to the heart. Both my sons had betrayed their sacred duty to Russia.

"I am going to see him," I told Olga, after Xenia sent us a telegram from Felix's estate, relaying Misha's refusal and decision to return to his regiment. "Nicky needs me now."

Olga watched in silence as I threw articles of clothing into valises and my staff hurried to prepare my train. Then she brought me to a halt. "What if you're too late?"

I didn't look at her, pausing over the heap of shawls and shoes in my open suitcase.

"What if nothing you do can change it?" she said. "Nicky has abdicated. They have his wife and children under their so-called protection, and he's undoubtedly their prisoner. What if they take you prisoner, too? What if they decide all of us should be imprisoned?"

I turned to her. "Three hundred years of Romanovs cannot be so easily discarded. We still have many supporters. We are not anyone's prisoner yet."

Olga gave me a troubled look. "Mama, I've always admired your courage, even when I thought you were wrong. You never admit defeat. But this time, you cannot win. Nicky did this to himself. To us. He was warned time and time again we were headed for disaster, and he—"

"Enough." I held up my hand. "His abdication was forced by the Duma and this horrid Soviet. They've seized power illegally. You sound like Miechen. I'll not tolerate it."

"Miechen might be many things," she replied, "but she's never been stupid."

I ignored her, flinging shut my bags and ordering my immediate departure. Not until I was on my train did I realize that I might have packed a hundred shawls and not a single pair of extra undergarments. I hadn't even looked over what I'd packed, and Sophie and Tania were so flustered by my determination to leave, I was sure they hadn't checked, either.

No matter. I settled into my carriage as the train lurched toward Mogilev. If I arrived at his base camp in my one petticoat, at least I would arrive.

I would save him from himself. While I had breath in my body, my son must rule.

⌒

A BLINDING SNOWSTORM turned the world into a white blur as my train pulled into the station at Mogilev after four long days of travel. I couldn't see anything outside the frosted windows, rubbing at the panes with my gloved hands until Sandro, attired in his uniform, came into my compartment. "They're bringing him to us. We're not allowed to disembark."

"So much for Olga's fear that I'd be taken prisoner." I snorted. "They fear me, as well they should. Were the troops to see their dowager empress, another cock might crow."

Sandro smiled wanly. "It might, indeed."

"Have every carriage light turned on. Let them see that I am here."

I had Tania and Sophie set me to rights, or as right as I could be under the circumstances. No jewels this time, no fancy gown. Stark. Simple. Black.

When Sandro returned to inform me that Nicky was coming down the platform, I insisted on going outside to greet him. The cold hit me like a fist. As I sucked in air that turned to icicles in my lungs, blinking my watery eyes against flurries of snow kicked up by the wind, I caught sight of him, escorted by revolutionary soldiers with red armbands. No Cossacks flanking him. None of the panoply of his rank. In his belted greatcoat with his cap tilted at an angle to shield his face, even with his beard he looked like the diffident boy he'd once been, so reduced in stature that I couldn't move, my voice catching in my throat.

"Mama." He embraced me, holding me close. I felt the bones of his shoulders through his coat as he whispered, "You shouldn't have come. It's not safe."

I drew back, looking into his eyes. He did not seem sad. Tired, yes—beyond fatigue, that weariness of the soul that plagued him now laying claim to him in its entirety—but not sad. Had I not known better, I might have thought he was relieved. "I had to come," I finally said, taking him by his arm. "Come. We'll have supper together on the train and talk."

He glanced at his escort. For a moment I feared they'd refuse us privacy, but they stepped aside to allow him to mount the train, Sandro behind us.

"Alone," I told Sandro, and my son-in-law retreated.

In my compartment, Nicky stood as if unsure of whether to sit, fishing out his cigarette case as I made myself say with as much calm as I could muster, "Now, tell me."

He gave a half shrug. "You must have heard everything by now. My generals advised me it was what I must do to save the country."

"Your generals do not rule Russia."

"Neither do I. Not anymore. Not ever, according to some," he replied, and before I could lift protest, he said softly, "I never wanted the burden. If this is to be my fate, I embrace it. I was born on the day of Job. Like him, I must now pass through my trial of faith."

I swallowed. He had done it willingly. He'd not been forced. He may have felt he had no alternative, but he hadn't resisted it. I knew then that Olga was right. I was indeed too late. Years too late. Alexandra had poisoned him as surely as if she'd dosed him with cyanide, as Felix had done to the mystic. I blamed her entirely, though I knew it was unfair, that my son could have prevented this calamity had he shown the strength of will required.

When he said nothing else, I asked, "What will you do?"

"Return to Sunny and the children, of course. They must be very frightened. My family needs me, and—"

"No. *Think,* Nicky. What will you do once they strip you of everything? There are Bolsheviks among them, calling for your head. You mustn't think that because you abdicated, their revolution is over. You must negotiate honorable terms for your surrender."

I couldn't believe I was speaking these words; I couldn't accept that what his father and his ancestors before him had fought to defend, he'd set aside like an ill-fitting garment. Vladimir, God rest his soul, had predicted it. He'd told me on that infamous Sunday after the protesters were fired upon outside the Winter Palace that my son was unfit. Sasha would have been ashamed. *I* was ashamed, but I couldn't say it. What good would it do?

"Such as?" He spoke as if he hadn't given the future any thought.

"Where you will go," I burst out. "How you and the rest of us will survive this."

"We'll stay here, of course," he said, to my amazement. "Russia is our home."

I gnawed at the inside of my lip; when I tasted my own blood, I said, "Russia will never be your home again. You abandoned it when you set aside your crown. You cannot stay. You must demand to be sent to England, be assured of safe passage, and depart at once. Negotiate for Alexandra and the children's removal from Tsarskoe Selo as soon as possible, as well; they have no escape from there. Have them sent to Peterhof. There's a harbor nearby in case they must flee. But you must go first. Without you, they mean nothing. With you, they're in as much danger as you are."

His face shifted, the weariness vanquished in an instant. "No."

"No?" I stared at him. "You will not negotiate for their protection?"

"Sunny telegrammed me before—before all this, to say the girls had contracted measles. She was nursing them when—" He reached to the inset ashtray by my seat to crush out his cigarette. "They had high fevers and are still convalescing; Sunny had to shave their heads. I'll not endanger their health. Later, once the situation settles, we'll see where we might go, if we must leave. But now is not the time." His voice darkened. "Misha has again proven a grave disappointment. I abdicated because I believed he'd assume the throne in my stead. None of this would be a concern if he'd only done as I asked."

"None of this would be a concern if you'd listened to me," I said. And then I saw it, the despair draining his expression. "You should have listened. It might never have occurred."

He sighed. "Or it might have anyway. Where's the use in reproaches now?"

"None. No use. But you still must listen to me. For the children's sake, if nothing else. Ask to meet with the British ambassador. King George is your cousin. He will—"

"George's parliament does not want me," he interrupted, with an arid smile. "Bloody Nicholas is not welcome in England. I've already been informed as much."

"It's a mistake." I came to my feet. "I will write to Alix myself. George mustn't realize the gravity of our circumstances, but once he's informed, he will behave accordingly. You must have safe haven. He is family. He treated you like a brother when you were children."

"All the more reason. No one wants a disgraced brother on their doorstep."

Sandro came to the compartment door. "It is time."

"Time?" I whirled to him. "He only just arrived!"

"I'll see you tomorrow." Nicky bent to me, kissing my cheek, then he strode out to his waiting escort as I stood there, stunned, looking in bewilderment at Sandro.

When my tears finally came, I could not stop them. They seeped down my cheeks as I let the sorrow overwhelm me, like the odious red flags now blanketing our country.

⁓

WE HAD THREE days together. We heard mass in Mogilev's chapel, where for the first time since my arrival in Russia, the names of the imperial family were not included in the blessing. Then we had to witness the revolutionary flag hoisted onto the pole in the camp, replacing our imperial standard. Nicky walked before his assembled troops. Some of the soldiers began to cry, begging to kiss his hand. In that brief moment, he was their Little Father again. His generals looked bereft, but none asked him to reconsider. It would have been futile. My son had given his word of honor that he would not seek to reclaim his throne.

After a sparse luncheon on my train, where words failed us, Sandro left us alone, escorting the members of Nicky's staff out—now dismissed, they'd donned the red armband for protection—and Nicky told me the Petrograd Soviet had granted him permission to return to Tsarskoe Selo and reunite with his family.

"You can still escape," I started to say, recalling the broken expressions of his troops and his generals. "There is still time—"

He shook his head, cutting off my plea. "The only thing left for me to do is be a loving father and husband. All the rest . . . it is finished."

On the platform, I clung to him. I couldn't control myself; I wouldn't let him go as he kissed me over and over, whispering, "Be strong for everyone, as you always are. We will see each other again soon," until he pulled away and Sandro stepped to my side. I forgot my dignity, leaning against my son-in-law and stifling my anguished cry as Nicky, escorted by rebel soldiers, proceeded to his train, the outline of his dismantled insignia still visible on the carriage doors.

Just as he started to board, he turned toward me. My heart leapt. I thought for a breathless moment that he'd decided to rally his men and make his escape. He lifted his gloved hand. Though he was too far away,

I could see his expression as if he stood before me, his sorrow evident now. Heartrending and absolute.

I might have sunk to my knees in the snow had Sandro not kept hold of me.

We did not move from the platform until his train had vanished into the endless horizon.

CHAPTER FORTY-TWO

In Kiev, the revolution had reached our threshold. Pushing past baleful civilians sporting red armbands or cockades in their hats, we had to hire a public carriage to the palace. Our guard of honor had been replaced by revolutionaries lounging in the guard hut, who did not rise to their feet to salute us. As I took one glance at the bare flagpole over the palace, my sorrow boiled into outrage. They had removed my standard.

Olga hurried out in her nursing uniform. Before she could speak, I said angrily, "Have my standard flown at once. This is still an imperial residence."

"Not here, Mama." Olga hauled me upstairs to our apartments, to the very drawing room where a year ago I'd received Miechen. I saw evidence of their loathsome intrusion: empty vodka bottles scattered about, soiled glasses on the tables, mud-crusted boot prints dirtying the parquet, and half of the extra furnishings we'd stored here upended or looted.

As I glared at her, Olga said in a hushed voice, "They're singing 'La Marseillaise' in the streets and freeing political prisoners, tearing down our crest from every building. Members of the Kiev Soviet came to inform me that they'll take over the palace and our infirmary in the name of the people."

Sandro went white. I snarled, "They would not dare."

"Mama." Olga looked as if she might clamp her hand over my mouth. "The Petrograd Soviet has issued a manifesto, calling us enemies of the state. They want to arrest us. All of us. Every member of the imperial family."

"They haven't arrested you," I pointed out.

"Because I'm married to a civilian," she replied, but there was no pride in her avowal. For the first time since the crisis began, my daughter sounded terrified.

She directed her next words at Sandro. "Xenia sent a letter; a Cossack risked his life to bring it to me. She's gone to Ai-Todor in the Crimea with your sons and the Yusupovs. She says they couldn't remain in Kursk. Lenin is on his way to Petrograd to assume charge of the revolution, and everyone is fleeing. Xenia begs us to join them as soon as we can. I was only waiting for your return."

"Never," I said, before Sandro could reply. "We are not going anywhere. We don't know what will happen yet. The people—not everyone is a revolutionary. Many love their tsar and will soon realize how much we need him. We're still at war with Germany. Without our emperor, who will lead our troops? Lenin?" I scoffed. "And what of our patients in the infirmary? I'm the president of the Red Cross. Absolutely not. We stay here."

"We cannot." Olga was trembling. "Mama, listen to me for once in your life. You are not the president of the Red Cross any longer. You are not the dowager empress and I am not a grand duchess. Did you not hear what I said? They're going to take over this palace and *arrest* us. I'm pregnant. I won't stay here with our very lives at risk."

This momentous news—at almost thirty-five, she'd shown no maternal inclination, so I hadn't expected it—gave me pause. "How far along are you?"

"Three months or so. We must leave. Sandro, can you help us?"

My son-in-law gave a wary nod. "I can try. We must have some supporters here—"

"Use my train," I said. "Take Olga with you. When you can, send it back to me."

"Minnie," he said. "If we return to the station, they'll know we're trying to leave. They've probably confiscated your train by now. Give me a few days to find another way."

"Do so. In the meantime, I will go to the hospital tomorrow to oversee the wards that my Red Cross financed. Then we shall see if I'm still the dowager empress."

Nothing Olga said could dissuade me; she was in near despair when

I left the following day with Tania in my carriage for Kiev's main hospital, where I'd gone many times to visit convalescing soldiers transferred for care we couldn't provide in our infirmary. The gates were shut. Despite my demands, the sentry on duty refused to admit me. Tania kept imploring me to leave, while I stood at the gates, my boots soaked through by the snow. Finally, the hospital director, a kind and perennially overworked man, hurried out. From behind the gates, he informed me that my services were no longer required.

"Since when?" I was so irate, I rapped my knuckles on the gate and bruised them through my gloves. "This hospital is still open because of my services."

"You must leave Kiev," he said, as the sentry yawned and turned back into his hut. The director lowered his voice. "They will come for Your Majesty. It's only a matter of time."

"How do you know? Are you one of them now?"

"I am not, but everyone knows. Please, Majesty, I beg you." He left me at the gates, staring after him.

As I ordered my coachman to return us to my palace, Tania grasped my bruised hand so tightly, I winced. "Don't you start. No one is going to arrest us."

But she wouldn't release my hand, and I no longer believed my own assertion.

⁓

WE CREPT OUT of Kiev in the dead of a freezing night, swathed in dark hooded cloaks, as the raucous shouts of drunken celebrations resounded throughout the city. The situation had descended so swiftly into anarchy—the police force abolished, jurisdiction given over to the Kiev Soviet—that I had difficulty accepting the fact that we were now being hunted like beasts, as my father-in-law had described his own stalking years ago by the Nihilists.

Though Olga was frantic to depart, I refused to leave any of our personal belongings behind, which meant her husband Kulikovsky, my loyal steward Obolensky, his wife Tania, and my Sophie staggered under the weight of our valises. In truth, my valises contained more than my china and photographs; we had our jewel coffers, and one of my precious Fabergé eggs: my Order of St. George egg, given to me by Nicky.

Once Sandro had told us he'd found the means to escape, Olga and I sewed our most valuable jewels into our corsets, doing it so quickly that the filigree settings, brooch pins, and latches poked our ribs with every step. Later, we'd find our flesh riddled with prick wounds, like stigmata.

On a deserted platform outside the city, we boarded the old train Sandro had commandeered from loyalists, pandering our name and a few jewels. None of us could draw a full breath until the train, belching black smoke, pulled out. Even as it gained speed toward the Crimea, where we must transfer to motorcars to reach Ai-Todor, we huddled together in a single compartment, my pug, Tip, squeezed between us, as we anticipated sudden detainment, the boarding of the train by Bolsheviks, and our subsequent arrest.

None of us slept. We did not eat and we barely drank. Like the refugees we'd become, we endured privation for three days, until we arrived in Sevastopol. Roaming bands of rebel sailors eyed us malevolently as we boarded the motorcars provided by the Military Aviation Academy, which had served under Sandro and rallied to his call, taking us on the winding roads to the Crimean estate.

I hadn't been to Ai-Todor in years, having barely visited the Crimea since Sasha's death. Livadia was deemed too dangerous; as our traditional vacation palace in this Black Sea coastal region, if they came looking for us, they'd go there first. I'd forgotten how lovely Ai-Todor was, its whitewashed complex comprised of several villas, with fluted turrets like an Arabian fantasy, encircled by wind-shaped cypress and gardens of jasmine.

Xenia came running out. My eldest daughter had lost too much weight, her eyes circled by shadows and her cheeks hollowed. I started to cry as she flew into my arms. Felix and Irina, and Xenia's six handsome sons, surrounded us. The boys embraced their father, Sandro, who couldn't hold back his own tears. Clinging to her colonel's hand, Olga seemed ready to fall to her knees to kiss the very ground in gratitude.

That evening, by candlelight with the curtains drawn, we ate a frugal meal as Xenia related their harrowing flight, as well as the fragmented tale—patched together by rumors, week-old letters, and the occasional telegram—of the exodus by others in the family.

"Cyril was the first to disavow us," she said. "That coward went to the Duma in person to rip off his imperial honors, pledging fealty to their provisional government."

"Trust a German to know when to switch her allegiances." I lit a cigarette, not caring to hide my smoking anymore. "Miechen made Cyril marry Ducky to suit herself and then sent him to do her dirty deed before the Duma. I suppose she thinks she can keep that garish palace of hers if she pretends she's no longer one of us."

"It did her no good," said Xenia. "She had to flee. We don't know where, but Cyril and her other sons joined her after they received warning they were about to be arrested."

I snorted. "Probably halfway across the Caucasus by now, if I know her. Disguised as a gypsy, with her Cartier diamonds stuffed into her corset."

Silence descended at my acerbic remark. Then Irina giggled, her two-year-old daughter, Bébé, on her lap, and Felix, who looked remarkably well, all things considered, drawled, "Grand Duchess Pavlovna would certainly not permit a revolution to deprive her of her Cartier. I don't intend to let them take anything of mine, either, not if I can help it."

We softly sang "God Save the Tsar" but didn't dare play the pianoforte in the drawing room, out of fear that the sound might carry. We had no delusion that we'd come here unperceived, but with the whispering sea outside and no demonstrators shouting nearby, it almost felt as if we were safe, protected by this place that had always been our haven. Felix assured us the Crimean Tartar regiment remained loyal, volunteering to patrol the estate.

After everyone went to bed, I stayed up with Xenia. Olga's pregnancy fatigued her; she kept nodding to sleep on her chair until I told her to go to bed. Her husband the colonel—whose first name was Nikolai, even if I refused to say it aloud lest he mistake it as a sign of familiarity—led her upstairs. Alone with my eldest daughter, I listened in silence as she told me she'd lost contact with Misha, last seen in Gatchina with Natalia and their son, and that she'd petitioned the provisional government in vain to visit Tsarskoe Selo.

"They refused me." She kneaded her hands. "I never had the chance to say goodbye to Nicky, Alicky, and the children." She went still, realizing what she'd just said. Then she whispered, "What will happen to them?"

"I don't know." I took her chafed hands in mine, hers like a servant's now from cooking meals and lugging bags, when once they'd been so tender she complained that her gloves pinched. "We mustn't lose hope. Nicky isn't their enemy. Not even Alexandra, for all her faults, wished any ill upon the people. We must do all we can for them, to see them freed and sent abroad."

"You do not think that . . ." Xenia's voice faltered.

"Do not say it," I said. "Do not even think it. What good would it do to harm a deposed tsar or his innocent family?"

⁓

SPRING BROUGHT OUT the rugged beauty of the Crimea, the weather turning balmy and the gardens exploding in bloom. We opened the terrace doors to let in the air, mixed with the scent of wild roses and spindrift. We took excursions in our motorcars, always with our Tartar guard, never straying too far. Irina and Felix had taken residence in the Yusupov villa, a short distance away, and came every evening to sup with us, often staying overnight. We were left alone, even if we soon learned it didn't mean we were forgotten. Our incomes, dispersed through the Imperial Ministry, were cut off; we now had to count our rubles. Xenia and Sandro sent away their remaining servants, as we couldn't afford to keep them. Sufficient food also became a mounting concern. There was little to be found, let alone for a pittance.

Then Felix announced that he would go to Petrograd, over Xenia and Sandro's horrified objections. He had money and jewels stashed in the Yusupov Palace, as well as valuables he could try to sell. As he wouldn't be deterred, I asked him to check on my Anichkov, for I'd been unable to communicate with my staff there. Irina insisted on accompanying him, leaving Bébé with me and Xenia. The child cried after her parents departed and toddled after me, sleeping in a cot in my room, though she had her nanny.

With summer upon us, we bathed in the sea and slept with our windows open. In August, Olga gave birth to a boy, christened Tikhon. In her typical manner, she didn't inform me that her labor pangs had even begun; as her belly grew larger, she'd reverted to her old self, unearthing a roll of canvas and a rickety easel from one of the villa closets. She filled her vivid paintings with riotous bougainvillea and views of the turquoise sea, making me think that of all of us, she'd adapt best to an ordinary life, having never been comfortable with our constraints. I rushed to her side as soon as Xenia told me she was in labor, so I was present for her child's birth. As a christening gift, I gave her one of my sapphire rings.

She smiled weakly. "Milk would be better, don't you think?"

"We have that, too," I said. "The local farmers have brought us crates of fresh produce, plenty of eggs, milk, and cheese. They insisted we accept it without pay. See? Not everyone is a revolutionary. We're still respected by some."

Olga cradled her boy. She looked at peace, blissful even, for the first time in her life.

Nevertheless, the unknown haunted us. Although we avoided any speculation that would salt our wounds, it was always there. We had no further word of Misha or of how Nicky and his family fared. And I was cut off from my family abroad. Telegraphing or sending letters was impossible. I could only hope my sister Alix, her son King George, and my relatives in Denmark were doing everything possible to assist us.

When Felix and Irina returned, driving up to the estate in a motorcar laden with trunks filled with cutlery, extra clothing, bedding, and supplies, including haunches of smoked ham and beef, we applauded as we might have a ballet at the Mariinsky. Xenia's six sons, ranging in age from twenty-year-old Andrei to ten-year-old Vasili—whose youth had resulted in a state of restlessness that had them leaping stark naked from the cliffs into the sea, to Xenia's dismay—were overjoyed to find books in one of the trunks. Avid readers, they'd pored through the library at Ai-Todor and now had something useful to occupy their time, rather than stomping over the kitchen garden we painstakingly nurtured.

Xenia thawed in her chastisement of Felix for endangering himself and Irina, once he showed her the necessities he'd brought. While Irina tried to entice wide-eyed Bébé from behind my skirts, my nephews wandered off with their books, Xenia and Olga went upstairs with the changes of linen for our beds, and Sandro took the food supplies to the kitchen.

Only then did Felix remark that the situation in Petrograd wasn't as terrible as had been reported. "The vice chairman of the Soviet, Kerensky, is a moderate," he said as I eyed him, for this same moderate had been one of those who'd called for Nicky's abdication. "He has declared Russia a republic and must appear to be on terms with the Bolsheviks, but he doesn't like the tumult. He wants to set matters to right. I also walked into our palaces without any trouble. Others do, as well, as the sentries supposedly guarding our gates aren't averse to bribes. But they let me go about my business."

The way he let slip that sentries were at our doors in the city but not deterring intruders caused me to narrow my gaze. "Are our homes being looted?"

Felix's grimace betrayed not all was as facile as he made it appear. "Not exactly. They've confiscated our palaces and everything in them. I had to slip into my Moika late at night to check if Mama's jewels were still in the vault. They were, but I didn't think it wise to remove all of them. Our trunks were searched at the station; transporting an excess of jewels seemed too dangerous, even for me. I did, however, fetch the best pieces and my Rembrandts. No one can afford to buy paintings now. Maybe later."

"And my Anichkov?" I asked, in dread. My home, where I'd lived with my husband and raised my children, now open to revolutionary riffraff.

"It's still standing and, for the most part, unharmed," he said. "It's been designated for some Soviet ministry. Your staff has been dismissed, but I went there as promised." He reached into one of the empty trunks, peeling back its lining to extract a paper-wrapped parcel; inside was a rolled-up canvas. "Irina told me how much you love it."

With hands that suddenly trembled, I unrolled the painting on the dining room table and went still, looking down at the portrait of Sasha in his blue Life Guards uniform. It had hung prominently over my sitting room mantel, my favorite portrait of him.

"It was all I could take for you," Felix said quietly. "I cut it out of the frame. They're destroying our portraits; I saw heaps of charred paintings in the squares. But not yours at the Smolny Institute. When the Soviet tried to remove it, the students formed a barricade around it."

"Thank you," I whispered. "This is far more valuable to me than any jewel."

"And this." Felix removed a crumpled envelope from within his boot, of all places. He pressed it into my hand. "From Nicholas."

As I clutched the envelope, Irina said, "Kerensky gave it to me in person." She sat on the couch with her daughter, who'd let herself be enticed onto her mother's lap. "It's a few months old and has been opened, of course, but he's safe. Kerensky assured me of it."

"You *saw* the vice chairman?" I was incredulous. The jaws of the wolf, indeed. My granddaughter, who'd wept when the German mob threw stones at our train in Berlin, had apparently walked right into them.

She nodded. "I petitioned him. He's living in the Winter Palace, with the servants and guards, even if their hideous red flag now flies over it. He received me in Great-Grandpère's study." As I flinched in revulsion that the Soviet vice chairman had appropriated my father-in-law's place of death, where Nicky himself had refused to work, she said, "Kerensky holds you in high esteem; he told me he'll try to have your income restored and promises to send half of whatever is due. He said, your rights as an emperor's widow should not be hindered. If you wish to send any letters abroad, he'll also do his utmost to see them dispatched." She smiled. "Go on. Read it. Felix carried it in his boot the entire trip back."

I held the letter to my chest like a talisman. "Later. Before the family," I said, resisting the urge to rip open the envelope. I searched Felix's face. "Any word of Misha?"

He shook his head. "All we know is that he was at Gatchina when the estate was taken over. No one knows where he is now. Irina asked Kerensky, because we'd heard a rumor that Misha had been arrested. Kerensky said he'd make inquiries."

"Inquiries?" Fear surged in me. "How can the very man who oversees the Petrograd Soviet not know where the tsar's brother is?"

Felix gave a pained sigh. "He may not have felt he could tell us. It was enough of a risk to receive Irina. Lenin is in Petrograd; he's taken the former mansion of that ballerina, Little K, and is giving speeches from the balcony. Kerensky is not a radical; as I said, he wishes us no harm. But he fears Lenin. That impudent little exile is calling for our arrest, and many are flocking to him. The people think Lenin will be their savior."

"Sasha had the little exile's brother executed," I said. "Lenin despises us. No matter what this letter or Kerensky claims, Nicky isn't safe. None of us are safe."

"For the moment we are," replied Felix. "Who knows for how long?"

I READ THE letter first in the privacy of my bedroom. It sundered me to see Nicky's handwriting; I could hear his voice in his words, even if what he wrote was obviously meant to be seen by others—a few brief paragraphs, relaying that the girls were on the mend from the measles, Alexei was well, and they'd planted a vegetable garden at the estate.

"An emperor," moaned Xenia. "Working the land like a serf."

"What of it?" I retorted. "We're doing the same here. At least he's occupied and spending time outdoors, which is good for him and the children. Nicky once told me he'd rather tend sheep than rule. He sounds happy enough." I was lying; he couldn't be happy, living under constant surveillance. And while he might put up a brave front for the children, Alexandra surely could not. She must be near hysteria that her idyllic world in the Alexander Palace had been turned upside down, for my son hadn't mentioned her once in his letter.

"We mustn't believe everything he says," ventured Sandro, giving voice to my thoughts. "They're not allowed to leave the estate, so they are definitely prisoners."

"They could be released soon." I made myself sound more confident than I felt. "We apparently have an ally in the Petrograd Soviet. Irina, tell them what Kerensky said."

The news heartened the others, although if even half of the money due to me arrived, it wouldn't be enough to sustain us. But it was a start. The revolution hadn't become quite the terror we'd feared. We still had supporters. We were here, together. Perhaps they would recognize the futility of holding Nicky captive and let him come to us.

Perhaps, given time, Russia would come to her senses.

CHAPTER FORTY-THREE

"Get up. Now."

The stranger's voice slashed through my shallow sleep; as I struggled upright in bed, I heard my Tip barking downstairs and Tania's irate protest in the corridor. In the diffused light coming through the doorway, I saw a hulking figure on my threshold, pointing at me as a group of faceless others leered behind him. I couldn't believe it as the man lumbered into my room, his boots pounding on the floor. His companions followed, one holding a kerosene lantern, casting greasy light as I yanked my sheet to my chest.

"And who have we here, eh?" The man gave me an ugly grin. He and his rebel friends wore a mishmash of clothing, shapeless greatcoats or sailor jackets coupled with army-regulation trousers, and frayed red armbands sagged about their sleeves. He was clearly the leader, for he stabbed his finger at me—"Get up. Or we'll drag you up"—as the others laughed. My heart started pounding so fast, I had to suppress a scream.

Bolsheviks. Here, in my room. They had finally come for us.

"She's the dowager empress," cried Tania from the hallway. "You cannot—"

"Empress?" The man guffawed. "I see no empress here. I see an old woman, cozy in bed in her villa, where there's enough room for ten families. We have no empresses in Russia anymore." His laughter faded. "I am Senior Commissar Spiro of the Sebastopol Soviet, so don't think of disrespecting me. What are you hiding in that bed, eh?" He took a step toward me. "Shall we search it while you're still in it? Would you like that, *comrade*?"

"How dare you." I meant to speak with assurance, only my voice trembled and he heard it. "I am the widow of Tsar Alexander III. You have no business here."

He cocked his hand at his hip, next to the pistol in a holster at his belt. "No business, she says. The Widow Feodorovna must think she's still in the Winter Palace. Old ladies get confused; we understand." He waved to my dressing screen in the corner. "You can wait there while we search. We know you're hiding something. Letters to your friends, no doubt, and who knows what else. Romanov vermin, the lot of you. Up. I won't ask again."

Tania managed to tear herself away from whomever detained her and burst into the room. "Give her privacy, please. We don't have anything. Just take what you like and go."

She moved toward me, holding out a shawl. Inching out of bed, I let her wrap the shawl around my shoulders, but as she started to guide me out, I said, "Let them search. I've nothing to hide." I made myself walk past the commissar to the dressing screen. "Do be careful," I told him. "I've very few things left. Whatever I still have, I treasure."

He brusquely motioned. His comrades, all seven of them, began ransacking my room. Tania and I cowered against each other behind the screen, wincing as we heard them yank out my bureau and desk drawers, upending my linens on the floor, ringing my alarm clock on my bedside table, tearing apart my bed, and riffling through my coffers.

Meeting Tania's terrified gaze, I gave her a thin smile. They wouldn't find any jewels or the sole Fabergé egg I'd brought with me from Kiev. We'd anticipated something like this. Xenia and I had hidden the jewels and the egg in cocoa tins Felix brought from the city, smothering our diamonds, sapphires, rubies, pearls, and emeralds in powdered chocolate.

"Nothing," I heard one of the men snarl. "No letters. Nothing worth a shit."

"Well, she's written them. We know she has. She sent some through that traitor Kerensky," said the commissar. I heard his boot crunch over something they'd broken. Then he growled at us, "Get dressed and come downstairs. Don't delay or we'll haul you down in your shift."

The men tromped out.

"Dear God," I breathed, as Tania quivered beside me and I peered past the screen to the mess they'd made. "I shouldn't have heeded Felix. He said it was safe to send letters via Kerensky, but they've questioned the vice chairman. He told them everything to save his skin."

"Kerensky and the Duma have fallen," whispered Tania. She moved jerkily, picking through my scattered clothing for a day gown. "They told Sandro when they barged in that Comrade Lenin has seized power. God save us, the Bolsheviks rule now, Majesty."

Once she fastened the dress on me, I shook her away to coil my graying tresses at my nape. I now looked every one of my seventy years. I didn't even keep a mirror in my room, disgusted by how precipitously I'd aged. The vibrant dowager who had seemed to stop time was now as much of a memory as our galas and balls.

"No 'Majesty,'" I told her. "Don't address me by my title, because they may shoot us."

As Tania gasped, I added sternly, "And you mustn't show them any fear. They're villains and louts. They'll expect us to beg for our lives. We will not."

My FAMILY WAS assembled in the drawing room, Xenia and Olga, with her baby in her arms, flanked by Xenia's sons, as well as Olga's husband and Sandro, both of whom were obviously trying to appear calm despite their worried expressions. The Yusupovs hadn't stayed with us tonight; I was glad of it. Gathering my cowering pug from under the piano, I took a seat beside my daughters, with Tip in my lap.

About a dozen men were loitering in our drawing room, handling our possessions, banging their elbows on the pianoforte keys with loud, discordant twangs—sailors in dirty coats, carrying pistols and bayonets. The sight of their weapons horrified me. I had to school myself to indifference. No fear. No matter what.

Commissar Spiro entered, brandishing a sheet of paper. He appeared to be one of those ubiquitous lower-level officers who'd deserted our cause to join the revolution, puffing out his cheeks and chest with his newfound authority as he declared, "I will call out your names, and you respond." He began reading from the paper in hand: "Alexander Mikhailovich," and Sandro nodded. "Xenia Alexandrovna," to which my daughter glared, and onward, citing Olga by her married surname. When he uttered my name, I refused to acknowledge it. He knew I was here.

"Everyone accounted for," he announced, to no one in particular. "Well, then. That was easy enough. By order of the Sevastopol Soviet, I'm hereby commanded to remove the following: Maria Feodorovna, Xenia Alexandrovna and her husband, Mikhailovich, their six sons named herein, as well as any of their servants, to the estate of Djulbar."

"Djulbar!" Sandro lost his precarious calm, though I went limp with relief, having expected much worse. "Whatever for? It's not far from here, and we have the Tartar regiment as our guard. There's no reason to move us—"

"Not anymore." Spiro regarded my son-in-law as if he wasn't sure whether to laugh or strike him. "You'll be housed under our authority by order of Comrade Lenin." At the mention of the "little exile," as Felix had dubbed him, Sandro went pale. "The Tartars are relieved of their voluntary duty," Spiro went on. "They have no business here, as the Widow Feodorovna informed us. You'll be protected by us in Djulbar. Start packing. We leave at once."

Forcing my voice out of my throat, I asked, "And Olga Kulikovsky?"

Spiro checked his roster. "She and her husband are free to stay here or go wherever they like. They're not designated as members of the former imperial family."

Before Olga could protest, I gave her a sharp glance. She went quiet. If she was left free because she'd wed a civilian, at least one of us would escape the roundup. Though she had a baby and could hardly move about, she might be able to help us.

"Can we pack our food?" I asked, hoping to secretly alert Olga to the cocoa tins she must somehow hide. Then I realized my mistake.

Spiro's gaze narrowed. "No. We have plenty of supplies in Djulbar."

They did not; I knew it at once. They were going to steal ours and leave us to fend for ourselves as best as we could. When I met his stare, his mouth parted in a sneer.

"You may count yourself fortunate, Widow Feodorovna. The Yalta Soviet wants all of you shot as traitors, but until Comrade Lenin himself authorizes it, you're safe with me."

None of us could move. The sailors paused in their meandering of the room, where they'd been examining objects at will, shoving whatever they liked into their pockets. I noted Sandro's finger was bare, his gold wedding ring stolen by one of them. By their surly expressions, I doubted they'd have any compunction in taking aim at us with their pistols.

A sudden commotion at the door caused Xenia to let out a stifled cry. With laughing assurance that he posed no threat, Felix strode in, wearing his hat and overcoat and, incongruously, red leather Moroccan slippers, the cuffs of his silk pajamas peeping over his ankles.

He met my gaze. He'd raced here in his motorcar, alerted to our arrest; no doubt he regretted encouraging me to write those letters, but I wished he'd stayed put. They had him now. He'd left Irina, Bébé, and Zenaida alone, with only a handful of servants to defend them.

"Who are you?" barked Spiro.

"Felix Yusupov," he answered, with an air of offense. As he watched the commissar check his paper in consternation, Felix said, "Am I not on your list? Good. I shouldn't be. I did our Mother Russia a great service not long ago."

I was holding my pug so tight that Tip wiggled, trying to get loose. Prince Yusupov, married to Princess Irina Alexandrovna, a member of the imperial family. Was Felix insane?

Spiro looked up thoughtfully. "Oh?"

"I killed Rasputin," declared Felix, and the sailors began to chortle. "I shot him with these two hands." Felix held up his palms. "Or with the one. I used the other to beat him about the head with the butt of the gun. The devil just refused to die until I threw him into the Neva, but he sank then. Like a stone. Right to the silt."

The sailors started applauding. Sensing he was about to lose control of the situation, Spiro barked, "Silence!" and unhooked his pistol from his holster. "Then I must also do our Mother Russia a service in return," he said, glowering at Felix. "Which of these enemies of the state do you suggest I shoot first? The widow, perhaps?"

As Spiro veered toward me, his pistol leveled, Felix said with remarkable calm, "Before you do, I suggest you check the cellars. An excellent vintage, favored by the tsar himself. Perhaps we should toast together the death of the mystic and our glorious revolution."

The sailors discarded all semblance of obedience. As I watched in amazement, they gave a bellowing cheer and propelled Felix between them to the cellars, asking him to tell them the story of how he'd killed Rasputin. Spiro looked after them in dumbfounded bewilderment, shoving his pistol back into the holster.

Felix was insane. Mad as only a prince of Russia could be. And he saved us that night. He set the sailors to carousing, getting drunk as gypsies on our most excellent vintage, while he strummed a guitar and they embarked on maudlin choruses until dawn. It took Spiro two full days to regain command over his unruly men, who emptied the cellars of every bottle and hoisted Felix onto their shoulders like a hero to parade him about.

The resultant chaos gave Xenia and Olga time to hide our cocoa tins under paving stones in the garden; we then hastily stitched our precious, smaller jewels into the lining of Olga's coat. When we said our tearful goodbyes at the gates of Ai-Todor, Olga clung to her colonel's arm, weighted by the remnants of our wealth.

⸻

DJULBAR HAD A high wall, patrolled by Soviet sailors with purloined German artillery, under the leadership of one Comrade Zadorozny. Massive and rough-mannered as Spiro, to whom he sent his weekly reports, he was fully invested in his charge. Yet unlike Spiro, he watched us in covert interest. I ignored him as much as possible, taking strolls with Tip in the parched garden inside the wall, despite the autumn chill, accompanied by Xenia and her eldest son, Andrei. After one of these walks, I caught Zadorozny staring.

"Do we seem so strange to you?" I asked him.

He averted his gaze. "I saw you once in Moscow when I was a boy. You seemed so . . . large. Like a statue. All covered in diamonds and silver. But you're really quite small."

I smiled. He'd seen me when he was a child. He had revered me and must retain some of that reverence still. A good sign. Unless he had a direct order, he wouldn't harm us.

With Olga's colonel and Felix free to move about, they arranged for weekly visits. Not with them, as they weren't allowed, but with little Bébé, brought by her nanny, as Zadorozny didn't think a child mattered. Olga pinned her letters inside my great-granddaughter's bib and we returned our replies the same way. Felix had a contact in Petrograd; thus did we learn that sometime while we'd still been in Ai-Todor, Nicky, Alexandra, and their five children had been taken from Tsarskoe Selo to the remote province of Tobolsk in Siberia.

I fell apart for the first time since the upheaval. Taking to my bed, all the sorrow and loss coalesced to sicken me. I developed bronchitis. As I hacked up what felt like my very lungs and shivered with fever, thinking I'd do better to die now in my bed rather than stay alive for whatever came next, Xenia tried to console me.

"The Duma ordered their transfer months ago," she said, plying me with a foul herb tonic she'd brewed herself. "For their own safety. They were already in Siberia when the Bolsheviks seized power; now we have the White Army fighting for us. Lenin can't harm Nicky when he has his hands full trying to salvage his revolution. It's better this way."

"How is it better for Russia to descend into civil war or Nicky and his family to suffer winter in Siberia?" I cried. "How is *any* of this better?"

I did not die, even if I wanted to. I slowly recovered, though I couldn't smoke nearly as much for the cough. Not that cigarettes were any easier to come by than decent food; Xenia was outraged when she caught me requesting a cigarette from one of the guards, chastising me for consorting with the enemy.

"He's a boy," I said, spitting out shreds from the cheap tobacco. "He's not even twenty. Look at them: They're all boys. Their revolution is a child's game. He doesn't hate us. None of them do. He told me so himself."

"Your boys will still shoot us if Lenin gives the order," she retorted. The next time my great-granddaughter visited, along with Olga's letter there were Turkish cigarettes from Felix, stashed in the pram. "If you must smoke," said Xenia, "smoke our kind."

In the spring of 1918, Zadorozny informed us that Lenin had negotiated an accord with the kaiser. Panic broke out among us; we waited in terror every day for word that we were to be transferred to Moscow, where Lenin had established his Bolshevik capital, with his own security force called the Cheka, which mandated the registration of every

Romanov. I worried most about Misha, from whom no one had heard a word. I kept asking about him, to no avail, until in a rare outburst for me, I railed at Zadorozny.

"I'm a mother," I cried. "To you, this may be freedom for the people, but to me, it's a calamity for my children."

He gave a solemn nod. "I swear to you, I know nothing about your son. I'm doing all I can. The Yalta Soviet wants you and the others delivered to them, but I will only answer to Comrade Lenin and the Petrograd Soviet."

In retaliation, the Yalta Soviet came to fetch us, under the guise of protecting us from approaching German troops, now sweeping in retreat to the Crimea. Zadorozny refused to unbolt the gates, manning the guns on the wall with Sandro and my grandsons. Deprived of their prize, the Yalta soldiers looted several villas nearby, including Ai-Todor, forcing Olga and her colonel to flee to the Yusupov estate, where Felix was dismantling jewels to pay local Tartars to protect his family. As the region collapsed into disorder and we expected to be rounded up and shot at any moment, Zadorozny decided to depart, lest he and his men face German reprisals. After he offered to take us with him and we declined, he gave over the guns on the wall to Sandro.

When he took his farewell, he kissed my hand with such startling gallantry, rousing a fleeting resurrection of my bygone glory, that it brought tears to my eyes.

"God be with you," he murmured. "My duty was to keep all of you safe."

A revolutionary he might be, but his Russian reverence ran deep. I almost missed him and his crude comrades when all of a sudden we found ourselves waiting, at the mercy of the Germans, about to be liberated or made prisoners again by the very kaiser who'd plunged most of Europe into a maelstrom of destruction.

I did not sleep. I stashed a knife under my pillow and paced my room.

When a German field marshal arrived with a detachment of soldiers to declare us under their protection, I wouldn't receive him. Sandro had to act as our go-between, conveying the kaiser's invitation of refuge in Germany and returning my indignant refusal.

"Why?" Sandro threw up his hands. "We can't stay here, hoping against hope that Nicky will be restored to the throne. White Army or not, it is over. We'll never be the imperial family again."

"We will always be the imperial family," I retorted. "Their offer is a formality. Lenin has made peace with the kaiser. Do you think rescuing us was a term of their accord? If they manage to get us out, it will only rouse Bolshevik antipathy toward those we leave behind."

With the Germans in charge of the region, Olga made haste to join us, with her colonel and her baby. Soon thereafter we left Djulbar for the villa of Harax—an English-style estate near Cap Ai-Todor, close to the port of Yalta. A lovely manor house overlooking the Black Sea, with terraces garlanded in honeysuckle, it belonged to Grand Duke George Mikhailovich, first cousin of my Sasha, now a captive of the Cheka. It reminded me of Hvidøre; I felt more at ease here, even if provisions were scarce as ever and the renewed influx of news did nothing to alleviate my fears.

Aristocrats fleeing behind the Germans flooded into the Crimea. Other family members joined us, including a battered and dispirited Nikolasha, whom Nicky had relieved of military command. For months he'd been in hiding, moving from place to place to avoid detection. He believed the Germans might arrest him for his part in the war, so Felix and Sandro arranged a Tartar bodyguard for us. More jewels were dismantled and dispersed, but not ours. Olga had crept back to Ai-Todor to retrieve our cocoa tins, and we hid them under floorboards in the manor; we might need the jewels to ransom our family, I told my daughters. Let Felix pawn off Zenaida's pieces. She'd left the bulk of her collection in her palace vault and might retrieve it one day. She'd not suffer the lack as we would.

Everyone had a dire story to tell, of hardship and terror. A few also had disquieting confirmations to impart. Felix, who received everyone, told me that Misha had indeed been arrested by the Cheka after the registration mandate. My son sent Natalia and their son into hiding, but he was apprehended with his secretary and dispatched to Perm, in the Ural Mountains bordering Siberia. I was frantic for him, unable to absorb the blow when I also learned that Alexandra's sister, Ella, and a fellow nun of her convent, along with Grand Duke Sergei Mikhailovich, Sasha's first cousin; Prince Vladimir, son of my brother-in-law Grand Duke Paul by his morganatic marriage; and the three sons of

Grand Duke Constantine, nephews of my late brother Willie's wife, Olga of Greece, had likewise been arrested and sent to Alapayevsk in the eastern Urals, where they'd disappeared without a trace.

Most disturbing was the news that Nicky and his family had been removed from Tobolsk, to no discernible purpose. Speculation ran wild that they'd been rescued by the Germans, which I thought improbable. A more credible and horrifying rumor was that Lenin had ordered Nicky brought to Moscow to stand trial but the fanatical Ural Soviet intercepted him and Alexandra en route, taking them captive and demanding that the children also be rendered into their custody.

"In the city of Yekaterinburg," said Felix. "They're being held in a merchant's house there."

"Allegedly," I countered. "No one has actually seen them that we know of."

"Not that we know of. But it's the most persistent rumor about them."

"There were persistent rumors that we'd been killed. Yet here we are. Alive."

Felix tried to summon his mordant humor. "If you can call it that."

"We are still breathing, aren't we? So are they. We must pray for them."

I did pray. Every hour of every day. During our paltry Easter celebration and on my knees in my bedroom at night, I prayed with every ounce of strength in my being. I prayed as I had never prayed before. The faith I thought I may have lost, of which Nicky had said Alexandra possessed a surfeit—that faith, tenuous and frayed, was all I had to sustain me.

This time, however, I prayed for a miracle.

CHAPTER FORTY-FOUR

September of 1918 was so infernal, only at night did the heat dissipate into sultry relief. We expanded our vegetable garden to have extra fresh foods on our table, as more refugees arrived to seek asylum in neighboring villas, hoping proximity to us would safeguard them. To entertain them, and distract us from our worries, I organized an outdoor luncheon. Although Olga regarded me as if I'd lost my mind, Xenia eagerly took to the idea. Anything, she said, was better than digging up weeds, rationing our pitiful supply of meat, and wondering when the next batch of week-old rumors might arrive.

On that very day, as we set up tables in the garden under sheets strung over clotheslines to shade our guests from the sun, Nikolasha came to inform us that a Canadian colonel had arrived on our threshold.

"He serves in the White Army," Nikolasha told me. "He says he's traveled across the country at great risk to bring us word from the British. It seems your sister Alix has prevailed upon King George to send a battleship for us, once the Germans evacuate."

Together with Olga and Xenia, I went into the drawing room, where this Canadian, Colonel Boyle, stood with Felix. Boyle gave us a pained bow. He must have been a handsome man once, over six feet tall, with impressive shoulders, but he appeared to have lost more than half his flesh. To me, he looked as if he'd walked across Russia, barely able to stay on his feet. Yet with a stoicism I admired, he did just that; upright, he accepted our offer of tea and replied to our questions, confirming that my sister had indeed persuaded her son to assist us.

When Xenia demanded, "And have you any word of my brother the tsar?" I saw Boyle's scarred hand flinch, nearly spilling his third cup of tea.

"I was in Yekaterinburg," he said carefully. He shifted his gaze to me as Xenia said in impatience, "Well? Were my brother and his family there?"

The colonel blinked under the grime on his face—he was filthy, in dire need of a long bath—and as he struggled for words, my heart shrank in my chest.

"Where are our manners!" I exclaimed, startling everyone. "Can't you see Colonel Boyle is exhausted? We must let him take his rest. We have our picnic this afternoon; he can join us later, if he likes. Come." I gestured to my daughters. "Let Felix and Nikolasha see to our guest."

Grimly, Xenia rose to follow me. Her husband was no longer with us. Despite my irate protests, Sandro had accepted the German offer to sail from Yalta with his eldest son, Andrei, to persuade the Allied powers of the severity of the crisis in Russia, as Lenin's accord with the kaiser did not signify peace for us.

"They won't listen," I'd warned him. "They're still at war. Do you think they're going to stop killing one another to see to our welfare? They haven't thus far."

Xenia likewise pleaded with him to stay, but Sandro had had enough. I was so upset at him for abandoning us, I did not say goodbye.

I now herded Olga and Xenia outside, leaving Boyle with Felix and Nikolasha. But a part of me remained in the drawing room, seared by the misery on Colonel Boyle's face.

About an hour or so later, as we set the tables with cutlery and plates, Xenia gripped my arm. She'd gone white as the sheets overhead. "Felix is on the terrace."

I turned with a hand at my brow to shield the glare. Felix was immobile; when he didn't make a move toward us, I said, "Whatever is the matter with him? Why is he just standing there?"

"Go to him," said Xenia, with a quaver in her voice. I glanced at Olga, who kept her head down, sorting out the cutlery. I almost chided her for setting the salad forks on the wrong side. Instead, I turned resolutely to the terrace.

As I neared, I saw that Felix had gone almost ashen, as if he'd received terrible news. And in that moment I no longer saw him or the faux-English manor behind him. I no longer heard the sough of the sea or Xenia's sons' cheers as they played a ball game before the luncheon. I heard my grandson Alexei instead, on that day he'd slipped at my An-ichkov:

I only stepped into the pond. I'm not bruised at all. See?

"Minnie." Felix's quiet voice broke into my reverie. "Please, come inside."

I moved with him into the cool of the house. The drawing room was empty, the reek of Nikolasha's cigar lingering in the air. Both he and Colonel Boyle were gone.

"I trust you saw that poor Canadian to a bathroom," I said. Step-ping to a table and a vase of wild hyacinths that Xenia had arranged, I leaned to the fragrant blooms, breathing deep, wanting to fill myself with their scent. As soon as I did, I recoiled, almost upsetting the vase.

The scent of lilac. Alexandra's favorite flower. The smell of her per-fume.

Felix cleared his throat. Before he could speak, I said, "Whatever it is, I warn you now: The Bolsheviks are liars. They lie and deceive to tor-ment us."

"Boyle is not a Bolshevik." Felix took a step toward me. "You heard him. He was there. In Yekaterinburg. The White Army laid siege to the city and forced the Reds out. They reached the house. The locals . . . they call it 'The House of Special Purpose.' That was how the Ural So-viet had designated it. It was empty. Nicky and his family weren't there."

A burst of laughter escaped me—harsh in that room, not my laugh at all. To my own ears, I sounded like a stranger, an embittered old lady, refusing to heed anything that might disturb her final idyll.

"Of course they weren't. They never were. Another rumor, like so many others."

He hesitated. I felt myself inch away from him, staking a precarious distance.

"There was evidence," he went on, his voice almost inaudible. "The rooms ransacked. Some of their belongings left behind. And in a cellar on the ground floor . . ." He paused, as if gathering his fortitude. "Bul-let holes in the wall. Bayonet gouges in the floor. Boyle recognized the marks. And dried blood, he said, hastily wiped up. He'd seen traces like it before, in battlefield infirmaries. He said there must have been a lot of it."

As this dreadful pronouncement thickened the air, I met his eyes. "You've always had a nerve, Felix Yusupov. More nerve than any man I've known. The nerve to kill a mystic and boast of it." As he flinched, I went on, "But you've exceeded your own nerve today, to have the effrontery to utter such a monstrous falsehood to me."

He held out his hands. "Minnie, no more. Please. You cannot deny it. You must accept it, for all our sakes. Boyle said the other soldiers with him saw it, too. One of them had a camera and took a photograph. He said they were going to send it to your nephew King George."

"Of a filthy cellar?" I did not raise my voice, but I felt my scream cresting inside of me, a wail that would shatter the entire world if I gave it release. "What proof is that?"

"That they're dead. The Bolsheviks murdered them and disposed of their bodies."

The room darkened around me. I swayed, unmoored; I had to grope toward the sofa as if I slipped across the deck of a floundering ship. Dropping onto the sofa, I saw my granddaughters at the Mariinsky in their new gowns, waving to the audience; Alexei frowning on the terrace at the Alexander Palace, wanting to run after hoops with his sisters; and then, with heart-wrenching clarity, Nicky on the platform at Mogilev, turning from his train to lift his hand in farewell.

Be strong for everyone, as you always are. We will see each other again soon.

"No," I whispered. "It cannot be. I don't believe it."

Felix sank to his knees before me. "No one wants to believe it. But they've not been seen for months. Something horrible must have happened to them in that house." He paused, meeting my eyes. "There's more."

"More?" I could barely look at him. He was no longer the impeccable dandy who'd set an Abyssinian at his door while he dawdled with Irina—his face was fallen, his eyes haunted, as if he'd witnessed too much. I saw myself in him. I realized all of us here must look the same.

"Boyle said other members of the White Army went on to Alapa-yevsk, where they heard that Ella, Constantine's three sons, Prince Vladimir Paley, and the others with them had been thrown down a mine shaft. Locals took them to the site. The soldiers lowered ropes into the shaft and found the remains. And Grand Dukes Nicholas and George Mikhailovich, Dmitri Constantinovich, and Grand Duke Paul, your own brother-in-law—Boyle claims the Cheka has ordered them returned to Petrograd from their exile in Vologda to be executed."

I was suffocating, starved for air. "Rumors. That's all it is. Rumors. Nothing more."

Felix seized my hands. "It is happening. To all of us. We're being exterminated."

I heard Spiro in my mind: *Romanov vermin, the lot of you . . .*

Then Felix hesitated. I felt it in his grip, a sudden laxness, as if he were holding back.

"Say it," I hissed. "Say it now or never speak of it to me again."

He whispered, "Misha," and I wrenched my hands from his.

"No." My cry wasn't loud. It was scarcely a sound, but tears started to slip down his haggard face as he said, "Taken into the forest near Perm and shot. Boyle heard it from another White Army soldier, who met someone in Perm who'd witnessed it. The Bolsheviks claim Misha was abducted and has disappeared, but no one believes them."

"No. No." I was shaking my head, wanting to shove him away. The details. How did Boyle know these horrible details? How could he know when we hadn't? "It's not true. It—"

"Enough." From the terrace doorway, Olga's voice sundered the room.

Felix turned on his knees to her. "She must hear it. She has to know. Sandro was right. You know it, too. They're coming for us next. Boyle came here to warn us—"

"I said, enough." Olga glared at him. I'd never seen her like this; she'd become the personification of Sasha, her shoulders squared, her chin thrust forward in that manner he had, as if she'd smash her way through any obstacle. "Go to Irina and let my mother be."

He staggered to his feet. "I'm sorry. I'm so sorry, Minnie." As he moved past Olga, I heard him sobbing. To my surprise, I spat out, "Stop blubbering like an infant. You'll terrify the others. Not a word, do you hear me? Not *one* word to any of them."

Olga came to me. Coiled in my rage and sorrow, I turned on her. "You knew it, too?"

"I feared it." Her voice was subdued. "I told you in Kiev that they'd called for our arrest. Our lives were at risk. But I didn't know this. How could I?"

"No one could, because it's impossible." My voice fractured. "Do you believe it?"

"Does it matter?" She regarded me with such tenderness, my youngest daughter, who'd rarely shown me affection or tolerance; she looked upon me now as she might her own babe after he'd thrown a tantrum and she must patiently suffer through the aftermath.

"Yes. It matters," I said. "If you believe it, if Felix, Nikolasha, and the others believe it, then they *are* dead. Whether it is true or not, we've killed them by losing hope."

"Mama." Her voice wavered—I could see how deeply affected she was—but she didn't offer me any comfort. She stood there, not awkward like Sasha when I'd flown into a temper, yet stolid like him, unwavering. "I ask if it matters because the only person who must believe it is you. None of us can leave without you, and you will never leave unless—"

"They are your brothers." Grasping at the couch, I hauled myself to my feet. "My sons. Our flesh and blood. How can you? How can you think of leaving when we don't know anything? We have no proof, no matter what that Canadian says. They could be anywhere, dependent on us to save them, while we're here debating whether or not to flee."

"We are not debating it," she said, and once again I realized how much I underestimated her. Despite her artistic notions and unsuitable spouse, she was more of a Romanov than I cared to admit. "The only one still debating it is you. We all think it must be true. Why else have they gone missing? Why has no one seen them or provided any proof they're still alive? But none of us will say it. None of us *can* say it, because we love you so much. Is the truth worse than letting you think you will see them again? Which is best to keep you safe with us?"

"The truth," I whispered. "I want only the truth," and as she gave a futile sigh, I crumpled. She gathered me in her arms—sturdy arms that enfolded me, the sole anchor I had left in my anguished, vanishing world.

"We may never know," she said. "But whatever you believe, we will believe it, too."

WINTER CAME AGAIN. In the Crimea, the wind had fangs, and the urgency of our predicament escalated, our supplies dwindling as the Germans consumed everything in sight. In November, the Allied powers hammered out an armistice with the kaiser, whose war machine had turned into wreckage. He suffered for his hubris: his regime toppled, his person exiled, his people forced into concessions that would starve Germany to its bones.

We did not rejoice. The Great War might be over, but in Russia our civil war raged on, with Lenin's Reds gaining ground. In late March 1919 a German general came to Harax to warn us of a Bolshevik takeover in the Crimea once his forces departed. They couldn't protect us any longer here, but my nephew King Christian had sent word that he would receive me in Denmark. Likewise, my nephew King George had confirmed dispatch of the HMS *Marlborough* to Yalta. Though I did not see or speak to him, the general emphasized to the others that we now had a narrow window for escape. Within the week, we must be ready to depart.

"We cannot be here when the Reds arrive," expounded Olga, when we gathered for a family conference on the very day of Xenia's forty-fourth birthday. My younger daughter was nine months' pregnant with her second child, yet she exhibited none of the listlessness of most women in her state; if anything, she was invigorated. "We have an offer of safe passage and we must take it. Sandro is now in Paris with Andrei. Xenia and their other sons can join him there. Mama, you can go to England and then on to Denmark."

"I assume you will be coming with us?" I said darkly. She'd promised to stay with me, believing whatever I did, but with the threat now upon us, I sensed she had other plans.

"Nikolai, Tikhon, and I will travel to the Caucasus. I can't endure a sea voyage in my condition, and Boyle has offered to take us into the mountains; the Whites have driven the revolutionaries out of the region. At least this way, our child will be born in Russia. Afterward, we'll make our way to Europe to meet up with you."

"You will not." I was infuriated. "I'm not going anywhere, so you can give birth right here. The White Army hasn't lost the war yet. And what of those who have sought refuge with us? We are still Romanovs. We are all that stands between order and chaos."

Xenia said, "Mama, you aren't listening. You heard the general—"

"I did not hear him. Germans. As deplorable as the Bolsheviks."

"God in heaven," Xenia cried. "That German you find so deplorable took the time and care to warn us! It's all been planned: only us, in absolute secrecy. I have my husband and our sons to think about. We've done as you asked, but we've heard nothing save horrors—"

She cut herself short when Olga gave her a scalding look. "You won't even look at the newspapers the Germans left us," Olga said, in a steadfast tone that devastated me. "They're holding memorial services for Nicky and his family all over Europe. To them, Russia is lost. They grieve us already. Do you want that to be our fate?"

I stared at her, then at Xenia, who couldn't contain her tears. Nikolasha kept his eyes downcast. Felix sat in silence with Irina, having avoided a single opinion since our confrontation over Colonel Boyle. At his side, his mother, Princess Zenaida, her former charm wasted by hunger and fear, met my eyes. She implored me without saying a word, this woman who'd been our most envied heiress, invitations to her palace balls the most esteemed after the court's. All of it: Lost. Like Nicky was, to them. Vanquished. Already mourned.

But not to me.

I came to my feet. "I am ashamed to call you my family."

Before they could protest again, I climbed the staircase to my rooms. Tania had shut the window against the evening; although spring neared, a chill crept in with the night. As I stood there, Tip watching me anxiously from my bed, I wanted to fling things against the walls. I felt inchoate rage churning up inside me. I had to clamp down on it, biting into my lip, the sting of it bringing me to reason as a tentative knock came at my door.

I did not look around. "Go away. I will never abandon my sons. Do you understand?"

"Yes, Grandmère." At the sound of Irina's soft voice, I started. She was a slip of a woman now, her fragile beauty turned gaunt. She ate less than a sparrow, hoarding her portions for Bébé. Yet despite her pallor and incised cheekbones, she was still ethereal, reminding me of my granddaughter Tatiana. "We will stay with you."

"No. You must take the British ship. Felix can sell his Rembrandts abroad. They're worth a fortune; those and whatever jewels remain to Zenaida will support your family."

She shook her head. "Felix says he has caused you great distress. He will not leave you alone. And I cannot leave without him."

I almost smiled. "With refugees here by the dozens? I assure you, I'll not be alone."

"What if they also decide to leave?"

"They cannot. You heard Xenia. The British have orders to evacuate only my immediate family and me. No one else."

She went silent for a moment before she said, "Perhaps you can persuade the British to amend their orders. If you refuse to leave without everyone, what else can they do?"

I knew what she was about. Despite his recent acquiescence, Felix had not forsaken his guile and had sent her to test me. I may no longer care what happened to me, but to be held responsible for those with us—he knew I wouldn't abide it. He also knew that citing it would force me to make the one decision I'd avoided all this time.

I finally assented. I had no other choice. "I suppose I can try."

$\sim$

"IT IS QUITE beyond my orders," declared the lieutenant commander of the HMS *Marlborough*. "His Majesty was specific. Only Your Majesty and your family."

"But you have more ships in the area? You're not here alone?" When he gave reluctant assent, I said, "These people are our subjects. Find a way or leave without us."

"Majesty, I am ordered to carry you on board by force, if need be," he replied, but he visibly blanched as he confronted me with my Tip in my arms, Tania and Sophie flanking me, amid our pile of luggage. A short distance away, Xenia and her sons, Nikolasha, Felix, Irina, and Zenaida, and their assortment of trunks, watched as I harangued this man whose sole purpose was to rescue us.

I lifted my chin toward my family. "Will you carry all of us on board by force?" Then I shifted my gaze to the horde on the docks. "You need only tell them that you're rescuing them because of me and they'll swim to your ships."

It was supposed to be a secret evacuation, but word had spread fast, and I'd not been remiss to hasten it. As soon as the refugees learned of our departure, panic erupted. They'd crammed Yalta with their own luggage, pets, and servants, some of our wealthiest nobles and landowners, reduced to whatever they could carry. Xenia shivered at my side, distraught that at the penultimate hour, after everyone had scrambled to pack in collective relief, I now set up another obstacle. Olga, who'd departed the previous day with her family for the Caucasus, would have expected nothing less, although I'd been furious at Kulikovsky for agreeing with her to embark on an arduous journey into the mountains, with her pregnancy so advanced. Olga herself had refused to heed me, as well. She might prefer to live without our imperial trappings, but she insisted that her child had Romanov blood and therefore must be born in Russia.

"Is Your Majesty quite decided?" the lieutenant asked with clipped British reserve. Even when faced with disobeying his sovereign's instructions, he did not reveal a hint of disquiet.

"I am. All of them and me. Or none of us."

He sighed. "I'll cable the fleet. I promise, everyone will get on board a ship. Now"—he held out his arm to accompany me onto the jetty—"will Your Majesty trust in my word?"

I accepted his gesture. "You'll never hear the end of it if you go back on it."

ON THE BATTLESHIP, I entrusted Tip to Tania. She and Sophie went belowdecks to prepare the cabin allotted to us. Xenia would share an adjacent cabin with Irina, Zenaida, and Bébé. My grandsons, Felix, and Nikolasha would bunk with the sailors. It wasn't a pleasure craft; we were under British naval authority until we reached Malta and transferred to another vessel for England. For a time, I'd seek comfort with Alix, but I already knew that eventually I must return to Denmark and Hvidøre, the only house I had left. If I must dwell in exile from the land I'd called my home for over fifty years, at least I would go to my grave in my native country.

The balm of the early-April morning rustled the Black Sea. I paced to the railings at the edge of the quarterdeck. Gazing toward the rocky escarpments of the Crimea, I envisioned those places I could no longer see: Livadia, where I'd bid goodbye too soon to my Sasha. Ai-Todor, where I'd fled from chaos. Djulbar, where I'd thought I might die. And Harax, where I'd learned of blood spilled that I could never concede aloud.

I saw every place, and beyond, to St. Petersburg and the splendor of the Winter Palace, to my beloved Anichkov, our fortress of Gatchina, and, finally, into the echoing emptiness of the Alexander Palace, where our forsaken future had hoped and despaired.

Expecting to weep as the ship heaved under me, preparing to depart, instead I caught sight of another ship passing nearby—a Russian steamer, crowded with volunteer recruits for the White Army. I stared, mesmerized, as it neared, so close I could discern the pinched anonymous faces of young men still willing to fight for us. The world they sought to preserve had already changed. Many, I knew, would perish defending our cause.

I rummaged in my pocket for a handkerchief. I only had this moment, one brief time as our ships crossed paths, when they could see me as I saw them. Lifting my handkerchief, I waved it. Let them see me. Let them know that though I was forced to leave, I would always remember. I was a mother; they too had mothers, who might never see them again.

Look at me. See your beloved *Matushka*. Let me know you will remember me.

And as my tears finally came, misting my eyes, they stared toward me. They jammed the railings of the steamer, raising their arms in the traditional salute. From across the lapping wash of our passing vessels, I heard their ragged voices swell as they sang out:

God save the Tsar!
Strong sovereign, reign for our glory
Reign to our foes' fear, Orthodox Tsar.
God save the Tsar!

At last, after everything denied, God answered my prayer. I was given this one miracle.

We would never be forgotten.

AFTERWORD

Following her arrival in Malta, where many of the refugees she helped to escape were left stranded but not forsaken by her, Minnie reached England in May 1919, together with Xenia and her sons. Minnie's reunion with her sister Alix must have been heartrending, yet she adopted her characteristically brave face for a world still reeling from the aftermath of the Great War and cataclysmic fall of Imperial Russia. In private, however, she faced a near-penniless existence, dependent on a charitable pension from the British royal family after having been one of the wealthiest women in the world.

Many came to see her, including Grand Duke Dmitri Pavlovich, who'd helped murder Rasputin and whose military service in Persia saved him from the Bolsheviks. All those who saw Minnie reported she was gracious as ever, if diminished by her circumstances.

For the rest of her life, she proved a relentless champion for Russian émigrés. She also interviewed visitors over the years about her missing family. In public, she never wavered in her faith that they may have survived, despite mounting evidence to the contrary. In addition to the slaughter of thousands of landowners and members of the aristocracy, of the fifty-three Romanovs alive in Russia when Nicholas II abdicated, eighteen were murdered and thirty-five escaped. In July 1918, fourteen Romanovs were killed; among these were Misha, shot in a forest near Perm with his secretary, and the tsar and his family, executed in Yekaterinburg at Ipatiev House.

Misha was the first Romanov to die at Bolshevik hands; his remains and those of his loyal British secretary, Brian Johnson, have never been found. Following Misha's exile to Perm, his wife, Natalia, smuggled their son, George, to Copenhagen. She remained in Russia, petitioning Bolshevik commissars, including Lenin himself, about Misha until they ordered her imprisonment, from which she escaped. The retreating Germans, believing Misha was alive and leading a counterrevolution, assisted Natalia and her daughter by her first marriage to flee to England in 1919, where George reunited with them. To support her family, Natalia accessed Misha's international bank accounts; like most exiles, she also sold her jewels. Conflicting rumors about Misha went unabated until 1924, when Natalia had him legally declared dead to inherit his estate in Britain, valued at a mere £95. She then moved to France to reduce her cost of living. In 1931, George died after a car accident, devastating her. By the outbreak of World War II, Natalia was destitute. She died in 1952 and is buried in the Passy Cemetery in Paris beside her son, Count Brasov, last male-line descendant of Tsar Alexander III.

Although photographs of the ravaged cellar in Ipatiev House had been in circulation since 1923, there's no evidence that any were presented to Minnie. It bears noting that Alexei's devoted spaniel, Joy, escaped the massacre, when two of the family dogs did not. A starving stray, Joy was found months later, wandering by the abandoned house. One of the former house guards recognized and took pity on the dog, caring for him until a colonel in the British Expeditionary Force rescued Joy as the White Army retreated from the Urals. The colonel returned to England with the spaniel, who was loved and died in Sefton Lawn in Windsor. In his memoirs, the colonel wrote that Joy never fully recovered his spirits.

Minnie must have learned of Joy's survival. She often said, "Nobody saw Nicky killed." Yet the evidence was irrefutable. What she thought in private can only be assumed. It seems doubtful that, knowing as much as she did, she believed her own assertion. Given Cyril's strident claim to the throne, perhaps she resolved that to preserve the dynastic succession in case of a miraculous survival, she must never admit her sons were dead.

Nevertheless, she lent financial support to Nikolai Sokolov, a White Army judicial investigator who traveled to Yekaterinburg eight months after the tsar and his family had vanished. The first to gather testimony on the regicide and explore the abandoned mine where the bodies had initially been taken, Sokolov concluded that no one in the imperial family had survived the House of Special Purpose. When he went into exile in France, he took his meticulous documentation with him; his archives later informed the 1993 investigation by Russian authorities into the events of July 16–17, 1918. Before his death, Sokolov prepared a report for the dowager empress. Minnie never met him in person and it is not known if she read his report. His book, *Ubiistvo Tsarskoi Semi* ("The Murder of the Royal Family"), was published posthumously in 1925.

Designated as a branch of the Ural Revolution Museum in 1927, Ipatiev House was demolished in 1977 under Boris Yeltsin's regime. Following the dissolution of the Soviet Union, the Church on the Blood was built on the site.

The disappearance of Nicholas, Alexandra, and their five children, along with four of their attendants, including Dr. Eugene Botkin and Alexandra's maidservant, Anna Demidova, gave rise to rampant tales of harrowing survival and numerous imposters. The most famous was the 1922 claim by Anna Anderson that she was Anastasia—a ruse engineered to inherit the legendary Romanov fortune. Anderson persisted in her claim until her death in 1984; she was proven a fraud by DNA analysis after the exhumation of the imperial family.

In 1979, amateur archaeologists made the clandestine discovery of the tangled skeletons of Nicholas, Alexandra, their daughters Olga, Tatiana, and Anastasia, as well as Botkin, Demidova, the family valet, and the cook, buried beneath railway planks under a dirt road near Yekaterinburg. The bones, bearing evidence of bullet holes and bayonet gouges, were discolored by the sulfuric acid used in vain by the executioners to dissolve the bodies. They were left in their makeshift grave until the Soviet Union collapsed in 1991.

DNA identification matched Alexandra to a sample provided by Prince Philip, Duke of Edinburgh, related to the tsarina through his maternal grandmother. Mitochondrial DNA from the body of Nicholas's brother, George, as well as from his father and grandfather, confirmed the tsar. Russia's Supreme Court ruled that Nicholas II and his family had been victims of political persecution; canonized as martyrs, the last tsar, tsarina, and the three grand duchesses were entombed in the St. Peter and Paul Cathedral. In 2007, a shallow pit not far from the original site revealed fragments of the missing Tsarevich Alexei and his sister, Grand Duchess Maria, separated from the others during the chaos to dispose of the bodies following the executions. New DNA testing in 2015 confirmed a 99 percent probability that the discovered bones belonged to the tsar and his family. To date, the Russian Orthodox Church has refused to recognize the results, confiscating the remains of Alexei and Maria and those of Nicholas and Alexandra from their crypt for further analysis. It is unknown when the family who lost their lives under such terrible circumstances will be reunited.

Minnie moved to Denmark in 1920, eventually settling in Hvidøre. She became the heart of the refugee community and an occasional thorn in the side of her nephew, King Christian X, for despite her penury she was extravagant and defiant. In 1925, her sister Alix died—the final loss. On October 13, 1928, Minnie died in Hvidøre at the age of eighty, having outlived four of her six children. She was interred in Roskilde Cathedral. Not until 2006, following negotiations between Denmark and Russia, was her wish to be interred beside Sasha honored. She returned to Russia one hundred forty years after her first arrival to be laid to rest in the St. Peter and Paul Cathedral, next to those she loved most.

Grand Duchess Marie Pavlovna, known as Miechen, was the last of the Romanovs to escape Russia. She remained in the Caucasus with her two younger sons throughout 1918 until the Bolshevik approach prompted their escape to Anapa on the north coast of the Black Sea. Miechen only agreed to leave Anapa in 1920 when she was told the White Army was losing the civil war. With her son Andrei, his mistress, the ballerina Little K, and their young son, she boarded a ship for Venice. Grand Duchess Olga happened upon her at the port of Novorossiysk and described Miechen's inimitable flair: "When even generals were lucky to find a cart, Aunt Miechen made the journey in her own train. It was battered—but it was hers. For the first time in my life, I found it a pleasure to kiss her." Miechen died in September 1920. She was sixty-six.

A family friend in the British Secret Service retrieved Miechen's jewels from her palace vault. Before her death, Miechen distributed her jewels among her children, who sold the most valuable pieces. Queen Mary, wife of George V, purchased her Bolin diamond-and-pearl tiara;

it remains in the British royal collection and has been worn by Queen Elizabeth II. The heiress Barbara Hutton purchased the grand duchess's prized emeralds from Van Cleef & Arpels, converting the necklace into a tiara. Actress Elizabeth Taylor later acquired the tiara and had the emeralds recut and set as a necklace and earrings. The luxury jeweler Bulgari, who had sold the emeralds to Ms. Taylor, reacquired them at the auction of the late actress's jewelry collection.

Despite the abolition of the Russian monarchy, Miechen's senior son, Grand Duke Cyril Vladimirovich, declared himself emperor from his exile in France. Minnie and her surviving family refuted his claim. Cyril died in 1938. His granddaughter, Grand Duchess Maria Vladimirovna, has likewise declared herself the rightful successor to the Romanov throne.

Minnie's eldest daughter, Xenia, settled in England, while her husband, Sandro, resided in Paris until his death in 1933. Xenia's finances were precarious and she was obliged to contend with the fraudulent claims of Anna Anderson until 1928, the ten-year anniversary of Nicholas's disappearance. With him and his family legally presumed dead, the much-contested Romanov fortune, which has never materialized, devolved to Xenia as her brother's heir. Upon her mother's death, she sold Hvidøre and the dowager empress's jewels for income. By 1937, Xenia was residing in the Wilderness House in Hampton Court Palace, where she died in 1960 at the age of eighty-five. Her youngest son, Prince Vasili, the last of her seven children, died in 1989.

Xenia's daughter, Irina, and her husband, Felix Yusupov, led a colorful existence after their exile, selling his Rembrandts to sustain the family and traveling throughout Italy before bribing an immigration officer with diamonds to enter France. In 1920, they established the couture house Irfé in Paris, but the venture was short-lived, their philanthropy and excessive lifestyle decimating their wealth. Felix won a 1932 lawsuit against MGM for a scurrilous movie titled *Rasputin and the Empress*. He also wrote his memoirs, capitalizing on his infamy as Rasputin's assassin. He had affairs with men, even while he and Irina enjoyed their marriage for more than fifty years. Felix died in 1967, and a grief-stricken Irina followed him to the grave three years later. They are buried in the Sainte-Geneviève-des-Bois Russian Cemetery in Paris.

Princess Zenaida was entrusted with raising her granddaughter,

Bébé, in Rome. After her husband's death, the princess moved to Paris to be with Irina and Felix, where she died in 1939. She never recovered the rest of her magnificent jewel collection from her Moika palace; the jewels were discovered and sold by the Bolsheviks in 1925. To support her family, Zenaida sold her major jewels, removed earlier by Felix from the vault. Bébé, whose title was Princess Irina Yusupova, married a Russian count and bore a daughter. She died in 1983 and is buried alongside her family.

Minnie's younger daughter, Olga, gave birth to her second son, Guri, in the Caucasus. In November 1919, she and her family fled to Novorossiysk. Sent to a refugee camp near Istanbul and evacuated to Belgrade, she arrived in Denmark with her family in 1920, where she became Minnie's reluctant secretary. Never the best of friends, mother and daughter clashed, and the dowager empress excluded Olga's husband from formal functions.

In 1925, Olga met Anna Anderson in Berlin. She was unconvinced by Anderson's claim. Anderson didn't speak Russian or English, languages that Anastasia had mastered, and the tsar's youngest daughter would have been twenty-four, while Olga found Anderson much older, with dissimilar features. Olga expressed sympathy for Anderson, sensing she was mentally unstable, primed by nefarious sources to "act the role in order to lay their hands on our nonexistent fortune," but she publicly denied that Anderson was her niece.

With her share of her mother's estate, Olga purchased a farm outside Copenhagen, where her family took to the rural life with vigor. Olga continued to paint. Her renditions of Russian and Danish scenes had exhibition auctions in European cities. She donated some of the proceeds to Russian charities.

During World War II, Olga's two sons served in the Danish Army and were briefly interned as POWs. At the end of the war, Soviet troops occupying eastern Denmark accused Olga of conspiracy against them. Fearing assassination or abduction by Stalin's regime, she and her family emigrated to Canada in 1948, purchasing a farm in Halton County, Ontario.

By 1952, Olga and her husband were elderly and had sold the farm, taking a small house in a Toronto suburb. An enduring symbol of Romanov appeal, the grand duchess was visited by dignitaries, including

Queen Elizabeth II and Prince Philip. Her husband's declining health prompted Olga to sell her remaining jewelry to pay for his care. His death in 1958 exacerbated her own infirmity. Toward the end of her life, she lived with émigré friends in an apartment above a beauty salon. Grand Duchess Olga died in 1960 at the age of seventy-eight and is buried next to her husband in York Cemetery, Toronto. Her son Tikhon founded the Russian Relief Program in her honor to exhibit selections of her work. Her paintings can be found in the collections of Queen Elizabeth II and the royal family of Norway. The Ballerup Museum in Denmark houses approximately one hundred of her works. Her son Guri died in 1984. Tikhon died in 1993.

There are over one hundred Romanov descendants alive today.

INNUMERABLE SOURCES GUIDED me in writing this novel. While not a full bibliography, I list below those works I consulted most often to portray Maria Feodorovna and her world:

Erickson, Carolly. *Alexandra: The Last Tsarina*. New York: St. Martin's Press, 2001.

Gelardi, Julia P. *From Splendor to Revolution*. New York: St. Martin's Press, 2011.

Hall, Coryne. *Little Mother of Russia*. New York: Holmes & Meier, 2001.

Hough, Richard. *Edward and Alexandra*. New York: St. Martin's Press, 1992.

King, Greg. *The Court of the Last Tsar*. Hoboken, NJ: John Wiley & Sons, 2006.

———. *The Last Empress*. New York: Birch Lane Press, 1994.

Massie, Robert K. *Nicholas and Alexandra*. New York: Random House, 1967.

Massie, Suzanne. *Land of the Firebird*. New York: Simon and Schuster, 1980.

Maylunas, Andrei, and Sergei Mironenko. *A Lifelong Passion*. New York: Doubleday, 1997.

Nelipa, Margarita. *Alexander III: His Life and Reign*. Ontario: Gilbert's Books, 2014.

Poliakoff, V. *Mother Dear*. New York: D. Appleton and Company, 1926.

Radzinsky, Edvard. *The Last Tsar*. New York: Doubleday, 1992.

Rappaport, Helen. *The Romanov Sisters*. New York: St. Martin's Press, 2014.

Rounding, Virginia. *Alix and Nicky*. New York: St. Martin's Press, 2011.

Tisdall, E.E.P. *Marie Fedorovna*. New York: The John Day Company, 1957.

ACKNOWLEDGMENTS

My fascination with the Romanovs began in my childhood with a coffee-table book that belonged to my mother, featuring their palaces, jewels, objets d'art, and photographs of them. I was enthralled in particular by Nicholas, Alexandra, and their children, whose physical beauty and tragic end roused romantic fantasies of an idealized world. Dwelling in unimaginable splendor, they epitomized the word "imperial." In reality, despite their privilege, their lives were fraught with the suffering, joy, and vulnerability we all share.

Though less celebrated today, Minnie was greatly admired in her lifetime. She indeed championed reform for the poor, funded the Society for the Protection of Animals in Russia, and tried as best as she could to curb her husband's despotic tendencies, including intervening on behalf of the Jews. She guided her son Nicholas II at the start of his reign until she lost her influence over him to Alexandra. Her exasperation with her daughter-in-law is well established. To Minnie, Alexandra was antithetical—unsuitable, ill equipped, and, most tragically, unwilling to assume the responsibilities of her rank. Minnie wasn't always kind or understanding of Alexandra's flaws. Like all of us, she was fallible.

Her survival is a testament to her resiliency and luck. Had she been in the capital when the 1917 Revolution erupted, she may have suffered a different fate, even if legend has it that Lenin held her in begrudging respect. Her plight in the Crimea may also have ended differently had she commanded less awe. A Canadian in the White Army did bring word that Nicholas and his family had been murdered, which she refused to believe, at least outwardly. And because she insisted that the British evacuate the refugees who'd joined the Romanovs in the Crimea, she saved many lives.

Documentation about the Romanovs abounds, including their diaries and letters. While I strived to remain faithful to the facts and the recorded personalities, I admit to certain liberties, such as occasional shifts in date or place to facilitate the narrative, a necessary omission of certain people and events in order to restrain my sprawling word count, and, naturally, my own insight into these characters, whose mythical stature can obscure their humanity.

Specifically, I combined Dr. Botkins; in reality, the father and later his son treated the tsars. I also did not detail the complexity of the various Dumas, as the political scenario of Imperial Russia's final years can be daunting. Though I've employed the title of "tsarina" for its overall familiarity to readers, in Russia, "tsaritsa" was the accurate term. "Tsarina" or "czarina" are Anglicized versions, derived from the German *czarin* or *zarin*. Since 1721, the official titles of Russia's monarchs were emperor (imperator) and empress (imperatritsa); the emperor's wife was known as empress consort. Officially, the last Russian tsaritsa was Peter the Great's first wife. Alexandra, wife of Nicholas II, was therefore the last empress consort of Russia. However, tsaritsa was also unofficially employed to describe the tsar's spouse.

My aim wasn't to elucidate the era in its entirety but to present a fictional portrait of one of its most enduring women. Any errors are inadvertent. I apologize in advance to experts or devotees who may disagree with my interpretations. The Romanovs can stir passionate debate. I understand and applaud it.

As always, I must thank my husband, who supports my obsession with the past and my haphazard domestic persona when in the throes of writing. I adore my rescue cats, Boy and Mommy, whose feline insouciance brings me love and laughter. I cannot thank my agent, Jennifer Weltz, enough. She is the lodestone of my career. Everyone at the Jean V. Naggar Literary Agency, Inc., endeavors to simplify the tribulations of being a professional writer.

My editor, Susanna Porter, remains unstinting and ever-gracious in her editorial acumen. My assistant editor, Emily Hartley, also contributed in significant ways. My copy editor, Kathy Lord, performed a very thorough examination of the manuscript. I couldn't ask for better guides at the publishing helm. Once again, I am grateful to Ballantine Books for continuing to believe in historical fiction in our increasingly challenging marketplace.

I owe special thanks to my beta readers and fellow authors Tasha Alexander, Michelle Moran, and Sarah Johnson, whose insightful comments helped refine my drafts. Likewise, I owe my gratitude to booksellers everywhere who continue to invite me to speak and recommend my books.

Most importantly, I thank you, my readers. Your kind comments on social media, your emails, and appearances at my events make the seclusion and piles of research worthwhile. Your trust in me as a storyteller remains my biggest surprise and gift.

Despite their hunting practices, most of the Romanovs loved nature. I share this respect for our fellow beings. We share our planet with sentient creatures who have no voice unless we speak up for them. Be their voice for change. Adopt a shelter pet. Donate to reputable organizations fighting to preserve wildlife. Be responsible with what you buy, as every product on our shelves is the result of sustainable practices or the destruction of irreplaceable habitat. The children of Earth need you. Thank you!

ABOUT THE AUTHOR

C. W. GORTNER holds an MFA in writing, with an emphasis on historical studies, from the New College of California. He is the internationally acclaimed and bestselling author of *Marlene, The Vatican Princess, Mademoiselle Chanel, The Queen's Vow, The Confessions of Catherine de Medici,* and *The Last Queen,* among other books. To learn more about his work and to schedule a book group chat with him, please visit his website.

cwgortner.com
Facebook.com/CWGortner
Twitter: @CWGortner

ABOUT THE TYPE

This book was set in Garamond, a typeface originally designed by the Parisian type cutter Claude Garamond (c. 1500–61). This version of Garamond was modeled on a 1592 specimen sheet from the Egenolff-Berner foundry, which was produced from types assumed to have been brought to Frankfurt by the punch cutter Jacques Sabon (c. 1520–80).

Claude Garamond's distinguished romans and italics first appeared in *Opera Ciceronis* in 1543–44. The Garamond types are clear, open, and elegant.